RAE RIVERS

I am an avid reader and writer with a passion for writing juicy romance novels. I live in Cape Town, South Africa, with my gorgeous husband, two beautiful children and a zoo of house pets.

Besides writing, I love family time, the outdoors, travelling, watching TV series, reading and chocolate.

For more information about my books, or me, please visit www.raerivers.com and follow me on Twitter @RaeRivers1.

The Keepers: Archer

Book 1 in The Keepers Trilogy

RAE RIVERS

Harper*Impulse* an imprint of
HarperCollins*Publishers Ltd*
77–85 Fulham Palace Road
Hammersmith, London W6 8JB

www.harpercollins.co.uk

A Paperback Original 2013

First published in Great Britain in ebook format by HarperImpulse 2013

Cover Images © Shutterstock.com

Rae Rivers asserts the moral right to
be identified as the author of this work

A catalogue record for this book
is available from the British Library

ISBN: 978-0-00-755971-8

This novel is entirely a work of fiction.
The names, characters and incidents portrayed in it are
the work of the author's imagination. Any resemblance to
actual persons, living or dead, events or localities is
entirely coincidental.

Automatically produced by Atomik ePublisher from Easypress

To Ryan, who is the hero in my own real-life story, and my beautiful children who were all very tolerant of all the hours I've spent writing this book. Thank you, my angels.

To my dearest friend, Lisa. Running through ideas for this series with you was as much fun as writing it! Thank you for all the laughter, encouragement and input.

Lastly, thank you to the team at Harper Impulse for saying yes and for believing in my series – and me.

The Keepers Trilogy

The Keepers: Sienna (Prequel)

The Keepers: Archer

The Keepers: Declan

The Keepers: Ethan

Before you read the first book in *The Keepers Trilogy*,
find out how it all began with this exclusive prequel

THE KEEPERS: SIENNA

CHAPTER ONE

The stillness of the forest unnerved her.

The rail of the bridge felt cool against her fingers, damp from the waterfall that gushed beneath them. Thick ferns surrounded them, rocks overgrown with moss and tall trees. The sun had just set, plunging the forest into dark isolation.

Sienna shifted her gaze between two drums on either side of the bridge. Feeling a whirl of gentle energy within, she drew from her centre, making a connection to the one element of nature that would relieve the darkness.

Fire.

Moments later, bright flames sprang to life in each drum, giving their surroundings a dim glow of orange beauty.

"Still not a fan of the dark, my powerful witch?" Archer murmured, a small grin playing on his lips.

She glanced at her Keeper, took in his handsome face and brooding green eyes. With neatly-cropped brown hair, olive skin and a muscular frame, the man shifted parts of her in a way that still unsettled her. "Not after all the stories my Keepers told me of the creepy things in these forests at night."

"Those were just meant to frighten you and besides, we were kids then."

"Maybe, but the stories stuck."

His grin widened. "Don't worry, I'll protect you."

"I know." She smiled, familiar with those words, and relished the comfort they brought her. Always her fierce protector.

"Ready?"

"No."

"Just relax," Archer said, coming up behind her, his voice a soft rumble against her back. Brushing aside a lock of wavy red hair, he leaned forward to kiss her neck, the motion sparking a thrill of excitement she fought to keep buried. His hands trailed down to her waist, fingers splayed against her hips. "You're a Beckham witch. This is a piece of cake for you."

She snorted. "A piece of cake stuffed with dynamite."

"You'll be fine. There's no better place than here for you to practice your magic."

"What if I set us alight? Or cause havoc with the weather? That'll ruin the school carnival and the kids will –"

"You're not going to do either."

She released a noisy sigh, knowing when to admit defeat. "Fine, but if I lose control and set your hair on fire, then it's all on you."

He moved closer, the rigid feel of his muscular chest pressing against her back, reassuring her, offering her a strength she had yet to feel. "Your new powers are a gift."

"More like a curse."

"You simply need to embrace them. The rest will follow."

"I've only ever known the element of fire. That's as natural to me as breathing, but to channel all four at once unnerves me."

Mild words, but she refused to admit just how much her newfound powers frightened her. Three types of witches resided in their world. Sienna had been one of the middle witches, with the power of one element. Her grandmother was the rarest and most powerful kind of witch, channelling all four elements at once: Fire, Air, Earth, and Water. Rose's ability to manipulate them simultaneously was incredible; her connection something Sienna had always envied.

But Rose had felt the need to pass her powers onto Sienna. Since then, they'd become nothing more than an unwanted burden that gnawed at her in hope of receiving the attention they deserved.

"Relax, Sienna," Archer whispered, dipping his head so that it rested beside hers. His hands slid around her waist, strong arms enveloping her in a hold that was so tender – a complete contrast to the power he was capable of.

His presence calmed her but, at the same time, sent her heart racing with an uncontrollable speed reserved for him. Unable to stop herself, she tilted her head slightly so that her cheek was against his face. The slight spray of stubble across a firm jaw brushed against her skin, the touch familiar, and the longing she always felt when he was close struck again.

She heard his sharp intake of breath; felt the way he responded, even though he hadn't moved.

He dipped his head, his mouth lingering dangerously close to hers, and just as she thought he would kiss her, a small smile edged the corner of gorgeous lips.

"Stop trying to distract us," he murmured against her mouth. "You have to do this."

"You're not tempted? Not even a little bit?"

His smile broke free and he gripped one hip, tugging her closer so she could feel just how tempted he was.

Her eyes widened and she couldn't resist a satisfied grin – but it vanished when his lips covered hers in a kiss so sensual, so caring; the rush of energy between them asking for trouble.

She tangled her fingers in his hair, savouring the kiss that she always sought but could never have. She pushed away the gentle warning nagging at her to stop. After all, this behaviour was forbidden between a witch and her Keeper.

They were both breathless when he broke away with a longing that matched hers. She caught a glimpse of frustration in his green eyes, hazed with yellow from the fire – but it disappeared as he grinned.

"No more distractions," he said, turning her to face the small pool of water below. He laced his fingers with hers and resumed his position behind her. "We don't have much time. My brothers are waiting for us at the carnival. In case you forgot, you have a shift at the hall of mirrors in an hour and I'm manning the beer tent."

"Remind me again why we volunteered?"

"Because our old school principal would have our hides if we didn't."

She smiled and leaned into him, enjoying the warmth. "I can't think when you're so close."

"Focus, Sienna." He brushed his mouth against her ear. "Forget about everything around you and focus on that energy brewing within."

"Rose's powers –"

"They're not Rose's powers anymore. They're yours. Close your eyes."

She responded with a soft sigh and closed them, trying to tune out everything that permeated her senses.

The soft trickle of water; an owl hooting in the distance; and the gentle screech of crickets. The smell of mossy rocks, the waterfall, and Archer's scent. His taste against her lips; the feel of the cool air against her skin.

One by one, everything melted away, until all that remained was peaceful silence. She kept her eyes closed, cocooned in the darkness and the newfound stillness.

"Listen to the water," Archer whispered against her ear.

She zeroed in on the small waterfall below them, surprised when she felt the connection to the one element that had previously evaded her.

Her stomach rolled as an untouched energy rumbled through her in waves that quickly grew stronger. Her breathing grew rapid and her heart pounded as the energy swirled in search of its outlet.

She was familiar with the sensation – had often felt it when using fire – but this time, the energy was amplified in a way that startled her.

A gust of air whooshed past them and the fires flared brighter, fed by an invisible surge of energy that had her gasping in response.

Within seconds, the force inside her became so heated, so powerful, that she began trembling. She tried to keep a grip on it but – feeding off her fear – it overwhelmed her.

She groaned as she felt the snap inside that signalled the loss of control.

The flames flared higher, rearing up to lick the tree branches overhead. The leaves sizzled for a brief moment before catching alight. A fresh burst of wind swept through the forest, unsettling the fern bushes, fuelling the fire into a roaring blaze. Within moments, the tree was crackling in an orange inferno.

The waterfall bubbled furiously, the stream gushing unevenly across the rocks and flooding the embankment; the sound no longer peaceful.

The wind grew stronger, sending a whispered hush through the tall trees. She felt the cool breeze across her skin, the wind in her hair – caught the hint that this shouldn't be happening – but she'd given so much of herself to the magic that her senses had blurred.

"Sienna, stop." She heard his voice and ignored its distant warning.

The energy burst was as exhilarating as it was terrifying; a flow of power she'd never felt before.

"Sienna!"

Archer's harsh tone snapped her to attention and her eyes flew open.

He stepped around her, casting a worried glance at the blazing tree, and spread out his arms across the water.

His connection was instant, the element moulding to his will – and within moments, lashes of water rose up to douse the burning tree.

His power of water.

Icy fingers wrapped around Sienna's heart when she saw the chaos she'd created. The bridge was a muddy mess of forest debris. The sandy banks were flooded; the waterfall gushed unevenly. Tree branches, previously green, were scorched by the flames. Smoke filled the air, along with a gentle sizzle that hinted of failure.

"Oh my God," she breathed, averting her gaze from the smouldering tree to look at Archer. "I could've killed us."

CHAPTER TWO

High-pitched screams, scraping metal and a whoosh of air pierced the darkness as Sienna walked toward the school hall.

She glanced up at the shrieking teenagers on the rollercoaster brought in for tonight's festival and smiled.

Nothing like a little adrenaline fix to get everyone's heart racing.

The school carnival was a firm favourite in Rapid Falls and the residents were out in full force in a mingle of fun and festivity. The sun had set early, bringing with it the cooler night air – a sure sign that winter was approaching – but the weather did nothing to hamper the excitement of the crowd.

Despite her stinging disappointment, it was hard not to feel the enthusiasm that rippled through the town. Sienna shook her head, refusing to think of her magical disaster in the forest, and looked around. The school field was a mass of activity and music, laughter and chatter filled the air. The school hall had been transformed into a dark cave with dimmed lights and endless mirrors, offering hours of confusion and amusement.

The door to the hall burst open in an explosion of candy floss and girly giggles and Sienna smiled as they brushed past her, oblivious to her presence in their excitement to get to the Ferris wheel.

Sienna's smile widened as Sarah Bennett, the youngest of her four Keepers, came up behind them. Judging by her friend's expression, she'd had her fill of screeching girls. Sarah wore a white shirt, skinny jeans and long black boots that accentuated her slim, muscular frame; in her hand she clasped a jacket.

Despite Sarah's duty to protect Sienna, they'd developed a sisterly friendship that had filled a deep void. With the death of Sienna's parents several years ago, her grandmother was her only family. Her friendships with the three Keeper brothers were special in their own way, but what she had with Sarah was like gold.

Sarah's infectious laugh, wide eyes and silly ideas eased the burden of being a Beckham witch with hours of crazy fun.

Right now, her exasperated expression was anything but fun.

"Thank God you're here," she said, relief etching her tone.

Sienna laughed. "A bit much?"

Sarah rolled her eyes and ran her fingers through her short black hair. "Squawking teenagers and dimmed lights. It's enough to make me want to pull my hair out. How the hell did we get pinned for supervision in this darn carnival?"

"That's what happens when we grow up and act all adult-like."

"It feels like moments ago we were running riot in the cave and now we're the ones manning them. When did that happen?"

"Would you prefer to be swapping school notes with Steve Bailey under the stage?"

Sarah laughed, the lyrical sound whipped away by another round of rollercoaster screeches. "That was the last thing on my mind in the dungeon with Steve."

Sienna smiled at the memories they shared.

The Bennetts had been Keepers to her family's lineage of witches for generations. Two families bound together by duty, love, and loyalty.

Sienna reached for the keys in Sarah's hand. "Your brothers are in the beer tent manning the bar. Knowing Declan, he's probably stashed some under the counter."

"Just like the old days. Is Archer here yet?"

The name of her Keeper brought an instant flush to Sienna, which she masked by turning away. "Yes, we came together. What do I need to do?"

"Keep an eye out for any rowdy kids, break up the smooching ones, and make sure that no one smashes any mirrors."

Sarah pulled on her denim jacket and Sienna caught a glimpse of her tattoo. Carefully crafted in black ink above her left breast was a pentagram that illustrated Sienna's magical connection to her Keepers. Four elements of nature – one for each Keeper – and the fifth element was Sienna, the spirit that bound them together.

"And keep them away from the stage doors," Sarah added. "The principal will have a fit if they get in there. Lots of dark corners for the frisky kids."

Sienna laughed. "You should know."

"And what a different perspective I have now." Sarah sighed and then grinned. "Go do your time and then meet me at the Ferris wheel. I feel like acting like a kid again."

Sienna groaned. "The last time you said that, we mixed that potion in Rose's kitchen that had us scrubbing the walls for hours."

"It was you who added the vinegar."

"Only because you told me it was water!"

"Rose was furious," Sarah said with a laugh. "I thought she was going to ban us from her kitchen."

Sienna smiled and waved as she headed for the door. "I'll see you in an hour."

She paused in the doorway as her eyes adjusted to the dim

lighting, amused by the mirrors reflecting her image in distorted fragments. Heading in, she manned the passageways as teenagers trickled through in a whirl of excited laughter.

A while later, Sienna looked at her watch, relieved to see that her shift was almost over. And now that she was done playing chaperone, the kids had disappeared, leaving the cave in a ghostly silence.

Tunnels of giggling school kids were one thing but darkened corridors filled with nothing but her own images were unnerving.

Sienna strolled through the tunnels, ignoring her reflection as she walked. She'd check the stage one more time before heading out to join her Keepers for a beer.

They'd also be finished with their shifts and Sienna looked forward to a lively evening with her friends.

With Archer.

The thought shouldn't send a flutter of butterflies through her stomach but it did. Repeatedly.

Before Sienna could scold herself, the dim lights flickered a few times before going out completely.

She froze, wide-eyed, and then blinked as her eyes adjusted to the darkness. The only light was a stream of moonlight that filtered through windows in the roof.

A shuffle of feet had her whirling around, her senses prickling in warning. "Who's there?" she called, pleased that her voice held no hint of her uneasiness.

In answer, a black cloaked image appeared in the mirror beside her and Sienna took a step backward, a soft gasp escaping before she could stop it. She paused, scanning the tunnel of mirrors for the real version, but confusion reigned; the placement of the mirrors having the desired effect.

"This isn't funny!" she snapped, hoping like hell that this was some silly teenage prank.

The figure disappeared and she exhaled, only to spin around when it appeared again – but this time there were multiple images reflected around her. Trying not to panic, she focused on the face clouded in a hoodie and darkened shadows. It was hard to tell if it was one person or several.

Feeling the rumbling of restless energy inside her, Sienna back-tracked away from him, searching for the person behind the reflections.

He edged closer to the strip of moonlight cast across the floor, the movement chasing away some of the shadows on his face. With a deep growl, he lifted his head.

The air whooshed out of her as though he'd struck her. She stared, a flash of paralyzing fear rooting her to the spot.

The face of a skeleton stared back at her. Dark soulless eyes, outlined in thick black smudges, seared into her. A black nose with hollow, black cheeks, and a long jawline of skeletal teeth.

Everything reeled and she screamed, staggering back into the mirror behind her. It fell backward, shattering to the ground with an eerie screech of splintering glass that snapped her attention from the intruder for a split second.

With another low growl, almost a gurgle, he charged forward. Sienna screamed again as the mirrors closed in on her, the appalling face coming at her from all angles.

And then he was gone.

Shoulders heaving, Sienna gulped air and looked around frantically. The only reflection she saw was hers.

She felt the grumble of magical energy brewing within and focused on her breathing in an attempt to control it.

In a world of ordinary humans where only a handful of people knew of their kind, an explosion of magical powers in a school hall would not go down well.

Oh, God. What the hell was that?

She clenched her fingers, trying to steady her shaking hands, her mind struggling to reconcile the image she'd seen with that of a teenage prank. If that face had been a mask, it was the scariest one she'd ever seen.

Not waiting for his reappearance, Sienna bolted through the closest door. The area below the stage was still as grim as she remembered it. Concert props and other paraphernalia lined the walls. The air was stuffy, the roof low and littered with cobwebs that had Sienna suppressing a shudder.

As she ran toward the exit, she heard the scraping of the inner door as it opened and closed after her.

The realization that she wasn't alone spurred her on and she burst out of the back door with a soft cry.

Relief flushed through her when several teenagers came walking past and she fell in line with them, glancing back at the shut door.

It remained closed and her breathing began to level, even though she was unable to dispel the face from her memory.

If that was some kind of sick joke to frighten her, it had worked. Her only consolation was that no one else had witnessed it.

As for volunteering for a shift at the school carnival again? Hell no.

CHAPTER THREE

Sienna leaned over the safety rail of their cart on the Ferris wheel to peer at the shrieking teenagers on the rollercoaster. Clearly, the ride was a hit.

The Ferris wheel came to a stop to board more people and their cart dangled above, offering the best view of Rapid Falls.

Well-known for its production of ice wine, nestled at the foot of the mountains and surrounded by vineyards, forests and rivers, the small town had been her family's home for generations.

The cart rocked as Sarah pointed to a flicker of lights in the distance. "I've always loved seeing our house from up here. It looks so peaceful."

"It is peaceful. Most of the time."

Sienna studied the soft glow that signalled the Bennett Estate. The huge mansion, surrounded by a thick wall of forests, was home to two witches and four Keepers.

An odd combination but they were her family and best friends. Everything dear in the world to her. Her familiars.

"You're way too moody," Sarah teased, elbowing her. "Tonight's supposed to be fun."

Between her magical blunder and the eerie experience in the hall of mirrors, it had been anything but.

Sarah settled dark blue eyes onto her, her expression sobering. "You've been acting weird ever since you finished your shift. Everything okay?"

Sienna shrugged, reluctant to recall the creepy face that had left behind a growing sense of unease.

Sarah poked her on the arm. "We agreed that for one night, we'd shelve the worry over all the animal attacks that have happened lately and simply have fun."

"Bit hard to do when we both know they weren't animal attacks."

"I know." Sarah's mood shifted and she sighed. "So are you going to tell me what's worrying you?"

Knowing she wouldn't be able to shrug off her friend, Sienna agreed with a brief nod. "There was some kid that pulled a Rocky Horror Show on me with the mirrors and it creeped me out."

"What kid?"

"I don't know. He was wearing a skeleton mask or something. It was dark and confusing as the lights went out and I was alone."

"Alone? Where were the others?"

"A lull between the groups I suppose. I thought it was weird too."

"Are you sure it was a kid?"

"Who else would get some sort of sick satisfaction at scaring me? Unless it was Declan messing around."

But she knew it wasn't. Although Declan was as devoted to protecting Sienna as her other three Keepers, he still loved teasing her – but the stunt in the hall went beyond that.

"No," Sarah said, shaking her head. "Declan's been at the beer tent this whole time."

Their gazes met and they stared at each other in a knowing silence.

"You're thinking it was one of the Brogan brothers?" Sienna said, trying to ignore the tug of worry that licked at her gut.

Too late. The mention of the two warlock brothers had slashed the last of her determination to have a worry-free night. Dammit.

"We suspected they'd show up soon." Sarah's brows drew together in a delicate frown. "I'm surprised they'd go after you with your Keepers nearby."

"They didn't exactly go after me. All they did was try to frighten me. Besides, we don't even know if it was them."

"After all their wicked stunts recently, my brothers are going to pop a couple of veins if they're here." Sarah scanned the ground below them.

"You really think they're here? They're evil, not stupid."

"Their craving for chaos overrides any rational thinking."

Sarah wasn't wrong. The Brogan brothers were hell-bent on continuing their parents' legacy of exposing their kind to the ordinary humans around them. They'd lost all common sense years ago.

The Beckham and Bennett families had devoted their lives to creating harmony amongst the people and there was no way in hell they were going to let the Brogan brothers destroy that.

It was far too risky. Exposing their supernatural kind would only spell panic and destruction – as their ancestors had discovered many years ago after a brave attempt at coming out to the world. The witch hunt had been brutal; their massacre a tragic event that had marked the existence of any supernatural being ever since.

Sienna shuddered at the thought of ever being discovered, yet Mason and Warrick kept threatening to expose them all.

"It's hard to think that we used to be such good friends," Sarah said.

"Warrick's just influenced by Mason – some sort of brotherly bond crap. I don't think it's Warrick we should be worried about."

"He's still a Brogan and can't be trusted." Sarah pointed to the ground at the edge of the carnival. "There's Rose and Lora."

Sienna followed her gaze to where her grandmother was walking beside her friend.

"You really need to talk to Rose, Sienna. She can help you adjust to your new powers."

"I know, but I'm still mad at her. She talks to me in code and it's driving me crazy. I wish she would be straight with me and explain why she gave them to me." Sienna frowned when the two witches disappeared into the forest. "Why are they headed into the woods?"

The Ferris wheel began turning again, the abrupt jar of movement causing them both to swing in their seats.

Sienna gripped the bar in front of her to steady herself. Sarah's expression brightened with a mischief Sienna knew too well and she began rocking her body in gentle swaying movements.

"Years later and you still can't resist the urge to rock the cart?" Sienna asked, all thoughts of the witches and warlock brothers momentarily shelved.

Sarah's grin widened and she increased her rocking. The cart followed suit, swaying to her movements, and Sienna pointed to the sign on the bar.

"Read the sign, Sarah. No rocking."

"But it's so much fun," Sarah retorted, increasing her pace.

Sienna laughed, holding onto the bar tighter. "Sure, for you maybe. You can jump from here to the ground with the ease of a cat jumping from a four storey building. I, on the other hand, will splatter like a normal person."

"Splatter?" Sarah mocked with a raised eyebrow and then laughed as she gave an extra rock for good measure.

"Sarah, stop it!"

Sarah's laughter was swept away by another round of frantic shrieks as the rollercoaster took off on another stomach-flipping ride. Still smiling at her witch, she stopped rocking as their cart reached the bottom.

"Now you stop?"

"Don't want Mr Taylor to boot us off here."

Sienna glanced at the old school caretaker manning the Ferris wheel. He was a large man with a love for people and donuts, neither of which he lacked in this town, and although his stern expression drew respect and caution from the kids, they all knew that he was as threatening as a Gummy Bear.

And standing beside the old man was Archer.

Her breath caught as her gaze met his and all thoughts of the caretaker disappeared. Archer wore jeans and a suede black jacket, his hands shoved casually into his pockets. He was tall, with broad shoulders and a sexy presence that had a group of teenage girls standing nearby swooning over him.

The fact that their relationship was forbidden, cursed, did little to calm the butterfly flip in her stomach. With a brief shake of the head, Sienna silently scolded herself for the direction of her thoughts.

He could never be hers. Ever.

"I'm going to be sick looking at you two ogling each other like that," Sarah said, feigning a gag. "You're going to have The Circle spitting snakes if you're not careful."

Sienna waved her off, not caring for the discussion that would follow. It was one they'd had far too often of late.

The Circle were a group of ancestral witches who governed the laws of magic, witches and their Keepers. Not wanting the emotional complication from a relationship between a witch and her Keeper that might influence their roles in maintaining the balance of nature, the old witches had long ago forbidden any romances.

So the handsome, charming and darn sexy Keeper was off-limits.

If only her womanly parts would listen to her head.

Sarah's harsh intake of breath and soft curse snapped Sienna's attention back from all thoughts of Archer and she glanced at her with a raised brow. "Sarah?"

She'd gone rigid, her previous playfulness abandoned, and stared at her brother with a harsh frown.

A frown that matched his.

"Sarah, what's wrong?" Sienna asked, knowing instinctively that trouble had reared its familiar head.

Damn it.

When she didn't reply, Sienna reached for Sarah's arm. "Sarah, what's happening? What do you hear?"

Without looking at her, Sarah shook her head. "Nothing."

"Then what's wrong?"

"Blood," she replied, her tone edged with an icy warning that sent chills down Sienna's spine. She pinned Sienna with a sharp gaze. "I smell blood."

CHAPTER FOUR

With growing agitation, Sarah led Sienna off the Ferris wheel and went straight to her brother.

"Where's Rose?" Archer asked as they reached him. His jaw was clenched, his body riddled with tension, and he took Sienna's arm to draw her closer.

"I'll find her," Sarah replied. "You take Sienna. What's happened?"

"I'll call you when I know. Declan and Ethan are on their way."

They separated, their night marred with everything they'd been hoping to avoid. Acting on instinct, Sarah headed straight for the forest.

Rose was up to something.

The older witch had been secretive and quiet the last few days, silently disappearing on her own for lengths of time, much of which was spent with Lora.

And Sarah had spent enough time with witches to know that when two of them were clouded in secrecy that trouble was brewing.

A quick glance at the full moon confirmed her suspicions. Witches loved forests, especially the ones in Rapid Falls, which were steeped with its own magical history. But the only thing that witches loved more than the forest was a full moon.

And tonight, the moon was at its ripest, offering all the energy they might need.

Sarah kept a keen eye on her surroundings to ensure no one was following her as she made her way into the forest, following their tracks with ease. She cherished the supernatural abilities that came with being a Keeper.

Finding the witches didn't take long, her heightened hearing easily tracking them in the dark, and every protective instinct had her wanting to bolt toward them and demand an explanation.

Instead, she held back, surprised to find them already amidst a ceremony.

They'd cast a circle and stood in the centre, holding hands. Surrounding them were four burning candles that illuminated their faces in a gentle glow of yellow. The air was permeated with soft whispers that immediately had Sarah on edge.

She considered leaving them alone but something about the secrecy of the ritual kept her rooted to the spot.

Performing a ritual in the middle of the forest on the same evening as the carnival meant that Rose was either doing something that couldn't wait or – knowing that everyone would be occupied – performing a ritual that no one would witness.

And she hadn't said a word to her Keepers.

Sarah looked at the two older witches, both oblivious to her presence. It was a surprise that Lora was taking part in the ritual as she'd made it clear many years ago that although she was a witch and a messenger of The Circle, she was no longer a practicing one. Not after her daughter and granddaughter had fled their life and cut all ties with her.

Sarah frowned at Rose, wondering what the older witch was up to. Rose was tall and slim with shoulder-length red hair, lighter than Sienna's, and kind eyes that Sarah had known her entire life. Tonight, her face was lined with worry and everything about the way she stood hinted at the weariness that lurked.

The soft chanting grew faster and more forceful, a rush of whispered words in the darkness. The air grew warmer and the flames from the candles burned brighter, feeding off the energy of the witches.

Rose's hands, still gripped firmly within Lora's, began to tremble, and Sarah's protective Keeper instincts bristled.

But she knew better than to startle witches amidst a ceremony.

The chanting grew louder and everything around them shifted. It was an odd sensation, but Sarah felt the energy change around them.

The ground within the circle began to stir, a gentle swirling of sand, and then settled to reveal four stones that rattled against each other.

And just like that, it was over and everything fell silent.

Rose released Lora's hands and went to her knees.

Unable to stop herself, Sarah was on the floor beside her before the older woman touched the ground.

Rose gasped. "Sarah!"

"What are you doing, Rose?" Sarah eyed the stones with suspicion as recognition sparked. "You've summoned the stones that unseal the Grimoires?"

Four magical stones and a spell from a Beckham witch were the keys to unsealing the Beckham and the Brogan Grimoires. Summoning the stones from the four witches who protected them wasn't something Rose did lightly. The fear of the books landing in the wrong hands always lingered. The fact that she'd done so now sent prickles of alarm through Sarah.

"Why?" Sarah asked, her stomach clenching. "You know that the Brogan brothers could return any minute!"

Rose fell silent, her eyes a mixture of wariness and determination. "I need my Grimoire open, Sarah."

"But those stones unseal their Grimoire too. Summoning them is a huge risk."

"It's a risk we have to take. I'm no use to any of you if I can't access my Grimoire."

"Why tonight? Why the sudden need?"

Rose's expression tightened and she lowered her eyes. "I don't know. I can't explain it."

Sienna's story of the faceless man in the mirrors came to mind and she slumped to her knees beside the witch. "Something horrible is about to happen, isn't it?"

CHAPTER FIVE

Archer and Sienna waved at Mr Taylor, who was grinning like a cat who had nabbed a canary, and went to find Declan and Ethan.

Which didn't take long.

The two brothers were already headed their way, wearing jeans, jackets and matching sombre expressions. They were so different, but each exuded a strength and confidence that had snagged the admiration of a nearby group of women.

Women who would never know each man the way Sienna did. Highly-trained warriors with heightened skills of movement, strength and hearing. Their Keeper status and abilities to channel an element of nature – one air, the other fire – were a secret shared with very few people.

Declan fell in line beside them, his longer jet-black hair more dishevelled than normal, and sandwiched Sienna between himself and Archer. All traces of the usual laughter found in his expressive blue eyes had vanished in a smouldering look that smacked of worry.

"Where's Sarah?" he asked.

"She's gone to find Rose," Archer replied, keeping his hand on Sienna's lower back as they walked. "Any idea where the blood's coming from?"

"The parking area," Ethan replied, giving a quick nod in the direction of the cars. He had sandy-brown hair and striking blue eyes, clouded with anger. All signs of his usual mischievous grin had vanished.

They headed straight for the stretch of parked cars on one side of the school. It didn't take her Keepers long to trace the blood and Sienna gasped at the sight of a man slumped against the tyre of a car. At a glance, he looked like a drunk passed out – but his twisted expression hinted of something more.

"Oh my God," she said, rushing forward, but Declan stepped in front of her. Wide eyes swung up to meet his and he shook his head.

"He's dead, Sienna."

"Maybe we can still help him."

"No."

"Check his pulse. He –"

"Sienna," Archer said, taking her hand and pulling her away from the car. "Underneath that thick jacket is a lot of blood. There's no pulse, no breathing."

Her gaze met his and she closed her eyes with a soft sigh. If there were any signs of life, her Keepers would have heard them. "It's a school parking lot. There are children here."

Ethan circled the car, scanning for signs of the perpetrator as he made a quick call to the sheriff. "Pam's headed straight here. Think this was supernatural?"

Archer shrugged, casting a quick glance at the nearby forest that would provide an easy escape route. "Maybe, but it's too clean a kill to be Mason's. This isn't like the others."

Sienna's air whooshed out of her lungs as the icy realization washed over her. She dragged her gaze away from the car and faced her Keepers. "It's Mason."

Three pairs of eyes turned on her to stare at her in stunned silence.

Archer cocked a sceptical brow. "There's been no sign of him for a while."

"This isn't Mason's work," Declan said, motioning to the car. "Archer's right. All the other bodies the sheriff uncovered were drained of blood and mangled."

Sienna's instincts prickled like crazy as she pictured the creepy face in the mirrors. She hadn't been sure at the time but there was no escaping the grim truth now.

Mason was back in town.

"It *is* Mason," she repeated, louder this time and pointed to the man on the ground. "Check his eyes."

Ethan knelt beside the body, lifting an eyelid. His grim expression confirmed her suspicions and drew a curse from Declan.

Declan took two strides toward her and she refused to flinch when he stopped directly in front of her. "His eyes are black, a typical Mason signature. What the hell do you know?"

"Mason was here. Or at least I think he was."

Archer reached for her arm. "Did he hurt you?"

No," Sienna said, shaking her head. "He didn't touch me."

"And you're only telling us now?" Declan asked, something sharp and fiery edging his tone.

"I wasn't sure."

"Did you see him?"

"I…I don't know. I didn't recognise his face." She explained the incident in the hall, unable to suppress a shudder. "I thought it was some teenagers trying to scare me but now I know that it wasn't. It was Mason."

"But you said you didn't recognise him."

"It wasn't his face. He wore a mask or something. Whatever it was, he wanted to frighten me and let me know that he's back. This," she said, pointing at the dead body, "is another message from him."

"No kidding."

Archer circled them, scanning their surroundings. The parking area was quiet and dimly lit by a few scattered street lamps. The forest that loomed behind it was pitch-black, offering all sorts of hiding places. He pointed to Ethan. "Try calling Sarah again. Warn her."

"Hopefully she's found Rose," Ethan said, already walking away, his body rigid and snapped to attention as he made the call.

Four teenage girls came walking out of the carnival, headed for their car, and Declan hurried to sidetrack them. Several giggles later, the girls turned back to the carnival.

Prince Charming at work.

Sienna glanced at the body, a feeling of dread settling in her stomach like lead. "We have to stop Mason."

"No shit," Declan said, coming up behind her.

"Now." She spun around and started walking down the sandy road, a fresh wave of anger feeding her determination.

Declan was in front of her in a whoosh of air and a speed that barely stopped her this time. "Uh, uh, witchy."

She tried to walk around the bulky frame but he side-stepped her, providing a wall of muscles that was impossible to penetrate.

"What are you going to do, Sienna? Walk up and slap him on the wrist? This is Mason, dammit!"

"Don't you think I know that? I know exactly what he's capable of and I'm sick of it. He just killed an innocent man at a school filled with children!"

"He's not innocent," Archer said, coming up behind them. "He has Mason's mark."

Sienna gaped at him. "He does?"

"On his wrist. Just like the others."

She thought of the four other men the sheriff had found murdered over the last month. They'd all been attacked by an animal – a horrible accident, were it not for their dark, withered eyes and the mark on their wrists.

The mark of the one warlock they all loathed.

"Why would Mason be killing off his warriors?" Declan asked.

"He's gone too far and they know that." Archer nodded in the direction of the dead man. "He's probably one of the better ones who tried to stop Mason."

"*We* have to stop Mason," Sienna interrupted, staring at the body slumped against the car tyre.

"We have to find him first, so if you have a warlock locator spell up your sleeve, now would be the time to pull it out," Declan said.

"My locator spells don't work like that, Declan. Besides, Mason would have thought of that already."

"You witches. So unreliable."

She pulled a face at him. "Careful, Bennett. I can think of a great toad-turning spell that I'm itching to use."

He flashed her a fake smile. "Just try me, witchy."

Archer stepped forward, always the peacemaker. "This isn't helping. We need to find Mason before he hurts someone else."

"He's long gone," Declan said.

"We don't know that!" Sienna argued.

"Sticking around after the stunt he's just pulled would be suicide. The man's a creepy murderer, not stupid."

Something in her eyes must have given her away because Declan waved a finger at her and shook his head.

"No solo missions, witchy. Whatever it is you're planning, you run it by us first, got it?"

She turned away and he grabbed her wrist, drawing her around so that she faced him again.

"Sienna."

"I've had it with this man," she snapped, yanking her wrist back. "I'm sick of all the wasted lives, the death, and the constant threat he poses to our kind."

"We'll figure out a way to stop him."

She blew out air and gave a brief nod, trying to quell the agitation inside. "We have friends here. Family. I just –"

"I get it, Sienna," Declan said, lowering his voice, his intense gaze meeting hers. "Trust me, I get it." They fell silent, the need for words unnecessary. They shared the same duties, the same worries, and fought the same battle.

Archer reached for her arm, glancing at the sheriff and two deputies heading their way. "Pam is here. We'll figure this out later."

"We have company," Declan grumbled, nodding to a group of teenagers headed towards them. One of the girls caught sight of the slumped body between the cars and froze in her tracks, snapping out a warning to her friends.

They all stopped, turned to gape at Sienna and her Keepers, and it took mere seconds for the grim reality to set in.

The girl screamed, the shrill sound intrusive in the quiet parking lot, instantly setting off two of her girlfriends.

Declan cursed, shot Sienna an annoyed look, and rolled his eyes as he began moving towards the teenagers. "Have I told you before just how much I hate screamers?"

CHAPTER SIX

Despite the sheriff's best attempts at keeping the murder quiet, it took all of five minutes before a crowd of onlookers had gathered.

"I'm going to wait in the car," Sienna told Archer.

His brows furrowed and he glanced at the growing crowd. With a curt nod, he dipped his head to hers. "Once we can get away, we'll figure out what to do with Mason. Together," he added, eyeing her as he handed over the keys.

Sienna went to the black SUV parked several cars down. Her mind raced with thoughts of the warlocks and what they wanted. They'd grown more reckless in their quest for power and control.

Their parents had started a war that had eventually cost Sienna and Archer's parents their lives. Images of the devastating fire that had killed them still plagued her dreams. The cause of the fire remained unknown and even though suspicion had fallen on the Brogan family, it had never been proven. Unfortunately, in their haste to escape the accusations, Mason's parents had been killed in a car accident, leaving two sons to continue their legacy.

Years later, the war their parents had started still waged on. The idea that it would never end nipped at her every time Mason struck, creating fear and panic amongst the ordinary people around them.

Sienna despised using magic to adjust memories and rectify the balance, but with Mason on a warpath, sometimes a little magic had been necessary to keep their secret. No one wanted a repeat of the witch hunt that had slaughtered so many of their kind. After all, their agreement with the small handful of people who knew about them was that they lived in harmony. No public displays of magic or supernatural abilities, and no one was to be hurt.

Mason had crossed that line so many times that a confrontation was inevitable. It wouldn't be long before he unsettled the balance their families had worked so hard to maintain and trashed their dreams of living a peaceful life.

Sienna unlocked the car, climbed inside and shut the door. The tinted black windows offered a dark cocoon that was a welcome barrier to the chaos outside.

Her senses immediately prickled with a dark and unwelcome energy.

An energy that wasn't hers.

Gulping air, she reached for the car door, fumbling against the handle that wouldn't budge. Smoke began to pour through the vents: a thin veil of grey that gathered momentum until the car was smouldering with thick black smoke.

Blackness enveloped her with a choking hold that made it impossible to breathe. Her throat burned and her eyes began to water. Scrambling for the door, she hit the windows and yanked on the handle, trying to hold her breath to ward off the acrid smell.

And just like that, it was gone.

Sienna coughed frantically as she gasped air. She spun around in her seat, trying to grasp reality, and looked at the blank air vents.

Uneasiness arrowed to her stomach and it clenched in response.

The smoke hadn't been a car defect. Or a prank.

No, that was all Mason.

Sienna's head popped up as the car door beside her opened and Sarah climbed in, breathless as though she'd been running.

"Where's Rose?" Sienna blurted, glancing around the car for her grandmother.

"She's with Ethan and Lora. He's driving them home." Sarah held out her hand for the car keys.

"What are you doing?"

She started the engine. "I'm taking you home. Archer and Declan will follow once the sheriff has got this crazy crowd under control."

Sienna's breathing began to level, even though her heartbeat hadn't, and she turned back in her seat, trying to spot her Keepers. The crowd of people had grown, burying them in the chaos and panic.

"Is Rose okay?" Sienna asked, tugging on her seatbelt and dropping her head back against the seat. She exhaled, trying to get her head around the way Mason's magic had tricked her.

Surely she was stronger than that?

"She's fine."

"Why were they in the forest?"

There was a brief pause. "They went for a walk."

"They shouldn't be in the forest at night without a Keeper."

"Tell that to the old ladies. They think they're invincible."

"They could get hurt."

"She's fine, Sienna." Sarah flashed her a reassuring smile and turned the car onto the main road. Because the Bennett estate was situated on the outskirts of town, the road home was dark and isolated, twisting and turning as it followed the shape of the mountain.

"Do you know if Rose has summoned the four stones?" Sarah asked, glancing in the rear view mirror.

Sienna raised a brow. "The stones that open our Grimoire? I doubt it. Why do you ask?"

"Rose has been acting all weird and Lora said she felt an unusual amount of energy tonight."

Sienna glanced out the window, only to be greeted with blackness outside and the soft glow of her own reflection on the window. "We always feel an energy spike when it's a full moon. Besides, it would take a lot for Rose to bring them out of hiding."

"So I've heard," Sarah grunted, the nip to her words causing Sienna to glance at her. She was staring straight ahead, her lips pinched in a thin line, and a small frown creased her forehead.

The chiming of Sienna's phone lit up the car with a soft yellow glow. As Sienna reached for it, her gaze fell on Sarah's reflection in the window beside her and she gasped, reeling back in her seat as Mason's skeletal face reflected back at her.

Sarah's head snapped to face her. "What the hell, Sienna?"

The phone stopped ringing, plunging the car into darkness. Sienna glanced around, blinking rapidly as a tinge of wariness spread through her like wild fire. "Nothing," she muttered, her gaze returning to her Keeper. "I'm edgy tonight."

"We all are, but jeepers, you nearly gave me a heart attack."

"Sorry, I didn't mean to startle you," Sienna murmured, feeling foolish. She must be tired, or Mason's pranks were wearing her down. She reached for her phone, turning it on to see who had tried calling.

"Archer?" Sarah asked.

Sienna nodded and began to dial but Sarah reached out and snatched the phone from her.

"Sarah!"

"I'm trying to drive, Sienna," Sarah snapped, her tone laced with irritation. "The light from your phone is so distracting. You know how dangerous these roads are at night."

Sienna frowned as wariness trickled into alarm. She ran her gaze along the length of Sarah and bit back a sharp intake of air at the sight of her left hand on the steering wheel.

A hand that no longer wore her Keeper ring.

CHAPTER SEVEN

Meanwhile, in the woods, Sarah walked back with Rose to the parking area to find her brothers. She was bubbling with questions but the memory of the blood had her prickling with the urge to get her witches home.

The weather had changed, bringing cooler air and a wave of clouds that began to patch the moon. The smell of rain permeated the air.

With a wave, Lora climbed into her car and drove away. Sarah watched her leave, uneasy that the witch was without protection, but Lora had refused any for years.

The snap of her name had Sarah turning around to find Archer and Declan rushing toward them. She could see by their harsh expressions that agitation and fury were stewing a lethal combination inside.

She felt it too.

This latest death had served as a mocking reminder that they were fast losing the battle against Mason.

Against everything they were destined to protect.

"Where's Sienna?" Declan asked, scanning the area for their witch.

Sarah's eyebrows shot up. "She's with you, isn't she? I haven't seen her since the Ferris wheel."

Archer gaped at her as though she was about to sprout a vicious monster. "Sarah, you said you were taking her home."

"No, I didn't."

Ethan arrived, eyeing the grey storm of clouds setting in, and raised a brow when he sensed their tension. "What's wrong?"

"Is Sienna with you?"

"No. She went with Sarah." Ethan glanced at his sister. "You said you'd take her home."

Sarah looked at her brothers as though they'd gone mad, and gasped as it suddenly reeled into place.

Her Keeper instincts snapped forward and she circled them, searching for her friend. "Oh, no," she breathed, turning to face them.

Archer pushed past his brothers and snatched her wrist, his eyes burning. "Sarah, where the hell is Sienna?"

"I don't know."

"You said you'd take her home!"

"It wasn't me!" she said, yanking her wrist free. "I was with Rose and Lora this entire time."

"You walked past me, and told me…Dammit!" Archer spun around, his gaze settling on Declan's as the cruel truth sunk in. "It's Mason. Mason has her."

CHAPTER EIGHT

Sienna's heartbeat raced, as if a herd of running horses had taken off inside her. A swirl of protective energy churned within, fuelled by her fear, and her mind grasped for an exit plan.

The sky rumbled with thunder, the sound loud and intrusive in the darkness. The beauty of the moon had slowly waned as dark, thick clouds rolled in, wrapping their town in a gloomy fog.

"Give me my phone, Sarah," she said, pleased that her voice held no hint of the shaking anger she felt inside. Leaning forward, she tried to reach for her phone but her hand was slapped away. "Sarah! Archer will be looking for me. You're being a bitch. Give it back!"

Sienna lunged forward and tried to grab the phone.

"Stop it!" Sarah yelled, slapping her back as the car swerved across the road. "It's about to start raining any second. You're going to kill us."

"What have you done with Sarah?" Sienna snarled, sliding back into her seat, her gaze pinned on the imposter beside her. "Where's my Keeper?"

A bolt of lightning lit up the sky, plunging the car into a brief flash of light and Sienna watched in horror as Sarah's image slipped away to reveal the darkness beneath.

Mason.

Without the mask and dressed casually in jeans and a white shirt, he looked almost ordinary – like the Mason she remembered. His messy black hair had grown to his shoulders and his expression was a combination of amusement and malice. His presence had her lurching forward but an intense heat seared through her, touching her in places she kept guarded. She cried out and, using one arm, he slammed her back against her seat. The man oozed aggression and harboured an intense hatred for her and the Bennett family.

An age-old feud.

And she'd walked right into his trap.

She fell silent, her shoulders heaving as she tried to reel in her rapid breathing – but almost baulked when Mason gave her a triumphant smile that barely hitched his lips.

"Miss me?" he murmured in a gravelly voice that sent chills straight down Sienna's spine.

"Like a migraine." She should have known the warlock would attempt to reach her tonight. But to approach her as Sarah, with her Keepers nearby, surrounded by the cops? Mason's boldness rattled her more than anything else. "Where's Sarah?"

"Sarah's fine." His smirk disappeared, dark eyes flickering between her and the road. He dipped his head to glance at the sky. "Awful weather coming in. Seems like the carnival will be a drag after all."

"Do we have you to thank for this sudden weather change?"

His lips twitched. "Perhaps. I've never been one for school carnivals – although it did offer the perfect backdrop for some fun."

"Is that what you're calling the stunt in the hall with the Halloween mask?"

"You mean this one?" he asked, staring straight ahead.

She felt the rush of energy that prickled along her skin, even though he made no sound, and she gasped as his image shifted from the Mason she knew to the scary face she'd seen earlier.

And this time, she knew that it wasn't a mask but a skull tattoo.

It looked as though his skin had disintegrated, exposing the bones and holes below. His nose and cheeks were hollow, surrounding a jaw of exposed teeth. Black markings on his neck hinted at more tapestry beneath the clothing. Bony fingers gripped the steering wheel. He turned his head with a vacant glare and she felt the chill wash over her. It was an image of the walking dead, but what frightened her most were his cold, black eyes, outlined in dark rings.

The eerie sight ripped a shudder through her and she recoiled into her seat, her hand scrambling for the door handle.

"See something you don't like?" He sped up the car and started to laugh, the gruff sound grating her nerves.

Torn by the urge to look away, she reached for control over the panic that gripped her. "Stop it, Mason!"

"Your terror proves you're not as untouchable as you think, my love."

"How are you doing that?"

"This is the easy part, sweet pea. It's maintaining my old look that takes some effort."

She waved a finger at his face. "This is the real you? You tattooed yourself to look like a dead person? That's just creepy." Whatever his reasons, it was disturbing.

"Rather fitting for me, don't you think?"

Damn right. "So why the two faces?"

"Seeing the real me might ruffle a few feathers. I can't have the town folk having baby chickens just yet."

"What are you up to, Mason?"

His lips pinched together, as though he was suppressing a smile. "How did you like the smoke in the car?" he asked, his voice far too cheerful for the occasion. "A clever trick I picked up recently."

"Clearly the smoke erased your common sense too. Confronting me with my Keepers and the sheriff nearby was anything but clever."

"Ah, but they were occupied."

"Yeah, dead bodies tend to do that, but when it comes to me, my Keepers are never occupied."

She drew on that to steady her nerves and reminded herself of powers she had yet to touch. If it came to it, she was more powerful than Mason and he knew nothing of her newfound strength from Rose. Trapped in a car on an isolated mountain road, it was her only advantage, and she intended to use it.

"I'm not worried about your Keepers, Sienna, although you're the one who should be."

"If you harm them, Mason, we'll never give you what you seek."

He turned his head to face her and the tattooed teeth that stretched across his jaw broke into a creepy smile. "The stones that open my Grimoire?"

"This is what this little charade is all about, right? You want us to lift the spell that binds it? Is that why you were questioning me earlier about the stones? Fishing is beneath you, Mason."

"Most things are beneath me."

"Careful, Mason. Over-confidence and arrogance are never a good mix."

"Oh, but they're such fun, don't you think?"

"Why do you want the book opened? You've already demonstrated that your powers are getting stronger without your Grimoire."

"And it would be wise for you to keep that in mind. I have a right to access my family's spells. Rose must break the bind your mother cast on our Grimoire."

"You really think you can barge into town, kidnap me, and simply demand that we open it? Rose would never break that spell."

"She might be persuaded if I had something worthwhile to bargain with."

"That's your plan? To trade me for opening the Grimoire?"

Lightning flashed again, illuminating his wicked grin – a cat playing with a mouse.

But she refused to be the mouse.

"Your mother bound the book and I want it opened," he said.

"Perhaps your family should have thought of that before they killed her."

He gave an exaggerated sigh. "That was never proven, love, so let's not start with the mudslinging."

"My mother cast a spell on the Grimoire to keep your family from accessing its power. It's no secret as to why she did that. Our Grimoires are meant for protecting the good, for fighting evil. You are the evil. There's no way in hell I'm going to lift the spell that will unlock everything you need to create even more chaos."

"It's not chaos I'm after."

"How long do you think it'll take them to figure out that it was you behind all those *animal* attacks? Try living a great life once they've connected those dots." She shook her head, exasperated that he refused to see sense. It was an old argument, one that had long ago grown stale. "Exposing our kind to the world would be suicide. Surely you can see that?"

"We have these powers for a reason and the truth is, Sienna," he glanced at her, slowing his words, "we *are* superior."

"Doesn't give you the right to control others."

He made a "tsk-tsk" sound and shook his head. "You're such a buzz kill. Just think of what fun we could have if we all came out of the closet?"

"A life where we're hunted down by the majority? You're one confused puppy, Mason."

Her phone began to ring and her heart soared when Archer's

picture popped onto the screen. Mason glanced at the phone and gave a sly grin before answering.

"Where are you?" Archer's voice snapped over the phone.

"Hello, Bennett," Mason replied with a triumphant hitch to his raspy voice that drew a curse from her Keeper.

"Where's Sienna?" Archer kept his voice steady, but venom dripped off his words.

He glanced at her. "She's here."

"Is she okay? Is she hurt?"

"Not yet."

"You touch her, Mason, and I'll kill you."

"Now, now, Bennett. Threats will only piss me off."

"Let me talk to her."

Mason chuckled and began to end the call, but Sienna lunged for the phone, calling her Keeper's name.

The car swerved, tyres screeching on the tar, mingling with the loud crack of thunder that ripped through the sky.

"Dammit, Sienna!" Mason cursed, shoving her back with one arm.

Panic soared and she launched for the phone clasped in bony fingers.

"Stop it!" he growled, baring teeth behind upturned lips, the expression amplified by his tattooed teeth.

She screamed and lashed out, her fury snapping forward as survival instincts kicked in.

The car swerved off the road and plunged into the forest with a reckless speed that had them blundering through bushes and small trees.

Realizing that Mason had lost control, she drew back, bracing herself for the inevitable crash. The car bobbed along at a furious pace, branches scratching the doors and windows with an eerie screech.

Sienna glanced at Mason who gripped the steering wheel, his attention on the dangerous path in front of them as he tried to regain control of the car.

The moment the car collided with the tree, the airbags deployed with a hiss of air that muffled the deafening crash, cushioning the blow. Her body lurched forward with the impact, but her safety belt dragged her back, slamming her against the seat with a force that winded her. The sound of shattering glass and metal crunching against wood echoed through the darkness.

And then it went silent.

CHAPTER NINE

Raw adrenaline pumped through Sienna's veins, cushioning the shock of the accident. Her breathing consisted of choppy gasps of air as she released her safety belt, shoved against the airbag, and tumbled out of the car. Stumbling to the back of the car, she yanked open the boot and felt for the duffel bag Archer kept there. She tugged on the zip, wrenched the bag open and cried out in relief when her fingers wrapped around the torch.

Thank God.

Mason's loud curse tore through the silence as he struggled to free himself from the car. "Sienna!"

In the distance, she heard the screech of car breaks and doors slamming, followed by hurried footsteps through the forest.

Knowing it was too soon for her Keepers and that Mason rarely worked alone, Sienna raced through the darkness, grateful for the torchlight and sporadic lightning. The tricky terrain slowed her down, the uneven ground treacherous, and she kept a keen eye to avoid the burrows and fallen trees. As she ran, she tried to remember the route home, how far they'd driven, where they'd crashed.

Confusion wrapped around her, irritation adding to the cocktail of emotions bubbling inside her, but she pushed on.

A rustle of bushes and a low growl from a nearby tree had Sienna whirling around. Her body still moving, she shone the torch around her, gasping as the beam caught a flash of movement nearby.

A wolf? Mason's warriors?

Not waiting to find out, she spun around and bolted, a fresh wave of adrenaline spurring her on. The whirl of energy inside grew stronger, pounded against her chest for recognition, but in her haste for freedom it went ignored.

Another rustle of bushes, followed by more growls, sent her senses reeling as she realized she was being followed.

Without stopping, she looked over her shoulders, screeching at the large black shadow running silently behind her. Although it was dark, she could see it was an animal, crouching low, growling as it approached her.

And it wasn't alone.

The beam of torch light flitted from one animal to the next, panic snatching her breath away as they circled her. They were the biggest cats she had ever seen, unnatural and not of this earth. Their fur was brown, smudged with black; they had square jaws with snarling, upturned lips. Their eyes were black, filled with raw determination as they glared at their prey.

Her.

And she could never outrun them.

The truth stung but standing her ground, Sienna drew on her centre to create a circle of fire around her. A whispered chant sealed the circle and she drew on its protection to even her breathing and gather her senses.

They surrounded her, snapping, backs crouched low. The fire kept them at bay but Sienna wasn't sure what they were capable of.

That thought frightened her more than anything else.

Determination spurred her on and she glared at the cat closest to her. It was pacing along the barrier of fire, its death-like stare zeroed in on her.

Raising her hand, she gathered a ball of fire that hovered in mid-air before flying across the circle toward the cat.

It roared as the fireball struck but the flames were quick to disappear. The cat reared up, its agitation at a peak. Sienna tried again, mystified when the fire did little to ward it off.

A movement ahead had her lifting the torch to illuminate Mason walking toward her. He seemed unhurried, unperturbed; but his black eyes zoned in on her, the skeleton face a vision of evil in the darkness.

She glanced at the cats, hoping they'd sense their new prey and leave her alone. But if anything, Mason's approach seemed to fuel their vicious snarls.

She groaned as everything reeled into place. The mysterious animal attacks in town suddenly made sense – as did the cats' failure to be harmed.

They were Mason's and he'd charmed them with a protection spell.

Dammit.

Mason paused a few feet from the fire and his tattooed teeth cracked a smile. "Ah, you've met my cats."

"What the hell have you created?"

He laughed, the sound mingling with their growls and the crackling of flames. "They are rather fierce, aren't they?"

"That's what's been hurting the town folk?"

"You didn't believe it was animal attacks?"

"No. I thought it was you."

"And get my hands bloody? Not likely, sweet pea."

"You may not have hurt those people yourself, Mason, but your hands are as bloody as they come."

He shrugged, dismissing the statement and the responsibility that came with it, and went to the cat closest to him. Stroking its head, he patted the cat on the back, dishing out praise for securing his prisoner. "Open my Grimoire and this will all be over."

"That's a bit hard to do from here."

"You can't stay there forever. How about you douse this fire and we strike a deal?"

"You can huff and puff all you like, Mason, but we both know that's never going to happen."

His tattooed mouth turned downward and he gave a dismissive shrug. Reaching into his pocket, he withdrew a small bag attached to a rope. "I figured you'd say that."

Sienna eyed the circle of flames as her mind raced for an escape plan. All she'd done was trap herself but at least it had kept her from being mauled. A shiver raced down her spine at the thought but she tipped her chin upward.

As her anger mounted, the ground began to rumble beneath their feet and a harsh gust of wind blasted through the forest – all signs of an angry witch. She dragged in air, trying to calm the rush of energy inside.

Lightning struck in the distance and a bolt of light flashed through a gap in the trees, highlighting six approaching men.

Mason's warriors.

Sienna's gut twisted and with quick hand movements, she sent lashes of fire their way. Their shouts of surprise ripped through the night and they scattered. Sienna responded with another round of ammunition that seemed to quicken Mason's movements.

He tied the rope around the cat's neck and went to the next one with another bag, repeating the movement. "There was an old witch I met recently in New Orleans," he shouted above the noise, showing her the bag before fastening it to the third cat. "She was a friend of my mother's and shares our vision for our kind. She gave me these three bags and I'm itching to see if they work."

Sienna knew immediately what he meant, felt the hitch in her energy the moment the third bag touched the cat's neck, and fought to maintain the protection spell. Ashwood. She'd never seen the debilitating herb before, but her mother had once mentioned it. Not well known, it bound a witch's powers if placed in a triangular form around her. That and Rose Thorn were two herbs every witch dreaded.

Mason straightened, dusted off his hands and gave her a wide grin that smacked of triumph. Their gazes met across the retreating flames and she kept her back rigid, her head held high.

"You might temporarily bind my powers, Mason, but you've forgotten one thing," she said with a quiet confidence, even though the circle of fire had begun to wither away.

"And what's that, love?"

"My Keepers will come for me."

"They don't know where you are."

"They will find me and they will come for me. *Always*."

The long line of skeletal teeth drew together as his smile lessened. Without the grin, his tattooed deadpan expression was even more eerie, blurring the lines between the living and the dead. His black eyes settled on her with such intensity that her stomach lurched. "That's exactly what I'm counting on."

CHAPTER TEN

Archer was charged with a rage Sarah had never witnessed before. They all felt the blow that came with the cold realization that Mason had Sienna. It meant he'd grown bolder in his quest for control and exposure. Taking Sienna right under their noses had ignited a war they'd all hoped to avoid.

But he'd crossed the boundary now, triggering all their Keeper instincts to the max. He'd known it would and it had been a clever move on his part. They had just never thought he'd dare.

"Here," Archer muttered, sitting upright in his seat. He pointed to the side of the road up ahead. "Stop here."

Sarah slowed down the SUV and pulled to a stop on the side of the road without questioning him. They all had a unique connection to Sienna. She was their best friend, their witch, and everything they were duty-bound to protect. But for Archer, it had always been different. He sensed her in a way none of the others could.

They all climbed out of the car and scanned the forest.

Declan took three strides and pointed to a small broken tree that had been ripped from its roots. Casting a quick scan around them, he nodded. "Tyre tracks."

Ethan walked toward some overgrown trees and pushed aside the branches to reveal an abandoned car. "Mason's henchmen?"

Archer took off with a speed that jarred Declan into action. The two brothers raced ahead, while Ethan and Sarah followed at a slower pace with Rose.

In a few minutes, they had returned, in a blur of speed and heightened worry.

"Did you find her?" Sarah asked, unable to keep the hope from her voice.

"No." Archer shook his head. "But we found my car. It's empty."

"That means she's alive."

"I know. I'd know if she wasn't." Although his words were said with such conviction, they all knew that Sienna's fate could change in an instant.

Mason was irrational, fearless, and driven by hatred.

"Have you picked up her trail?"

Archer nodded in the direction of the forest and reached for Rose's hand. "Sienna's in trouble and we have to move fast."

Rose's expression shifted from worry to eagerness. "Of course."

"Archer, wait," Sarah said, with some trepidation, reaching for Rose's bag. Slowly, she withdrew the four stones Rose had summoned in the forest.

"What the hell?" Declan muttered, taking a stone and waving it at Rose. "Really, Rose? You summoned the stones on a night like tonight?"

Ethan's eyebrows shot up. "And we're about to head smack bang into what is most likely an ambush with the very stones that Mason seeks. A little heads-up would have been nice."

"Consider this your heads-up." Sarah stepped between them and handed out the stones to her brothers. She knew that they despised it when their witches took risks. "Since when do either of you question Rose?"

She wouldn't dare tell them that she had, too.

"Since Sienna was kidnapped by a damn warlock!" Archer

snapped, clenching his fists around the stone.

"I had my reasons for summoning them." Rose slung her bag over her shoulder and lifted her chin, not in the least bit perturbed by her Keepers' reactions. "I have a connection to my Grimoire that you'll never understand and I sensed I'd need its power."

"But those stones open the Brogan Grimoire too," Archer said, unclenching his fingers to glare at the offensive stone.

"Yes, but only with the spell from a Beckham witch. It'll take a hell of lot for us to break the spell that binds his book."

"He has Sienna, Rose. I think it's safe to say we know where this is heading."

"And I'm no help if I can't access my own Grimoire." Rose shifted her weight so that she stood in front of Archer. Reaching up, she closed his fingers around the stone again. "I don't know how all this is going to end, but I'm trusting my instincts and taking my guidance from The Circle. You have no choice but to trust me."

Archer nodded, exhaling through gritted teeth and pocketed the stone. "Fair enough, but next time you have the urge for witchy ceremonies on a full moon, it might be best that your Keepers are nearby."

Rose nodded and slipped into his arms that came up automatically around her. He lifted her in his arms, cradling her against him. "Watch the trees, Bennett. I've never been a fan of your speed."

Despite his frustration, Archer's lips twitched in the hint of a smile and he nodded at his siblings.

They took off at a speed only familiar to them and within seconds they'd tracked Sienna.

She was surrounded by Mason, six of his warriors, and three massive, grotesque-looking cats of a kind Sarah had never seen before. Mason's skeletal face unnerved her, just as it had Sienna.

Archer inhaled sharply and released Rose, tucking her behind them.

"Brother, wait," Declan murmured, stepping in front of Archer. "We need to be smart about this. We're outnumbered."

"Look at her! He has her surrounded by his damn wildcats!"

"I know."

Archer pushed forward but Declan and Ethan stopped him again. "I have to get to her."

"We get it." Declan slammed his hand against Archer's chest, his furious gaze matching his brother's. "We want her back as much as you do. Look at her. She's trapped, but she's fine. She's stronger than him and he needs her alive."

Rose pointed to the smouldering circle of fire that surrounded Sienna. "She had a protection circle but it's broken. Why would she break the spell?"

Sarah frowned, zoning in on the cats, and exhaled noisily when she spotted the bags around their necks. "She can't use her magic."

Four pairs of eyes swung back to look at her and she nodded to the cats. "Look at their necks. They're carrying Ashwood."

All talk of the herb came to a grinding halt when the argument between Mason and Sienna escalated, causing the warriors to edge nearer. The cats grew restless, circling Sienna, closing in on her.

A cloud of doom washed over them and a look of understanding passed between them. Moments later, they split up.

They had a witch to protect and a warlock needing a lesson about the dangers of messing with one of their kind.

CHAPTER ELEVEN

The binding of Sienna's powers left her with an emptiness she had never experienced before. She felt vulnerable, as though something vital had been ripped from her soul.

Although she was still trying to come to terms with Rose's powers, she had been connected to fire for as long as she could remember.

Sienna's gaze flickered, not sure what worried her more – the vicious cats or the power-hungry warriors itching to gain favours with their leader.

"Scared?" Mason taunted, his lips twitching.

"You won't hurt me, Mason."

"Snapping your neck would be a pleasure."

"So why haven't you? By killing me you'd absorb my powers."

"Tempting thought, but that's not what I'm after. There are other witches to destroy for my power supply."

His words challenged everything she stood for and she was quick to reel in the flash of anger. Another thought struck her and she frowned, eyeing him carefully. "What's in the Grimoire that you so desperately need?"

Although his expression didn't alter, she felt his flush of excitement. It was all the explanation she needed and everything inside her clenched in objection. "It's not the spells you want. You're after the location of the witch massacre, aren't you?"

A chuckle broke free. "That little secret is a goldmine of power. We can skip this entire process if you tell me where it is."

"That's what this is about? You want to access the energy at the site of the massacre!" Anger flared at the thought of the power he would gain from the murdered witches. Swallowing her horror, she gave him her most intimidating glare. "We will never let that happen, Mason, and we both know that you're no match for us."

His expression hardened and he took two strides toward her. Grabbing both of her arms, he yanked her against him. "I despise your kind. You think you're so righteous."

"We are here to maintain the balance between good and evil. You're the one constantly trying to tip it in your favour. This is your damn war!"

A frown creased the black circles around his eyes, and his grip softened. Lifting one hand, he trailed a finger along her jaw, his gaze settling on her mouth. "We could have made an indestructible team, my love. But you had to ruin it with your choices."

"I will die before joining forces with you."

"So you've told me countless times," he grumbled and rolled his eyes. "Bad me for not taking any notice." He dipped his head so that his lips were beside her ear, the contact making her recoil. "I'm done hiding and being governed by people beneath me. Do you want to know why I did this to my face?"

She didn't reply, his breathy words sending a bolt of panic through her, and she cringed at his touch.

"It's a permanent reminder of everything I want for you, your Keepers, and the people that stand against me. *Death*," he whispered as his grip tightened around her, bony fingers digging into her skin. He lifted his head to glower at her with such hatred that she had to bite down the urge to flinch again. "And just so you know what you're missing..."

A rustle of energy shifted inside, surprising her. She tried to move but couldn't, her gaze bound to Mason's in a way that terrified her.

A gloomy energy invaded her body, touching her in places she'd only reserved for the greater good, bringing along with it a darkness and despair that were completely new to her.

She tried to pull away but his sick magic had taken over, rooting her to the spot.

He whipped out a quick spell, repeating the words in a whispered gush that brought a wicked smile to his mouth – before releasing her.

She gulped air as the connection broke, unable to stop the cry of relief when the dark energy left her body. Horrified that he'd raided her body with his magic, she slapped him in the face.

"How dare you!"

His head shot to the side from the force of the blow, exposing a black cheek tattooed to look hollow. The smile widened and a hand shot out to stop one of his warriors, who'd taken a step closer. Turning to face her, he palmed his cheek.

"My magic offends you? How predictable."

The magical assault had shaken her more than the physical attack itself. He'd touched a sacred part of her that had left her feeling raw and exposed.

Sienna caught a glimpse of the tattoo on his inner arm. She sucked in air and grabbed it, ripping back the sleeve to expose the rest of the black mark. A wave of nausea washed over her as she stared at the bold letters carved into his arm.

Sienna.

"You tattooed my name on your arm?" Her words came out in a quiet hiss of disbelief and disgust.

Before he could respond, a roar from one of his warriors had him yanking her against him.

A ball of fire flew past them, hitting a small bush nearby. The cats began to growl and pace. There were shouts from Mason's men as they snapped into defensive mode, screaming orders as they rallied around their leader.

The area surrounding them lit up in a glow of orange inferno as more fireballs slashed past them in quick succession, hitting the ground in an explosion of embers and flames.

The ground rumbled beneath them, and the crackling of tree branches signalled new life. Roots ripped through the soil, slithering along the ground, aiming for the warriors. They shouted in response, dodging the roots as they slid around them, snapping at their heels.

A shower of stones and forest debris headed their way, raining down upon the warriors without mercy. Moments later, a whirlwind of thick dust wrapped around them, blinding them and destroying any means of escape.

And out of the haze, Sienna saw them approaching.

Her Keepers.

Her heart soared and a bolt of relief and pride washed through her.

Her four Keepers circled them, their presence wrapping around her like a protective shield, exuding a strength and power that horrified Mason's men.

Ethan and Archer hung back, bodies grounded in warlike stances, while Declan and Sarah wielded their magic in a series of skilled hand movements only known to them. Their expressions were even but she recognized the fury that burned in their eyes.

They were beautiful, their powerful force familiar to her. Despite the chaos that came with the arrival of her Keepers, Mason remained calm. Clearly, he'd been expecting them.

The dust settled and Mason snapped out a warning to his

warriors to reel them in. The cats growled, pacing between them, black eyes pinned on her Keepers.

"Your witch is unharmed," Mason called out, his tone laced with amusement.

"Release her, Brogan," Archer ordered. If Mason's tattooed face surprised him, he didn't show it.

Mason released Sienna. He waved a hand at her and stepped back, giving a bow of fake compliance. "She's all yours. Come and get her."

"Archer no!" Sienna shouted. "It's a trap!" It had to be. Mason had always feared her Keepers but his willingness to surrender her with such ease smacked of an ambush.

Mason grabbed her arm, pushing her forward. Sienna stumbled and one of the cats pounced.

Archer was there in a flash, ripping the cat away with a growl of his own. The cat responded with snarls, hair raised, canines flaring in warning. Archer glared at the animal as he helped Sienna to her feet, moving her behind him. "Call off your cats, Brogan."

"And ruin the fun? Unlikely."

"You should know better than to touch Sienna."

"It's not Sienna I'm after," he said, looking at Rose.

Archer's forehead tightened into a frown, suspicion flashing through narrowed eyes. "What are you up to, Mason?"

"Nothing. Take your witch."

Reaching for Sienna's hand, Archer backed away, releasing her only when Declan stepped forward.

Sienna couldn't stop the sigh of relief once she was with her Keepers again but a fresh bolt of fear trickled through her. Mason wouldn't have hurt her but he wouldn't hesitate to hurt them.

Away from the cats and the Ashwood they carried, she felt the swirl of energy within, inhaling sharply at the familiar sensation.

"I have a proposition for you," Mason said.

"We don't make deals with evil."

"You might have no choice. Meet me at the abandoned church tomb at midnight. It's a full moon. Bring the old witch and the stones. Warrick will bring the Grimoire."

Archer snapped out a laugh of disbelief. "You're insane, Brogan. There's no way in hell that's going to happen."

Mason shrugged. "We'll see. Midnight," he said sharply and turned away. The warriors retreated, the cats still circling them, and they all followed their leader.

Archer was in front of him in a flash of movement, his muscular frame an instant barrier. "What the hell is this?"

Mason lashed out a harsh shove, which sparked vicious growls from the cats. The warriors closed in, the tension dripping between them. Archer responded by grabbing Mason's shirt, hauling him so close that their noses were almost touching.

"Midnight, Bennett," Mason said. "You fuck with me and Sienna's dead."

Archer grabbed Mason by the throat. "You touch her again and I will kill you."

Sienna gasped as her throat contracted in a harsh grip around her neck. She clawed her throat and spun around to see who'd attacked her but there was no one. The grip tightened around her with a strength that could easily snap her neck. Choking air, she glared at Mason as horror set in.

She was now his.

CHAPTER TWELVE

Sarah reached Sienna as she dropped to her knees, everything inside her rebelling to see her friend in pain. "What's wrong? What's happening?"

Sienna struggled for air, one hand clutching her throat. With a strangled cry, she waved her other hand at Mason and Archer.

Sarah took in Archer's rough grip around the warlock's throat and cursed. "Archer, stop it!"

Not releasing Mason, Archer flicked Sarah a glance over his shoulder. Confusion crossed his expression when he saw Sienna and he shoved forward. "What have you done to her?"

Mason's laugh came out in a strangled gasp of air. Simultaneously, Sienna released a ghastly gurgle as air evaded her.

"He's linked them!" Sarah screamed. "Stop it, Archer! You're hurting Sienna!"

Her words immediately broke Archer's grip and he stepped back, glaring at Mason, who alternated between chuckling and coughing as he tried to catch his breath. Panting, Mason straightened as a wide grin broke free. He reached into his pocket and pulled out a knife, slashing the palm of his hand.

Sienna grunted and stared at the blood that gushed from hers. Rage flashed across her face at the idea that she was now tied to the one man they all despised. "You linked us? That's your master plan? You ass!"

Mason chuckled and attempted to slash his palm again but Archer snatched his wrist mid-air and glowered at him. "*Don't you dare.*"

"Everything you do to me will happen to her. A nifty spell, isn't it?" Mason goaded. He rolled his shoulders, straightened his shirt, and glanced back at Sienna. "So, how about we make that deal?"

Silence fell, a sure sign that their options were limited, and Sarah's heart sank at the stark reality of it all.

"The spell is my insurance policy. You know how this works, right?" Mason glared at them, all primed to annihilate him should he hurt their witch.

A witch out of Sarah's reach, despite the fact that she was right beside her.

That knowledge alone sent a bolt of terror straight to Sarah's gut and she drew in air, her mind grasping for another plan.

Dammit!

Whatever they did to Mason – or whatever he did to himself – would happen to Sienna.

That put him in charge.

"So what now, Mason?" Sienna snapped.

"Meet me at the tomb at midnight. Break the spell on the book and I'll leave town."

"And you'll run straight to the location of the witch hunt."

"Your options are limited, love."

"And the linking spell?"

"Stays in place until I'm sure you and your bodyguards are no longer a threat to us." He turned back to Archer, a grin on his tattooed face. "You have no choice here, Bennett. Deviate from what I want, change the plan in any way, and I will start dicing myself in ways you'd loathe."

Archer's expression was all control, despite the hatred that oozed off him. "Mason, you'll get your damn book open, but if you hurt Sienna again, there will be nowhere on this earth that you can hide."

Mason snapped out a harsh laugh that mocked the tension and nodded to his warriors before walking away, his cats nipping at his heels.

Archer was beside Sienna in an instant.

"I'm fine." She got to her feet and spun around. "Where's Rose?"

"I'm here." Rose rushed forward, her eyes a cloud of worry, and reached for her granddaughter. "Oh my God, Sienna. Are you okay?"

Sienna nodded and was quick to pull away. "Gran, the curse you told me about ... is it really possible?"

Recognition flashed, along with an instant wariness that had Archer raising a brow. "Yes, but it's too risky."

"I'll take my chances."

CHAPTER THIRTEEN

Sienna found Archer in the living room, staring at the three daggers on the wall above the fireplace. He'd had a shower and the smell of soap and man permeated the room, an aroma that was quick to dispel some of the gloom she felt.

He turned when she entered, a small smile easing some of the tension in his face. "Are you okay?" he asked, his voice a soft grumble of sexiness.

She nodded and went to him, glancing at the daggers that unlocked the room that concealed her family's Grimoire. The ancient book contained every spell, ritual or potion ever performed by the generation of witches in her family. It was sacred, its whereabouts a guarded secret, and Sienna had never been able to bury the anxiety that came with taking it out of its hiding place.

Archer swept a strand of hair away from her face, his Keeper ring brushing against her cheek. The antique silver ring stood for everything he meant to her and it tugged at the part of her that cherished that connection. She could see that he was worried.

"It'll be fine, Archer," she said softly, covering her hand with his. "Rose and I can do this."

"I don't trust Mason. We have no guarantee that he will break the spell that binds you to him once you've released his Grimoire."

"Hopefully, we won't have to worry about that. It's risky, but we've covered as many angles as we can possibly think of."

He went quiet and his jaw tightened, as though he was choosing his next words with care.

And she wasn't wrong.

"Sienna, you need to settle your argument with Rose. She gave you her powers for a reason."

"I will, just not now. If I'm going to pull off the spell tonight then I can't have that energy in the way." She tilted his hand toward her mouth, kissing him on the knuckles. "I will deal with that when this is over."

"You don't need to do this alone. Rose can help you." He tipped her chin upward. "With time and practice you'll do great."

"Oh, absolutely. I'm going to kick ass," she said brightly, but he saw right through her and she sighed. "The strength of what I'm capable of frightens me."

"You're a Beckham witch. You'll do this."

And she would. Just not tonight.

He leaned forward, his lips almost touching hers with a small smile. "I'll have to remind Declan not to pick a fight with you."

A smile broke free as his mouth covered hers and she slid her arms around his neck with a longing to hold him and never let go.

Heat fired from her stomach to her thighs and she groaned softly as his hands slid down her body, grasping her hips, tugging her closer. His hardness excited her; muscular, strong, and powerful.

When he broke away a moment later, they were both breathless, touched with guilt, knowing they had crossed another line.

He captured her cheeks in his hands and kissed her softly, the movement lined with such tenderness that she ached for more. "How can something that feels so right be so wrong?" he asked.

She closed her eyes, his words washing over her as a stark reminder of everything she felt. Everything she could never have. "I know," she whispered, opening her eyes.

An unsettling energy swept through her, serving as an instant barrier between them. Her skin prickled with a wave of uneasiness and she pulled away.

"Sienna?"

"Oh no," she whispered, stepping away from him. The odd sensations grew stronger.

"What's wrong?" Archer scowled, scanning her body with a quick glance before reaching for her again.

"Don't." She moved out of his reach, her heart pounding in warning. Fear trickled through her, crushing the tenderness she'd felt in his arms moments ago.

"Sienna!"

"The Circle," she whispered, her gaze meeting his. "They're angry."

They'd crossed the line despite knowing the punishment that lingered because of it and her body rattled with a furious energy that wasn't hers.

Oh, no.

Something sharp pierced her forearm and she inhaled sharply, ripping back her sleeve, confused to find nothing there. Her skin indented and she cried out as a slash appeared, blood oozing from the wound. "Archer!" she gasped, gaping at him.

"This isn't The Circle." He grabbed her arm and looked around. "What the hell?"

She grimaced as the cutting continued but the eeriness of the moment sent a bolt of fear through her, overruling the pain. Archer cursed as a bloodied, jagged word began to form on her arm.

MASON.

With a cry, she swiped at the blood, hoping to wipe away his name, his brand; but blood smeared across the word.

"It's okay," Archer murmured and she heard the shaking anger in his voice. He ripped his shirt, using the material to cover the wound, and it instantly turned red.

Her body began trembling and she clawed at her arm, an intense desire to rid Mason's name from her body.

"Sienna, stop it! You're going to hurt yourself even more," Archer said, louder this time, and reached for her hands, tugging her closer. His hands came up to cup her face and she could feel the tremor against her cheeks. He was as rattled as she was. "Calm down, baby. It's just a ploy to frighten you."

She blinked, refusing to cry, but she couldn't dismiss the sick feeling that came with the thought of being branded by evil – or being at Mason's mercy. She shuddered and when Archer pulled her into his arms, she went willingly, needing his strength and purity to wipe away the smear of the warlock.

"He's reminding us of his claim on you, but it's not for long, Sienna," Archer said, pulling back to look at her. "He will never have you. We'll end this tonight and he'll pay for this, I promise."

She nodded and exhaled, reaching for calm.

When he lifted her arm to examine the wound, his expression clouded with fury. He disappeared and returned moments later with a damp towel and a few first aid supplies. He remained silent, his brows drawn together in a harsh frown.

Her spirits lifted as he gently wiped away the blood and patched her arm, his tender actions easing the invasion of Mason.

When he was done, he slid his hands across her shoulders, down her arms, and captured her fingers with his. "Are you okay?"

She nodded.

Planting a gentle kiss on her lips, he pulled back and glanced at the daggers on the wall. "We should go. My brothers are on their way down."

Sienna took in a deep, quiet breath and faced the wall. She reached for the daggers, whispering a spell as she adjusted the blades in a pattern that would open the entrance to the Grimoire. A guarded secret, only known to the Beckham women and their Keepers.

The bookshelf across the room rumbled in response and shifted half a metre to reveal a dark hole set within the wall. It was dusty, hadn't seen the light of day for a long time, but in the middle of the hole was the Grimoire.

Old, tatty, treasured.

Sienna realized she'd stopped breathing when she went to the book and reached for it. She blew out air, trying to calm the butterflies in her stomach, and hugged it against her chest.

Her mother and grandmother had used the book for all sorts of magical rituals, as had all the Beckham women that had come before them, and holding it against her now filled her with pride.

She turned to Archer, their eyes meeting across the room, and she swallowed.

"Ready?" he asked.

"As ever."

CHAPTER FOURTEEN

Sarah's insides twisted as they climbed the rocky steps of the platform that marked the location of the tombs. The moon was at its fullest, offering a gentle glow of light that eased the darkness of the forest.

Waiting on the platform in guard-like stances were Mason's warriors and all three cats. Tension soared between the men and the cats pacing along the cement floor, their lips hovering above exposed canines.

One of the warriors nodded to Sienna and Rose. "They go inside alone."

"Like hell," Archer snarled, pushing forward with a quiet determination that had the warrior backing down.

Sarah glanced at her brother and bit back a smile. In defence mode, when it came to Sienna, her brother's size, muscular frame and deathly glare were intimidating. No wonder the warrior hadn't challenged him.

The other warrior pushed open the heavy door that served as the only entrance to the underground tombs, eyeing them with caution. The tunnel was dark and musty. Once an old church tomb, it was now abandoned and overgrown, left to the likes of secret rituals such as this one. Very few people knew of its existence and even fewer were able to access it, which made it the perfect place for what they were about to do tonight.

Using her connection to fire, Sienna sent a trail of light along the lanterns hanging from rusty nails in the ceiling, easing the creepiness of the tunnel. Declan went inside first and Sarah followed, casting a quick glance at Sienna, who had the Grimoire clutched to her chest as though it were gold.

Her fire-red hair was tied back in a loose knot at the nape of her neck and several stray strands had escaped to frame her face. She had been quiet on the drive here, her face masked in a tension felt by them all.

Rose followed, casting longing looks at her granddaughter. The tension between them was still ripe, but worry had taken over for now.

The deeper they went, the stuffier it got, and Sarah drew in air as they entered the main tomb. Several fire torches burned against the wall.

The tomb was built of stone with sandy floors and a low ceiling. In the far wall was a doorway that led to a smaller tomb.

Sienna moved to the middle of the room and cast a circle. Rose stepped forward, placing the four stones in the centre of the circle.

"It's almost midnight," Sienna said. "Mason should –"

Senses prickling, Sarah silenced her with a finger to her lips and gave a quick shake of her head before tapping her ear. Taking in a steady breath, she glanced at the entrance of the smaller tomb. "Hello, Mason."

A skeleton emerged from the shadows of the smaller tomb, wearing black clothes, heavy boots, and a smirk. His curly black hair had succumbed to the hot airless tomb and clung to his face in a wet mess – a testament to how long he'd been there. He appeared calm, amused; but his black eyes were filled with challenge and aggression. In his hands was a thick brown book, spelled shut by

Sienna's mother many years ago.

Warrick came up behind him, his appearance similar to his brother's; but his hair was lighter, shorter, and he'd shelved the smirk. His clamped jaw, pale face, and clenched fists hinted at hostility.

Suspicion stirred and Sarah did a quick scan of the room, searching for any signs that might hint at their intentions.

"You're early," Sienna said, her tone clipped with irritation.

Mason flicked the Keepers a casual glance and rolled his eyes. "You're here. How unsurprising."

"You knew we'd be here," Archer said.

"Well then," Mason said, his tone hitched with a mocking boredom, "let's get started. Open my Grimoire."

"Manners, Mason," Sienna cautioned and pointed to the centre of the circle. "Place the Grimoire on the floor in front of you."

Sarah glanced at the women, hearing the sound of the witches' pounding hearts. Her friends were nervous, adrenaline coursing through their bodies, their senses primed; but despite the under-lying anger, they both appeared calm.

Mason didn't immediately comply. Clearly, his suspicion of the witches marred his eagerness to have his book of spells returned. He looked at Sienna and then faced Rose warily. After all, the warlock had no idea that Rose had transferred her powers to her granddaughter. "Try any witchy crap tonight and you'll regret it."

"Power struggles and threats don't scare me, Mason," Rose retorted.

He reached for the fire torch closest to him. "Something you should know by now, Rose, is that I'm all power and threats."

"Makes me question our decision to open your Grimoire."

"Of course," he replied, dousing the flames of the torch. "That's precisely why I cast the spell on Sienna linking her to me. She's my…insurance policy." A small smile broke free as he pushed the sizzling torch into his palm.

"No!" Sarah yelled, reaching for Sienna as her anguished cry ripped through the room. In perfect unison, Ethan and Archer charged Mason but he swung the torch at them before placing it near his neck. The motion was enough warning to halt them in their tracks but Sarah knew the strength it took for her brothers to restrain themselves from ripping into him.

Looking up from her injured hand, Sienna gave Mason a fierce glare, her expression hardening with fresh anger. "You've hurt me three times now, Mason. You try that again and you will never, ever, see your Grimoire open."

"Those are the stones?" Mason said to Sienna, glancing at the four stones in the centre of the circle.

Sienna nodded. "Yes."

"Considering their power, I was expecting something a little more dramatic."

"Dynamite and small packages, Mason. Let's get this over with."

CHAPTER FIFTEEN

Sienna went to stand beside Rose.

Two women on the same side of nature, one bound to the warlock in a way that could alter everything.

Rose stroked the symbol on the front of the Beckham Grimoire, closed her eyes, and whispered the spell that would unseal the book. Opening it, she flipped through the thick pages until she found the spell they needed. Turning to Sienna, they started reading, their hushed words rolling around the room in an eerie whisper. The energy in the room shifted and they focused on the stones with an intensity that added fuel to the burning torches.

Mason and Warrick were both staring at the Brogan Grimoire on the ground between the stones, their glee for the impending outcome so obvious that it made Sienna want to bite something.

Instead, she blocked out everything around her and focused on the spell that would finally end the madness.

Despite the lack of air, a strange wind blew through the tunnels and circled the room, fuelling the fire and unsettling years of sand and dust. The torches burned brighter, the whispered chanting grew faster, louder, the eeriness of the moment spiking to a peak.

Sienna felt the heat within her and hoped like hell it wouldn't swallow her whole. Not now. Not here. She breathed deeply, concentrating on the flow of magic, connecting to her central power, channelling it with ease.

Uncomfortable with the heat invading his body, Mason shifted beside her, tugging at his t-shirt as droplets of sweat pooled on his forehead. His brows drew together into a pinched frown and his narrowed eyes became glassy as he dug deeper for his own magic. His own strength.

He grimaced but remained silent, his struggle to maintain the spell that linked them betrayed by his intense expression.

Hope fired in Sienna, only to be washed away by the heightened force within her, and she chanted on, drawing on everything inside her to sustain the heat.

The ground began to shake, a soft rumble around them that drew frowns from all her Keepers and a growl from Mason. He swiped at his forehead, clawed at his neck.

But he fought on, determined to win their power struggle, real-izing that the only way he'd accomplish that was if he maintained the linking spell.

She sensed his resistance, his fear, and it sparked her own determination to overwhelm him. She drew on her heated energy in a way she'd never done before, and dug deeper when she felt it weaken him.

Moments later, with a loud grunt, he snapped out of his trance with a low growl, his shoulders heaving as he gasped air.

"Sienna," Mason snapped, swiping his brow. "What are you doing?"

Sensing the weakening of his strength and the spell that bound him to Sienna, the witches chanted on, simultaneously changing to the spell they'd reserved for this moment. More vigour. More power. More energy.

Sienna's nose began to bleed and she felt the heat, grimaced, but fought on, ignoring the burning sensations running through her. She was drenched, and it had nothing to do with the stuffy tomb or the burning flames. It was a heat within that only she felt.

And Mason.

"Sienna, stop it!" Mason choked, gasping for air. He was wet, his t-shirt soaked with sweat. He reached for her and grunted as her skin scalded his hand.

And just as Sienna thought she might combust from the heat, the spell was finished.

She broke away from Rose with a huge gasp of her own, her trance broken. Exhausted, she pinned Mason with a satisfied glare.

"What have you done?" Mason asked, sinking to his knees with a guttural groan.

"Mason!" Warrick bolted forward but Archer and Declan were ready for him, grabbing him in perfect sync, slamming his body against the wall. Warrick squirmed against their hold but was no match for her Keepers' strength. "Dammit, Sienna! What have you done to him?"

"What I should have done a long time ago," she replied.

"Sienna, stop!" Mason hissed through gritted teeth. His skeleton skin tightened, contracting as though something was sucking the very essence out of him. Amidst the tattooed bones, the veins on his face and neck began to bulge. The black circles around his eyes narrowed and dark eyes stared in horror.

"Mason! MASON!" Warrick shouted.

"How are you doing this?" Mason wheezed, clutching his heart.

Sienna watched the warlock wither away as his heart rate began to fade and his blood grew thicker, slowing his movements. "Linking us was a bad, bad idea, Mason. There was one thing you forgot." Sienna sank to her knees beside the warlock, leaning closer so that her mouth was against his ear. "A linking spell works both ways. Whatever I feel, you feel too."

And she'd used that connection to overwhelm him enough to

break the hold he had on her. Once the linking spell was broken, they'd cast a spell of their own, a curse, that would bind him to the tomb forever.

"The power, the heat. How –"

"Remember Rose's powers? They're now mine, so when you chose to link yourself with a witch, you picked the wrong one."

"The Grimoire. The stones –"

"This meeting was never about opening your Grimoire." She drew on an inner strength not to flinch at the horrific sight of the desiccating warlock. "So how does all that power feel, Mason?"

"Screw you," he snarled, his words a fierce whisper in the room. He tried to grab her, but his movements were slower, and his eyes bulged as he realized the full impact of what they'd done.

When he finally grew still, staring blankly at her with cold, dark eyes, Warrick's howl of fury snapped her attention back.

Rage fuelling his strength, he fought fiercely, shoving Declan off him before whirling on Archer.

Sienna's instincts snapped to the forefront and she straightened, her gaze pinned on the raging warlock.

She held out her hand and began whispering a spell that had Rose joining in. Their whispered chants stayed level, a quiet hush of voices drowned out by Warrick's shouts.

"Sienna, no!" he yelled, reigning in his anger. When she ignored him, he held out a hand to plead with her. "I'm nothing like Mason. You know that."

Sienna's gaze flickered to meet his, a brief hitch in her whispered chant, but she pushed on with the spell.

"No! Sienna, we were once friends. I know you haven't forgotten that." His voice held a tinge of desperation as he fought against receiving the same fate as his brother. "Please, Sienna!"

She fell silent and moments later, Rose's voice faded away too. "You chose to side with Mason despite my attempts to change your mind."

"I had no choice! You know how powerful he is. I did what I had to do to stay alive." His gaze shifted to his brother on the ground. "But after what you've done to him, I'm free. I don't have to bend to his will anymore."

"Warrick —"

"Please, Sienna! I had no choice!"

Sienna felt the tug of his plea and the suspicion that came with it. She glanced at Rose and sensed her grandmother's struggle. Their gazes met in silent understanding and Rose gave a brief nod. Without looking away from Warrick, Sienna began to whisper a spell.

It didn't take long for Rose to join in and their whispered chanting grew louder and faster as they fell in sync.

Warrick's anger flared when he connected to their words — a binding spell — and with a powerful roar, he ripped out of Archer's grip and charged at the witches.

Before he reached them, a gust of wind swept through the tomb, stirring up a whirlwind of sand that wrapped around the warlock. He waved his arms, fighting the confusion and muffled vision.

Sarah stepped forward, eyeing him with fierce intensity as she worked her magic. The whirlwind grew faster, engulfing the warlock in more layers of sand. Warrick tripped and stumbled to the ground. Sarah retreated, as did the whirlwind.

Coughing and cursing, Warrick struggled to his feet and charged again, his movements dazed. Ethan was there in an instant, stepping in front of the women with a swinging punch that hurled the warlock across the room. Warrick slammed against the wall with a grunt and slumped to the ground.

"Is he dead?" Archer asked.

Declan went to Warrick and shook his head. "No. Out cold." He flashed Ethan a grin. "That was some punch, brother."

"Damn right."

Declan hitched a brow at Sienna. "What the hell did you do to him?"

"A binding spell, but not as strong as Mason's. He'll be free, but without his powers, he'll be weak."

Leaving the unconscious man with his brothers, Archer took two large strides to Sienna.

"Are you okay?" Archer asked, strong hands cradling her face. His eyes held a storm of turmoil and he reached for her injured hand.

"I'm fine," she whispered with a slight nod. Exhausted, raw, but fine.

They all were.

Sienna's head fell forward to rest on her Keeper's shoulder and she exhaled. "It worked. Mason couldn't handle the strength of my powers. It's finally over."

CHAPTER SIXTEEN

Was it?

Sarah glanced at Warrick and frowned at the unconscious man slumped against the wall. They'd bound his powers and sealed his desiccated brother in a tomb. Would Warrick really let this go?

The energy that had whipped through the tomb had subsided, leaving the room in a ghostly silence.

Archer nodded to Ethan. "Let's go, brother. There are still a few clueless warriors outside, and those cats are ugly."

Ethan grinned and joined his brother. "Fine. I'll take the warriors. You take the cats."

"Why do I get partnered with the cats? They're creepy."

"The cats will have vanished," Sienna said. "They were spelled by Mason. Some sort of sick ancient magic used to amplify animals."

"So you're off the hook," Ethan said and followed Archer outside, leaving Sarah and Declan with the witches while they closed the circle.

"You should have done the same to Warrick," Sarah said, unable to identify the flash of unease that trickled through her.

Sienna reached for the Grimoire. "Mason's the bigger evil. Warrick was simply influenced."

"You're so sure of that?"

"His powers are bound. Hopefully without them, he'll have some sense shaken into him."

"You really believe that?"

Sienna shrugged. "It's his choice. If he decides to follow in his brother's footsteps, we'll be ready for him."

"He's going to be furious when he wakes up."

"Maybe, but he's seen what we can do. That should caution him." Sienna looked at the Grimoire, closed the heavy book and bound it with the Beckham spell.

"We're done here. I need some air," Rose said, pocketing the four stones. Fatigue lined her expression, her eyes filled with wariness. Rose might have once been a powerful witch but despite the fact that she looked ten years younger than she was, she appeared to still feel the strain of the magic. "I'm going to wait with Archer and Ethan."

"We'll meet you outside," Declan said, coming up behind Sarah to nudge her on the arm. He flipped a casual nod toward the smaller tomb. "Help me seal the door on big bro."

Sarah hesitated, casting a quick glance at Rose as she disappeared into the tunnel, and went to help her brother. With little effort, they moved the heavy stone door across the entrance of the tomb. That, combined with the spell Rose and Sienna had performed to bind the tomb shut, would seal Mason's fate.

"Are you sure this will hold him?" Sarah asked, looking at Sienna.

Sienna nodded without hesitation. "He's just shy of a corpse so he's not going anywhere. Without the co-operation of a Beckham witch, our Grimoire and the four stones that open it, that door is impenetrable."

"Mason's going to be spitting cobras at us."

"A fitting punishment."

"Damn right. Need help with Warrick?" Sarah asked Declan, glancing at the unconscious man on the floor.

"Nah, I'll sling baby bro over my shoulder and dump him in the forest. By the looks of it, he'll be sleeping with Bambi for a while until he recovers from Ethan's blow." He grinned and turned to douse one of the torches. "No powers, a headache, and sandblasted. He's not going to be a happy camper."

"Serves him right. I'm going to check on Rose." Sarah headed for the door and disappeared into the tunnel, only to whirl around when she heard Sienna scream.

Icy cold shivers washed over her and she tore into the main tomb just in time to see Warrick charging at Declan, a dagger clasped in one hand.

"DECLAN!" Sarah leapt forward, slamming her body between them. She felt the blade pierce her skin, sucked in air that suddenly seemed to evade her, and collapsed against Declan.

"Sarah!" Declan shouted, his voice ripping through the stunned silence. He reached for her, his expression twisting in horror as he lowered her to the ground.

Sienna screamed, rushing forward, but Warrick spun around, shoved a hand against her throat and slid behind her, yanking her against him.

"Revenge is sweet, witch, and in this case, it's even sweeter." Warrick's voice came out in breathless rumbles of anger. Declan stood up, tearing his eyes away from Sarah, and Warrick tightened his grip around Sienna's throat in warning. "You were a fool for believing the crap I spewed earlier. Of course my brother and I share the same vision!"

Sienna choked, clawing against his hands as she gasped for air.

With a deafening roar, Declan lunged for Warrick, slamming his full weight against the warlock. They all slid across the floor, colliding with the wall. In a flash of movement that left Sienna dazed, Declan separated her from their fight. She sank to her knees, clutching her throat and sucking in air.

"I will hunt you all down until my brother is freed!" Warrick bellowed, staggering to his feet and swinging toward Declan.

"You won't live to try," Declan huffed, dodging Warrick's attempt to punch him. Warrick charged and the two men tumbled backward, wrapped in a struggle of thrashing fists, hatred and rage.

The pain tore through Sarah, slashing away everything else, and she tried to focus on the fight. "Declan!" she gasped, her voice a mere whisper. Everything around her began to spin and she was vaguely aware of Sienna on her knees beside her.

"Sarah!" Sienna's hands moved frantically across her body, fingers splayed around the knife in her heart. "Oh, no! No, no, no! Declan, she's hurt!"

Her brother's roar rattled through the room, along with the eerie rumble of shaking ground that hinted at Sienna's fury. The torches flared to life so powerfully that a whoosh of air exploded through the tomb. The room lit up with a vicious glare that had Sarah closing her eyes.

Blackness threatened, her breathing gulping and shallow. She closed her fingers around her friend's hand. "Sienna…"

"SARAH!"

CHAPTER SEVENTEEN

The flames tore through the tomb with a reckless vengeance, endangering everything in their path. The heat was unbearable, threatening to envelope Sienna in its relentless path of destruction.

Flames sparked by her grief but they couldn't touch her.

Nothing could touch her.

Heat flooded her cheeks, her veins bulged, her heart raced uncontrollably; her body had been overrun by a force she had no control over. Driven by rage, grief and devastation, Sienna had given in to the powerful energy within.

She sank to her knees, exhausted and depleted, but the fire inside her raged on as much as the fire surrounding her.

In the distance, she heard the moaning of her name through the crackling of flames; groans of pain.

But she couldn't stop it, couldn't snap out of it.

There was a blur of movement around her as the groans faded away. Drawn to oblivion, she edged toward the heat of the fire.

A strong pair of arms reached for her through the orange glow of angry flames; drew her back from the inferno that threatened to devour her. "Sienna!"

Somewhere in the distance, far beyond a darkness she'd never experienced before, she heard Archer's voice. It jerked her back, beckoned her, and the haze slowly began to lift as she emerged from her trance.

"Sienna, stop it!" Archer dragged her out of the tomb and into the tunnel, coughing from the thick blanket of smoke that filled the air. He dropped to his knees, grabbed her chin in his hands and snapped her name again. "Come back to me, baby."

She blinked as his face came into focus. Dark eyes, full of concern, were pinned on her. His brows were furrowed in a harsh frown, his jaw clenched in a grimace of pain.

Archer.

She glanced around them, cringing at the flames that licked the walls in the main tomb. She shifted her gaze back to his, confusion twisting everything around her.

And then it hit her like a dark, dirty reminder that would never let go.

Sarah was dead.

Her wail of anguish joined the sounds of the crackling flames and she began to cry; uncontrollable sobs that ripped through her.

With the sound of a caged animal, Archer yanked her toward him, crushing her against him. Trembling furiously, he staggered to his feet, drenched from the heat, and gathered her in his arms. Cradling her, he stumbled through the tunnel, his own devastation splashed across his face, lacing his muttered ramblings.

They tumbled out of the tunnel into the cold night air, gasping for the fresh air that had evaded them in the tomb.

In the distance, Sienna was vaguely aware of her grandmother rushing toward them. "Sienna! Oh my God, Sienna!"

Archer swayed down the stairs of the platform and, in a clumsy movement, lay her down on the forest debris. Grunting, he collapsed on his side next to her, his shoulders heaving as he tried to catch his breath.

The smell of burnt flesh snapped her attention away from his face and she recoiled at a black mesh of scorched skin on his right arm. She glanced around them, trying to make sense of her surroundings in the darkness, and cried out when she saw the still frames of Declan and Ethan on the ground nearby. They were dirty, drenched in sweat, their clothes a singed, torn mess; their bodies blackened from the heavy smoke.

She scrambled over to them, shouting their names, squealing with relief when she found movement.

Weak, drained, but alive.

And then the cold realization struck with a force that threatened to devour her and she stared in horror at her three Keepers, shame washing over her in a way that could never be cleansed.

"Oh my God," she gasped, steely fingers wrapping around her heart. She looked at the two men before settling her gaze on Archer. "I did this?"

Archer glanced at his brothers. Panting, he straightened until he was on his knees. He didn't reply and she struggled to breathe as the impact of what she'd done finally sank in.

"I channelled them," she whispered, her voice sounding foreign to her own ears. "My powers, our connection…My God, I could have killed them!"

"Sienna."

"Warrick –"

Archer shook his head. "He bolted."

She scrambled to her feet, gaping at her Keepers, reaching for fragments of memory that might clear the blur of what had happened. Her powers had overwhelmed her, an easy task once her guard was down and rage had set in. She'd lost herself to the magic and destroyed the tomb. And when she'd drained her own energy, she'd used the sacred bond she had with her Keepers to channel theirs. It was a special connection, seldom used because of the dangers that came with it.

But she hadn't had the strength to stop herself.

Mortified, she squeezed her eyes shut, unable to shoulder the horror of almost having destroyed what she treasured most in the world.

Her Keepers.

CHAPTER EIGHTEEN

The necklace felt heavy clasped within Sienna's hand and she unfolded her fingers, staring at the family heirloom, once her mother's. A chunky, antique pendant in the shape of a pentagram hung from a silver chain. It was simply designed but the perfect illustration of her connection with her Keepers. She'd never worn it and holding it in her hands again triggered unwanted memories.

Her mother. Sarah. Her Keepers.

Reaching for the welcome numbness she'd relied on since Sarah's death, Sienna walked to the three daggers on the living room wall. She reached up, shifted the weapons and turned around with a satisfied nod when the doorway concealing the Beckham Grimoire opened.

She glanced at the four stones beside the book, relieved that Rose hadn't returned them yet. Sienna whispered the words that would unlock the Grimoire and flipped through the ancient book until she found the page she sought.

A disconnection spell.

Not giving the nagging voice in the back of her mind a chance to rear its head, she placed the necklace and the book on a nearby table.

Inhaling several deep breaths, she held out her hands over the necklace and began whispering in a hushed undertone.

She felt the swirl of energy but it was gone in a flash and she smiled at the simplicity of the spell.

God, how she loved simple magic.

Something that had become totally foreign to her since inheriting her grandmother's powers.

Powers she would shun until the day she died.

Sienna returned the Grimoire to its rightful place and cast the spell to seal it, unable to resist a final lingering glance. She fastened the necklace around her neck, knowing that once she did, her connection to Archer would be altered.

He'd always been able to sense her, but the necklace would sever their connection and keep him from tracking her. Despite the numbness, Sienna still felt the pang of anguish that came with the thought of leaving Archer.

Oh God.

The soft hum of a car engine stopping outside the front door had her glancing at her packed bag in the doorway. It was black and almost empty.

Just like her.

She took four strides to the daggers where she retraced their places on the wall. The soft scrape of wood against the floor indicated the sealing of the Grimoire.

The murmur of voices in the kitchen hinted at her Keepers' arrival, jarring her into action. She had to leave. Now.

Ignoring the flash of fear, she grabbed the bag, slipped quietly into the hallway and out the front door, where the cab was waiting at the bottom of the stairs. Ignoring the sound of her name, she climbed into the car.

"Go," she issued the driver, closing the door behind her. "Just go."

The car pulled off into the long driveway and Sienna turned in her seat to glance out the back window.

Archer raced to the top of the stairs, his heavy frown and hurried movements an indication of his confusion. "Sienna!"

Declan and Ethan came out of the house and she saw the bolt of betrayal and disbelief slam home, their expressions tightening when they realized she was leaving.

Three men. Tall, powerful, and breathtaking in their own way. They were her best friends, her partners, her Keepers.

And she'd almost killed them.

She looked at Archer, the man who'd stolen her heart, aching with the knowledge he'd never be hers. Sarah's death had driven a wedge of grief and guilt between them impossible to ignore. Perhaps The Circle had cursed them after all.

Archer charged down the stairs. "SIENNA!"

The anguished shout of her name stung and a small sob escaped her. Shifting in her seat, Sienna met his gaze as the cab drove away, feeling as though something had been ripped from her soul.

"Everything okay, miss?" the cab driver asked.

Sienna swivelled around, breaking the connection with Archer, and turned her back on them.

"Yes," she whispered, refusing to lay claim to the wreckage in her heart. "Everything's fine."

Liar, liar.

THE KEEPERS: ARCHER

CHAPTER ONE

She was under a microscope.

A silly notion, one she'd never admit to anyone. Her logical mind challenged the thought but Sienna Beckham knew – just knew – that she was being watched.

Sitting on the grass, she scanned the busy park. A casual, fleeting glance, nothing too obvious.

Nope. Nothing out of the ordinary.

Just the normal crowd – different faces than the day before, but normal nonetheless. Joggers, strollers, a few picnics, several ball games – all the same. The warm weather and sunshine had drawn out the nature lovers who appeared reluctant to leave despite the setting sun. The park, once lush and green, had turned a magical shade of orange, yellow, and red, a sign that fall had arrived with fervour.

Her instincts bristled; her gut clenched.

Paranoid? Crazy?

She pushed herself off the grass, drained the last of her water, and tossed the bottle in a nearby bin.

The sun hovered above the horizon, illuminating the tall

buildings around the park in a gentle orange glow. The lake had turned a soft shade of pink. One last lap around the park and she'd make her way home to shower and change before heading out to Terroirs for drinks with two of her colleagues from the bookshop. She hadn't wanted to go out tonight but it was Saturday, a day they were determined to celebrate.

She pulled her fiery red hair into a ponytail and set off at a gentle pace. Within moments, she was flying across the park with a feeling of lightness. Jogging always did that to her, but today she felt…different.

Hell, she'd always felt different, but today she felt strange.

Her parents?

The anniversary of her parents' deaths loomed dangerously around the corner, threatening to jolt her back into a time she'd rather not remember.

But her uneasiness hinted at something more, something she hadn't been able to identify all week.

With a shake of the head, she scolded herself for being so serious, for thinking too much, and concentrated on running with a clear mind.

She soon lost herself to the fresh air, the warm glow of the fading sunlight, the wind in her face, and the thoughtless running.

It wasn't until she'd neared the end of the lake and rounded a bend marked with several large, overgrown bushes that he pounced.

Strong, powerful, and terrifying.

His hands grabbed her and in a fluid motion, she was absorbed into a clearing in the bushes, into him.

She tried to scream but the heavy hand covered her mouth, smothering her cries. She couldn't breathe, couldn't see.

The more she struggled, the more force he used. His aggression pressed against her back like hot lead, evil and angry, and terror took a powerful grip.

Oh, God.

She lashed out, her elbow connecting to his ribs. He grunted, and she broke free. Before she could move, he charged, and for the first time, she saw his eyes.

Black, cold, evil.

She'd seen those eyes before, and they smacked of the life she'd once shunned.

"What do you want with me?" she cried as he lunged for her. They tumbled to the ground, her arms beating, pushing, shoving.

But he was stronger and he hit back.

"Stop!" she cried. "You're hurting me!"

"Be still, witch," he snapped in a tone so cold that she felt the chill wash over her.

The result was instant. She froze and gaped at him. "Witch?"

"Surprised?" He grinned, without humour. "Surely you knew it was only a matter of time before we came for you?"

"I don't know what you mean." She blinked, trying to clear the fog in her mind.

He shook her, not caring as her head connected with the ground. "Feigning ignorance won't help you."

"Why are you here? What do you want?"

"We've come for you. For the book."

And just like that, in a blink of an eye, the life she'd once fled came crashing down around her.

A life as a powerful Beckham witch, fiercely protected by three Keepers. She'd always known it would catch up with her. Now that it had, fear and a crippling sense of pain and loss threatened to choke her all over again.

"Let me go!" she yelled.

A slap to the face left her dizzy and confused and when she fought back, he continued with the punches until she stopped struggling.

Silent, she closed her eyes as fury washed over her, and began to tremble.

Her body quivered from the inside out as the trembling intensified…stronger, stranger, bolder.

With a soft cry, she flung out her arms, drawing on an inner strength that had been silenced for too long. Air whooshed past her ears with a force that made her wince. A moment later, without touching him, her attacker hurled through the air like a limp puppy.

Oh, God. Her powers. It had been so long since she'd used them and they almost terrified her more than the attack itself.

He flew backward, hitting the tree behind him, and stared at her, seemingly unsurprised. With a soft growl, he jumped up and began to circle her.

"Are you insane?" she snapped, struggling to her feet, her entire body shaking. Although shock still riddled her from the surprise attack, anger had wedged itself deep inside, enough to clear the murkiness that lurked. "This is a public park. There are people here. You know the rules."

"We've taken care of that. No one will hear you cry."

"Clearly, whoever sent you failed to warn you about messing with a Beckham witch."

"Ah, but the witch walks without her mighty Keepers. A fact that has had many tongues wagging."

An image of her Keepers came to mind. Three powerful warrior brothers who'd been her protectors, friends, and allies fending off anything dark and evil that had upset the balance of nature. Despite having run from them, from that life, she couldn't deny the sense of longing that came whenever she remembered.

Dismissing all thoughts of her Keepers, she straightened her shoulders and summoned up a confidence she didn't quite feel. "And yet it's taken this long for someone to come for me. That makes you either super courageous or incredibly stupid."

His eyes narrowed at the taunt. "You don't scare me, witch."

"We'll see how you feel when I turn you into a toad," she said, keeping her tone light. His eyes widened, and she almost smiled at the brief flash of apprehension. Almost. It wouldn't help to tell him that toad turning wasn't her style. Instead, she swallowed her own unease, her mind racing for an escape route.

A rustling in the bushes had her whirling around and her heart sank when two more men stepped forward. Like her first attacker, they were both dressed in black and wore expressions of evil.

"Who are you?" she cried, her voice quivering at the realization that this was one fight she might not win. Not without some help. Two years ago, she had sworn off her powers for good and hadn't tapped into them since. But the three men outnumbered her in more ways than she cared to admit, and no amount of traditional self-defence would save her.

They circled her like a pride of lions, and she swore she could hear them growling.

Insane. Maybe she was crazy after all.

She shook her head, choking on fear, but refusing to back down. She wouldn't go down without a fight. And just like that, they attacked.

****

Archer Bennett had known an attack on Sienna was imminent. The darker world had been quiet for far too long and he'd been biding time until the moment hit.

But now that it had, fear curled in his gut like an unwelcome visitor. Adrenaline soared through him, triggering every protective Keeper instinct he possessed.

From his perch in the trees above them, Archer watched as the three men circled Sienna, rage bubbling inside him. They'd set up the perfect ambush – at the edge of the lake, void of spectators, overgrown with a wall of trees and bushes – and she'd run straight into their trap.

Her screech pierced the air and tore through him, and he readied himself to jump. Sienna fought on, kicking and punching, reaching for half-forgotten spells – determined not to back down.

Typical of a Beckham witch.

It was no good – the men were closing in. Archer pushed forward, flew through the air with the rapid speed of a Keeper, and landed on the ground below with a soft thud.

Not waiting to determine if they'd sensed his presence, he launched himself toward them.

The fight was uneven, but he drew on his heightened strength, power, and hatred for the men preying on the frightened woman.

Bodies entwined, fists connected with flesh, and blood-curdling growls filled the air. A cloud of dust surrounded them, muffling the visual impact of the fight.

With a swift movement and a possessive roar, he lunged for Sienna and placed himself in front of her as – exhausted and unseeing – she crumpled to the ground. The three men growled and snarled while he swiftly scanned the lake behind them. With a sense of calm that always came when he tapped into a sacred part of himself, a sacred part of her, he slowly raised his arms toward the lake.

Controlled and deliberate. He had a message to deliver, a witch to protect, and three men needing a lesson on the consequences of messing with a Beckham witch and her Keepers.

A soft trickle of water had all three men glancing behind them as understanding dawned. Clearly, from the horror that quickly twisted their expressions, they knew all about the Keeper with the power to manipulate water. Before they were able to react, the trickle turned into a loud rumble of waves as the water rose up to form a solid wall. Archer moved his hands in circular motions and the water instantly split into three separate balls, each one tightly compacted together to form a lethal weapon.

Sienna's first attacker jerked toward her, hoping to use her as leverage against the inevitable attack, but Archer was too quick for him.

A ball of water bulleted through the air and hit him on the back with a force that sent him reeling against the tree with a rumble of filthy curses. In swift succession, two more water missiles flew toward his accomplices, knocking them off their feet with ease.

With another swift motion of the arms, Archer readied the water with a fresh supply of lethal missiles and hovered, hoping the dark forces had had their fill of chilly lake water.

Drenched, panting, knowing when to admit defeat, the men fell silent and glared at him, their bodies heaving breathlessly with unleashed adrenaline. There was a pregnant pause as they sized him up, weighed their options.

"You can't protect her forever," the first attacker said.

"I will always protect her," Archer told them, his voice level and unyielding.

"Then you will both die."

Sensing defeat, and without waiting for a response, they rushed for the bushes and vanished.

Archer dropped his arms, the water crashing into the lake with a loud splutter, and immediately lurched forward. He sank to his knees beside Sienna, silently scanning her body to check for injuries – an action that came as naturally to him as breathing. She seemed confused, disorientated from the vicious slaps she'd received, and her tiny body trembled from the shock of the surprise attack. Seeing her like this fuelled his anger and hatred for the men responsible and something cold and steely wrapped itself around his heart.

They'd be back. He knew that with every instinct he possessed. Defeating them wouldn't be a problem – the challenge would be convincing Sienna to accept his help.

"Are you okay?" he asked, fighting against the urge to pull her into his arms.

"Don't touch me!" she shrieked, scrambling away from him.

Her right hand shot out at the same time the excruciating pain shot through his head – a pain so powerful it threatened to cripple him. His head pounded from the vicious onslaught of heat channelled through her central power – fire. She'd done this before, damn her, and the pain had almost killed him.

A Beckham witch's ultimate defence.

Eyes shut to ward off the pain and holding his head in agony, he sank to his knees with a guttural groan.

"Sienna," he said between gritted teeth. "It's me. It's Archer."

The mental violation and pain stopped the instant he said his name.

She gaped at him, shock unhinging her jaw. "Archer?"

"It's me," he repeated and struggled to his feet, still holding his head. Damn, she still had the power to fry his brain. He blinked, trying to clear the haze, and looked at her with a harsh frown. "Damn it, Sienna. What the hell was that for?"

"I thought you were trying to hurt me." She rushed to him and cupped her hands over each of his. "I thought you were one of them."

"Do I look like a warlock's minion?"

"I'm sorry. They rattled me, caught me off guard." She fell silent and inhaled softly. "Archer, you're here. You found me."

"I'm your Keeper and I vowed the day you left that I'd find you."

She didn't reply and frowned when he grimaced. "Are you okay?" Worry lined her features and her green eyes flashed with concern. She looked a mess, a complete contrast to her usual poised self. Her hair hung in a dull, dusty, tangled mess around her shoulders. Her right cheek, glowing and swollen, showed early signs of a bruise.

God, how he'd missed her. It had been so damn long.

Fire sparked deep in his gut as fresh anger washed over him. The two years he'd spent searching for her had almost driven him to the brink of madness. The constant worry, the daily longing, and the permanent reminders of her back home had been torture. Torn between the urge to hug her and throttle her, a quick nod was all he could manage.

"I'm sorry," she said softly, tugging his hands away from his head.

"Promise me you'll never try that voodoo mind fry on me ever again."

"It's the quickest defence I have against you."

"You don't need any damn defences against me."

"I'm still not agreeing."

Stubborn minx. Nothing had changed. He ran his thumb across her swollen cheek and tried to ignore the rush of emotions that flooded him. He'd found her. After two long torturous and empty years, he'd finally tracked her down. The relief was immense and he had to resist everything inside him that ached to wrench her against him and never let her go. "Does it hurt?"

"He knew how to pack a punch but I'll live." Her shoulders fell, and she met his gaze. "They weren't human, were they?"

"Not entirely, no."

"Did anyone see us?"

"No. Our secret is safe."

As it should be. And when it wasn't, a little magic would usually rectify even the soundest memory, but only as a last resort. Surrounded by a world of ordinary humans where only a few selected people knew of their supernatural existence, they'd been bound to keep their presence a secret without harming anyone in exchange for being left alone.

It wasn't always that simple but that was the agreement, the rule, and breaking it would initiate consequences Archer would rather avoid.

"It's been quiet for so long. Why now?" Sienna asked.

"You're a Beckham witch," he replied, annoyed with the question. 'It's no surprise they've come for you."

"That's not who I am anymore."

"You'll always be a witch, Sienna, and they'll be back for you." The image of Sienna surrounded by the three men flashed through his mind, and he frowned. "They surprised you," he noted quietly. "And you held back from using your powers."

"You won't understand."

"Damn right I won't. You come from a family of powerful witches. Those men were no match for your powers. Why would you hesitate to use them?"

Her age-old defences fell into place as the wall returned. He'd seen how her emotions had changed from relief to surprise, then horror as she'd realized that he'd finally found her, despite all her efforts at keeping him away.

Her eyes flashed with disbelief, and she stepped back.

"Sienna, don't."

"I have to go," she said, pushing past him, heading for the opening in the trees.

He caught her wrist in one quick movement. When she lifted her eyes to meet his, he raised an eyebrow. "Seriously? You really think I'm going to let you leave?"

CHAPTER TWO

Sienna looked at the man she'd once considered a friend, trying to make sense of what had just happened. One moment she'd been running in the park, the next moment her life had been thrown back into the turmoil she'd tried so hard to get away from.

And Archer Bennett stood for everything she'd run from.

A world she was bound by duty and honour to defend, where grief and guilt were constant companions, and an intense, forbidden attraction that had almost destroyed them.

It was hard to determine which surprised her more – the sudden attack by complete strangers or Archer's reappearance in her life.

Her heart slammed against her chest and she knew it had nothing to do with the attack and everything to do with the man. Physically, outwardly, he hadn't changed at all. Tall, broad shoulders, short brown hair, and a face so handsome that it hinted at perfection. And he still wreaked havoc with her senses. But the way he clenched his jaw and the tortured look in his brooding green eyes gave her a glimpse of the anguish that lay beneath the layers, catching her off guard. He'd always had an intensity about him, but the darkness had intensified since she'd last seen him. It shouldn't surprise her. He'd lost, suffered, mourned.

Like they all had.

In their world danger often lurked in a way that ordinary humans wouldn't understand and often resulted in pain and suffering that came with the loss of losing one of their own.

Sarah. Their parents.

She sighed, refusing to think about the loss. The anguish that came with their memories always left her raw. "Why are you here, Archer?"

He shot her a look that questioned if she really needed an answer to that.

After all, he was a Bennett brother and destined to protect a Beckham witch at all costs. He still wore his ring – the ring of a Keeper. The heavy, antique silver ring symbolized everything he stood for, everything he was. Her Keeper, her Guardian. She'd never seen him without it and seeing it again now tugged at a part of her that she'd buried a long time ago – a part of her that was in complete contrast to the life she'd run to.

Sienna wasn't just any witch. She was a Beckham witch with a powerful lineage. Her grandmother, Rose, had been one of the most greatest witches on earth. Scattered across the world in a combined effort to maintain the balance of nature were three orders: ordinary witches, who dabbled in spells and potions; elemental witches, who drew their energy from the elements of nature – and witches like Rose. Whereas most elemental witches were able draw their power from one element of nature, Rose was able to channel all four. Herself being the fifth - the spirit that bound fire, water, earth, air. In the witch world, the ability to draw energy from all the elements of nature was a rarity and any witch able to master such power was honoured, respected, and fiercely protected.

For the longest time, Sienna had embraced her heritage, her destiny, and her simple powers as an elemental witch. Until the day Rose had passed on her full powers to her and she'd run from it.

But now it had all come crashing around her like an unwanted curse.

"So you finally found me," she said, closing her fingers around the chunky pendant hanging around her neck.

"It took a while."

She glanced toward the lake, dark pink from the reflection of the sunset. "So why now?"

"You needed me."

"Ah, ever the White Knight."

He ignored the jab, never one for jesting about his duties. "They would've taken you, Sienna. Don't you see that?"

"They surprised me, but I can take care of myself."

"And yet you hesitated."

"I was fine, Archer."

"Then explain this," he said and touched her swollen cheek. "Any other woman would be no match for their brutal strength and aggression. You, on the other hand, have the advantage other women don't. Why would you even let them near you? Why did you wait before using your powers to defend yourself?"

"Let it go, Archer," she said and pulled away.

It didn't take long for him to figure it out. His hand shot out to grab her arm, and he tugged her round so she was facing him again. "You haven't used your powers since you left Rapid Falls, have you?"

No. For two years she hadn't cast a single spell, she'd started fires with a match and not her mind, and she'd opened doors with her hands and not her thoughts. Protection consisted of a security company and a mace spray, not three burly Keepers and magic.

Her silence seemed to confirm his suspicion, and his eyes narrowed.

"Why?" His voice softened, and she heard the confusion that lingered. "Inheriting Rose's powers made you one of the most powerful witches in the world. Why aren't you taking advantage of that?"

"Because Rose's powers scare the hell out of me!" Sienna yanked her wrist free and took a step back, needing the distance between them – and the masculine sexiness that still wreaked havoc with her body. Her pulse was on a runaway mission and parts of her tingled that had hadn't tingled in a very long time.

Damn him.

"Sienna, they're not Rose's powers anymore," he said softly. "They're yours."

She glanced away, knowing that he was right, and hating it. How could he know the fear that came with her powers, the anger toward her grandmother for passing them onto her without an explanation, or the guilt that gnawed at her for what she'd done the first time she'd tapped into her newfound powers?

Her gaze fell to his scarred hand, and she dragged in a deep breath.

"I have to go, Archer," she said, knowing he'd never allow it.

"Like hell."

No surprise. "You're not a part of my life anymore, and I can't go back. For the first time in years, I've known peace." Liar, liar.

He studied her, adding a touch of frost to his gaze. "I'm one of your Keepers, Sienna, and that makes me a part of you until the day you die."

"How did you find me?"

"Rose sensed you were in danger. Clearly, she was right."

"My grandmother sent you?" Sienna had always known the older witch would one day give her away. Her hand returned to her necklace, and she frowned. "How…?"

He shrugged, and she tried not to concentrate on all that muscle beneath the ripped black shirt. "Emotions fuel her remaining powers and when she sensed you were in danger, there was enough anger and worry to frighten even me. A simple locator spell led us here."

"That easy, huh?"

Something dark and angry clouded his features. "No, Sienna. Finding you has been anything but easy." In two strides, he closed the gap between them. "Do you have any idea what it's been like for us to lose you?"

"So you and your brothers lost your witch. Big deal. Find a new one."

"It's not that simple and you know it," he said, tightening his grip.

She knew. They were all bound together by destiny and a magical connection that could only be broken by death. It wasn't something she could easily forget, no matter how hard she'd tried. It was a life neither of them had asked for but had accepted as part of their duty and family legacy, as had their parents and generations of grandparents before them. And when it had become too much for her, she'd run.

Coward.

"Two years, Sienna. Two years I've been searching for you. How the hell did you keep me away?" His eyes fell on her necklace and his jaw clenched. Before she could stop him, he reached out and closed his fingers around the bulky pendant. "It's the necklace, isn't it? That's why I've been unable to sense you." He looked up, dark eyes burning into hers. "That's why it's taken me so long to track you down."

"I cast a spell on the necklace. It was the only way you'd stay away."

Anger oozed off him in waves and his fingers tightened around the pendant. For a brief moment, she feared he would rip it from her neck.

She placed her hands around his, willing him not to. "Don't."

He fingered the pendant, glaring at it with a harsh frown. A pentagram with five points that symbolized the five elements of nature, that symbolized them. It was the perfect illustration of what they stood for. Four Keepers who each had the power to manipulate an element of nature. Earth, fire, air, and water. And she was the fifth element that bound them all together. Without her, their elemental powers were useless. Interlinked in a way few people could ever understand, they shared the same destiny and a mutual purpose of maintaining the balance of nature.

His gaze lifted to meet hers and the raw emotion she saw in his dark green eyes rattled her. "This necklace depicts everything we stand for. Everything we are. How could you use it to keep us apart?"

"I left that life behind. I can't go back, Archer."

"Sienna" he said softly, forcefully. "You're a Beckham witch. That's not something you can hide from."

"I'm not that person anymore. I have a life here, one that doesn't involve magic, evil warlocks, or powers so potent that I can't control them. Or death," she added, her voice quietening as memories of their last encounter resurfaced. Memories she'd run from. "I can't be a part of all that anymore."

She saw the moment it all fell into place for him. His expression softened, and they stared at each other in silence.

"My sister's death wasn't your fault," he said softly, releasing the pendant.

Sienna took a step back, not wanting the discussion that would follow such a statement.

"You can't hide from who you are."

"It worked for the last two years."

"Only because the balance in the paranormal world has been in our favour. That's changed and you're in danger."

Ah, so he'd found her because his duty as her Keeper had him wanting to protect her. And what about the man finding a woman he'd almost made his?

"You have to come home, Sienna. We'll help you, protect you."

Something cold and determined washed over her, and she lifted her chin defiantly. "You're crazy if you think I'm going to let another one of my Keepers die protecting me."

"Sarah's death was not your fault."

Unable to stop herself, her gaze fell to his scarred hand. "But I hurt you. I hurt you all, and there's no guarantee that I won't do it again. I refuse to put you or your brothers at risk again."

"And you're crazy if you think I'm going to let you go off alone on this stupid Kamikaze mission. The fact that they've targeted you and tracked you down means they need a Beckham witch. They also know that you haven't mastered your powers yet so they will come for you, repeatedly, until they have you."

He was right. Few people ever messed with Rose because of the power she could wield. It was one of the reasons that she needed less protection than Sienna. But since passing on her powers, Rose was an ordinary witch like all others. Still in high regard because of her Beckham status, but her powers had lessened. Archer was right. To them Sienna, her full powers still untouched, was the inexperienced witch needed to unleash their own evil. They would be wary of her, perhaps a bit fearful because of her Beckham name, but it wouldn't stop them.

Of course, that would all change once she learned how to channel all her powers simultaneously.

Never.

She stepped back, the familiar fear slamming home at the thought of ever using her full powers again.

Archer narrowed his eyes, and he reached for her. "You know I'm right. You have no choice, I'm taking you home."

She raised an eyebrow, refusing to be forced back to a life that frightened her. "You said it yourself, Archer. I'm a powerful witch. You might want to keep that in mind when you threaten to caveman me home."

"Now who's threatening?"

Her smile was slow, cheeky, and challenged him in a way that only he would understand. He straightened, readying himself for whatever she was about to throw at him.

"Sienna, don't you dare," he warned softly.

Apparently, he knew her well.

Although she loathed using her powers, she also knew that they were the only way she'd get away from Archer. Shoving aside the fear, Sienna drew on them and took a step back. Archer cursed when a wall of fire sprang to life in front of him, cutting him off. His reaction was lightning fast but she was faster and a moment later, a circle of fire surrounded him, a striking glow in the darkness.

Fire. Her central power.

"Sienna, stop this Hocus Pocus crap." There was no mistaking the fury in his voice.

She raised the flames, quietly chanting a spell to seal the circle. She knew that if he chose to use his powers, she'd have a fair fight on her hands. Her magic topped his, but he was stronger, angrier, and hard-wired to protect her. That alone was a power on its own. The rage that burned in his eyes spelt trouble and when his gaze shifted to the lake behind her, she knew she had to leave. Quickly.

He lurched forward but stumbled back when the heat of the flames hit him. "Sienna!"

"Stop resisting and the flames will die."

As there was no chance in hell he'd accept his prison of fire, she knew the flames would hold and keep him from following her.

"Don't ever look for me again, Archer."

His jaw flexed, and he clenched each fist. Slowly, he pinned her with a heated glare. "I will find you, Sienna. Don't fool yourself."

With a shaky smile, she backtracked away from him. "You're the fool for thinking you could broomstick me back home."

She turned away, needing to flee before he saw the crack in her powers as her body wasn't yet strong enough to maintain them.

And the fear of losing control always lingered.

"Sienna." The change in his tone had her glancing back at him over her shoulder. His eyes narrowed and his mouth curled into a small smile. "Game on."

****

It was only later, when Sienna felt the syringe slam into her neck in the darkness of her apartment, that she wished she'd allowed Archer to take off her necklace.

This time, she really was on her own.

CHAPTER THREE

When the cold arm wrapped around his neck with a vicious grip, Archer wasn't surprised.

Thanks to his heightened senses, alive with warning, he'd heard and smelt the intruder the moment he'd entered his house. Driven by instinct and armed with exceptional reflexes, Archer whirled around and rammed his fingers around his attacker's neck in a deathly grip. He charged forward, slamming the intruder against the wooden wall of the living room, not caring when the wood splintered beneath the impact, his arm shoved against his neck. The action sparked a series of choking gasps of air.

"Your name." When silence met his question, Archer added more pressure.

"Hunter," the intruder gasped between clenched teeth. "My name is Hunter. Now get off me."

Like hell. "What do you want?" Archer demanded, adding another quick slam against the wall.

"I have a message for you."

"And you had to deliver it personally."

Hunter straightened his body in a brief act of bravery. "It's about your witch."

The mention of Sienna's name fuelled Archer's rage more than the attack itself. Go figure. "Leave Sienna out of this."

"We know where she is."

With lightening speed, Archer grabbed Hunter by the shirt and hurled him across the living room. The resounding crash resonated through the room with a sickening crunch of splintering glass. Three long daggers pinned against the wall rattled against the wood. Without flinching, Archer bolted and landed on his attacker with a low growl.

He spotted the branded tattoo on Hunter's wrist, and his gut clenched. The mark of the one warlock he'd hoped would never return.

Warrick Brogan.

Damn.

"You're here for Warrick," he said, reining in his searing anger.

"He's issuing a challenge to the Bennett brothers," Hunter choked, flinching at the weight of the solid man on top of him.

"And what challenge would that be?"

"He dares you to find the witch before he does."

Archer's stomach rolled at the mention of Sienna's name in the same sentence as Warrick's. The feeling was almost unbearable – blind fury and the instinctive urge to protect shot through his body, fusing together in intense heat.

"Tell Warrick that I have a message for him." The colour in Hunter's face had changed to a distressed blue. When his eyes started rolling back in his head, Archer softened his grip. After all, he needed a messenger. "If anyone so much as lifts a finger to Sienna, the Bennett brothers will retaliate with so much wrath that it'll make hell seem like an attractive place."

Hunter gave a sly grin. "Warrick wants the Grimoire."

Of course. "Tell him to get in line."

"But he wants the witch even more."

"Like hell."

"You won't be able to protect her forever." His words, said with such malice and confidence, hit Archer straight in the gut.

The Keeper of the Wise. His ancestral duty was to protect the Beckham witches from the evils of men like Warrick Brogan and his minions. So far, he'd already failed dismally where Sienna was concerned.

Two years later and she was still in hiding. Damn her.

He'd also failed his sister, his parents, and Sienna's parents too, and their deaths had sparked a bitter quest for vengeance.

He leaned forward. "Touch her and you'll die," he said in an undertone that cut like a knife.

"Warrick won't back down, Bennett."

"And neither will we." With herculean strength, Archer flung Hunter forward. "Get your evil ass out of my home," he ordered and tossed Hunter through the jagged window. More glass shattered, and Hunter landed on the lawn outside with a loud curse.

"You'll pay for this, Bennett," Hunter said, wiping blood from his mouth with the sleeve of his shirt. "We're coming for the Grimoire and the witch, and the Bennett brothers won't stop us."

Archer's anger soared, and he bolted through the window, landing on the grass with the ease of a cat jumping from a four-story window. "I dare you to say that again."

Hunter stumbled to his feet with a string of curses that would make his mother blush. Not that men like him had mothers. No, they were the spawn of…evil.

A rustle of bushes drew Archer's attention to the shrubbery beside him. A Golden Retriever circled their visitor with a soft growl.

"Ah, you've pissed off Levi." Archer suppressed a grin at Hunter's expression. The retriever's growl deepened. "And Levi hates trespassers even more than we do."

"Call off your dog." Hunter quickly stepped back. "I'll deliver your damn message, but you should know that Warrick won't let this go."

The dog's low growl turned into a series of quick, loud snarls that sent Hunter soaring off and away.

Archer couldn't blame him. In defensive mode, Levi did look rather frightening – nothing like the gorgeous, fury, friendly, and protective dog she was.

On edge with restless energy from the surprise attack, Archer blew out air and flexed his shoulders. His gaze travelled to the broken glass on the lawn, and he frowned. Broken doors and windows at the Bennett Estate were nothing new, but still sent a bolt of fury and resentment through him. Attacks from Warrick Brogan and others like him had been part of their life since they'd taken over the Keeper role from their parents before their deaths several years ago. But every time a dark force entered the estate uninvited, it stirred something vicious inside.

Situated in a small mystical town renowned for the production of ice wine, the mansion had been home to the Bennett family for decades, carefully restored by each generation. It was an impressive house, luxurious, and large enough to house several families. Thousands of trees, shrubs, and flowers filled their grounds. It was nestled in the centre of massive spans of land, surrounded by thick forests and a glistening river on the one side, and endless rows of grape vineyards on the other. The estate itself was very old, and steeped in magical energy. Storage buildings and underground tunnels filtered through the estate and the forest surrounding it. They'd all been abandoned or destroyed when the Bennett family had moved in.

Currently, the mansion was home to two of the three Bennett

brothers. Still no sign of Declan.

Levi returned moments later, chasing an Aston Martin down the driveway.

Ethan.

When the car pulled to a stop in front of the house, the youngest Bennett brother emerged with a sheepish grin. "Seriously? Did you use Levi to frighten our visitors again?"

Archer smiled. "No. Levi offered. And it worked, didn't it? One look at the crazy dog and he bolted."

Ethan dropped to his knees and patted the cheerful dog. "Nobody messes with Levi, do they girl?"

Archer took in his brother's ragged appearance and cocked a brow. Yesterday's jeans and a rumpled blue T-shirt, messy sandy brown hair, and unshaven. A far cry from his immaculate appearance the night before. "Late night?"

Ethan nodded, his grin widening.

"Looks like you didn't get much sleep last night."

"Nope."

Figures. With his carefree grin and endless charm, Ethan was never without a woman at his side. The youngest Bennett brother loved parties, alcohol, and women – and they loved him right back. The man had stamina that even put Hercules to shame.

Ethan's silly grin disappeared as he glanced at the broken window. "So who was our visitor?"

Archer frowned, thinking about his intruder and every threat he stood for. "Remind me to arrange for some damn security," he said, although he knew that ordinary security could do very little to keep the likes of Warrick and his gang away. Supernatural powers trumped conventional security measures any day.

"What did he want?"

"Warrick Brogan sent us a message."

The mention of the warlock's name was enough to jar the

expected reaction from his brother. Any trace of amusement vanished and thick silence hung between them.

"Gargamel's back?" Ethan frowned. "What does he want?"

"The Beckham Grimoire."

"Oh, hell. They're starting that again?"

"They never stopped. They were simply biding time until Warrick's numbers were up. According to Fly Boy that I sent through our window, Warrick's numbers are up. That's not all," Archer said in a soft tone that had Ethan look at him. "They want Sienna."

"They won't find her."

"Apparently they know where she is."

Ethan gave a brief snort. "We're her Keepers. If we don't know where Sienna is, then how the hell would they?"

Archer shrugged his shoulders, not bothering to hide his concern. His brother knew how he felt about Sienna, how her disappearance tormented him.

And two days ago, Archer had found her – only to have her blindside him and vanish again. He swore that if he ever saw her again, he'd wring her pretty little neck himself.

Keeper's promise be damned.

"Still no sensing her?" Ethan asked, rolling up his sleeves.

None. Zero. Zilch. "No. She still wears her necklace. Until she removes it, I can't track her or reach her."

The necklace blocked him from her in a way that drove him crazy. He'd always had a connection to her unlike his brothers, until she'd cast a spell on her necklace, severing their connection eternally.

"Rose could do another locator spell?"

"Sienna's already covered that angle, but I'll chat to Rose again."

"Any readings from Fly Boy?"

"Only that he works for Warrick." Archer spun around to face his brother as a thought struck him. "If they know where she is, then I should be able to sense her through him." He'd been too surprised to discover Warrick's name that it hadn't occurred to him at the time of the attack.

Ethan looked doubtful and glanced at the mess on the ground. "Not unless Fly Boy left a gift behind. Without something of his, you won't make the connection." He knelt, reached for a piece of broken glass, and studied it in silence. Straightening, he turned to look at Archer with a wide smile, and held out his hand to reveal the blood stained glass. "Blood should work?"

"You bet your ass it'll work."

Several minutes later, Archer's fingers closed over the bloody glass with such force that his knuckles turned white. "Oh, God."

Ethan's gaze shot up to meet Archer's, and he frowned when he saw his brother's expression. "What's wrong?"

"They have her." Archer swallowed, trying to get a grip on the emotions triggered by the thought. "Those bastards have Sienna."

CHAPTER FOUR

Damn. Her attackers had given her Rose Thorn.

A useless herb for most, but to witches, the tiny plant had the ability to weaken and strip her of her powers.

Sienna was furious. For two years, she'd packaged her powers in a neat little box and stored them away until the day she'd need them again.

Today, she needed them – really needed them – but the herb had ravished her, destroying any chances of accessing them. For now anyway.

The loss of control unnerved her. It was one thing choosing not to channel her powers. Being stripped of that choice was another thing entirely.

She glanced around the room, trying to make sense of where they'd taken her. An abandoned house – sparsely furnished, darkened windows. The stuff horror movies were made of. Of everything, the quiet surroundings frightened her. Without her powers, she had little chance of freeing herself from these men and a little neighbourly assistance would have been nice.

"She's awake," her first attacker said, the man from the park, motioning toward her.

"Who are you?" she asked, but had to clear her throat. God,

she was so thirsty.

"Call me Harper."

She eyed Harper, sizing him up. Where he lacked height, he made up with bulk and attitude. The man had a menacing aura around him that had Sienna immediately on edge. She glanced at the other two men skulking in the background. It didn't take rocket science to figure out who was running this circus.

Trying not to wince, she struggled to her feet, but her legs buckled beneath her and she slumped against the tattered couch. Before she could try again, Harper had his booted foot on her back.

"Down, witch."

"Brave to mess with a Beckham witch, aren't you?"

"Stupid to walk without your Keepers, aren't you?"

"What do you want with me?"

He smiled, but the smile held more evil than amusement. "Warrick Brogan has big plans for you."

The warlock's name sent an instant chill down her spine and Sienna had to concentrate on masking her surprise. It was hard to think that the man had once been a friend to her and the Bennett brothers. Now, the mention of his name made her stomach clench. "Warrick Brogan can kiss my ass."

"Now who's brave?"

"I'm not afraid of you." She was pleased that her voice sounded steady, even though her insides were rolling.

Harper waved the syringe at her. "You should be. Without your powers, you're no challenge to us."

"And without me, my powers are of no use to you so why am I here?"

"You haven't figured it out yet?" He sat on the table in front of her, the ancient wood creaking beneath his weight, and leaned closer. "You're a witch from a lineage of even more powerful witches. What's the one thing we could possibly want?"

The Beckham Grimoire.

Sienna's heart sank. Of course. She should've known this was about the damn book. She was destined to keep her family's Grimoire safe – a thick book of handwritten notes that listed all the rituals, spells, potions, formulas, and magical properties ever used by a Beckham witch. To someone like Warrick Brogan, the book was lethal.

And everything her parents and Archer's parents had fought for, and eventually died for, would be for nothing.

Their vision of a life where supernatural people could live in harmony with ordinary people would truly be up in flames.

Over a century ago, six families: the Bennetts, the Beckhams, the Brogans, and three other ordinary families had founded Rapid Falls, a small abandoned area once thought to have an abundance of mystical energy. Over time, they'd established a thriving community.

Their agreement had been simple. They lived and worked in harmony and kept any supernatural tendencies a secret. No harming humans, no public displays of supernatural abilities. For the longest time, their agreement had worked, until a few generations later; Warrick's parents had developed a different vision. Instead of a peaceful existence, their vision consisted of freedom, control, and exposure. A feud had broken out, altering their friendship circle forever. In the end, her parents and Archer's parents had lost the battle.

Sienna still remembered the fire as vividly as though it had just happened. The image of her house engulfed in thick orange flames and the horror of knowing their parents were inside had affected her forever.

When suspicion had fallen on Warrick's parents, they'd left town. Then, in a brutal car accident, they died – leaving Mason and Warrick as orphans, and taking the truth of the fire to the grave.

It hadn't been long before the two brothers had made it clear that they shared the same views as their parents and would do anything, hurt anyone, in order to have the freedom and control their parents had fought for.

Like hell.

She would die before she handed over her Grimoire.

"I don't have it," she said firmly, shoving away the anger and resentment stewing inside.

"But you know where it is and according to the legend, we need a Beckham witch to open it. Warrick seems to think you'll also know the location of all four stones."

"Chasing the book is like chasing a rainbow. You'll never get close, and you'll certainly never hit gold."

"It exists and we'll not only find it, Sienna, we'll open it."

She touched a hand to her pounding head, willing the pain away. The blinding headache only clouded her already murky thoughts. It was hard enough to think clearly with Harper pointing a syringe of Rose Thorn at her. The damn headache had to go.

She knew precisely why Warrick wanted the Grimoire. She was simply surprised he'd taken so long to come for it.

Two years ago, in a desperate attempt to bring an end to the wicked hold the Brogan brothers had on everyone, Sienna and her grandmother had cast a spell. Mason Brogan, the older and bigger evil of the two brothers, was spelled into an abandoned underground church tomb deep inside the forests of their hometown, cursed to live as the dead until ever freed. As for the younger brother, Warrick Brogan, they'd cast a spell on him to diminish his powers, underestimating his evilness.

Warrick had retaliated, killing Sarah Bennett, her fourth Keeper and dearest friend. That night had altered the course of their lives and the reality of Sarah's death had sent everything reeling out of place.

Without his brother or his powers, Warrick had simply vanished. Until now.

If Warrick ever got his hands on the book and the four stones that were the key to opening it, he'd access the spell binding Mason, and could then unseal the curse.

"Have you found the other stones yet?" Sienna asked, her stomach rolling at the thought.

He grinned, meeting her eyes. "We're working on it."

"Even if you find the book, you'll never be able to open it."

"They all warned me that I'd never catch a Beckham witch, but here you are." He kicked at the rope around her ankles. "Bound, weak, useless." Pleased with himself, he started to chuckle.

"I'll never help you."

"You will or people will die. You're a witch so you'll never let that happen." He trailed a calloused finger along her jaw and down to the silver necklace around her neck, his touch light, yet harsh at the same time. "Beautiful necklace." His fingers clasped around the solid pendant and toyed for a moment before yanking it off her.

"No!" Eyes widened in disbelief as her hands flew to the spot on her neck where the necklace had hung for the last two years.

"A family heirloom?"

His mocking tone stirred the lull inside of her and fury sparked a sudden burst of renewed strength. Sienna pushed at his chest and he stumbled backward. Stronger than her, he recovered with the speed of a demon and pounced.

His slap was brutal. "You're weak, Sienna. Nothing you do can harm me."

"I won't always be weak," she said, hating that he was right. The effects from the Rose Thorn still ravaged her and until the dreaded herb left her system, she would never be able to fight him off.

"But just to be sure…" he said with a wicked smile and brought the syringe toward her.

She baulked in fear, panic taking its destructive grip. "You can't!" She tried to back away from him, but stumbled against the couch behind her. "A second dose so soon could be deadly."

He grinned and closed in on her. "A gamble."

"No!" she screamed as all three men held her down and injected her with the dreaded herb. The affect was instant and her body went completely limp. She fought for consciousness, tried to claw her way out of the blackness.

And lost.

Much later, she resurfaced long enough to hear the shouting, breaking glass and violence - terrifying sounds that rattled her to the core. She tried to open her eyes, to make sense of the chaos around her, but sleep beckoned.

Then silence fell.

Confusion reigned and she couldn't move, couldn't fight back. Alone. She was so alone and at the mercy of these three men.

And out of the darkness, she saw him.

Archer.

"Sienna," Archer murmured, kneeling beside her. "It's over."

"Archer?"

"It's okay, we're here. You're safe now."

Strong arms drew her in as the blackness engulfed her again.

Her Keepers had found her.

CHAPTER FIVE

"Archer?" His name, whispered in the darkness, had Archer bolting from the chair in the corner of the bedroom.

"Sienna." Archer sat on the bed beside her, relief washing over him. A quick study along the length of her reassured him that she was fine. Pale and thin, but she was awake – and safe. She looked lost in the massive bed and for a moment, he wasn't sure if the bed was ridiculously too big or if she was simply too damn small. "You had us scared to death."

"Remind me to hunt down every last Rose Thorn tree and destroy it." She grunted and tried to sit up, blinking to clear the cloudiness. "That herb packs a powerful punch."

"It'll take a while for the effects to wear off and for your body to heal." Archer reached for her, adjusted the pillows. Her arms felt tiny in his hands, almost as though they were silly little branches that could be snapped without any effort at all.

She settled back against the pillows and ran her fingers through her long hair, the colour of fire, in an attempt to tame the wavy curls. "Where am I?"

"We brought you home." And about time too. The huge mansion nestled on a quiet estate in the hills had never been the same since she'd left. Private, peaceful, surrounded by forests that had frequently been her favourite escape over the years.

Green eyes widened in surprise, and she quickly glanced around the bedroom. "Here? To Rapid falls?"

"It's the safest place and it's your home."

"Was my home." She covered her face with her hands and released a frustrated groan. "Dammit, Archer. Why did you bring me here? This is the last place I want to be and you know that."

"That's a conversation we'll have when the Rose Thorn is no longer mulling your senses."

"The Rose Thorn doesn't change how I feel about this place."

Her words stung but he kept a straight face. Her determination to stay away surprised him. She really hadn't wanted them to find her. It annoyed him until he saw the underlying fear in her eyes.

She was scared.

Of coming home? He knew she carried her own demons and coming home meant facing them but did she really think she could run forever?

He of all people knew all about relentless demons. They always caught up in the end.

Sienna massaged her temples and looked at him, the frown that creased her brows softening. "You found me again."

He dangled the necklace in front of her for a brief second but quickly palmed it when she reached out. "No way, Sienna. The spell you cast on the necklace keeps me from sensing you. Until Warrick's off your back, it stays with me."

"Dammit, Archer. Give me my necklace."

"So that you can disappear again? Hell no."

Sienna winced at an attempt to settle back into the pillows. Not caring for her reaction, he manoeuvred himself behind her and pulled her into his arms. Surprisingly, despite the tension and uncertainty he sensed in her, she relaxed against him. "I think we've already established that you need us, Sienna, and you're better off here than with Warrick and his bootlickers."

"He's gathered some minions?"

"It appears so."

"They're after the Grimoire."

"I know." His gut clenched at the thought.

"Archer?" Her voice was soft, barely above a whisper, and chased away all thoughts of the warlock. "Just so you know, I didn't take off my necklace, they did."

"Why didn't you?'

"You would've come for me."

"Of course." And it had nothing to do with the fact that he was duty bound to protect her. How could he explain that ever since their parents had died in the fire on the estate, that she'd become the very essence of his world? She was his best friend and knew him in a way that few others did. They'd always shared a special connection but the tragedy of losing their parents at such a young age and in such a horrific way had cemented their bond forever. He pressed his face into her hair and inhaled. The action stirred heaps of memories and against his will, his body stirred viciously in response to her.

"Thank you."

He tipped her head back so that she faced him. "Would this be a bad time to give you grief about running again?"

"Hell yes."

"Two years, Sienna."

Two long, frustrating years. Damn her.

"After your sister died, I had to leave. And you let me go, Archer."

"Had I known you were planning to vanish, that would have been different."

"I did what I thought was best at the time and I could never bring myself to return. When this is over, I'll be leaving again."

The thought brought a fresh bout of unease but he simply

nodded, not surprised or even willing to challenge her. "We'll see. For now, I'll leave you to rest." He made a move to go but a gentle palm placed against his chest stopped him.

"Please stay. Just for a minute."

He toyed with the idea. He had to track down Ethan and devise a plan. A fierce warlock was after their witch and the brothers would stop at nothing to protect her. In order to do that, they needed a game plan.

"Please."

Her simple plea tugged at the wall he'd erected around himself, a wall developed to keep some distance between them. But resisting her would take an ocean of strength he didn't have. With a small sigh, he nodded and relaxed against the pillows. "Just for a minute."

****

Two hours later, Sienna finally stirred. As she swept the cobwebs out of her murky brain, she became vaguely aware of the hard bulge of muscles beneath her cheek.

"Rise and shine, slumber queen."

The voice had her bolting forward, and she whirled around to face Archer. For a moment, she gaped at him until her mind started piecing everything together and it all came rushing back to her. "You stayed?"

"You asked me to."

With a quick glance, she took in his neatly-cropped brown hair, the dark eyebrows drawn together in a slight frown, and the brooding green eyes coloured with concern.

"How're you feeling?" The tenderness in his voice was a far cry from his piercing war cries when he'd come to her rescue.

"I'll live." She sank onto the pillows beside him, embarrassed she'd slept in his arms. Such an intimate act belonged to lovers, not estranged friends. She cast a quick glance around the spacious room, one she'd often occupied. Against the far wall was a massive fireplace that was now a big gaping hole in its emptiness. Come winter, her Keepers kept her fire roaring, a gesture she'd always appreciated in the cold winter nights. Large windows covered with drapes blocked out the late afternoon sunlight that usually streamed across the four-poster bed. Not much had changed since she'd left. The realization that they'd kept the room the way she'd left it, untouched, tugged at something vague and guarded inside.

"Rose was worried sick. She hated the way things ended between you before you left."

Her grandmother lived in the guesthouse on the Bennett estate. It had been Rose's home for decades and when Sienna's parents had died, it had become her home too and she'd loved it. Since fleeing home – fleeing Archer – Sienna hadn't been back and realized now with a pang of sadness how much she'd missed home. The warmth of her grandmother's touch, the laughter she'd shared with the three brothers, the massive forest between their homes, and the feeling of…belonging. She'd left in such a rush, confused, and riddled with guilt and anger.

Sienna shifted her gaze to meet Archer's, realizing how much she'd missed him. "I know, so did I. I need to see her."

"We didn't want to wake you, but Rose was here earlier and will be back later." A scarred hand reached out to stroke the bruise on her cheek, and she inhaled quietly at the reminder. His touch was gentle and warm. Soothing. It surprised her and she shook her head, trying to reconcile the kindness in his eyes with the hatred she'd witnessed there when he'd fought off her attackers in the park.

"Are your brothers here?"

"Only Ethan, and he's been busting at the balls to see you again."

"Are they mad?"

"We're all mad, Sienna, but Ethan won't rag you about it."

"And Declan?"

His gaze hardened, and he slowly shook his head. "We haven't seen Declan since Sarah died."

"What do you mean you haven't seen Declan?" The idea of the three brothers having lost contact was absurd – not the brothers she'd once known. They were inseparable, best friends.

"He went off the rails after Sarah died. It was better for him to leave."

Sienna met his eyes, searching for an explanation of the hidden anger she heard in his voice. "Where is he?"

"No idea."

"You're angry with him."

"Hell, yeah, but I'm mad at you too, yet here you are." His tone had softened and she sensed he'd done it deliberately, not wanting to discuss his brother. He stood and moved to the window, ripping open the curtains.

Sienna groaned as bright sunlight destroyed the haze around her. "Jeepers, Archer. That's harsh."

"You need food. You look like you haven't eaten for a month."

"Ouch."

"Can you stand?" he asked, stepping closer but not touching her.

She nodded and tried to stand but stumbled against him. Strong arms flew out to steady her and gratefully, unashamed, she leaned into him, drawing on his strength. Judging by the rippled muscles and broad shoulders that struggled beneath his grey shirt, the man was all strength. Not that she'd forgotten.

"Damn, I'm such a girl," she said against his chest. She was a mess and trying to make light of it. After all, weakness was an attribute she despised, an emotion she always resisted. A meek reaction to an unexpected attack was no different.

"Sienna, you were kidnapped, drugged, and bludgeoned," he said, tipping her head back so she was looking at him. "It's okay to be upset by what they did to you. You don't have to hide it from me."

Of course not. Besides, he'd know if she was hurting. Their bond went far deeper than the magical connection they shared.

"I'm okay. I'm still trying to shake off the Rose Thorn and I'm a little pissed at myself. I should've known they'd be back."

"You made it easy for them. They're after the book and the four stones. Everyone knows that a Beckham witch is the only one who's able to use the stones to open the book. Imagine their delight when they discovered you've been separated with your Keepers."

When he said it like that, she felt crazy for ever having contemplated walking alone. "Thank you for helping me."

"I will always be here for you, Sienna."

And he would. They all would. Individually, they were powerful in their own unique way. Together, they were ruthless.

Their magical connection was something she'd always treasured until the day she'd used it to almost kill them.

"Sienna," Archer said softly, his thumb stroking her chin in a gentle movement. His dark eyes were full of an intensity that kept her captive, unable to look away.

Wow, the man was mesmerizing.

Sienna felt something vaguely familiar roll through her, quiet and unsettling, and realized with a harsh intake of breath that it had nothing to do with the Rose Thorn. No, this had everything to do with Archer.

His finger trailed along her jaw, his heated gaze never faltering from hers.

"You're safe here, Sienna, and you'll be fine now that you're back in my bed."

"You mean my bed."

His lips twitched with a hint of a smile. "It's my house so technically, my bed."

"I was never in your bed, Archer."

"It was close."

"But it doesn't count."

He edged nearer, his body almost touching hers, heat radiating off him in a way that sent her heart racing. He dipped his head beside hers as his fingers toyed with hers. "Oh," he breathed against her cheek, "it counts, Sienna. Everything that happened between us counts."

"No."

Her whispered denial came out in a breathless whoosh of air. Everything inside her tingled at the intimate act and her racing heart was a dead giveaway to the effect he had on her.

"Your heart is pounding."

"You can tell that by simply touching my hand?"

"I can hear it."

Of course. "Archer, stop it."

His hand slid to her hip, pulling her firmly against him. "Still want to tell me it doesn't count?" he whispered against her ear.

The closeness of him, his scent, and his touch sent a familiar thrill straight through her. She closed her eyes and quietly exhaled.

He was right. Everything counted. Everything.

Including the fact that he'd never tried to stop her from leaving. Memories of their fight two years ago tumbled back and she shut her eyes to ward them off.

"Sienna?"

Not trusting herself to speak, she merely shook her head and stepped back.

He didn't push, thank God, and released her. "I have some work to attend to. Are you sure you're okay?"

"Yes."

"You'll find some painkillers on the nightstand beside your bed. That'll numb any pain for a few hours. I also bought you a new phone. They trashed your old one.”

“Thanks.” She glanced down at the male shirt she wore and slowly closed her eyes. Lovely. “Where are my clothes, Archer?”

“Binned. They were all kidnappy and gross.”

“Do I dare ask who undressed me?”

He didn’t reply but a small smile toyed at the corner of his mouth. God, the man was breathtaking when he smiled.

“You undressed me.”

“It was either me or Ethan,” he replied, catching the pillow she tossed at him. “You’ll find fresh shirts in the drawer.” He nodded at the wooden chest of drawers against the far wall.

“I can’t walk around all day wearing nothing but your damn shirt.”

He grinned. “This way, you can’t leave the house. For now, you need to lay low.”

She raised an eyebrow and folded her arms across her breasts, issuing a sly challenge.

His eyes narrowed. “Don’t even think about it.”

“I need to see my grandmother. She won’t be very impressed if I arrive on her doorstep wearing nothing but your shirt.”

“You’re not leaving the house. At least not until you’re stronger. Rose will come here.”

So he wasn’t going to make this easy for her. She dragged her fingers through her red mass of untamed hair and sighed. “Fine. I’ll wear your shirts. For now.”

“Good. Ethan will be home later, and we’ll all have dinner.”

She tossed another pillow at him as he walked out the door. “With a bare ass wearing nothing but a damn shirt. How Sharon Stone of me.”

CHAPTER SIX

The silence of the forest was comforting, a brief respite from the crazy turn her life had taken since her attack in the park a few days ago. Sienna knew the path between her grandmother's cottage and the Bennett estate by heart, a path she'd walked for years. Her feet crunched along the forest debris along the ground, the sound noisy in the silence around her. The smell of pine needles filled the air, triggering old memories of when she'd played in the forest with her Keepers at a time when they'd been nothing more than friends.

And now she was at odds with them all.

Sienna felt the weariness wash over her at the thought and settled her gaze on the stone walled cottage ahead. The sound of water gently trickling nearby hinted that she was close. When she'd been a child, the rocky stream that surrounded Rose's cottage had often given Sienna the impression that they were on their own island. An island in the middle of a magical forest.

Her heart thudded noisily in her chest when the cottage came into view. A double story cottage with a thatch roof. Rose's white rose bushes, her pride and joy, edged along the neat wooden picket fence that ran along the front of the house. The chimney that peeped out through the thatch hinted of years of use, black with age. The front door was open, a sign that her grandmother was home. Conflicted with excitement and sadness, Sienna stopped in front of the cottage and simply stared. Sweet Rose with the strawberry blonde hair, kind eyes, and fierce spirit. Sienna knew she shouldn't blame her for losing control of her powers the night they'd spelled Mason into a tomb. The fault was all hers for channelling them in the first place, but seeing Sarah die in front of her had evoked such devastation that something inside her had snapped. She opened the small wooden gate, the soft creaking of the aching hinges a dead giveaway of her arrival. Rose appeared in the doorway dressed in a long flowing blue skirt and a white blouse. Rose's hair, several shades lighter than her own, hung loose around her tiny shoulders in a flutter of soft waves.

"Gran?"

Rose's face brightened at the sight of Sienna, and the older woman rushed down the porch steps to embrace her granddaughter. "I'm so glad you came!"

Sienna didn't reply but held onto her grandmother for the several moments it took to regain her composure. Holding her again was like gold.

Rose pulled away and gave Sienna's outfit a quick once over. "Sienna, dear, you starting a new fashion or something?"

"Archer's afraid I'll run so he won't give me any new clothes."

"So you traipsed through the forests in his shirt and gumboots?"

"It's not far and no one saw me." With a wide smile, she pulled her grandmother into her arms again. "I missed you so much."

Rose wrapped her frail arms around her granddaughter and smiled. "I knew you'd find your way back home."

"More like home found me."

"And in the nick of time too." Rose pulled away to reveal bold green eyes filled with love and wisdom. She grimaced at the fading bruise on Sienna's cheek. "Are you okay?"

"Yes. Archer gave me some painkillers that have taken the edge off the aches and pains."

"Do you know who did this?"

Sienna followed her grandmother into the kitchen and inhaled the familiar smell of home. Earthy and fresh, with the faint aroma of herbs. Typical of a witch's kitchen. Some of Sienna's happiest childhood memories were of her time spent here. "He said his name is Harper."

"And you couldn't fry his ass?"

Sienna shook her head and filled the kettle. "Rose Thorn."

"I've had a dose or two of Rose Thorn in my life time," Rose replied with an all-knowing nod. "Wicked herb. Is he one of Warrick's minions?"

"Yes. Has Archer filled you in?"

Rose sank into the chair at the kitchen window and sighed. "Of course. I'm glad you're home, Sienna."

Sienna offered Rose a warm smile. "It's good to be back." Her time away had been fraught with constant worry for her grandmother. Rose had aged, and even though her powers as an ordinary witch were still strong, her body wasn't.

"You still have some clothes in your old room," Rose said, giving Sienna's shirt and gumboots another glance.

"Ah, I could do with some underwear."

Rose chuckled merrily as Sienna disappeared through the house.

Sienna's smile quickly faded the moment she opened the door to her bedroom. It smelt musty, starved of air, as though it had remained sealed since she'd left. It was exactly as she'd left it. Only dustier. The bed was still made, the curtains still drawn, and memories of her life still splashed across the room. Sienna swallowed, trying to push away the emotions that suddenly choked her. She wondered how she'd ever had the courage to leave.

With a brief shake of the head to clear her thoughts, Sienna quickly gathered a few items. She opted for only the essentials, as she'd have to haul everything across the forest. Also, a huge load of clothes would look awfully suspicious – a dead giveaway that she'd gone to see her grandmother.

Naughty, naughty.

When she returned to the kitchen, Rose's expression brightened. "Tell me about your trip," she said, placing two steaming mugs of coffee on the kitchen table.

Sienna reached for the coffee with an appreciative smile, not commenting on her grandmother's choice of words. She'd hardly call a two-year absence a "trip."

Several hours later, when Sienna suggested that she stay over, Rose wouldn't hear of it.

"You're better off with your Keepers, Sienna." She glanced out the window. "And the sun is setting so you'd best be making your way home. It's almost time for dinner."

Sienna would have argued, but as fatigue still reigned, dinner and sleep sounded like an attractive idea. "I'll come see you tomorrow."

"Of course." Rose placed a hand on Sienna's arm, her touch light and gentle. "I'm surprised the boys let you come here alone." When Sienna remained silent and simply reached for her gumboots, Rose's jaw dropped. "Sienna, they don't know you're here?"

"If they knew they'd be here."

Rose gave a low chuckle. "Archer's going to pop a vein, girl."

"As if I care."

The expression on her grandmother's face cooled. "You don't fool me, Sienna."

"I'm fine," Sienna replied, never having doubted it. She'd always been transparent with Rose.

"And Archer?"

The smile disappeared. "Archer's also fine."

"That's not what I meant."

"I know."

"You two were always together." Rose's eyes were ripe with concern. "It must have been hard to be apart for so long."

"He was my best friend." Always had been. After all, his parents had been her mother's Keepers. At first, they'd spent every day together as neighbourhood friends. Later, after their parents' deaths when he'd inherited the role as her Keeper from his parents, they were inseparable. But their attraction had grown to the point that it bordered on the forbidden. "I miss him. I miss the way we used to be."

Rose stood and embraced the younger woman. "Are you ever going to tell me what happened between you two?"

"Nothing happened."

The older woman pulled back to look at Sienna. "Did it have something to do with Sarah's death?"

"Mostly."

"I know Sarah's death was hard on you both but I suspect it had something to do with The Circle's curse."

Yes. "No."

"It may be hard for you to understand why The Circle forbids a witch to get involved with her Keeper, Sienna. They don't want that kind of emotional connection interfering with your choices in maintaining the balance of nature."

"Those old hags shouldn't have a say in my love life!" Sienna snapped and then quickly drew herself back. Challenging a bunch of ancestral witches that governed the rules around witchcraft was not something she usually did. "And besides, my leaving after Sarah's death involved a lot more than just my relationship with Archer."

"Sarah's death wasn't your fault, Sienna. That was all Warrick Brogan."

"She was there because of me." Her tone had taken on an edge of venom to it, despite her resolve not to. "And when Warrick killed her, I lost it to the point that I hurt my Keepers. That's not something that'll ever leave me."

Rose placed a wrinkled hand on Sienna's arm. "It was a mistake, Sienna."

"I almost killed them!"

"But you didn't."

"I could have. I was so angry, so devastated when Sarah died. I destroyed the tomb with powers I had no idea how to control and once I became weak, I drew my strength from Declan and Ethan to the point that I almost killed them. What kind of witch does that make me?" Sienna turned away, struck with the images of the chaos she'd created that night.

"The reason witches have that connection to their Keepers is for that very reason, Sienna. We're supposed to be able to draw energy from each other."

"Not to the point that I kill them. I couldn't stop," she said, her voice filled with the anguish that had taunted her for years. An image of Archer trapped in the fire in the tomb whilst trying to stop her came to mind, ripping open old wounds. "And Archer was burned in the fire I created. His hand still carries the scars." Unlike the rest of his scars, this one would never disappear as it was caused by a witch, by her.

Rose's hands came up to cup Sienna's face so that they were facing each other. "Sienna, you made a mistake. One that you can't change but eventually, you'll learn to live with it."

"I wasn't ready."

Everything fell quiet, the elephant in the room having reared its head. For a moment, neither of them spoke, but when her grandmother wrapped her arms around her, Sienna couldn't help but let her.

"You have to trust me," Rose said quietly against her granddaughter's hair. "Receiving such power is enough to frighten anyone. I know because I was also once in your position."

"How did you learn to control them?"

"With practice, a lot of whiskey to numb my nerves, and plenty of time spent alone in nature."

Sienna gave her grandmother a brief smile. Rose might be heading toward seventy, but the old woman still loved her whiskey.

"You simply need some time, Sienna. Play with your magic, practice your skills, and embrace them. They're a gift."

"They're nothing but a curse."

"Sienna, don't say that."

"Magic destroys, Gran. My parents, Sarah, the way I harmed my Keepers." Sienna pulled back, the familiar urge to run making her feel agitated. "I should leave before Archer comes looking for me."

Rose placed a gentle kiss on Sienna's cheek and pulled back to look at her. "You don't understand why I transferred my powers to you, Sienna, but one day you will. You have your own destiny to fulfil, just as I did. But it's your journey to discover." She pulled away, offering a weak smile that was oddly comforting. "Your Keepers are waiting."

Sienna glanced outside at the fading afternoon sunlight and nodded. "Yes, I should go." She hugged Rose one more time before making her way to the door. She hesitated in the doorway and turned to look at her grandmother. "What would it take to break The Circle's curse on a Keeper and his witch?"

Rose met her gaze, her eyes flashing with a brief glimpse of sorrow. "It's complicated."

"But it can be done?"

"Yes."

Hope fired, despite the warning voice that niggled. "How?"

"With a counteracting spell and a blood sacrifice. A death."

And just like that, all Sienna's hopes went up in flames. There was no way she'd ever offer a blood sacrifice if it meant death. Sienna bit back a response and simply nodded. "I'll see you tomorrow."

By the time Sienna made her way through the forest toward the Manor House, the sun had begun setting at a rapid pace. The fading light didn't worry her; the darkness was well suited to her mood.

Archer. Sarah. Her parents. Rose.

Not a day went by that she didn't think of her parents or Sarah Bennett, her fourth Keeper. And every day, the pain that came with the memory surrounding their deaths still twisted her soul. She'd simply discovered how to muffle the pain and move on.

Her parents, solid and kind, full of wisdom and love. They'd made her feel safe, treasured, and she'd blossomed under their care. Her father had been the town sheriff of Rapid Falls, her mother a Beckham witch. An odd couple but together, they'd fought for order and harmony in their town.

Sadly, it was their quest for peace that had eventually destroyed them.

Sarah too, with her kind eyes, contagious laugh, and endless chatter. She'd been like a sister to Sienna and living in such close proximity with three strong males had called for some female companionship to balance the odds. They'd shared so much love and laughter and losing Sarah was like losing a treasured part of herself.

Sienna swiped at her tears, cursing them. She'd be damned if she'd put Rose or another one of her Keepers in danger protecting her. They were all she had left.

But Archer was right.

She did need the Bennett brothers and the protection they offered. She'd missed them and a small part of her was thrilled they'd found her. The thought unsettled her and she frowned, rubbing her arms with her hands to ward off the chill.

The snapping of a nearby twig had her whirling around.

"Hello?"

Silence greeted her and she swallowed, trying to ignore the sudden uneasiness that had taken hold of her. Her instincts prickled, and she cast a quick glance toward the Manor House. She was close but even at a fast run she would never reach it in time.

In time for what?

Before being mauled by the likes of Harper? A wolf? Before she could contemplate which option would be the lesser evil, two dark shadows stepped out from the shadows of the night.

Senses in prime form, Sienna heard the soft whoosh of the dart gun before the dart reached her. She dropped to the ground, out of its lethal aim, and grunted with satisfaction when the dart disappeared in the darkness. With the skills of a trained warrior, she sprang to her feet, her eyes pinned on the men.

"Rose Thorn?" she asked, glancing at the offensive gun. A rumble of powers stirred inside as her body went into defensive mode. In response, the trees began to rustle around them.

"Worked last time."

Sienna's stomach rolled as she recognized the voice. "Harper. Back so soon?"

Harper stepped forward, wearing a leather jacket and a wicked smile, and reloaded. "I would've thought you'd be expecting me."

"On the Bennett property? You must have a death wish."

His brief laugh sounded more like mockery than amusement. "What better plan than to steal their witch from right under their nose?"

"Ah. There's only one problem though."

"And that would be?"

"You're fresh out of Rose Thorn," she replied, raising unsteady arms in his direction. A strong gust of wind rose up around them but vanished before she could channel it.

Harper gave her a satisfied smile. "Is that all you have, witchy? Even without the Rose Thorn, your powers are still sketchy."

With shaking hands, Sienna tried again. The air shifted, creating a slight whirlwind of forest debris. She raised her arms and sent the whirlwind their way but it whooshed past them, missing them completely.

Harper laughed and edged closer, raising the gun in her direction.

Sienna dragged in air, as the stupid tears welled in her eyes. This is what her fears had reduced her to?

His accomplice broke away to circle her, the motion sparking her defences all over again.

She moved backward as they closed in on her and panic welled up inside her. Giving in to the survival mode that overrode everything else, Sienna flung out her arms with a soft cry. A strong gust of wind slammed against Harper, catching him off guard, and sent the gun smashing against a nearby tree, destroying the batch of dreaded herb. Harper's accomplice produced a second gun with lightning speed, but he quickly retreated a few steps when the gun exploded and landed at his feet.

Feeling empowered from the magic she still shunned, Sienna started chanting in a fierce tone that had both men stop and take notice. The chanting became louder, quicker, and more forceful, a fierce combination of fury and self-preservation brewing a deadly cocktail within, overriding her fear of the magic.

"Cut the crap, witch," Harper ordered and slowly backed away.

The fear in his voice enthralled her, rather than stopped her, and Sienna flung out her arms with more purpose. A spark ignited into a ring of fire and chased off with neat precision, immediately forming a perfect circle around the two men.

They'd kept her prisoner. She was about to return the favour.

Instinctively, both men charged forward in hope of scaling the small wall of fire, but Sienna had already anticipated their move. With a quick raise of the arms, the wall of flames heightened.

"Don't even try," she warned. "I've spelled the circle." When they backed down with loud curses, she gave them a wicked grin. "Not so brave now, are you?"

Even as she said it, she felt the briefest crack in her armour. Her powers were as strong as ever, but her body still lagged from the tail end effects of the Rose Thorn and despite the sudden unwelcome satisfaction at using magic again, the fear of losing control still lingered.

The bright flames flickered and Sienna had to concentrate on maintaining the intensity of heat. The circle of fire raged on, a deep glow of red in a circle of darkness.

She wouldn't be able to hold them for much longer. With a grimace, she sank to her knees but held her head high.

There was no way she'd allow Harper see just how badly the Rose Thorn, or her demons, had tormented her.

Hell no.

****

Archer walked to the edge of the patio and scanned the grounds, a familiar discomfort of warning tugging at his gut. He sensed fear and aggression.

And it wasn't his.

As if to confirm his uneasiness, Levi stood on quiet alert at the top of the stairs, staring into the darkness.

"Levi?"

The retriever tilted her head and whined.

Archer discarded the drink and frowned when he saw the soft glow of flames licking at the haze of darkness in the distance.

Before he could process the sight, Ethan walked up behind him.

"What the hell is that?" Ethan asked, motioning to the fire with the glass in his hand. "Rose have some voodoo witchy crap going on?"

Archer narrowed his eyes, doubtful. "Why would Rose have a roaring fire in the middle of the forest?" The nagging sensation in his gut heightened, demanding he sit up and take action. And then it dawned on him. "It's Sienna. Something's wrong."

"Isn't she up in her room?" Ethan asked, quickly setting his glass on the table beside him. "Have you checked on her again?"

"I'm going to kill her," Archer said, and bolted down the stairs, Levi directly beside him.

With their supernatural speed, it took mere moments for both brothers to reach the fire.

Archer slapped a hand across Ethan's chest, putting an abrupt stop to his haste. With his other hand, he reined in the unsettled dog.

With a brief nod, Ethan motioned to the circle of flames ahead of them. "Voodoo witchy crap. What the hell are they doing?"

"I have no idea." But the smell of raw aggression punched him in the gut. And fear. Sienna's fear. Archer looked around, his fists clenched at his sides. The fire blazed sharply, eliminating the dullness of the darkening forest. Nearby leaves of several tree branches sizzled into a crackling oblivion. His stomach rolled when he saw the silhouettes of the two men trapped in the middle of the fire.

Barking furiously, Levi broke away from Archer and bolted.

And then he saw her.

Sienna.

The sight of Sienna on her knees, drawing on the remains of her strength to keep the two men trapped in their fire prison, sent immediate chills down his spine.

"Sienna!"

Levi was already all over her. Sienna's head whipped around, and he saw the relief cross her face.

"What took you so long?" she asked casually, but he heard the strain in her voice.

"What happened?" Archer asked, kneeling beside her.

"Harper."

His head flung up, and he glared at the two men. "They came here?"

"Bold, aren't they?"

"Are you okay?"

She gave a brief nod at the same time the intensity of the flames lessened.

"Sienna, stop," he said, placing a hand on her arm. The trembling he felt beneath his fingers brought on a fresh wave of anger. "We're here. You can stop."

The fire didn't let up and he moved closer to her. A quick glance at Ethan told him what he needed to know. His brother nodded in response, ready for the attack that would follow the moment the wall of fire came down.

"Sienna," Archer said, sliding his arms around her shoulders, "stop."

Just like that, the fire disappeared, leaving the two men exposed to the wrath of her Keepers.

"Go inside," he told her, tugging her to her feet. When she hesitated, he pinned her with a glare, half-warning, half-pleading. "We've got this."

She nodded and backed away at the same time the two entrapped men sprang into action.

It was only when she disappeared into the darkness, Levi hot on her heels, that Archer whirled toward them.

CHAPTER SEVEN

With a burning sensation chewing at his gut, Archer marched through the house in search of Sienna.

He found her in the kitchen, draining a bottle of water, a bloodied tissue clasped in one hand. Nose bleed, no doubt. Whenever her powers had taken too strong a toll on her body, she'd develop either a migraine or a nosebleed.

Despite his rage, he couldn't help but notice her, and hesitated in the doorway. Her red hair, a striking contrast to the white shirt she wore, hung loose around her shoulders. Her shirt had hitched up her waist to reveal long, toned legs and a white scrap of lace that barely covered her ass.

All skin and woman.

The sight struck him right where it mattered most, and he felt an instant tightening between his thighs. Only Sienna could fend off attackers in gumboots and still look sexy. Something inside stirred beside the rage, mingled for a brief moment, and was pushed aside.

Reminding himself that he was, in fact, still very mad at her, Archer shoved open the door and tossed the small bag of clothes she'd collected from Rose onto a nearby couch.

She lowered the water bottle and spun around. "Archer."

"What the hell were you thinking?" he demanded, coming to a stop in front of her.

"I'm in no mood for a lecture, so back the hell down."

He caught her chin and tilted her face to either side. A mild nosebleed as he'd suspected. Her attempt to pull away only tightened his grip on her. She was upset and a fire raged in her eyes that he hadn't seen in a very long time. Good. "Are you okay?"

"I'm fine."

"What part of 'stay in the house' got lost in translation?"

Sienna slapped at his hands and drew back. "I went to see Rose."

"Rose would've come here."

"I can't stay here and hide forever."

"No, but you'll have to be careful until Warrick and his warriors can be dealt with."

She gave a defiant lift of her chin. "I'm not the weak little witch girl you make me out to be, Archer. In case you hadn't noticed, I handled them."

"Any longer and you would've crumbled." He saw the denial on her face and had the urge to shake some sense into her. Instead, he planted his hands firmly on her shoulders, forcing her to face him. "No one doubts your powers but you refuse to embrace them and that makes you weak. Don't for one moment think those assholes don't know that."

"I'm fine!" She shoved his chest, packing a powerful punch for someone so small.

Damn, she's infuriating.

Frustration prickled and pushing past her, he slammed on the tap with a little more force than intended.

Sienna's eyes widened when she saw him vigorously scrubbing his hands, blood rinsing down the drain. "You're hurt."

"I'll live."

She came up behind him, took hold of his hand in hers, and

winced. "It's a bad one."

He tugged his hand away, not caring to examine the thin cut on his inner arm. He'd had worse. "I'm fine, Sienna." The wound had already begun to heal and once again, Archer was grateful for the accelerated healing that came with his powers. It had saved his hide several times.

"Archer."

"I heal quickly," he said, grabbing a nearby towel and wiping the wound dry. "You, on the other hand, don't."

"And you're hurt because of me."

"So stay in the damn house."

"I can't talk to you when you're like this." Her attempt to side step him failed, and she blew out her breath. "Let me go, Archer."

Reaching between them, he took her hand and held it against his shoulder where his Keeper tattoo was branded on his flesh. The action brought an instant flash of recognition in her eyes, and she lifted her gaze to meet his. "You know how this all works, Sienna. Without you, our elemental powers are useless. But without us, your elemental powers will weaken. You will weaken." His voice clouded with a thick emotion he couldn't prevent, and he swallowed. The very thought of something happening to her sent his entire body into a rip-roaring rollercoaster of anger, misery, and denial.

"Archer, stop."

"No. You need to get how serious this is."

"Don't you think I know that?"

"By your actions tonight, no. I don't think you do." She tried to break away but he grabbed her wrists and held them between their bodies. "If you're hell bent on risky manoeuvres, then we're all at risk. And I'll be damned if our parents died for nothing."

"Don't you think I feel that, too?" she cried, her voice trembling as her eyes filled with unshed tears. "Every damn day is a reminder of them, of Sarah, and I blame myself. I keep losing people, no matter how hard I fight for them."

He gave a mocking laugh of disbelief and yanked her toward him. "You call this fighting? All I see is you running away and taking stupid risks. You're a Beckham witch, Sienna, so start acting like one!"

"Why do you think I loathe using my powers? You're all I have left and I almost destroyed you and although we have no proof, I'm pretty damn sure it was magic that killed our parents."

"It wasn't the magic that killed them!" he yelled, frustration whipping away his usual control. "It was Warrick's parents!"

His words snapped her into silence and she blew out air and closed her eyes. A single tear trailed down her cheek and everything inside Archer twisted. "We don't know that for sure."

"Smoke, fire. They won't stop," he said, lowering his voice. "The Bennett brothers have vowed to protect you. Why hide? Why've you resisted us for the last two years?"

Her eyes blazed something sharp, and she looked away, swiping away the fallen tear.

"Tell me."

She shook her head. "Now's not the time for that conversation. It's been a long night."

But he refused to let it go. He'd waited two years for an explanation, and now seemed like the perfect time. "Why did you run?"

She became still, and he felt the fight lessen. "You know what would've happened if I'd stayed."

"Say it," he said softly.

"No."

There was a subtle shift of energy between them as their gazes met in an unyielding challenge. Two unmovable forces, a lifetime of history, and undeniable passion hung between them.

"Say the words, Sienna," he insisted softly.

"You know why."

"Say it."

She didn't reply, but didn't have to. He saw the raw longing in the depth of her green eyes, conflicted with sadness, full of wanting.

Archer stared at her lips, caught by the urge to lay claim to them, and tried to push aside the vague voice that screamed a familiar warning at him. They'd been down this road before. Almost. And look where the hell they'd ended up.

But his universe shrank around him the moment her gaze fell to his lips.

Throwing caution to the wind, his mouth came down on hers, avid and hungry, and everything else fell away.

Except her.

CHAPTER EIGHT

An instinct older than civilization yelled at Sienna to run, but her whole body started tingling the moment Archer's mouth touched hers.

Instead, she gave in to the tender pressure of his lips, and tangled her fingers in his hair.

The kiss that followed was so intense and rocked her world in a way that unnerved her.

His clever hands were all over her, deliciously rough against her flawless skin, and her girlie tingling instantly turned into insatiable throbbing. Exotic little fires of need kindled inside her and she pressed herself into him, demanding more.

It had been a long time since she'd felt like this.

"I'd hoped things had changed," she groaned between kisses.

He smiled against her lips. "Have they?"

She shook her head.

"Damn right they haven't," he said, nibbling her neck. His mouth moved across her cheekbone, along her chin. He dropped soft kisses across her jaw and into her neck, and she hung her head back to give him full access.

"I've never stopped wanting you, Sienna."

His words, whispered against her ear, sent her imagination

racing, and she smiled in anticipation. She hungered for more and clung to him as he took control of her body and overpowered her senses. His stomach pressed against her in a way that sent her libido roaring and brought an instant flush to her cheeks.

Raw primal need took over, destroying all rational thought, and with a swift motion, Archer hitched his palms against her lower back and hoisted her against him.

Her legs came up around him in reflex response and she sought out his mouth, needing the onslaught of delicious kisses only he could give her.

"God, you're beautiful," he whispered, plundering her mouth with his.

He kicked the door closed behind him and took three strides toward the kitchen counter. With a quick swipe of his arm, he sent the fruit bowl scattering across the floor, before placing her seated on the counter top.

His raw, masculine aura of power and strength was overwhelming.

"We shouldn't be doing this," Archer said softly between kisses, sliding his hands under the hem of her shirt to cup her hips and pull her closer.

"We really shouldn't be doing this."

He tipped his head back long enough to give her a slow, predatory smile before capturing her mouth with his again in a kiss so heated, so exciting, that she almost squealed with delight.

The man was built for speed, sex, and pleasure. The thought made her entire body burn, and she threw her head back with a soft sigh.

The sound of the kitchen door opening across the room sent a vague warning through her, but she ignored it.

"What the hell?"

Sienna's eyes flew open and she pulled back to stare at Archer. He drew in a deep, aggravated breath and tilted his head toward the kitchen door. "Your timing sucks, brother."

Sienna blinked, trying to catch her breath and find her senses. She felt like a whirlwind had ripped through her – a whirlwind of pure masculine heat and sexiness.

With a quick glance past Archer's body, she saw Ethan walk further into the kitchen. Like his brother, he was tall and muscular, but had a lightness about him that Sienna had always loved. He wore his sandy brown hair in shorter spikes, the casual look suiting his carefree personality. Usually, his striking blue eyes were filled with laughter and kindness. Tonight, the Ethan that stood glaring at her was a far cry from the Ethan she knew. Fury had erased the laughter in his eyes, a deep frown creased his brow, and his mouth was set in a tight grimace of complete disapproval. There was nothing light about Ethan now.

Sienna closed her eyes with a soft groan and dropped her head against Archer's chest, hoping that Ethan would simply turn around and leave.

But no.

"Archer," Ethan said in a low tone, the single word signalling the start of a heated lecture.

Archer kept his back to his brother and remained positioned between her legs, quietly casting a quick scan across her body to ensure she was decent. With a frown, he straightened her shirt and exhaled. "Not now, Ethan."

Ethan grabbed the discarded fruit bowl off the floor and gaped at his brother. "Seriously?"

"Not now, Ethan."

"Archer."

"Ethan," Archer said quietly, his tone serving as a warning on its own, "leave. Now."

With an unaccustomed scowl, Ethan picked up the various fruit strewn across the kitchen floor and threw them back into the fruit bowl. "You two miss the part about this sort of behaviour being forbidden between a Keeper and his witch? You'll have The Circle spitting cobras."

Ethan's words brought reality crashing around Sienna's feet with a thunderous roar.

The damn Circle.

A relationship between a Keeper and his witch was so strongly frowned upon that the witches had cast a spell, cursing any budding relationship. They had their uses, their rules and regulations were needed, but right now, Sienna resented the hell out of them. It was hard to think that a bunch of dead witches still ruled her life.

Sienna felt Archer withdraw, even though he hadn't moved.

Thanks to Ethan's stark reminder, the curse that kept her and Archer apart two years ago would continue to keep them apart.

"Ethan, this is none of your business," Archer said, whirling around to face his brother.

"When it comes to Sienna, everything about her is my business."

"Not this."

Ethan took three strides and stood in front of his brother. "You're her Keeper, Archer, and you don't want to mess with a bunch of dead witches." He jabbed a finger into Archer's chest. "Besides, she's no match for your physical strength. You could hurt her."

"Ethan, stop it," Sienna said softly.

Ethan whirled to face her. "If he doesn't control himself, he'll hurt you."

"Oh, please," she scoffed. "Archer's the poster boy for control. You really think he's going to hurt me?"

Ethan's expression eased. "Playing with fire equals getting burned. Not a good idea."

"We're not children, so back off."

Ethan glanced at them both and then nodded. "Fine. You two

figure it out. But when the dead Aunty Hilda's come seeking punishment, don't come knocking on my door for help." He walked to the liquor cabinet, pulled out two glasses, and poured Bourbon into both. He handed Archer a glass. "Drink up, brother. You look like you need one."

Archer's jaw flexed. "Get out of here, Ethan."

Ethan tossed back the whiskey, refilled the glass, and headed for the door. "You guys need to figure this shit out before someone gets hurt," he threw over his shoulder as he left.

Archer was frowning when he turned back to Sienna. "Are you okay?"

She nodded and slid off the counter, trying to keep herself from blushing at the thought of the hot, needy kiss they'd shared moments ago. Had Ethan not interrupted them, she would easily have forgotten the rules set by The Circle and given Archer free reign on her.

Wow.

Archer reached for her but she stopped him with a shake of the head. "Ethan's right, Archer. The Circle will be spitting cobras if we take this further."

"Sienna."

They fell silent, the undeniable truth adding distance between them even though neither one of them had moved.

Anger flooded through her, and Sienna choked back a scream. There had once been a time when her destiny and Beckham heritage had felt like an honour, now felt like an annoying burden she simply couldn't shake.

And right now, despite their best intentions, she hated The Circle with everything in her.

Inhaling softly, she lifted her chin in quiet determination, trying to calm the resentment inside. "It's late. We should get some sleep. Tomorrow's going to be a busy day."

Archer lifted a brow. "You have plans?"

"Yes." She pushed past him and moved toward the door. "I know it's a long trip back to New York but I need to sort out a few things at my apartment and pack a few bags. I'm happy to make the trip alone but I'm assuming you'll want to tag along."

"I'll come with you, Sienna."

She nodded, never having doubted otherwise, and stopped at the doorway to frown at the shattered lamp on the floor. When had that happened?

Her breath caught as memories of Archer's kiss clouded her mind, but she was quick to push them away. She looked back at Archer and blushed when she saw his lip curl into a slight grin. He would be able to sense her quick flush of excitement sparked by the memory of their kiss and judging by his grin, he found brief amusement in her reaction to the memory. "Stop it," she said, jabbing a finger in Archer's direction.

"Stop what?"

"I want my damn necklace."

"But this is way more fun."

"For you maybe. I'm going to bed."

"You haven't eaten yet."

"I'm not hungry."

"Lucky you." A sexy gleam entered his eyes and a silly grin played on his lips. "Because unlike you, I am hungry, Sienna, but it's not food I'm after."

Sienna gaped at him for a second, spun around, and fled to her room.

CHAPTER NINE

The dream had Sienna bolting out of bed with a soft cry. Heart pounding and gasping choppy breaths of air, she whirled around in the darkness and blinked rapidly in an effort to calm the frenzy of emotions that threatened to overwhelm her.

Breathe. Breathe.

The night times were the worst, as she had no control over the memories that sparked the vicious nightmares.

Someone had once told her that time healed all wounds. Bull. Wide-awake and restless, Sienna pulled on a cardigan to ward off the cool night air, and silently made her way toward the kitchen. She doubted tea would do much to calm the fierceness that lurked inside, but it would give her something to do.

The spacious kitchen was in darkness and she left it that way, needing the blackness to smother her thoughts.

Sienna filled the kettle with water and turned it on. While waiting for it to boil, she strolled outside to the undercover patio that led onto the pool area. It was still dark but the garden lights illuminated the patio and the pool with a soft glow that comforted her. The patio consisted of a fireplace, several comfortable couches, a table with several chairs, and a breathtaking view of the estate's back garden. It was homely, immaculate, and a popular gathering spot for the Bennett brothers. The bright blue light inside the pool added a cool inviting feel to the water.

Of all the brothers, Archer had always been the lover of water. Not surprising considering his connection with it.

She envied the natural connection her Keepers had to their elemental powers. When channelling their powers, they exerted such confidence and control, something totally foreign to her. Archer could do things with water and manipulate the droplets in a way that never failed to amaze her, Declan could wield fire with impressive ease, and Ethan handled the wind as though it were child's play.

You're a Beckham witch, Sienna, so start acting like one.

Archer's words came to mind, stirring the emotions she'd avoided until now. Although he hadn't elaborated, she'd known what he'd meant. She'd spent years watching her mother and grandmother in witch mode and she'd learned from an early age that Beckham witches were fighters. They were strong and they fought for what they believed in. They were kind, loving, respected, often feared, and lived their lives to maintain order. They weren't afraid of their powers and embraced it as a gift, using their magic to make the world a better, safer place.

An instant flush broke out through Sienna as shame trickled through her. She closed her eyes and allowed the truth to sink in.

She'd spent the last two years being everything a Beckham witch wasn't.

Sienna opened her eyes and stared at the water for a long while before moving silently toward it. Maybe, just maybe, if she acted like a powerful, confident Beckham witch, she might actually start to feel like one. She was reaching but there had to be something better than the anguish and fear that had been her permanent sorrow buddies for the last few years.

A small whirlwind of energy began to quiver inside her, a gentle fluttering that symbolized hope. The awakening of her powers?

There was only one way to find out.

With careful ease, her heart pounding against her ribcage, Sienna quietly raised her arms toward the pool and gave way to the trance that usually took over when channelling her powers.

The water swirled inside the pool, slowly and softly at first. Once she'd gathered momentum, she raised her arms slightly. A low wall of water followed suit, hovering quietly above the pool before collapsing with a loud splash. Two attempts later, Sienna was ready to scream with annoyance.

I can do this, dammit!

Drawing in a deep breath, she pushed aside the frustration and tried again, this time, giving more of herself to the magic. The water swirled slowly at first but soon caught momentum and moments later, it was swirling faster and harder. With a gentle movement of her arms, the water rose up to form another wall that remained hovering in mid-air.

The ability to make the water do as she pleased was incredible, and a brief jolt of euphoria landed in her gut. When Harper had attacked her in the forest, she'd used two powers to subdue him. Air and fire. It had taken a few tries and she'd channelled both elements with difficulty, but with a control that had surprised her.

Curiosity and confidence spiked, Sienna concentrated on keeping the water mid air with one hand whilst stirring up a whirlwind in the forest beyond with the other hand. Moments later, she had a whirlwind of forest debris heading her way. The sight frightened her, only briefly, but bold instincts had taken over, driving Sienna to a depth she'd been too afraid to touch.

The whirlwind picked up speed as it approached, gathering fuel along the way. Once she had both elements of nature side by side, she twirled her arms in circular motions, her mind and body completely in tune with the elements. Both elements immediately began swirling in circular motions, faster and faster until Sienna herself was panting.

And feeling even bolder, Sienna slammed her hands together, creating a full-blown collision of water against wind. Water and forest debris exploded into an impressive scene around her, leaving her breathless.

Gasping for air, her shoulders heaving from the unleashed adrenaline, Sienna stared at the chaos she'd created. Water, stones, sticks, leaves, small plants, and even a tiny tree littered the pool area that had only moments ago been spotless. Now it looked as though a mini tornado had taken place while they'd all slept.

But the moment of the collision had been incredible, the realization that she had controlled both elements at once even more so.

Taking a few calming breaths, Sienna smiled at her accomplishment and went inside to make the tea. The brief exertion of power had been exhilarating but exhausting at the same time.

It was almost dawn and the sun would be up soon. As would the two Bennett brothers.

Ethan she could handle. As for Archer…

All thoughts of Archer vanished the moment Sienna realized she wasn't alone.

Age-old instincts sparking a familiar warning, she spun around in time to see the silhouette of a man approaching her.

She screamed, the shrill sound shattering the silence of the night, and lashed out. Her hands met a thick wall of muscled chest, and strong arms came up around her. They stumbled across the counter, knocking over the wooden block of carving knives that crashed to the floor with a sickening clang. She cried out and launched herself toward the discarded weapons. There was a struggle, a fierce growl, and she fought with all the strength she had.

But her tiny body was no match for his size or strength. In a heartbeat, he had her pinned beneath him, her arms trapped above her head.

"Let me go!" she demanded, tugging one arm free. Her heart soared with hope as her fumbling fingers touched something sharp. With a fierce cry, she drove the knife deep into her attacker's back, and shoved against him.

There was a flash of movement in the darkness followed by a fierce, low growl as her attacker was hoisted off her and sent flying across the room. He crashed into the wooden drawers against the wall, shattering a lamp, and fell to the floor with a loud curse.

Gasping, Sienna looked up at the silhouette of a second man towering in the darkness above her.

Archer.

He growled, his eyes pinned on the intruder, and readied himself for the fight to follow. "What the hell are you doing here?" he asked between gritted teeth.

"I live here, dammit."

Archer stepped forward, his breathing rapid, his fists clenched beside each thigh. Sienna heard him exhale as the tension subsided. "Declan?"

The tall figure at the back of the room struggled to his feet. "Hell, brother, your hospitality sucks."

Light flooded the room and Sienna blinked, trying to adjust to the harsh light, to the two Bennett brothers staring at each other in stunned silence.

Archer moved first. He was barefoot and had tugged on a pair of jeans. He held out a hand to Sienna and pulled her to her feet. "Are you hurt?"

She shook her head and turned to Declan, the middle Bennett brother. "Declan?"

Declan.

Another Bennett brother that stirred an ocean of memories and conflicting emotions. Longer dishevelled jet-black hair, expressive blue eyes and a bad boy image he'd never shed. He wore black jeans, an olive green t-shirt, and a black leather jacket, a firm favourite of his.

With a grimace, Declan Bennett stepped forward, his hands clawing at his back in a desperate attempt to remove the knife.

"Oh, my, God. You're hurt," Sienna said, rushing to him.

"You stabbed me with a damn knife," he growled, dropping to his knees with a guttural groan.

"You attacked me."

"Like hell. You attacked me."

Sienna dropped to her knees and reached for the knife. "You scared the life out of me." With a small cry, she tugged the invasive weapon out of his back. She grimaced as his flesh released the knife with a sickly sucking sound, oozing blood everywhere. Declan scowled at her as he shrugged off his jacket.

Archer appeared beside her with a towel, and Sienna quickly pressed it against the wound.

"I'm so sorry," she said, her free hand flying to her mouth. "Dammit, Declan, I could've killed you."

"You stabbed me," Declan repeated, staring at her.

"That'll teach you to creep up behind me in the darkness," she said. Despite trying to make her tone sound light, her voice still shook. She pulled the towel away and breathed a sigh of relief. The bleeding had stopped. "It's healing."

"Still doesn't take away the pain."

"Don't be such a girl."

Declan winced and held out his hand to his brother. "Help me up, brother. I need a drink."

Archer pulled him to his feet. "What are you doing here?"

Sienna looked up at Archer and lifted a brow, caught off guard at the anger she heard in his voice.

"Don't be so hostile," Declan said and tugged off his t-shirt.

He turned to toss the t-shirt onto the counter and Sienna caught a glimpse of the striking black tattoo spread across his shoulder blades. It was the image of a pentagram, creatively crafted, designed with care. The mark of a Keeper.

Her Keeper.

Pushing herself to her feet, Sienna retrieved a fresh towel from the kitchen drawer, wet it, and held it out to Declan. "Clean up, Bennett, you look all bloody and gross." Not that it did anything to hide the hard wad of muscles he'd unveiled when he'd tossed his t-shirt.

Declan cocked a brow. "Not surprising considering you stabbed me."

"You're damn lucky the surprise attack left me without time to use some witchy joo joo on you. What were you thinking sneaking up on an unstable witch in the dark?"

A sly smile spread across Declan's face, and Sienna had the urge to shove him. Had it not been for the knife she'd found, she could've caused a lot more damage if she'd used her powers.

"I wasn't sneaking. I live here."

"You haven't lived here for two years. You came back." A rush of relief flooded her, surprising her, and she realized how much she'd missed him. Over the years, she'd formed a separate bond and a unique relationship with each of her Keepers. With Declan, their shared understanding of the weight of responsibility they both carried in being a powerful witch and a dedicated Keeper had sealed their bond, different to her relationship with the other two brothers. Sometimes their world rocked, other times it didn't. Declan got both. His dark, mischievous, troublemaker, bad boy attitude annoyed Archer who was the complete opposite in nature, but for Sienna, Declan had always added some colour to her journey as a Beckham witch.

"Declan," Archer said softly, breaking the silence. "Why've you come back?"

Declan tilted his head to look at Sienna. "Duty calls, so I'm here."

"After two years, you've decided to honour your duty as a Keeper?"

"Can't be a Keeper if there's no witch to keep. Sienna's back so I'm back."

"We don't need any more trouble, Declan."

Declan's smile was slow and full of mischief. "Where's the fun in that then, brother?"

"You haven't changed, have you?"

"Oh, I've changed, Archer," Declan replied in a low tone that held more weight behind the words than anticipated. He opened the liquor cabinet and hauled out a bottle and a glass. He poured himself a drink, swallowed it, and poured another. "Two years of therapy, loads of women, and an endless supply of bourbon. I'm a transformed man."

"You're full of crap."

Declan laughed. "Okay, no therapy, but I wasn't lying about the bourbon."

"Can you be serious for a minute?"

"Or the women."

"Declan."

"What, brother? Just because you're all broody and serious all the time doesn't mean I should follow suit." Declan motioned to Archer's harsh frown. "I happen to like a wrinkle free forehead."

Archer waved a hand across the room. "Someone has to keep all this together."

"Which is why I left."

"You didn't leave, Declan. You ran."

"You were relieved when I left, Archer." Declan's tone was clipped with a brief hint of anger that quickly disappeared when he smiled. "But you should ease up on the frowning, brother. It's a very crowded forehead you have there."

Archer's jaw worked and he stepped forward, staring at his brother with such anger that it came off him in waves. "We couldn't all have the luxury of stuffing the pain of what happened to Sarah in a box and running off to God knows where to drown our sorrows in women and alcohol. You screwed up, Declan, and you left us to clean up your mess. I've earned the crowded forehead."

Declan reeled back as though Archer had struck him. Silence reigned, thick and prickly, and both brothers stared at each other.

Without breaking eye contact, Declan lifted the glass and mock toasted his brother. "Didn't take long for the elephant in the room to let out a mighty roar."

Despite their anger and tension between the two brothers, Sienna's heart sank. Sarah. It all came back to Sarah. Would any of them ever be able to get over her death? The horror of losing Sarah Bennett had struck them all in different ways, yet with the same result.

Absolute destruction.

Archer's frown became more pronounced. "You should go, Declan."

"Like hell. I live here."

"Sienna's been marked, and you're no good to her if you're hell bent on revenge and trouble."

"Revenge? A given considering our sister is dead and our witch has been marked. Trouble? That's reserved for enemies so you might want to determine which side you're on, Archer."

"The only side I'm on is the one that protects Sienna."

Declan smiled, without amusement, and sipped his drink. "Then that puts me squarely on team you," he said, crossing the room to where Archer stood. For a brief moment, the brothers looked at each other in prickly silence.

Declan sighed and spoke first. "We may have a difference in

opinion but we agree on one thing, brother. Sienna's wellbeing comes first."

"And why do I find it hard to trust anything you say?"

"Ouch."

Sienna stepped between them, slamming a fist against each burly chest. The anger that burned between the two men was overwhelming, and she drew in a deep breath. "Stop this," she said, her voice steady, even though their hostility to each other had shaken her to the core. "We can't fight each other."

Without breaking eye contact and in perfect unison, each brother took Sienna by the arm and hoisted her out of their way.

"Like I said," Archer murmured, turning back to his brother, closing the space between them. "You should go."

"You need me, Archer. Warrick plans to get into that tomb and Sienna's his way in. There's no chance in hell I can leave and you know it."

"You're not much help to us if you're still caught up in revenge and guilt, Declan."

Declan shrugged and gave a half smile. "Nothing a little alcohol can't numb."

"Will you be serious for one damn minute?"

Their level of tension and testosterone had reached a peak that unnerved Sienna. She stared at the two handsome brothers and sighed.

Two men, each with a remarkable strength and power of their own, sized each other up. Both dark, both handsome, and both rattling with anger and resentment. But so different. Their loyalty and dedication to their legacy, to her, was the only thing they shared. Archer held a deep intensity and fierceness about him that Sienna had always found incredibly sexy. Declan, on the hand, consisted of smouldering dark looks and heaps of attitude. Whereas Archer had neat cut hair, Declan had grown his to the point that it almost touched his shoulders. A perfect illustration of their different personalities. Archer had always been the more controlled brother of the two, and Declan more reckless. Water and fire. This wasn't the first time they'd butted heads and wouldn't be the last, but Sienna found their hostility and aggression to each other disturbing.

"Stop it." Her voice was low and insistent but failed to catch their attention. Deciding she'd had enough of their fiery banter, she raised her hands and drew on her centre.

Both brothers immediately grabbed their heads, groaning and cursing, and stumbled to their knees.

"Sienna, dammit," Archer ground out, clutching his head.

Sienna's hand fell to her sides, putting an instant stop to the mental torment, and lifted a brow. "Will you stop the fighting?"

Still holding a hand to his head, Archer got to his feet. "I told you never to use that witchy crap on me again."

"It got your attention, didn't it?"

Declan rose, wincing as he rubbed his forehead, and peered at her through narrowed eyes. "Damn, Sienna. It's been a while since you mind blasted me with your witch's joo joo. That hurt, dammit."

"It's supposed to hurt or it wouldn't be a useful tool for breaking up stupid male driven, testosterone loaded fights, now would it?" She lifted her chin and straightened her shoulders, needing all the height she could muster to face the two brothers glaring at her. "If we're going to stop the Brogan brothers, we have to work together." She looked at Archer. "You were the one who told me I was crazy for thinking I had to do this alone, Archer. Now who's the crazy one for thinking you can do this without your brothers?"

"Sienna –"

Ignoring him, Sienna pinned Declan with a steely gaze. "Sarah's death was not your fault, Declan. She was in that damn tomb protecting me. We were blindsided and nothing you did could've saved her." She saw the flash of sadness in Declan's eyes, followed by his quick attempt to mask it. "Sarah wouldn't want this. Before her death, the five of us were inseparable, ready to take on any crap the Brogan brothers threw at us. Now, we're divided and don't for one minute think that Warrick Brogan doesn't know that." Her shoulders fell and her tone softened. "Don't you see? We owe it to Sarah to pull together to protect everything she died for. Everything our parents died for. If we keep the seal of the curse in place, the Brogan brothers will continue to live out that curse until their deaths. That alone is revenge in itself."

Declan tilted his head, the word "revenge" striking a core. He slowly nodded. "She's right, Archer."

"I know. Still don't have to like it."

"Neither do I."

Two pairs of eyes met in an unspoken truce.

Declan was the first to look away, turning to Sienna. "Sienna, you try that mind fry on me again, and I'll personally feed you some damn Rose Thorn."

"Yeah, as if that's going to happen."

He arched a brow. "Try me."

"Oh, you're just jealous because my powers top yours."

"Is that a challenge?"

"Declan, that's enough," Archer said, stepping forward.

Declan glanced at his brother and smiled. "Still her big protector, aren't you brother? Glad to see nothing's changed."

"Stop being an ass."

Declan scooped his bloody t-shirt off the counter and dumped it in the bin. "The three Bennett brothers and their witch are back, and all's well in Rapid Falls."

"Where're you going?" Archer asked as Declan moved to the kitchen door.

"I'm assuming you haven't torched my room so I'm going to

bed."

"It's almost morning."

"Who cares?" Declan threw over his shoulder and walked out the door without looking back.

Archer exhaled softly before turning to face Sienna. "Are you okay?"

She nodded. "At least he's back."

"He's a pain in the ass."

"He always has been, but he's your brother."

"It's the only thing that's kept me from ripping his spleen through his throat."

Sienna smiled at the empty threat, not unfamiliar with them, and then her expression cleared. She sobered and wrapped her arms around herself. "I was wrong to run two years ago."

"We've all been running. In different ways."

"Declan blames himself for Sarah's death."

"We all blame ourselves."

"No, Archer. You weren't there the moment it happened. It's different for Declan."

And it was. Memories of the moment Warrick Brogan had targeted Sarah shortly after the ceremony they'd performed to cast the spell came to mind. Archer and Ethan had taken Rose above ground, leaving Declan and Sarah with her. One Brogan brother sealed in the tomb, the other sprawled unconscious on the floor. Their defences were down as everything had fallen silent, the spell was over, and the curse was in place. As they were about to walk away, Warrick Brogan charged Declan with a warlike cry and a vintage dagger clasped in one hand. Acting on instinct, Sarah had flung herself in the way, protecting her brother, and taking the stab to the heart meant for him.

The only way to kill a Keeper was to attack the heart.

And the dagger had gone straight into Sarah's, killing her

instantly.

A violent fight had broken out between Warrick and Declan and everything after that was a blur to Sienna. Overwhelmed with grief and fuelled by rage, she'd tapped into a very deep, raw part of herself and had allowed her powers to consume her. When she'd finally snapped out of her trance, exhausted and depleted of energy, the tomb was on fire, Warrick was gone, and Declan and Ethan were unconscious. She'd channelled their elemental powers, fire and air, draining them of their energy source. Almost killing them. Thanks to Archer who'd dragged them all out of the tomb, they had escaped the flames. Archer hadn't been so fortunate.

"Sienna." Archer's words, spoken softly in the quiet room, speared the memories of that horrible night and brought her mind back to the present. "You've got to let it go."

She shrugged and shook her head. "I hurt my Keepers. I can't let it go, Archer, and neither can Declan. We both feel responsible. Sarah was there to protect me and died protecting Declan." A tragedy that had bonded Declan to her forever.

"I get it, Sienna. Trust me, I get it."

"So cut him some slack, okay?"

"Only if you cut yourself some slack."

The mood shifted between them when he stepped forward, tangling his fingers in her hair. His thumb stroked the faded bruise on her cheek, his gaze flickering from hers to her lips, as if contemplating whether to kiss her.

"Archer, don't," she whispered, wrapping her hands around his to stop him.

"Sienna –"

"No. We can't. Ethan was right. We shouldn't do this."

He shifted his grip and captured both her hands in his. "Can you really walk away from this?"

She knew what he meant, and her entire body reacted at the

thought. Her heartbeat raced, her stomach clenched, and she dragged in a choppy gasp of air.

"Can you, Sienna?"

He was looking at her with an intensity that held her fixed to the spot and everything that sizzled when they were together sprang to the surface.

"You can't kiss me again," she said softly.

"But you want me to."

She wouldn't deny it. "Our relationship is cursed, you know that. Last time we got too close, you lost a sister and I lost my best friend." She tipped her head to the side. "You know I'm right, Archer."

"I'm willing to fight for it."

"But I'm not." She couldn't risk losing again and she'd had enough of the bad that the good didn't seem worth fighting for anymore.

"Sienna."

"No."

He closed his eyes and exhaled softly. When he opened them a moment later, she saw the struggle reflected there. With a final nod, he turned around and walked to the door.

Sienna ached to stop him, to call his name, but she held back.

Her breath caught when he paused in the doorway, spun around and took three quick, determined strides toward her.

Capturing her face in his hands, his lips caught hers in a kiss so powerful, so urgent, and so full of emotion that it stunned her into stillness.

Fire ignited, along with the familiar longing that always came when he touched her. When he pulled back moments later, she stared at him in breathless silence.

His hands still cradling her face, he dipped his head to meet her gaze. "That's just a reminder of what you refuse to fight for."

And just like that, he left her alone.

CHAPTER TEN

Following morning
Sienna's apartment, New York City

Her hideout. After all this time, Sienna had opted for a simple apartment in the city. A far cry from the rambling gardens, endless vineyards, and small town life of Rapid Falls, but perfect for a woman needing to vanish.

Sienna put a finger to her lips as they stepped off the elevator. "I don't want Alex to hear that I'm back or we'll never get out of here."

"Who is Alex?" Archer asked, automatically scanning the hallway to ensure there were no lurkers nearby.

"A friend from across the hall."

"Is he a problem?" His stomach clenched at the thought but he kept a straight face as he followed her to her door.

She shot him a small smile. "Not unless you're afraid of little old ladies."

Archer ignored Declan's chuckle behind them. "Who is she?"

"She's my friend and worked with me at the bookshop."

"You worked at a bookshop all this time?"

"It was peaceful, gave me something to do, and Alex needed

173

the help."

"So why are we hiding from her?"

"If she sees us, she'll want to feed us and I'm not in the mood for food or chit chats with little old ladies right now, no matter how sweet dear old Alex has been to me."

He smiled and watched as she opened the apartment door. In a way, it pleased him that she'd had someone to watch out for her in the time she'd lived here.

When Archer saw the chaos and destruction of Sienna's apartment, everything inside him shifted. Torn couches, slashed pillows, books tossed from the bookshelves, broken glass, and shattered lamps. It looked as though a whirlwind or a tornado – some natural disaster – had ripped through the apartment and destroyed everything in its path.

Except it hadn't been a natural disaster.

With a low whistle, Declan disappeared into the rest of the apartment as Sienna came up behind him, peering over his shoulder.

Archer heard her sharp intake of breath, felt the bolt of horror that shot through her the moment she saw the destruction.

"Oh, my," she whispered as her hands flew to her mouth. She stepped further into the room and looked around in silence.

Archer left her side and pulled open the curtains. Light filtered through the large windows, chasing away some of the gloom. Knowing Sienna, the small apartment had once been warm, neat, and homely. Now it was impossible to tell as they'd searched, moved, and destroyed everything.

Sienna turned to look at him. "They really thought I'd be stupid enough to keep my Grimoire here?"

"They probably knew it wouldn't be here but still had to try."

"You've got to give them points for their thoroughness."

"And desperation."

Declan returned with a grim expression, and Archer didn't need to be told that the path of destruction followed the same throughout the apartment. A silent look passed between them, and Archer stepped behind Sienna, placing a hand at her lower back.

"Sienna, we should go. There's nothing left for you here."

She nodded and dragged in a deep breath.

He went with her to the bedroom, another disaster, and frowned at her expression as she looked around sadly at the life she'd once had, a life destroyed.

Clothes, shoes, and other paraphernalia littered the floor amongst the dozens of feathers from the torn duvet. Shattered mirrors, wrecked lights, doors torn from their hinges.

With a soft moan, she gathered a broken photo frame from the floor and shook off the shards of glass.

"Why would they do this?" she said softly, looking at the photograph in her hands. "They knew the Grimoire wouldn't be in a damn photo frame. Why destroy them?" Her eyes shifted to the rest of the ruined frames scattered on the floor. "Why destroy everything?"

"They're angry, Sienna. We've taken so much from them and they have to fight an ocean of resistance in order to achieve their goals."

"All they've done is piss me off and make me more determined to keep them from getting what they want. Do they seriously think that every witch and her Keeper will stand back and allow them to achieve their vision for control? Our kind may be stronger and more powerful but we are so outnumbered by the ordinary people around us. Exposing our abilities and existence to everyone would be suicide."

"I know." He came up behind her to peer over her shoulder at the photograph in her hands.

He recognized it immediately and felt the tug of nostalgia as the faces of the four Bennett siblings stared back at him. A time when they'd all been together, laughing, happy. A silly picture taken at a silly moment and treasured by them all.

"You kept this," he said, taking the photograph from her. Something stirred inside, quiet and reassuring, and he rubbed a thumb across the four faces.

"It was a happy day."

"Sarah had just announced that she was planning to open the restaurant."

There'd been huge celebrations and brainstorming that day. Archer brushed his thumb across his sister's face, familiar with the longing that always came when he thought of her. She'd never had the chance to realize her dream but Ethan was determined to renovate the old pub in town into the restaurant she'd envisioned. Her dream would be a reality even if she wasn't here to see it herself.

Without saying anything more, Sienna gave him a brief reassuring squeeze on the arm before walking into the closet. She slowly turned around, surveying the damage. "There's not much here to rescue."

"Leave it," he said, placing the photograph on the drawer and looking up. "We'll stop at the store and get you some things." The thought of her wearing any of the clothes handled by the intruders made him shudder.

She nodded and with a final glance around the room, she headed for the door.

He followed closely behind but collided with her when she suddenly whirled around to face him. His hands shot out to steady her, and he raised an eyebrow.

"I forgot something," she said, quickly looking away in an attempt to hide the unshed tears.

"Sienna." Archer captured her chin with his fingers and tilted her face to his. She tried to pull away but his other hand slid behind her back, keeping her in place. "Look at me."

"I'm fine, Archer."

"I know."

She reached for the photograph on the drawer beside them and held it against her chest. "We should go."

He studied her in silence, his thumb stroking the fading bruise on her cheek. Of everything she'd come for, the only thing she was walking away with was a photograph of his family. He leaned forward and kissed her forehead. "Everything's going to be okay."

She closed her eyes, resting her head against his. "Warrick should know better than to piss off a Beckham witch."

True, but in fact, Warrick had done him a favour. Thanks to his meddling, Sienna seemed to be slipping back into her defend the world mode. He smiled, slid an arm around her shoulders, and led her back to the living area.

Declan's eyes narrowed when he saw Sienna, and he glanced at his brother. "Is she okay?" he mouthed.

Archer nodded. "Let's go."

"We don't have to clean this mess?"

Sienna smiled at the relief in Declan's voice. "Leave it. When this is over I'll come back to sort it out. And don't look so damn pleased with yourself."

"Trust me, honey. Pleased is the last thing I feel right now," Declan said and followed her out the door.

****

Sienna had never been a fan of road trip bonding but the tension between the two brothers hung in the air like an unwelcome aunt.

Her efforts to break the silence during the long drive home had resulted in quick one-worded answers, and she'd eventually given up and made peace with the fact that the trip back to Rapid Falls would be far from exciting.

For two brothers that had once been inseparable, the rift between them was unnerving.

The darkness had added to her boredom, making her road trip pure torture. At least with the light, she'd been able to watch the passing scenery.

Her relief came an hour later when they finally stopped for fuel and refreshments. Determined to mellow them both, she returned to the car loaded with enough drinks and food that had both men raising an eyebrow at her.

She ignored them and held back a smile once they were back on the road, and both brothers attacked her stash of road trip munchies with fervour.

She'd figured they'd be hungry. All that muscle and testosterone in the front of the car needed fuelling, didn't it?

"Have either of you spoken to Ethan?" Sienna asked from the back of the car and handed out hot coffee.

Declan took a sip and wiped his mouth with the back of his hand. "He's with Rose. They're alerting the four witches who have the stones and their Keepers."

"I wonder how long it'll be before Warrick strikes at one of them."

"If he's able to track them down, I say we should let him."

Archer choked back his coffee and cleared his throat. "Hell no. Someone could get killed."

"I meant we should let him strike, not that we should let him succeed," Declan replied, rolling his eyes.

"You want to use one of the four witches as bait? That's absurd."

"Worth a try, don't you think?"

"We can't anticipate his moves, Declan. It's too risky. He has no use for any of the four witches other than to get the stones they harbour. He'd kill them in a heartbeat."

"So what else would you suggest? That we sit back on our asses and wait for him to come to us? Either we use a witch to draw him out or we go find him ourselves."

"We wouldn't even know where to look."

"Can't you or Rose use a locator spell or something?" Declan glanced at Sienna, blue eyes flashing with hope. "Surely one of you Beckham witches can track him?"

Sienna shook her head and hauled out a chocolate. If she was going to deal with all this testosterone, she might as well enjoy it with a sugar rush. "Warrick's not one of us, Declan, you know that. Locator spells don't work for evil."

"Yes, but isn't there a loop hole or something?"

"It's magic. You're not going to find loopholes."

Declan reached back and snatched the chocolate from her. Settling back in his seat, he bit into the chocolate, chewed, and swallowed. "I still think we should draw him out."

"We're not using a witch," Archer said firmly and everything about his rigid posture and the way he gripped the steering wheel, staring straight ahead, made it clear that he wouldn't budge on this one.

And Sienna knew the handsome Keeper well enough to know that he was as stubborn as a cat about to have a bath.

Especially when it came to witches.

Declan shot Archer an impatient look. "Since when are you scared of Warrick?"

"I'm not afraid of Warrick, Declan. If anything, I'd love to rip his heart out."

"And yet you choose to sit back and do nothing."

"I can't risk someone else getting hurt."

"If we leave Warrick to his free reign, someone will get hurt."

"That's why we've alerted the four witches and their Keepers. They'll be safe. Their Keepers won't let anything happen to them.

And once we find Warrick, his days are numbered, but we'll find him without using the witches as bait."

"Fine, then we'll leave the witches out of it. After all, the only witch he wants is sitting in the back seat of this car." Declan turned to face Sienna, and something about the way he looked at her had her freezing mid bite.

And it had nothing to do with his glorious blue eyes or chiselled, perfect features.

"Declan, don't even think about it," Archer said.

Apparently, Archer knew his brother well as the gleam in Declan's eyes brightened and a wicked smile played at the corners of his mouth.

Sienna lowered the chocolate and licked her lips. "You want me to be the bait?"

Declan shrugged and turned back in his seat. "It might be the only way."

"There's no way in hell we're using Sienna to draw him out, Declan," Archer said through gritted teeth and slapped a hand across the back of Declan's head. "What the hell are you thinking?"

"What? We'd be there to watch out for her." Declan swatted Archer's hand away and ran his fingers through his thick mane of hair.

A muscle worked in Archer's jaw. "Seriously?"

"Your bait is listening to every word you say, so stop talking as though I'm not here," Sienna interrupted, shifting forward in her seat. "Declan has a point, Archer."

"A crazy point, that is."

She should've known he'd never go for it. "We draw Warrick out and end this power trip of his before anyone gets hurt."

"You could get hurt, Sienna."

"We all could, but it's a risk we'll have to take in order to protect the seal of the curse."

"We have no idea who's working with Warrick or what powers they possess. We wouldn't even know where to find Warrick."

"No, but his minions do, and they seem to be hot on my trail lately. It'd be easy to send a message."

"Saying what? Inviting him for tea?"

Sienna smiled. "I doubt a man like Warrick even drinks tea. Way too civilized for him."

"Yeah, he probably drinks the blood of newborn babies," Declan said, taking another bite of chocolate.

"He's not a vampire, Declan."

"Who knows what he does in his leisure time?"

Archer scowled at her in the rear-view mirror. "We're not using anyone as bait to draw Warrick out."

"Fine," Sienna said, slumping back in her seat with a noisy sigh. "Let me know when you come up with a better plan."

"I will," he said in a low tone. "And it'll be a far better plan than you offering yourself up as a sacrificial lamb."

Sienna rolled her eyes and turned her attention to the window, relieved to see they were approaching Rapid Falls.

Home.

She'd grown up here, had friends here. Her family had lived here for generations – they were one of the founding members of the town, along with the Bennett family and several others.

And even though she'd resisted coming home with every fibre of her being, now that she was here, she wondered how she'd ever left.

A peaceful hamlet situated in an area well known for producing excellent ice wine, with rolling hills rich in all types of greenery, endless rows of vineyards, and surrounded by mountains and forests. A place that maintained and celebrated their traditions every year, and where the town folk were friendly, warm, and sociable. Within the village itself, historical buildings restored to a new modern beauty, thatched cottages, and several quaint shops stood amidst an avenue of beautiful gardens and oaked lined streets. In the centre of town, was the restaurant the Bennett brothers were renovating, the project mostly driven by Ethan. Those needing a calmer approach to life sought out the neighbourhood, known for its safety and tranquillity and quiet streets, with either low fencing or no fencing at all.

Situated on the outskirts of town stood the Bennett estate. It held its own charm – private, peaceful, and boasted massive spans of protected grape vineyards, gardens and forests.

And three very handsome, very muscular bachelors.

Although the vineyards on the Bennett estate produced the vast majority of grapes for the infamous ice wine produced by the local town winery, the three brothers had very little to do with the actual production of the wine itself. They had employed sufficient staff and an excellent manager, Tara Reed, who kept everything running smoothly. Tara's family had been a founding member of the town and she knew of their special abilities, but she kept to their agreement and very seldom brought it up. She'd been good for the brothers, taking over the business side of the estate with an ease that gave the three men a lot of freedom.

The Bennett estate supplied the grapes, year after year, to the winery in town that processed them into an expensive, sought after wine. Come January, when the temperature dropped to the perfect degree, it was all hands on deck and they'd all be trudging through the snowy vineyards kitted out in full winter gear to pick the frozen grapes.

Harvesting time had been one of Sarah's favourite times of the year. The town went into an absolute frenzy to harvest the grapes, always working through the night, and once every last grape was picked, the entire town put on a festival of fun and celebrations that often drew visitors from far away.

Sienna smiled. Even though her return signalled the start of a familiar battle of the wicked, it was good to be back.

"Still want to stop at Lora's store?" Archer asked, glancing at her in the rear-view mirror.

Sienna nodded. "The few items of clothing I brought from Rose's house won't get me very far, so unless you want me prancing around in your shirt tomorrow…"

He grinned. "The look suited you. It's late, maybe we should come back tomorrow?"

"Archer, stop the damn car."

With a chuckle, Archer manoeuvred the car into the parking area and stopped outside a quaint woman's clothing boutique – Sienna's favourite. The owner, Lora Williams, knew exactly what suited Sienna, thus making a shopping trip a painless and quick experience.

Sienna smiled as she caught sight of Lora through the window. The older woman with blonde hair and a friendly face stood in front of a shelf, quietly folding several t-shirts. They probably didn't need any folding, but Lora had never been one to sit still for long. Lora was a messenger of The Circle and also a powerful elemental witch, but no longer a practicing one. A shame, as Lora had the heart and soul of an excellent witch – wisdom that Sienna had frequently turned to when she was younger. But several years ago, Lora's daughter, like Sienna, had fled Rapid Falls in fear of the witchcraft she'd been born into, taking her young daughter, Kate, with her.

The blow had been brutal for Lora, and she'd stopped practicing as a witch the moment her daughter had left town.

Sienna pushed open the door to the store, eager to see her friend. It had been a long time since she'd had any contact with her friends from Rapid Falls, and she'd missed them.

"Sienna?" Lora gasped, whirling around with a delighted smile. "Oh, my goodness. Come here, sweet child!"

Sienna went into Lora's open arms with a laugh. "How are you?"

"I'm fine. When did you get back into town?"

"A few days ago."

"And you're only coming to say hello now?"

Sienna's shoulders fell, and she stepped back to look at Lora. "We've been busy. I'm sorry."

"We?" Lora asked, peering over her shoulders through the window outside. "Ah, the Bennett brothers. Glad to see you're on speaking terms again."

Sienna followed Lora's gaze, not surprised to see that several town folk had gathered around the two brothers on the sidewalk across the street. After all, it was a friendly town and the Bennett brothers were very popular.

Most of them weren't unfamiliar with Sienna's handsome entourage but would be surprised to see them together again after so long. They'd always thought that the Bennett brothers were simply smitten with her. How could they know that she was a witch and they were her fierce protectors when their families had spent more than a century hiding it from them? Only a few selected people of the town, the sheriff and descendants of the founding families, knew about the paranormal activity that occasionally reared its head. Together, they worked hard to keep it quiet and maintain order and harmony.

Sure, the town was rich with dark rumours and folk lore of times when mystical creatures had roamed their streets, but that was a long, long time ago. Now it just made for fascinating bedtime stories. Except for Sienna those stories were her reality.

"They seem happy enough," Lora said, taking her arm and leading her to the clothing. "And you seem like you need some new clothes."

Sienna grimaced. "My apartment was ransacked and everything was destroyed. I need a few essentials for now."

"Trouble?"

"You really want to know?"

Lora shrugged. "It won't matter. My girls are never coming home."

"Still no hope?"

"No. Jane keeps in basic contact and sends pictures of Kate sometimes, but she refuses to come home. This town, this world, terrifies her and she refuses to have Kate be any part of it. She won't even let me visit them."

"I'm sorry, Lora. Must be hard on you."

"I have a granddaughter I don't even know and a daughter who won't come home. Tragic, isn't it?" Lora squeezed Sienna's shoulder and brightened. "Now, shall we get you some essentials? A woman can't return to town after a two year absence looking like that." With a grin and a twinkle in her eyes, Lora trailed a cheeky gaze over the length of Sienna. "I know just what you need. Wait here."

The older woman disappeared into the storeroom, and Sienna wondered around the large store. Lora stocked everything a woman could need – hats, bags, underwear, shoes, clothing, accessories. Casual and practical but with a touch of elegance. The fact that a dear friend who knew her basic needs owned the store was a bonus. The store consisted of four rooms that all flowed onto a charming courtyard that offered a water feature and a small garden. The doors were all open and Sienna wandered outside, her mind drifting to the many times she'd shared coffee with Lora in the beautiful garden.

It was tranquil here and offered a perfect pause to the tiresome act of shopping.

An unexpected wave of warning washed over Sienna before she felt the presence behind her. She closed her eyes and drew in a silent breath, needing all the composure she could muster. Without making a sound, she slowly turned, already knowing whom she'd find.

After all, there were several degrees of evil a witch could sense. And this was one of the biggest degrees of all.

CHAPTER ELEVEN

"Warrick."

"I never took you for a woman who likes to shop," Warrick Brogan said with a half smile. He wore black pants and a casual grey shirt. With his curly dark blond hair and charismatic smile, he looked ridiculously normal.

Only, he wasn't.

"Thanks to the mess you made of my apartment, I had no choice."

"Never leave a stone unturned and all that crap. I heard things got a bit messy."

"You really think I'd be stupid enough to keep the Beckham Grimoire in my apartment?"

"It was worth a try."

"What are you doing here?" Sienna glanced over her shoulder, quietly searching for her Keepers.

"They're outside," Warrick said. He kept his voice low, out of range of her Keepers' sharp hearing.

"How did you get past them?"

"Another entrance."

"Where's Lora?"

"Occupied."

Sienna stepped forward, her eyes widening. "If you've hurt her —"

Warrick's hand shot out, grabbing her wrist. "She's fine, Sienna."

Pinning him with a level look, Sienna yanked her arm out of his grip. "Brave to confront me alone."

"Who says I'm alone?" He tilted his head to the side, and Sienna caught sight of two men hovering nearby. Both dressed in black, both with fierce expressions.

"You should know better than to mess with a Beckham witch," she said, straightening her shoulders and stepping back.

"And you should've known better than to mess with the Brogan brothers." His eyes flashed something harsh, and his body grew rigid at the memory of what the witches had done to him.

"I won't undo the spell."

His expression eased, and he smiled. "Ah, that's a discussion for another time."

She hesitated, wary, but not afraid. Her powers topped his any day and even with his sidekicks standing nearby, she'd handle herself. A simple scream would have her Keepers at her side before either of them could blink. That knowledge settled around her like a protective cloak, giving her the courage she needed to face the man she hated with everything in her. "Why are you back in town?" she asked.

"I have some scores to settle." He circled her, like a shark circling its prey, and cast a quiet glance along the length of her. "You haven't changed much."

"Why are you here?"

"I have something to discuss with you."

"I'm not up for a discussion with you, Warrick. Ever."

He laughed, but the sound held no trace of amusement. "Oh, trust me. You'll want to hear what I have to say."

"Like hell."

"For the sake of your Keepers, your grandmother, Lora and everyone you've ever loved, you'll listen to me, witch," Warrick said casually. "I've already killed one Keeper and I'd enjoy killing another."

His words struck her where it mattered most, and she drew on all her strength not to flinch at the threat.

"Fine," she said, looking at him, adding a touch of frost to her gaze. The man gave her the creeps.

Warrick picked up three pebbles in a nearby pot and kneaded them between his fingers and palm. "Ah, much better. I far prefer it when you're pliable."

"Spill, Warrick. If my Keepers catch you here, they'll be anything but pliable."

"Oh, don't be such a buzz kill," he said with a fake frown. "I happen to be enjoying myself."

"Makes one of us. Now spill or I walk."

"I want to strike a deal."

"I don't make deals with the devil."

"You might if your Keepers were threatened."

"We're not afraid of you."

"Stupid."

"So what's the deal?"

"We'll discuss that later." A slow smile spread across his face – a face that some people might find attractive. To Sienna, the evil she saw there washed away anything good about him. "I've sent you a gift and an invitation." She opened her mouth to protest, but he held up a finger. "You will open it, you will accept, and you will come. Alone. We'll discuss my proposal over drinks. That's all I'm asking."

Sienna raised an eyebrow. "For me to join you for drinks?"

"For you to hear me out."

"So talk now."

He smiled again. "Not here. I have something more memorable planned for us. I'll see you tomorrow and we'll talk then." He moved toward her, his smile fading. "And if you refuse, I'll strike where it'll hurt most."

Her family, her friends. Sienna's gut clenched at the thought, but she didn't look away. "Between you and your parents, you've already struck where it hurts most."

"It was never proved that my parents were involved in the fire. Besides, everything that's happened between our families could all have been avoided had you lot sided with us."

"Your parents threatened everything our families had worked so hard to build simply because of their greed and desire for control. Humans are not meant to be controlled, Warrick."

"They shouldn't dictate to us when and how we should live."

"They don't. All they ask for is some discretion. Exposing us would strike fear and panic everywhere and be sure to sign our death warrants. Try living a normal life once that's out there."

"My brother and I still share my parents' vision for our kind, Sienna, and clearly we're still on opposing teams. Let me be clear. I intend to get my brother back and once I do, we're going to continue our mission and have every damn human see us for who we are and bow down to us." His face twisted with anger and bitter resentment. "I hate this town for what it's done to my family so we'll start with Rapid Falls first and we'll move from there. Person by person, town by town."

"Is that what this is about? Revenge? Your parents caused havoc in town, possibly murdered the four people who tried to stop them, and when suspicion turned to them, they crashed their car into a tree trying to get away. Only a small handful of people in this town know what really happened back then and none of them are to blame for anything that happened. That's all on your family."

His frown deepened, his jaw clenched, and he glared at her with hatred. "I will avenge my family, Sienna, and I'm determined to see their vision realized. Our days of living in silence are over."

"And the people that object?"

"They'll be used as an example to the ones still sitting on the fence."

She straightened her shoulders, his words striking rage in her. "Over my dead body, Warrick. Besides, you have no powers."

Her words didn't seem to perturb him and he held out his hand, exposing the round pebbles in his palm. With his other hand, he grabbed hers, tilting it so that her palm faced upward. "We'll see. You come see me tomorrow or another death will be on your hands."

"My Keepers would never allow it."

"Make a plan," he quipped, placing the three pebbles in her hand and closing her fingers around them.

Sienna's eyes widened and she gasped as hot energy speared through her, touching her in places she'd thought protected. She reeled back, staring at Warrick wide-eyed.

He laughed. "No powers? Don't underestimate me, Sienna. Everything you need to know about our meeting is being delivered to your house as we speak." His gaze narrowed in warning. "And everything you fear is on the tail end of your rejection to my invitation."

She kept silent, not trusting herself to speak. Her body felt violated, touched with a magic other than hers. She opened her hand and dropped the stones, inhaling sharply at the three burn marks they'd left behind.

Warrick flashed her a triumphant grin. "I look forward to our meeting tomorrow, my dear."

"There's no chance in hell I'm meeting with you tomorrow, Warrick."

Her words triggered his rage, shattering the calm façade he'd had since first seeing her. He charged toward her and stopped only inches away from her face. "You will do this, Sienna. You owe me."

"I don't owe you a damn thing."

His hand shot up to the collar of his shirt and quickly loosened a few buttons. He pushed the shirt aside, exposing scarred flesh across one side of his chest and across his shoulder. "You did this to me. Trust me when I say, you owe me. And just for the record, I don't take it lightly when someone crosses me."

Sienna ignored his intense glare, loaded with malice, and the evil that emanated off him. She'd seen this side of him before and seeing it again only fuelled her own anger. She jutted out her chin, and instead of backing away, she pushed herself closer to him. "I'm not afraid of you, Warrick. Your brother was evil and he hurt a lot of people before we spelled him. Had I known you were just as twisted, I would have sent your ass with him. You got everything you deserved that night in the tomb and if I could go back, I'd do it all over again." Well, almost all of it. "You saw that night what I'm capable of so you might want to back the hell away before I lose my temper again."

"We both know that you won't easily use your powers again, Sienna. You're terrified of them."

"Want to tempt me?" she challenged, hating that he was right. His statement annoyed her, but she quickly dismissed it. A few days ago, his words had held a ring of truth to them, but since returning to Rapid Falls, Sienna felt a renewed connection with the powers she'd once shunned. She was still wary and still had a lot to learn, but for now, curiosity and determination had her open to the connection. "It's men like you that make us so powerful, Warrick. You feed our determination, our power, to rid the world of assholes like you."

"And I'll believe that when you back that sassy mouth of yours with some kick ass powers," he said with a fake smile before backing down. "Until then, I'll see you tomorrow."

Sienna waited until he was at the door before she snapped his name. "Just for the record, Warrick, I don't take being crossed lightly either and I don't socialize with evil so there's no way in hell I'm accepting any invitation of yours."

He paused in the doorway to look back at her. "Well, then drive safely, Sienna." His eyes narrowed and a smug smile broke free. "I hear the roads up to the Bennett estate can be treacherous in the dark."

The moment he walked away, Sienna sank into the chair behind her and gasped.

Oh, no.

****

A trickle of apprehension ran down Archer's spine even before Sienna walked out of the back entrance of the store empty handed. His senses flashed with the warning that something was wrong. With practiced ease, he excused himself from the small crowd of neighbours and old school friends gathered on the sidewalk and went to her.

"What's wrong?" he asked, casually glancing around.

"Nothing. I'll come back tomorrow."

"What happened?"

"Nothing." She nodded her head in the direction of their friends. "Please let's go home before they spot me. I'm not up for the onslaught of questions I'd get if they see me here."

With a quick nod to Declan, he unlocked the black Land Cruiser and opened the door for her. Without looking at him, she pushed past him but he stepped forward, blocking her.

"Archer, I'm tired and it's late. Please can we go home?"

He raised a brow. "I know you're not a shopaholic, Sienna, but

I also know how much you hate not having your own clothes. What happened in there?"

"I'll get by with what I have at the house for now." She met his eyes briefly before lowering them. "Please take me home."

"Are you hurt?"

"No."

She was lying. His instincts and senses sparked the way they always did when Sienna was afraid or hurting.

She climbed into the car, ignoring him, but he caught her hand. Her soft gasp and sudden withdrawal as she tugged away had him frowning. He reached for her hand and turned it over in his, inhaling sharply when he saw the three small burn marks.

"Sienna," he said quietly through gritted teeth. "What happened?"

She pulled away, rubbing her injured hand. "I want my damn necklace, Archer."

Declan approached and lifted a brow when he sensed the tension. "Something wrong?"

Archer tilted his head and the brothers shared an all-knowing gaze. Sienna ignored them both and got into the car, shutting the door before either of them could say anything more.

"What happened?" Declan asked, walking around the car. He climbed into the front seat and glanced back at Sienna. "You okay?"

She nodded. "I'm tired. And hungry. Do either of you know what Ethan's making for dinner?"

"You're translucent when you're deflecting, Sienna," Archer said, starting the engine.

"And you're reaching. I'm fine, so please focus less on me and more on your driving. These roads are tricky at night."

"What happened to your hand?"

"I knocked over Lora's cup of tea," Sienna said, and Archer sensed a small crack in her armour. "And I'm upset because Lora's hurting over the loss of her daughter and granddaughter. Could you please put the protective crap aside long enough for me to have my moment?"

Archer glanced at her in his rear-view mirror. It was hard to read her in the darkness but he could feel the worry and fear brewing within her. Why she refused to unload on them, he wasn't sure, but he decided to back down. If something had happened, she'd come out with it later. "Are you sure that's all that happened?"

"Yes. Now please take me home."

Liar.

CHAPTER TWELVE

The darkness on the drive home was a blessing Sienna was grateful for. It offered her a cloak to hide the fear and emotions sparked by her brief confrontation with Warrick Brogan. The thing he'd done with the stones had frightened her more than his threats had. It proved that his powers were returning – maybe not all of them, but enough to send a flare of warning.

And knowing that, she had to take his threats seriously.

With a soft sigh, she looked at each of the Bennett brothers, destined to protect her. And somehow, she was as bound by duty and love to protect them.

She would tell them what had happened – after she'd seen what Warrick had delivered to her.

A bright light from behind them lit up the car with a sudden velocity that had Sienna's attention jolting back to the present.

"We have company," Archer said, keeping his hands firmly on the steering wheel, his level gaze flickering between the road ahead and his rear-view mirror.

"What the hell?" Sienna held up a hand to shield her eyes from the glare of the imposing headlights, Warrick's warning fresh in her mind.

The car revved, hovering dangerously close to the back of the

Land Cruiser.

"It's probably some kids, Archer," Declan said, glancing behind him.

"Sienna, has this got anything to do with what happened at Lora's?" Archer asked softly.

She heard the prickle in his voice. "I don't know."

"Not the answer I was hoping for. Get down."

Before Sienna could react, the grey SUV overtook them with a speed and recklessness that sent her heart rate soaring.

Music blared from the car, even through the darkness and sealed windows, and the car took off ahead of them, quickly disappearing into the distance.

Sienna sank back in her seat with a relieved sigh. "Jeepers, Archer. Not everything's a threat. Just some local teens out for some R & R."

Declan ran his hands through his hair and stretched. "We should follow suit. We could sure use some decent hometown rest and relaxation."

"There's no rest for the wicked, Declan."

He flashed her a grin. "The wicked don't need the rest, just the relaxation."

And if any of them knew how to do that, it was Declan.

Archer cleared his throat. "Are you going to tell us what really happened in that damn store?"

"Back off, Archer," Sienna replied, instinctively knowing that if she did, they'd turn the car around and high tail it straight back to town in search of the warlock. Warrick would be back in hiding by now, and all it would do is stir up a lot of anger and resentment. The car rounded a bend and in a flash of panic, they spotted the grey SUV stopped in the middle of the road.

"Archer!" Sienna shouted as their car swerved to avoid the inevitable impact.

The two cars collided with a sickening crash of metal against metal, a thud of heavy bulk against even heavier bulk. Their car ricocheted off the SUV, spun around twice in a whirl of screeching tires and shattered glass, and plummeted down the embankment into the river.

Sienna screamed as water gushed into the car with frightening speed, pulling them further into the depths of the river. It was icy cold and took her breath away. Hands shaking, she fumbled with her seatbelt and bolted to the front seat.

"Declan!" she cried, grabbing his shoulders and pushing him back against his seat. He was out cold, blood streaming from a wound on his forehead. She slapped his cheeks and shook him, aware of the water rapidly closing in around them. "Declan! Wake up." She reeled back and looked around, gasping when she couldn't find Archer. "Archer!"

She struggled with Declan's seatbelt and gave a triumphant cry when it came loose. They were running out of time. The water had reached chest level, threatening to swallow them whole.

The car shifted, pushed by the force of the flowing water, and Sienna felt her world shrink as the water engulfed them.

Silence fell, in complete contrast to the craziness of the crash.

And the only thing going through her mind was that there was no way in hell she could leave Declan.

A combination of horror and determination sent a fresh bolt of renewed energy through her and drawing on a strength that surprised her, she slid her arms under Declan's and hoisted him toward her. It was dark, the water murky, and confusion reigned, but she managed to exit through the shattered windscreen and bring them both to the surface.

The roaring of the water muffled her loud gasp of air, and she wrapped her arms around Declan's shoulders and clung to him with all her strength. Swept away with the tide, and struggling against the current, she fought to keep them both above the water, kicking and splashing toward the edge of the river.

She screamed as a pair of strong arms encircled her waist.

"It's okay, it's me!" Archer shouted, drawing her close.

Archer!

"Hold on to me," Archer said, reaching around her to grab his brother. With a powerful leap, he hoisted them out of the water and onto the safety of the riverbank. "Are you hurt?" he asked, grabbing her and checking her over.

"No." Breathing hard and gasping for air, Sienna scrambled to Declan's side. Her heart soared when he started coughing and struggled onto one elbow.

"Sienna?" he said, looking around, trying to catch his breath.

"Declan!" she cried, throwing her arms around his neck. "Oh, my God, are you okay?"

"I'm fine. What the hell happened?"

"We were in an accident."

His eyes widened, and he tried to push himself up but settled back when she touched his chest. "No, you're bleeding." She ripped his shirt and used the material to swipe at the blood on his forehead.

He pushed her hand away. "It'll heal quickly. Are you hurt?"

She captured his hand in hers and kissed his knuckles. "No."

Declan's head bolted up. "Where's my brother?"

"He's fine." She heard his sharp intake of breath and tightened her grip around his hand. "We're all fine, Declan."

Archer dropped to his knees beside them, dripping water and oozing anger. "They're gone."

"The SUV?"

"Trashed and abandoned but the driver's gone. Someone must've called in the accident. I hear sirens."

She couldn't hear them, but she often never heard the things they did – not at that distance. She sank to the ground, giving way to the trembling, and gulped air.

Archer put a hand on her shoulder. "Sienna, are you okay?"

No.

"Yes," she whispered in a breathy gasp of air as guilt ripped through her.

She was to blame for this. She'd defied Warrick and ignored his warning. This was all her fault.

CHAPTER THIRTEEN

Sienna grimaced as she swallowed the painkillers for the pounding headache she'd had since the accident.

Warrick's sudden return to Rapid Falls had frightened her, his actions proving that he was bold, reckless, and out for revenge. She should have taken his threats more seriously and she was mad at herself for ignoring them.

Sienna flexed her hand that still smarted from the mild burn caused from the pebbles. What was with that? Had he spelled them? Used Rose Thorn?

She dragged in a deep breath and faced the row of kitchen windows, all wooden arches, all designed for maximum sunlight and optimal views of the garden outside. The kitchen was immaculate and shiny, the advantage of living with men who loved to cook.

Her Keepers. The very idea that Warrick had threatened them sent fear spiralling through her. The thought of something happening to one of them terrified her. She couldn't lose another Keeper, another friend – and it had nothing to do with the fact that she'd already lost one Keeper, which had weakened the strength of her power, weakened her. Losing another Keeper would weaken her even more. No, the anxiety that Warrick's return had provoked had nothing to do with that. They were her family, everything she'd ever known, and she loved them. Sarah's death had gutted her, leaving a wake of sadness and emptiness that hadn't healed. Because of their magical connection, protecting Sienna meant their individual elemental powers would still exist, but the three brothers were hell bent on protecting her and it had nothing to with their powers. No, their fierce protection and loyalty came from a sense of duty, of love.

Sienna straightened when she caught sight of Archer's reflection behind her as he walked into the kitchen. He wore jeans and an expression she couldn't decipher. He paused in the doorway to watch her in silence, muscular arms folded across his naked chest. All that muscle gleamed at her, lean and smooth, and she was thankful she had her back to him.

The man was pure masculine beauty.

And played havoc with her senses with his shirt on. Without the shirt, her insides did a little jiggle.

Not what she needed right now.

"Sienna."

The way he said her name sent a spiral of electric energy through her, his words a soft rumble of sexiness in the silence of the room. She turned around and mustered a smile.

Her gaze fell on his bold tattoo, and she stared at it, unable to look away. Carefully crafted in black ink across his left shoulder was the creative image of a pentagram surrounded with a beautifully crafted circle design. The mark of a Keeper.

"I thought you'd gone to bed," he said, sauntering into the room, arms dropping to his sides.

She shifted her gaze from his tattoo to the scarred flesh along his right arm, and quickly swallowed the familiar tug of regret before looking away. "I couldn't sleep."

"Not surprising." He disappeared into the small wine cellar adjacent to the kitchen and returned a moment later with a vintage bottle of red wine from their collection. He retrieved two wine glasses and eyed her hand as he opened the wine. "How's the hand?"

"Healing." She coughed again and cleared her throat, very aware of the half-naked man. His hair was wet from the shower and he smelt of soap and man, a scent that quickly awakened her senses. "Where are your brothers?"

"Ethan's on his way back from the restaurant. Knowing Declan, he's probably holed up in the study planning a revenge tactic." He handed her a glass of wine and looked at her. "Are you okay?"

She nodded. "The wound on Declan's head has healed?"

"Yes." His voice was low, raspy, and tinted with an emotion he usually concealed. Dark green eyes met hers. "Thank you for pulling my brother out of the car. Once you both went under, I couldn't find the car in the dark."

Her throat closed with emotion, and she quickly swallowed. "You would've both done the same for me. Did the sheriff track the owner of the other car yet?"

"Pam's working on it." He took a large sip of wine and set the glass on the counter. "Sienna, you know who's responsible for this."

It wasn't a question and Sienna blinked but held her ground. "Archer, please don't start this."

Not now.

Archer removed the glass from her hand and placed it on the counter beside his, his brows furrowing into a tight frown. "Someone sent us spiralling into that damn river tonight. I just can't figure out if they wanted us harmed or warned."

"It was an accident."

"I know you don't believe that."

The way he towered over her signalled the start of an argument she'd rather avoid, but he surprised her by stepping closer and reaching for her hands.

"Something scared you tonight. At Lora's. And then the accident happened." Strong fingers threaded with hers, and he tugged her closer. "You're afraid."

He knew.

Of course, he'd know. Even without trying, he'd always been able to know exactly what was going on with her. She looked away, not wanting him to see the truth, but knowing that he would. "Archer, don't."

"What frightened you tonight?"

"I don't want to discuss this now."

He released her hands and cupped her face, tilting her head so she could see how serious he was. "What are you afraid of?"

"Of losing another Keeper," she whispered, "of losing you."

"You're not going to lose me, Sienna."

"With Warrick out for retribution, who knows what'll happen? All I know is that tonight left a ball of fear in my gut that I can't seem to shake. The thought of losing you like we lost Sarah terrifies me."

"Where's all this coming from?"

"It's always been there. The accident simply made me want to voice it." And the meeting with Warrick, but she didn't tell him that.

"Sienna."

She licked her lips, her pulse racing a steady, thick beat inside her chest. Parts of her tingled at the idea of what might happen if she let go and gave in to the irresistible pull between them.

The Circle's curse be damned.

"You said you didn't want this," he reminded her, his gaze flickering between her eyes and her lips. "What's changed?"

"I was afraid of the curse on a relationship between a Keeper and his witch. When we got close two years ago and Sarah died, I put it down to punishment from The Circle for breaking their rule. Tonight, I realized that bad things happen no matter what we do." Sienna reached out and slid her hands on either side of his neck. "I could've lost you tonight, Archer."

"But you didn't."

"No, but I could've. That thought alone made me realize that I want to fight for us, for this." She looked at his lips, overwhelmed by the urge to kiss him.

His jaw flexed and he studied her in silence, his thumb stroking her cheek. "Are you sure?" he asked, dipping his head toward hers.

Her mind screamed no, but her body had already started responding to him – a thought that made her entire body burn with anticipation.

Unable to find the words, she leaned forward and kissed him.

****

Archer hesitated, caught off guard by her kiss, wanting her to be sure. But her exciting womanly scent and the luxurious softness of her warm body against his sent messages to parts of him that wiped out all rational thought. She tangled her fingers in his hair, and he felt the answering surge inside himself.

Wrapping his arms around her, he pulled her closer and kissed her. Slowly at first, relishing the feel of her against him, but the kiss quickly became more urgent, heated, as years of longing and need came together in an explosive hunger for each other. With a low, deep growl in the back of his throat, he kissed her so possessively until they were both breathless. Heat fired between his thighs, and his body stirred fiercely in response to hers.

It always had.

"God, you're beautiful," he whispered between heated kisses.

He felt her longing, sensed her need, and shuddered at the idea of the raw, exhausting sex they both sought.

But no. He would savour her – all of her.

He pulled back, drawing in a deep appreciative breath at the sight of her full lips and flushed cheeks. She was breathing rapidly, her eyes pinned on him.

He plunged his fingers in her hair and tipped her head back so he could lay claim to the delicious skin he found there. She groaned when he nuzzled the nape of her neck, and trembled when he left a trail of kisses along her jaw.

His hand slid under her shirt, his fingers grazing her spine. He smiled when he heard her sharp intake of breath, and caught her mouth with his in a kiss so sweet, so heated, that the rhythm of it sent electric surges through them both.

With growing excitement, their bodies collided in raw hunger – years of wanting and waiting drawing them together with an intensity that left them both gasping for air.

He gripped her arms and walked her backward until they reached the couch behind her. In a fluid movement, she sank back against the cushions, pulling him on top of her. She captured his mouth with hers, giving him all.

Her hands were all over him, her skin deliciously soft against his, and he growled against her lips.

He felt the surge of power inside him, something he could usually control, and plundered her mouth with his. Grabbing her wrists, he pushed them above her head and held them there. With his knee, his nudged her legs apart, wanting her in complete surrender and at his mercy.

The things he could give her, do to her, make her feel. The very idea of it sent a renewed burst of hunger through him and he ravished her until she was writhing beneath him, her head thrown back, whispering his name. Her voice was raspy, her eyes clouded with an emotion, a desire, he'd never seen before. And the very essence of her drove him wild.

His breathing was rapid, his body trembling. "Upstairs," he murmured between hungry kisses, pulling her to her feet. "Now."

CHAPTER FOURTEEN

Everything in Sienna screamed at her that she needed this man with a hunger that only he could satisfy. He'd invaded all her senses, completely overwhelming her with his masculine heat and sexy aura. With his perfect features, brooding green eyes, and wall of sleek, strong muscles, he was built for sex and pleasure.

And she shuddered at the very thought of it.

He surrounded her with the hardness of his body, his strength, his powers, and she ached for more. She gasped when he stopped at the kitchen door, swung her around, and laid claim to her mouth in a kiss so possessive, so urgent, that she quivered in his arms.

Sidetracked by his kisses and the desire that burned between them, he shoved her against the wall, and drew her legs up around his waist with a satisfied growl.

The soft sound sent fresh shivers through her, and she threw her head back with a sigh.

And cried out when he suddenly froze.

"What's wrong?" she gasped as his body went rigid.

"My brothers," he grunted. With a scowl, he quickly separated them. "I'm sorry."

She gaped at him. "They can't see me like this." Everything about her screamed that she was sex starved and flushed with desire.

Archer gave her one last kiss, his lips lingering for a moment with promises of later. He smiled at her when he pulled away, tugged her shirt back in place, and ran his fingers through her hair to tame her curls. "They're here," he whispered as the kitchen door swung open and his two brothers marched into the room.

The three dark, handsome, and powerful men together in one room shifted the atmosphere almost immediately. Their mere presence seemed to shrink the space around her and Sienna quietly breathed in air, overwhelmed with the glorious trio of male splendour.

At least two of the three brothers were properly dressed in jeans with shirts.

"You must have consumed too much river water, Declan." Ethan walked to the counter island in the middle of the kitchen. He carried a rectangular white box and dumped it on the counter with an insignificant toss.

Declan followed, acknowledging Archer and Sienna with a curt nod. "I know it was Warrick, Ethan."

Apparently, the brothers' argument made them oblivious to the signs of the heated love scene that had just occurred.

Sienna blushed at the thought of what would have happened had Archer's brothers not interrupted them.

Ethan spread his hands in the air, palms facing upward. "Why would he send his witch into the river? That's insane."

"I know," Declan grumbled, running his hands through his hair. "But someone in that SUV caused the accident, and I bet the keys to my Harley that our wormhole friend was responsible."

"So why don't we find the dick and ask him?" Ethan said with a cool tone and reached for the bottle of wine on the counter.

"We wouldn't even know where to find Warrick. His ass has been in hiding since Sarah's death. He wouldn't dare come out of hiding and sends his minions to do his dirty work."

Sienna gulped as the opening reared its head, demanding she say something.

But she didn't.

Instead, she stood still, her eyes rooted to the package on the kitchen counter.

Ethan poured them both a glass of wine, handed it to Declan. "Bottoms up, brother. It'll take the edge off."

"I'm going to need something far stronger than wine to do that."

"Suit yourself." Ethan lowered the glass but smiled when Declan snatched it out of his hand, downed the entire glass in one gulp, and held it out for a refill. "Feel better?"

"Hell no."

Ethan laughed, the sound deep and sexy, and refilled his glass.

A trace of a smile hovered on Declan's lips, and he nodded at the white box. "What's with the box?"

"No idea. It was at the front door earlier." Ethan reached for it, sliding it across the counter toward him. He ripped open the card and frowned. "Looks like we have a new neighbour."

"And why would I care?"

Ethan held out the card. "It's always good to know who you're borrowing your eggs from."

"As if I'd borrow eggs," Declan scoffed. "Don't even eat them."

"Read the damn card, Declan."

He did and the frown that creased his forehead was instant and fierce.

Archer stepped forward, raising an eyebrow at his brother's reaction. "What's wrong?"

Declan swore softly and gaped at them. "What the hell's this?"

"Looks like you won't have to look far for Warrick after all," Ethan said and sipped his wine.

Archer frowned and folded his arms across his chest. "What do you mean?"

"Read the card. Warrick's back in town."

Sienna's stomach rolled, and she drew in a quiet breath. Say something, she told herself, unsure why she was hesitating. Dammit.

Declan crumbled the card in his hand. "And he's staying at the old Mallory property at the end of the river."

"So that explains the sudden renewed interest over that property." Archer reached for the crumpled card. "I thought they were tearing it down."

"Apparently not."

"So what's this?"

"Warrick's having a formal dinner dance." Ethan mock toasted his brothers. "And he's invited Sienna to join him."

Archer's head bolted up. "What?"

Sienna pushed herself away from the wall, having gathered her composure enough to face the three brothers. "Since when do you open my mail?" she asked Ethan, snatching the card out of Archer's hand.

Ethan shrugged, spread his hands in defence, and flashed a boyish grin. "How was I supposed to know it was meant for you?"

"By the name written on the envelope?"

In a simple, neat typed card, Warrick Brogan had invited her for a formal dinner, champagne, and dancing in celebration of his return to Rapid Falls.

And as most of the town folk had no idea of the evil he was capable of, they would all go. They'd eat his food, drink his stupid champagne, and slap several welcoming pats on the warlock's back.

It made her sick to her stomach.

Without saying anything, she dropped the card on the counter and reached for the white box. Archer was beside her in a flash that startled her.

"No," he said, covering her hand with his.

"I want to know what's in there."

"Let me."

She raised an eyebrow.

"We have no idea what's in there, Sienna. Puppies, snakes – who knows what Warrick's capable of?"

"I doubt he's sent me either. Just open the damn box."

Archer carefully lifted the lid and peered inside. The muttered curse and harsh frown that followed had her peering over his shoulder.

An evening gown.

She glanced at Archer who was staring at the blue material as though it would sprout several snakeheads and bite them. "Archer, it's only a dress," she said softly, touching his arm. "It doesn't mean anything."

His jaw worked, and he gestured wearily at the gown. "It means everything, Sienna. He sent you a dress."

"So we'll dump it."

"Hell yes." He balled the material in his fist and pulled it free from the box. A small handwritten note fluttered into the air and landed at his feet. He bent, reached for it, and opened the folded note. Heat fired in his eyes, and he spun around to face her. "Sienna," he read, his words laced with anger, "I hope our meeting earlier today was fruitful. Save me a dance. Warrick." He waved the note at her. "What the hell is this?"

Oh, brother.

Three men, wearing expressions of varying degrees of anger, stared at her for an explanation.

Sienna's gut twisted, but she held her ground. She knew their reaction came out of a loathing for Warrick Brogan and a love for her, but her defensive wall prickled at the feeling of being cornered. She crumpled the note in her hand, lifted her chin in a quiet act of defiance, and pinned them each with an intimidating stare of her own.

She was reaching, but she needed all the ammunition she could get to juggle all this damn testosterone and anger directed at her.

"You saw Warrick tonight?" Archer asked, something sharp and fiery clipping the edge of his soft tone.

"That's what spooked you out of Lora's store," Declan said with a fake laugh of disbelief, but his expression quickly clouded with confusion. "He came to you, with us standing outside?"

Sienna nodded.

"What the hell did he want?"

"To make sure I'd accept his invitation to the party," she said softly, drawing on her strength for the outburst that would follow.

And she wasn't wrong.

"Why the hell didn't you say anything?" Ethan asked, surprising her with the bite in his tone. It was seldom that he lost his temper or snapped at her.

Unlike his two brothers.

Declan grabbed the bottle of wine and poured so quickly that wine splashed onto the counter. "Sienna, we were in a car accident after your little hush-hush reunion and you never thought to tell us?"

"We don't know for sure that Warrick was responsible."

"Yeah, right. As if we have more than one psycho freak show after us. Why would you keep that from us?"

"Because I knew you'd all go King Kong on me and react this way!"

"Hell yeah. You know what Warrick's capable of. King Kong is mild compared to what I feel right now."

"Oh, calm down, Declan."

"Don't treat me like I'm an overprotective big brother, Sienna. You put all our lives at risk by not telling us that you met with Warrick."

"He caught me off guard, Declan."

"Yeah, well a little whisper, a scream, a sign – anything – would've been nice to warn us that Warrick is back in town and brushing toes with our witch right under our damn noses."

"Don't be snarky, Declan."

"Oh, I've earned several hits of snarky," he snapped. "You lied to us tonight and almost got us killed in the process."

"That's not fair."

"You shouldn't have lied, Sienna!"

"I didn't lie."

"Lie. Omission. Same thing."

"I was not about to let you go all crazy on him in the middle of Lora's store, Declan. There were people around."

"You should've told us!" he roared.

"Don't yell at me!" she shouted back and then lowered her voice. "He surprised me. I needed time to process our conversation before I told you."

"Yeah? An evil warlock's back in town. What the hell's there to process?"

"You weren't there."

"We were," he said, scowling at her. "And thanks to your need for processing, Archer had to haul us out of the damn river tonight. Was losing one Keeper not enough for you?"

Sienna reeled back as though he'd struck her.

"Declan, that's enough," Archer said, stepping between them. He pinned Declan with a sharp gaze, indicating to his brother that he'd crossed a line.

"Archer's right, Declan," Ethan said, pushing his brother away. "Back off."

Declan inhaled slowly, staring at Sienna with a cold, steely gaze. He slammed his wine glass on the counter, the sound resonating in the sudden silence of the room, and took three strides toward her.

Sienna was vaguely aware of Archer who quietly sidled closer to her, ready to step between them if his brother pushed too far.

Ever her protector.

She refused to back away or flinch when Declan stopped directly in front of her, his face close against hers. They stared at each other in silence, challenge dripping between them.

"Don't ever lie to me again," Declan murmured in a low, insistent tone that made her stomach clench. He levelled her with a hostile look and turned to face his brothers. "You're both fools if you allow her to attend the party."

"Allow me?" Sienna repeated, raising an eyebrow. "Since when do either of you get to decide what I can and can't do? Accepting this invitation is my decision."

Declan sent her another heated look that would intimidate most people. "Great. Of all the damn witches out there, we get stuck with the one hell bent on killing herself." His lips curled into a fake smile. "And guess what? You might just succeed."

"Declan, stop it," Archer said in a low tone that held all the warning needed to silence his brother. He stepped forward and placed a hand on Declan's shoulders. "That's enough."

Declan spun around and jabbed a finger into Archer's chest. "Whatever happens tomorrow at this crazy-assed party is on you. As for you, witchy," he said with another fake smile aimed at Sienna, "you best remember that playing with fire equals getting burned." With a muttered curse, he grabbed a new bottle of wine from the cellar, and stalked out the kitchen.

Archer nodded to Ethan. "Go after him and make sure he doesn't do anything stupid."

With an exaggerated sigh, Ethan pushed himself away from the counter and spread his palms. "Oh, great. You partner yourself with the witch, and I get partnered with a disgruntled King Kong. Fair deal, brother."

"Just keep him in line, Ethan. He's furious, and he's unstable when it comes to Warrick."

"Next time, I get the witch and you get the Kong," he called over his shoulder as he swiped the bottle of wine off the kitchen counter and disappeared out the door.

CHAPTER FIFTEEN

Archer turned to face Sienna. "Are you okay?"

"I'm sorry. He just makes me so damn mad sometimes."

"A given where Declan's concerned," Archer replied, pushing himself away from the counter. "He's riled. He –"

"No, don't," Sienna said, shaking her head. "He's right. I should've told you."

"Why didn't you?"

She met his sharp gaze, heard the snap in his tone, but didn't say anything.

"Sienna, we can't keep you safe if you're not straight with us."

She nodded, knowing he was just as annoyed with her as Declan, but Archer had always been better equipped at controlling his anger and emotional outbursts. Declan, on the other hand, had no filter when it came to expressing his thoughts and emotions. "I know, but you have to trust that I know what I'm doing."

"It's not that we don't trust you," Archer said, taking out a new bottle of wine and fresh glasses. "It's evil Jafar hell bent on revenge that we don't trust."

She smiled at Archer's name for Warrick. It suited the warlock, except the character in real life was far scarier.

"Declan can be such an ass sometimes," she said, exhaling

slowly, relieved they were alone. Usually she could handle the three brothers in all their testosterone glory but the events of her day had left her tired and rattled.

"Declan's an ass most of the time, but he loves you and he's scared of losing you."

"Warrick's no match for me."

"We all know how strong your powers are, but you haven't used them in a long time. You shouldn't be taking any chances."

"I don't intend to, but what am I supposed to do? Sit back and let everything unfold until it's too late to do anything to stop it?"

"No," he said, handing her a glass. "But attending Warrick's party could be dangerous for you. The fox has invited the hen back to his hole, and we all know how that scenario ends."

"I'm not about to be fox food, Archer," she said with a smirk and took a large sip of wine, needing the twinge of numbness the red liquid promised. "There's no way he'd be stupid enough to hurt me if we're surrounded by people and he'd never risk exposure without having Mason by his side."

"His judgment is clouded with revenge and the goal of breaking the curse on his brother. Who knows what he's thinking?" He glanced at her, his eyes narrowing. "What exactly did he say to you tonight?"

Time to take her head out of the sand and come clean.

She lifted her chin and met his gaze. "That I should accept his invitation to the party. That he has a proposal for me and wants me to hear him out."

"So why throw a party?"

"The party's a distraction, a statement aimed to let us know he doesn't intend going away." She shrugged. "By putting down roots here he'll be in our face every day and at some point, someone will have to give."

"It won't be us."

"Then where does that leave us?

"You can't seriously be thinking of negotiating with him?"

She turned away, thinking about the warning Warrick had issued against her Keepers. The car accident had sent a message that she'd heard loud and clear.

Warrick Brogan wasn't messing around.

But neither was she.

Warrick wanted the curse broken and the spell lifted, and would do anything to achieve his goal. Sienna would do everything to stop him, but if it meant sacrificing one of her Keepers in the process, she wasn't sure she could.

"Did he hurt you?" Archer asked softly, glancing at her hand.

She shook her head, but he moved toward her anyway. He reached for her hand, reeling her in when she pulled away.

"Don't," she whispered, trying to tug free, but his grip tightened and he stared down at the three round burn marks on her hand. She'd cleaned the wound and it hurt less, but still served as a fresh reminder of what Warrick was capable of.

"He did this to you?"

"It's nothing."

"What happened?"

She told him about the pebbles, about the power she'd felt when he'd placed them in her hand.

Archer's frown returned. "He wasn't channelling you?"

"No. Besides my Keepers, only another witch can channel me, and that's only if she has something of mine to make the connection."

"But the spell, the curse?"

She shrugged and pulled her hand free. "The spell binds the curse and only the witch who spelled it can undo it. As I haven't broken the spell yet, it would still be in place."

"So how's he channelling his powers?"

"I don't know. Could be a spell. Witches draw energy from the elements around us. How Warrick's drawing his energy, enough to heat those stones to actually burn me, is anyone's guess. Besides, the curse should prevent him from doing that."

Archer's eyes shifted nervously. "The fact that he's showing signs of power again concerns me on several levels."

"All the more reason for me to meet with him again."

"All the more reason not to."

"I have to, Archer."

"Why would you want to walk into a lion's den?"

"Because I've been invited to. Because I want to hear what he has to say."

Because he'll hurt the ones I love if I don't. She looked away, not wanting him to see the truth in her eyes.

"Then we'll go with you."

"He said to come alone."

"Right," Archer said with a forged smile. "As if that'll ever happen."

His reply didn't surprise her. "Archer, he won't harm me. Most of the people in town will be at his party."

"It's too dangerous, Sienna."

"You've always let me make my own decisions, despite your overprotective urges. Why's this different?"

He didn't reply but brushed his thumb along her chin. Their gazes locked and one unspoken word hung between them.

Sarah.

Sienna reached up and entwined her fingers with his. "You have to trust me."

He studied her with a long, pensive gaze before nodding. "Fine."

Just like that?

Sienna tilted her head, her eyes narrowing. "You won't stop me or interfere?"

"No."

A small smiled tugged the corner of her mouth. "You hate this."

He smiled and then turned it off instantly. "Absolutely."

She leaned forward and kissed him. "Thank you."

"Just don't do anything stupid, Sienna," he said, drawing her into his arms and kissing her head. "Then I'll be the one dealing with Declan."

Sienna smiled into his chest as something quiet and comforting rolled through her. The warmth and calm she found in Archer's arms chased away the crippling exhaustion of her crazy day, and she wanted to savour the unfamiliar feeling. "Declan's scary when he's angry."

"He's scary even when he's not."

CHAPTER SIXTEEN

Their names were on the guest list.

Even after warning Sienna to come alone, Warrick Brogan had expected the Bennett brothers. He'd known they'd never leave her unprotected – no matter how powerful she was or what promises he'd made.

Archer scanned the massive marquee in hope of spotting the elusive warlock. The party was in full swing and there was still no sign of their guest of honour. Archer knew most of the guests, the usual key players that Warrick called friends – and they returned the friendship out of ignorance.

Laughter and excited chatter broke the stillness of the night and echoed across the massive spans of lawn outside Warrick's home. Everyone seemed in high spirits – pleased for a reason to dress up and eager to celebrate the return of the son of a founding family of their town.

Archer wondered how they'd react if he told them just how wicked Warrick Brogan could be.

And that he'd murdered their sister, Sarah.

His lips drew together in a tight line and his nostrils flared. Inhaling quietly, he calmed from the anger summoned from that thought and did another quick scan of the marquee.

Warrick had gone all out – a band, music, fairy lights, silverware, catering, and an endless supply of champagne. Evening gowns glittered, jewellery shimmered, tongues wagged, and people mingled in a festive whirl of celebration and fun.

And yet, the lead weight feeling in Archer's stomach was anything but celebration and fun. No, he wanted to be anywhere but here, and he sure as hell didn't want Sienna here either.

But she'd insisted.

Despite everything inside him that cringed at the thought of Warrick speaking to her tonight, he was still curious at what Warrick had up his sleeve. Know thy enemy and all that crap.

Not that he believed Warrick would be straight with any of them – the man had as much integrity as a banana.

Declan approached in a black tuxedo that matched the one Archer wore; his dishevelled hair tamed for the occasion, and pushed a glass of champagne into Archer's hand. "Has Sienna arrived yet?"

"No."

Declan nudged his brother with an elbow and grinned. "I like it when you go rogue. Beats the crap out of your usual responsible, brooding self."

Archer smiled, staring at the guests around them. "We both knew there was no chance in hell that Sienna would attend this alone."

"And yet she thinks she is."

"That she does."

Declan chuckled. "She's going to be super pissed when she sees us."

"She'll get over it."

"Hm, but she's a witch and an angry witch pissed at a broken promise is one I'd rather avoid."

"I never promised her I wouldn't attend the party."

"You didn't?"

"And risk the wrath of an angry witch pissed at a broken promise?" He grinned. "Hell no."

"So what did you say to her to make her think you'd backed down?"

"It's not what I said. It's what I didn't say."

Declan laughed and tipped his glass toward his brother's. "Ah, clever, brother." He averted his gaze to scope out the room and froze, glass mid-air. "Isn't that–?"

"Yes, Warrick Brogan." Archer's body went rigid as he studied the blonde man. Dressed in a black tuxedo, a drink clasped in one hand and a smile plastered across his face, the man looked far too normal. A crowd of people had gathered around their host, dishing out hugs and welcoming slaps on the back. "And he's smiling at his guests as though he's running for mayor and lobbying for their votes."

"Evil can't find time for mundane duties like being a town mayor. But yes, his smile does make me want to punch him."

"Easy brother. No scenes tonight, remember? We weren't even officially invited."

"Warrick knew we'd be here."

At that moment, Warrick caught sight of them across the make-shift room. His face broke out in a wide, cheeky grin and he raised his glass at the two brothers.

"Play the game, Declan." Archer tipped his glass upward, straining to keep his temper in check. The blonde-haired man with the mocking eyes had taken so much from him. It took every ounce of strength Archer had not to tear into him and rip his head off.

"The bastard needs that smile adjusted," Declan grumbled.

"In time. For now, we want to know why he wants Sienna here tonight."

"He can't see her alone."

"He won't see her with three bodyguards hanging around."

"You think she can handle him?"

"Yes."

"And if he tries something, I can break his neck?"

"We'll flip a coin."

Ethan arrived, a glass of whiskey in one hand, a glass of champagne in the other, and Rose directly behind him. "I'd rather be anywhere but here right now."

Declan shot him a look that challenged his brother's statement. "You're the one usually scouring an event like this looking for some decent arm candy."

"I don't look for the arm candy, they look for me."

Archer's lips twitched at his brother's cocky reply. So typical of Ethan. And so true.

Ethan grimaced and sipped his drink. "Besides, tonight's different. I'm too damn wound up to even care."

"We all are, brother." Archer stepped forward to embrace Rose. "Rose, you look lovely."

It was the truth. The older woman wore a simple black floor length evening gown and oozed an elegance, confidence, and pride that few other women her age had. She had strawberry blonde hair, several shades lighter than Sienna's, smooth skin with few wrinkles etched around big green eyes riddled with wisdom and knowledge. She looked like a poster model for youth defying vitamins or anti-aging creams. Impressive considering her age.

Rose kissed Archer's cheek and smiled. "You three boys look ever so handsome. Something tells me my granddaughter might not be as pleased to see you as I am."

"You know why we're here."

"Same reason I am." She turned her attention on Warrick Brogan who was still mingling at the bar with several guests.

"Has he made contact with either of you?"

"Not yet. I doubt he will. It's Sienna he's after."

"He's crazy if he thinks we'll reverse our spell."

"Has he approached you?"

"He'd be bold to try."

Archer grinned. Rose's powers had lessened since the transfer ceremony, which made her more vulnerable, but it appeared her legacy still kept some of the evil at a distance. For now at least. "We'll watch out for her, Rose."

"Of course. And if Warrick tries anything, I'll have his testicles in a jar before he can even blink."

Archer did blink. Several times. And then he laughed. "I like your thinking, Rose."

Ethan held out the glass of champagne to Rose, but the woman raised an eyebrow and reached for the glass of whiskey instead. Ethan grinned, gave a shrug of resignation, and downed the bubbly liquid in one go.

Not his poison of choice but Archer figured any alcohol would suit his brother tonight.

"If you'll excuse me, but I see Lora and would like to hear if she's heard from her daughter again," Rose said, stepping forward. She turned, tilted her head at the three brothers, and wrinkled her eyes. 'Now you boys behave. No violence or unnecessary scenes, you hear?"

They all nodded.

"Unless of course," she added with a more sombre expression, "Warrick tries something with Sienna. Then you have my full permission to slaughter him."

They were all grinning when she walked away.

"She's scary," Declan said.

All talk of Rose came to a grinding halt as a woman wearing a flashy red cocktail dress and a bright smile approached them.

She cast a fleeting glance across the three brothers before her eyes zeroed in on Declan. Tara Reed, their estate manager – and an old flame of Declan's. Short blonde hair, sexy, and fun – one of the more daring and mischievous women Declan had ever dated. In that way, they'd been perfect for each other, but Declan had abruptly ended their fling before leaving town two years ago.

"Well, well, the Bennett brothers are together again." Tara nodded a greeting to each of them before sidling up to Declan. "I heard you're back in town and wondered how long it would take before you came to see me."

Declan grinned and kissed her cheek. "I've only just got into town. How are you?"

"Better now that I know you're here. It's been a while since I heard from you."

"It's been a while since anyone's heard from him, Tara," Archer added. "My brother fails miserably at keeping in contact when he's away."

She nodded. "Hm, I know, but this was different."

True, it had been different. And Tara had no idea precisely why.

A cool, familiar sensation slowly washed over Archer, alerting him to Sienna's arrival. He'd always been able to sense her presence, even before his brothers. Archer tilted his head to the doors at the top of the stairs. "Sienna's here."

His breath caught the moment she walked through the patio doors and paused at the top of the steps, dripping with confidence, power, and a beauty that struck him with an intensity that made everything inside him sit up and take notice.

Her hair hung in a mass of fiery red waves around her shoulders, and her eyes were darker with the heavier eye make up she'd chosen. She'd opted for a stunning champagne gown with thin straps over the shoulders that plunged into a V-neckline edged with silver sequins. The rest of the soft material flowed around her dangerous curves, ending at her feet in a subtle array of champagne material and sequined edging. A matching wrap draped casually around delicate shoulders to ward off the cool evening air.

She looked exquisite - and way sexy.

All feminine and all woman.

"What brought you back to town?" Tara asked Declan but his brother didn't reply. Instead, his gaze was transfixed on Sienna at the top of the steps. Tara turned to follow Declan's gaze and sighed softly when she saw their fascination. "I should have known," she said softly. "Sienna."

"Wow," Ethan murmured in Archer's ear, his eyes on their witch.

Declan nudged Archer in the ribs. "Archer, stop looking at her like that."

"Like what?"

"Like you're hungry and she's about to be dinner."

Ethan chuckled. "Or dessert."

"Cut the crap," Archer grumbled, frowning, vaguely aware that his heart rate was suddenly through the roof.

They both laughed, but the sound quickly faded as they spotted Warrick approach Sienna with a mild grin and mischievous eyes.

Archer automatically stepped forward, but both brothers stopped him.

"No, Archer," Declan said, gripping Archer's arm. He glanced at Tara before dipping his head against Archer's and lowering his voice. "As much as I hate this, now's not the time for Sienna to see us. Warrick can't know that we're at odds about her coming here tonight."

Archer hesitated, everything inside him rebelling at the idea of Warrick going anywhere near Sienna.

"Tara," Declan said, stepping back and reaching for Tara's arm. "I think I owe you a drink."

"I think you owe me an explanation, Bennett," she replied but went along with him.

"Yeah, but I'd rather start with the drink. Way more fun."

She laughed and they disappeared into the crowd.

Ethan placed a hand on Archer's shoulder. "Easy, brother."

Archer blew out air, trying to get a grip on the turmoil that ripped through him, and kept his eyes transfixed on the woman across the room. His woman.

"Are you worried about the witch or the woman?" Ethan asked softly.

Ethan's word struck a chord within him that he quickly pushed aside. "Both."

"She'll be fine."

She appeared fine. And apparently, quite willing to accept Warrick's extended arm and follow him onto the dance floor.

As though magically timed, the band changed its tempo and opted for a slower tune that automatically drew the dancing couples into each other's arms.

Warrick and Sienna included.

Damn it.

CHAPTER SEVENTEEN

Sienna kept her mask in place, hell bent on maintaining the cool, sickly sweet façade that she and Warrick Brogan had going.

"You look stunning tonight," Warrick said, holding an arm around her waist and swaying to the rhythm of the music. "And you opted against the gown I sent?"

"I never allow men to buy me clothes."

"I'll keep that in mind."

They moved around the dance floor in silence and Sienna took the moment to steady her nerves and absorb her environment. The night air was cool but the skies were clear, the weather perfect for an outdoor party. Warrick's home was impressive, as was his boldness at settling back in town after what had happened two years ago. A rambling home surrounded by high walls and few neighbours, perfectly crafted gardens, rolling lawns, and ample space. A perfect hideout for someone like Warrick.

Several people were watching them, whispering, smiling.

Not surprising.

They'd both returned after a long absence and people who lived in small towns loved to have everyone together.

And after all, she was dancing with a man who oozed charisma and charm. And a bachelor, at that. No wonder the single women were staring at Warrick as though he were a piece of chocolate cake. Ugh. But she could see the attraction. And it had nothing to do with his looks. Although he lacked the handsome gene, there was something about his attitude and confidence that attracted women by the hoards. A wealthy, charming bachelor with the ability to whip out a mischievous smile on a whim. What woman wouldn't want that?

If only they knew the monster that lurked near the surface.

Despite her determination to maintain her calm façade, Sienna bristled. This was all so wrong on so many levels. Evil shouldn't be allowed to roam the streets, renovate a house, move into her hometown, and throw a damn party.

But in her world, where evil lurked in secret, men like Warrick were free to live a normal life and create their own quiet chaos.

Over her dead body.

Sienna pushed away her irritation and returned a few forced smiles to their admirers. A waving hand from the opposite side of the dance floor caught Sienna's attention and this time, she offered a genuine smile. It was Maggie Bates, an old school friend who had taken over the local town florist. Maggie had always been a breath of fresh air for Sienna, friendly, bubbly, and full of laughter. Using her fingers to gesture a phone, Maggie placed them beside her ear and mouthed the words, "call me", before being dragged off the dance floor by her partner in search of a drink.

Sienna turned her attention back to Warrick, her smile fading. "Seems like everyone's fallen under your charms once again. They're all having fun and blissfully unaware of the chaos and evil their host is capable of."

Amusement flickered through Warrick's eyes, and his lips curled up at the corners. "Careful, Sienna, your fangs might show."

"We wouldn't want that now, would we?"

"You accepted my invite. I assume you come in peace."

"You gave me no choice and the word 'peace' isn't part of your vocabulary."

"We'll see. I heard you ran into some car trouble last night."

"Nothing we couldn't handle," she replied, choosing to ignore the dig and the spark of anger that came with it. "What do you want, Warrick?"

He cocked a brow and tilted his head to look at her. "You really have to ask me that?"

"What do you want tonight? Here. Now. Why am I here at this stupid party?" She followed his lead and moved through the rhythm of the dancing, stepping away and allowing him to twirl her around. When she flowed back into his arms, she frowned at him. "You wanted to talk to me, so talk."

"Not here. There are too many ears on us."

Sienna nodded. "So let's go inside and get your little chat over with. I'd like to go home."

"After dinner," he replied with a confident grin. "I'm told it's a delicious menu."

"I don't eat live spiders so I think I'll skip dinner."

He chuckled and shifted his gaze to someone behind her. His expression tightened, and then cleared. "Ah, ever your White Knight."

Sienna cocked her head to the side. "You're no White Knight, Warrick."

"I wasn't referring to myself," he replied and spun her around. Instead of pulling her back, he released her, and Sienna felt a fresh pair of arms embrace her.

Her eyes rounded, and she let her breath swoosh from her lungs in surprise. "Archer."

Archer kept his smouldering green eyes on her and gave a brief nod.

With his tanned skin, short brown hair, and dressed in a black tuxedo with a crisp white shirt, the man was breathtaking. He possessed a control and intensity about him that was incredibly dark and alluring and tonight, given his surroundings, those traits were magnified.

All man and all sexy.

Her heart thudded several times in warning, and her body stiffened. She should've known he'd be here.

Anger flashed through her but she quickly pushed it aside, aware of Warrick's watchful eyes. Instead, her shoulders slumped in resignation, and she relaxed in Archer's arms as they started dancing.

Of all the arms at the party tonight, she figured his were the best ones to have around her. And although she'd never admit it, a part of her was relieved to have her Keepers nearby. Her encounter with Warrick had rattled her calm façade, and she'd had to employ a wealth of strength to keep the façade in place.

She scanned the room with a fleeting glance. "I assume your sidekicks aren't far?"

Archer's lips curled into a faint smile. "Declan will be horrified to hear you refer to him as a sidekick." With practiced ease, he spun her around and drew her near again; dark eyes pinned on her face. "You look beautiful tonight."

"Thanks."

"Nice gown."

"One you bought for me a long time ago."

"I thought you don't allow men to buy you clothes."

Of course he'd been listening to her conversation with Warrick.

"This is different." She smiled. "It's you."

"Glad to know I'm on your approved list of suppliers."

"Oh, you're on my approved list of many things," she said, her smile fading, "but right now, there's a little less approval and a lot more irritation."

"You're angry that we're here."

"Shouldn't surprise you."

"And you shouldn't be surprised that we are. We're hard wired to protect you. Sitting at home drinking margaritas whilst you're dancing with Warrick Brogan is hardly something you can expect from us."

She nodded. "Fair enough. But you promised you wouldn't interfere."

"And I haven't."

Ah, clever. Word play at its best.

"So what now?" she asked.

"You do what you have to. If Warrick keeps his promise and doesn't harm you, you won't even know we're here."

All that muscle, heated looks, and attitude? Right.

"Promise me that if Warrick has a trick up his sleeve that you'll let me deal with him first." She put her fingers to his lips to silence his protest. "No, listen to me. If I need your help, you'll know. But I need to show Warrick that I can handle whatever he throws at me."

His hands came up to capture hers and he drew her closer, studying her in silence. A muscle worked in his jaw and a moment later, he nodded. "Fair enough."

"You know I'm right."

"Doesn't mean I have to like it."

"I'll be fine."

"I know," he said softly, kissing her knuckles and releasing her.

A woman's laughter drew their attention to the back of the dance floor where Declan and Tara were dancing.

"Tara's here?" Sienna asked and Archer nodded. "Wow, and already she's sought out Declan."

"Didn't take her long. Old flame and all that."

"You think that's a flame that might be rekindled?"

"Judging by the way Tara was looking at Declan, then yes."

Sienna nodded. "Too bad."

"Too bad? For Declan or for Tara?"

"For Tara. There's no way Declan will settle down with her."

"You're right, but Declan's always been clear on that when it comes to his relationships. Or flings," he added, smiling at the idea of Declan in a relationship. Not a status they'd ever really used for his brother.

Sienna put a hand on Archer's arm. "I'm going to find Warrick and get him to talk to me so we can go home."

He responded by sliding both hands behind her lower back and pulling her tighter against him so that her body was flush against his. She gasped at the sudden close contact and the intensity of his grip on her and tried to pull back to see his expression.

"Just a minute more," he whispered in her ear, keeping her in place as they swayed to the music. Her body shivered in response, his breathy words scattering her thoughts in an instant.

"Careful, Archer, any closer and people will start thinking I'm your woman."

"You are my woman."

She'd meant to tease him, to ease the sudden possessive grip he had on her, but when his mouth edged toward hers, the gentle scrape of his lips against her skin and his whispered words ripped a soft shudder through her.

"No."

"Not yet. In time, you will be."

She smiled against him. "Confident tonight, are you?"

"I call it like I see it." His fingers toyed with the seam of her dress at her lower back, and his lips hovered dangerously close to hers.

"You know we can't."

"I'm not in the mood to please The Circle right now and besides, some of the best things in life are the things that are forbidden."

"What are we, Adam and Eve?"

His face softened in a breathtaking grin and in a gentle movement, he released her, twirled her around, and drew her back to cradle her in a possessive hold that enthralled rather than annoyed her.

She longed to throw caution to the wind and kiss him, take what he offered, and lose herself in this gorgeous man. Screw the consequences.

Instead, she opted for the safe route. "Stop it, Archer."

"Scared to admit the truth?"

"No."

"Liar," he breathed against her lips before pulling back.

She blinked, trying to ignore the flash of desire that raced through her body and pretend her senses hadn't just been overrun by pure male sexiness.

Wow.

"I should go," she said, needing some distance between them. After all, she was here for a reason and it wasn't to spend the night in Archer's arms – on the dance floor or otherwise.

The silent motion of his head agreed with her, but she could see that he was worried.

She didn't blame him. Beneath her cool façade, even she was worried.

But she had a plan. One she wouldn't share with her Keepers just yet.

And she hoped to hell it worked.

****

Archer left Sienna with Rose and went to find a drink. God knows he could use one. Everything about tonight had him on the defensive, and he was as coiled as a Cobra ready to strike.

Seeing Warrick again had ripped open old wounds, exposing

the nasty aftertaste of resentment and bitterness.

The man had killed his sister. Beautiful, caring, and lovable Sarah with the infectious laugh and kind eyes. Gone. In one cruel swoop of a knife, Warrick had taken her from them.

Anger reared its familiar head at the memory, threatening to rattle the calm veneer he'd created for tonight's party.

It was all bullshit.

He was anything but calm and the idea that Warrick had gone from being a cold-hearted murderer to dancing with Sienna was absurd.

But he would pay.

Archer smiled when the barman approached with a whiskey and welcoming pat on the back. Jonathan Malloy was an old friend who'd opted to return to Rapid Falls several years ago after a long absence abroad.

"Archer, my friend, I'm surprised you made it," Jonathan said with a wide grin. "You haven't been out in the circles lately."

"Been busy, Jon."

"The grapes giving you a hard time?"

Everyone knew that everything about ice wine was a tricky business.

Archer nodded and reached for his glass, tossed back the whiskey and held it out for a refill. "Keep it coming tonight, buddy."

Jonathan laughed, refilled the glass and moved on to other customers.

"Rough night?"

Archer's stomach churned but he didn't look up. He'd know that voice anywhere, and his senses flickered with warnings of everything impure. He dug deep, reining in the anger that scorched everything inside him.

Warrick settled beside Archer at the bar, gesturing to Jonathan to pour a duplicate drink. "It's been a busy week for you, Bennett.

Your witch, your brother, and your greatest rival reappearing in your life after a two-year hiatus."

"Forgive me for not throwing out the welcome mat to you."

"This party's my welcome mat." Warrick grinned. "The town folk are lapping up my return like it's the new millennium."

"All they've done is set the wolf loose among their sheep."

"Ah, but I come in peace."

"Cut the crap and the niceties." Archer tilted his head and settled his enemy with a lethal, silent stare. "What do you want with Sienna?"

At the mention of Sienna's name, Warrick shifted his gaze across the room to seek her out. "You care about her."

"She's my witch. I'm bound to protect her."

"And we both know it's not out of obligation, Bennett." Warrick turned his head and matched Archer's stare. "You love her."

"Why did you invite her here?"

"Deflection? Oldest trick in the book." Warrick held up his glass, a smug smile making his lips curl. "I'm surprised you'd risk it, Keeper's curse and all. Forbidden fruit, but yet you've willingly sampled the apple." He shrugged and held the glass to his lips. "Gutsy, but stupid."

"You're reaching, Warrick."

His eyebrows shot upward. "Am I? You forget that we were once friends, Archer. I know how you felt about her then. I saw the way you were looking at her tonight. The way you touched her." He smiled and drained his glass. "It's all rather ironic. You're her protector and her weakness all rolled into one package."

Archer abandoned his drink and straightened, determined not to take the bait. "Mess with Sienna or Rose and you mess with the Bennett brothers. Again."

"Ah, Sarah."

"You remember her?" Archer said in a cool, sarcastic tone. He stepped closer to Warrick, shoving his face so close to the warlock's face that their noses were almost touching. "Don't for one minute confuse the fact that we haven't set you alight yet for forgiveness. We don't forget or forgive when we lose one of our own." Warrick shifted and tried to back away, but Archer gripped the warlock's arm, keeping him in place. The resistance, the strength, he felt beneath his grip surprised Archer, but he was quick to dismiss it. "Watch your back, Warrick. You're one. We're three, and we have two kick ass Beckham witches on our side. We're equally protective of our own, and you've messed with both. Together, we're all chomping at the bit to get a piece of you for what you did to Sarah."

Warrick quietly swallowed, his Adam's apple bobbing up and down in his throat. "Pursue your relationship with Sienna and you're down two members of your little fabulous five."

"My relationship with Sienna is none of your damn business," Archer said through gritted teeth and released him with a subtle shove.

No point in creating a scene, but he'd made his point and delivered a message.

And by the look on Warrick's face, he'd heard it loud and clear.

"Perhaps you should leave, Bennett," Warrick suggested, straightening his jacket.

"Suits the hell out of me. But Sienna comes with me."

"We have unfinished business."

Archer put a hand on Warrick's shoulder, leaned forward, and put his mouth close to Warrick's ear. "Then finish it," he said with razor sharp edging to his tone. "Because when I leave, I'm taking her with me."

With a final, firm squeeze to Warrick's shoulder, Archer backed off and went to find Sienna and his brothers.

It didn't take long to find them – surrounded by several friends – and it took a wad of effort for Archer to bury his fury and regain his calm veneer before joining them.

In the end, the party wasn't a complete dud.

At least it had given them all an opportunity to catch up with old friends, a rarity in their daily schedules and different circumstances.

When Sienna quietly disappeared from the crowd to seek out Warrick, the Bennett brothers were quick to follow.

Ethan spotted them first. "Up there," he said, gesturing to the top of the steps.

Warrick had a hand against Sienna's lower back, guiding her toward the house. Thanks to the large glass windows, it was easy to track their movements through the house. When they disappeared into a room at the back of the house, Archer realized he'd stopped breathing.

Everything inside him had to fight the urge to charge after her.

"Let's surround the back room," Archer said, moving forward. He tilted his head to Declan. "And please try being as inconspicuous as possible, Declan. We don't need Warrick and his minions knowing that we're listening in on their conversation."

"Inconspicuous? Oh please," he said, pushing past his brother and taking the lead. "When it comes to an evil warlock conversing with our witch, I can be damn near invisible."

"Whatever, just don't mess this up."

Declan spun around so fast that he drew raised eyebrows from both his brothers. "If anyone's going to mess this up it'll be you, Archer."

"Declan, it's Sienna."

"Precisely," Declan replied, jabbing a finger against Archer's chest. "Make sure you're thinking with your head and not your heart or you're going to get her killed."

"What's that supposed to mean?"

"We'll all protect Sienna but we'll protect each other and everything we stand for too. For you, it's different. It's only about Sienna."

Archer blinked several times, staring at his brother. Damn, what was it with everyone tackling his relationship with Sienna tonight?

Was it that obvious?

And what annoyed him more was that Declan was right. Crossing the line with Sienna put them all in danger. She wasn't simply his witch, his charge, anymore.

And that knowledge alone changed everything.

Ethan stepped between them. "Now's not the time for this conversation. Come," he said, edging them forward. "Sienna's already been alone with Warrick too long."

With a curt nod, both brothers followed.

CHAPTER EIGHTEEN

Warrick's mansion was as impressive on the inside as it was on the outside. High ceilings with extravagant chandeliers, wide windows and doors, and large rooms decorated with an exorbitant taste in furniture, accessories, and electronic equipment. He'd spared no expense, a testament to the endless zeros in his bank account.

Evil, power, and money made for all sorts of wicked results and Warrick was the perfect example of what a man could be if he had all three.

Sienna walked into the study and glanced around. A massive desk that held a laptop and a phone sat in the centre of the room, facing several brown leather couches that still smelt new. Dark mahogany bookshelves, filled to capacity with various books in different shapes and sizes, adorned the entire back wall. Wide floor to ceiling windows lined with wooden blinds made up the wall to her right, and to her left was a solid door that led to a large walk-in safe. Filled with loads of secrets, no doubt. Several lamps and unlit candles were randomly scattered around the study, the dim lighting suited to the mood of the gloomy room.

Warrick came up behind her, quickly shutting the double-edged door behind them. She heard him turn the lock, saw him pocket the key, but she didn't comment. The lock would be no hindrance to her or her Keepers and Warrick knew that – which made her wonder if he was simply trying to unnerve her.

It would take a lot more than a locked door to frighten her.

She was tired, cranky, her feet ached from the ridiculous heels she'd chosen, and her Keepers were on edge about this little visit which made her want to get this over with before either of them did anything stupid. She couldn't blame them. It couldn't be easy for them to be here, with the man who'd murdered their sister, knowing he was with their witch.

Sienna whirled around, her gown swishing with the sudden movement. "Fine, we're alone. Spill."

Warrick shrugged out of his jacket and tie and tossed it to the couch, one side of his mouth curling into a half smile. "What's the rush?"

"This isn't a social call, Warrick. If you have something to say, then say it."

He walked to the window, scanning the grounds outside. "I suspect your Keepers aren't far?"

"They won't interfere unless you try hurting me."

"Ah, you have them on a leash." He went to the liquor cabinet and pulled out a bottle of brandy and two glasses. Crystal, of course. "Drink?"

"No thanks."

"It's only Brandy."

"Right. Bottoms up then."

He returned the one glass to the shelf and took his time pouring brandy into the other one. "They can't get in here even if they tried, Sienna."

Sienna kept her voice steady and her gaze level. "What's that supposed to mean?"

"And you can't get out." He smiled, more of a ploy to frighten her than anything else.

"I'm not afraid of you, Warrick, and I'll never reverse my spell to break your stupid curse."

He swirled his brandy around in the glass and took a large sip. "I thought you might say that, and I was hoping I wouldn't have to force you."

She laughed, but the sound held no trace of humour. "No one forces a Beckham witch to do anything."

"Careful, Sienna. Over confidence often leads to a man's downfall."

"I'm not a man, and I'm all confidence."

He was in front of her in an instant, and although inwardly she recoiled at his sudden approach, outwardly she remained still. He discarded his glass to the table beside them and captured her hand in his. She didn't pull away, didn't step back. "I've always liked a confident woman who knows what she wants."

"Pity they don't like you."

He barked a quick laugh. "And here I was hoping for neutral corners."

"Warrick, you've trapped me in a room without my Keepers, you've threatened me, and now you're holding my hand. There are no neutral corners in your world."

"I always thought we'd make a remarkable team together."

"I think someone like Cruella de Vil would be more your type. You both like to prey on the innocent."

"Ah, but she likes puppies. I like people."

"You like to hurt people, Warrick. There's a difference."

"Only if they stand in my way. And of course, there are those, like Sarah, that are collateral damage."

The icy chill ran down Sienna's back at the mention of Sarah in such a callous statement, but she kept her game face intact. "All the more reason why I'd never undo the spell."

He ignored her and ran a finger along the length of her arm.

"Just think of all the power we'd have if we combined ours."

"Who'd want your puny powers?" she shot back, deliberately baiting him. She needed to know for sure if he had any powers, and the only way to do that was to force him to use them. A risky plan, but one she was sure would work. She knew him well enough to know which buttons would set him off and she was determined to press them all if she had to.

It worked, because even though his expression remained even, his tone had a lethal undercurrent. "You're so sure I have no powers?"

"I suspect you've been dabbling with fire spells and popping poor unsuspecting bunnies out of a hat, but I know you have no powers. In case you forgot, I was the one who bound you."

His body grew rigid, and his hands tightened around her arms. Frowning, he tugged her nearer until her face was close to his. The faint smell of brandy and cigars teased her nostrils, but she refused to pull away. "I've never forgotten, witch."

The chill in his words sent a flare of warning through her, but she pushed it aside. Her gaze flickered to the scar on his neck that peeked out from beneath his collar, a permanent reminder of their last encounter together. "Good. Then you'll remember what I'm capable of. So stop with the scare tactics and stupid games, and let me go."

"I want my brother. And I want my powers back. All of them."

"Hell no."

"Figured you'd say that. So the question is, what will make you agreeable?" He walked to the window and pulled the cord to lower the blinds, no doubt an attempt to block her Keepers from watching them. She couldn't see them but she knew they were out there, watching, listening, and ready to pounce. Without saying anything, Warrick moved across the glass and repeated the action until all the windows in the room were covered.

He turned, his shoulders erect, his gaze steady. "It didn't take Einstein to realize you'd never break the spell by choice. But everyone has a weakness, Sienna. Even you."

"I'm not afraid of you, Warrick. You can't hurt me."

"You may be a powerful Beckham witch, Sienna, but you best remember that with every great power comes a weakness. For you it's Rose Thorn and your grandmother. But neither of those two options appealed to me. And then we ransacked your apartment. One look at your photograph display in your bedroom and it struck me." A slow, wicked smile crossed his face. "I found your weakness."

It wasn't hard to figure where he was headed with this. The thought made her stomach roll, repeatedly, but she inhaled quietly and fought for control.

Warrick walked to his desk, produced a thick key to unlock one of the drawers, and pulled out a photo frame. He gestured to the photo with his free hand. "Your fearless courage is admirable, Sienna, but it's also damn annoying. It took me a while to discover what would frighten you enough to make you relent and all this time, it's been right here in front of me."

She recognized the photo frame from her collection, a cherished photo of herself surrounded by her four Keepers.

"Besides your powers, your Keepers are supposed to be your biggest ally, your biggest strength, and your most potent protectors. Isn't it ironic that in the end, they might be your greatest weakness?"

"You're a fool to think you can threaten my Keepers, Warrick."

He studied her over the rim of his glass, challenge oozing from his posture. "I've yet to come across a link that can't be broken. Imagine a world where Keepers don't exist? A world where witches are left to fend for themselves?" He smiled, the idea making his eyes sparkle. "Makes me think of a kid in a candy store."

"Ah, so there's your deal. Break the spell, and you'll spare my Keepers." Anger fired, and she took a step toward him. "We're not afraid of you, Warrick. You can huff and you can puff all you want but I'll never unbind your powers. Your minions are no match for us." She gave him a quick, mocking once-over. "And neither are you."

"And you're still so sure I have no powers?"

"As I'm not interested in seeing you pull bunnies out of your hat, I'd like to go." She moved to the door and gasped when he appeared in front of her in a flash, stopping her in her tracks.

What the hell? She blinked and stepped back, quickly masking her surprise. Since when did Warrick have the power of accelerated movement – an ability she'd only ever seen in her Keepers?

He grinned. "I have something to show you."

"So show me."

He held out his hand, palm facing upward, to reveal a silver antique ring. The ring of a Keeper.

Sienna recognized it immediately and sucked in air. Sarah's ring. "How did you get this?"

"You should know by now how resourceful I can be."

They'd always wondered what had happened to Sarah's ring in the confusion surrounding her death. Warrick.

With a casual shrug of his shoulders, he closed his fingers around the ring, flipped his fist, and held out his hand to Sienna. "Here."

A possessive reflex had her reaching for the ring without further thought, but she cried out and quickly retracted her hand when the silver burnt her skin. The ring fell to the floor and rolled across the room. When she shifted her gaze to meet Warrick's, all she saw was wicked amusement.

He has Sarah's powers.

Sienna frowned. A warlock could absorb a witch's powers if he killed her. But a Keeper's powers?

Warrick smiled as understanding crossed her expression. "Thanks to the annoying spell you and Rose cast on me, I may not have the full use of my powers, but Sarah's have been enough to tide me over until now."

The thought sent several waves of fury through her, and everything inside Sienna began to prickle. He was using powers meant for protecting the good for his evil gain.

It was such a violation of everything pure about Sarah's memory.

She thrust her chin upward and met his ridiculously cheerful gaze. "So you have the powers of a Keeper. One Keeper. You have three more above you – and the wrath of one very pissed-off witch."

Muttering a string of soft curses, she flung her arms out and sent Warrick flying backward in a whoosh of air that slammed past her ears. He crashed against the desk, the impact dislodging the open drawer, and slumped to the floor. The drawer slid across the ground, scattering its contents along its path.

Sienna zoned in on the photographs splashed across the wooden floor, the punch of horror taking her breath away. Strewn around him were pictures of young men and women, newspaper clippings, and various keepsakes.

With a shaking hand and a pounding heart, she kept him rooted to the spot, unable to move, and edged closer to the mess.

Several faces of unsuspecting and innocent people stared back at her. She gasped when she recognized the faces of two women, their recent disappearances splashed across the news for weeks.

"All these people in these photographs…" she breathed, staring at their smiling faces. "This was all you? Did you hurt them? What did you do?"

"Whatever I wanted." With a speed that didn't surprise her this time, he was on his feet, eyes flaring, fists clenched. He struggled against the invisible bind that kept him in place and flicked her an irritated glare.

"Are they dead?"

He simply smiled. "As if I'd ever tell you."

Rage flared, mingled with a fresh bout of panic, and she whirled around to face him with an aggression that sparked every powerful instinct she possessed.

"I refuse to let you harm any more people, Warrick, and before you threaten me or my Keepers, you'd best remember that I hold the one thing that is your weakness." She lowered her hand slightly, the motion causing him to drop to his knees with a low grunt. "Mason."

"I will hunt down every damn Keeper I know until they are all dead and once I've claimed their powers, I'll start on the witches." Everything about his tone, the determined look in his eyes, and the rigid stance of his shoulders proved that he meant every word. "Unless, of course, you're willing to strike a deal. Give me Mason and unbind my powers, and we'll leave Rapid Falls forever. We won't harm anyone you care about."

It was a tempting deal, one he might even honour, and the idea of keeping the Bennett brothers unharmed and never seeing the Brogan brothers again appealed to her.

Sienna glanced at the photographs scattered across the floor and shook her head. "I told you before, Warrick. I don't make deals with the Devil."

"Then you've just signed the death warrant of every Keeper you know."

His words twisted her gut, and her breath caught in her chest as she fully processed them.

Somehow, she managed not to flinch. "The spell remains, the curse holds. Your brother is dead to the world as evil should be. You on the other hand, should've had the same fate. I was stupid to think that you were different and that by binding your powers you'd have some sense shaken into you. I was wrong. You've become as evil as Mason." She flashed him a fake smile, her tone softening. "And we both know what I did to Mason, don't we?"

"You're trying to find my fuse, Sienna. It won't work."

"Oh, not only do I intend to find your fuse, Warrick, but I intend to light it."

Without shifting her gaze from his, she narrowed her eyes, and drew on the one power she was famous for.

Fire.

A moment later, all the candles in the room suddenly caught alight.

He laughed. "You would never hurt me, Sienna. Not with everyone outside."

"You threatened my Keepers, Warrick. Don't be so sure of that."

With her free hand, she motioned to the bottle of brandy and sent it flying through the air to shatter on the ceiling above his head. Shards of glass and alcohol splattered around him, on him, and he quickly slumped back. She saw the flash of fear in his eyes, and the quick attempt to cover it.

The cupboards to the liquor cabinet burst open and several bottles of alcohol slammed against the far walls. Spirits splashed everywhere, dripped down the walls and onto the floor. Fuelled by the spatters of the alcohol, the flames from the candles flickered brighter, stronger, until sparks were flying in all directions.

Within moments, flames licked at the walls surrounding them, fire hissing through the room like a snake about to consume its prey.

The blazing chaos triggered a brief flash of recognition for them both, but Sienna kept her focus. This time there wouldn't be any uncertainty or zoning out. This time, she was all control. And it was exhilarating.

"Sienna, stop!" Warrick shouted, afraid to move in case the flames chased the splatters of brandy she'd spilled on him.

She kept her eyes pinned on him, almost enjoying herself now. It had been a long time since she'd used her powers to this extent, especially to instil fear in another person, but instincts ruled.

He'd threatened her Keepers and she had a message to deliver.

Not blinking at the flames that licked the walls around her, Sienna sauntered toward the couch where he'd tossed his jacket. She reached into the pocket and withdrew a single bronze key. Then she scooped Sarah's ring off the floor. The heat had faded from the silver, and Sienna was able to slip it onto her finger.

"Sienna!"

When she reached the large wooden doors, she turned around and settled Warrick with a hard, unbending stare. "You will never get what you seek, Warrick, and don't ever threaten me or my Keepers again."

Shoving the key into the lock, she yanked open the heavy door and walked out.

At the same time, the flames vanished.

CHAPTER NINETEEN

When Declan bolted forward the moment Sienna left Warrick's study, his brothers were ready for him.

"Declan, no." Archer grabbed his brother by the arm, not surprised by the strength of the resistance he felt beneath his grip. They were outside and had heard everything.

Ethan stepped in front of Declan, blocking a quick escape. "Don't be stupid, Declan,"

"Back off, brothers," Declan grumbled, shrugging them off. He was running on the hot fumes of fury and pain, all rational thought extinct as he fought for the one thing he had to have in order to put Sarah's death behind him.

Revenge.

With both hands, Archer shoved Declan backward. He stumbled, straightened, and cursed when Archer grabbed the front of his shirt, balling the material into his fists. "Calm the hell down," Archer said through gritted teeth, his face close to Declan's. "We promised Sienna we wouldn't interfere."

"You promised Sienna you wouldn't interfere. She's had her turn with Warrick. Now it's my turn."

Archer slammed a hand against Declan's chest, pushing him backward. "And what are you planning to do, huh? Charge in there and rip his head off with a bunch of town folk watching?"

"At least it's better than sitting on our asses doing nothing while Warrick creates a full-blown war around us. Our parents, Sarah, they're all dead and it's thanks to that heartless asshole and his family! I can't sit around anymore, dammit!"

Ethan put a hand on Declan's shoulder. "Now's not the time for revenge, Declan. Warrick's got a house full of people."

"And it's about time this party ended," Declan said in a fierce tone.

The cold, steely, and eerily familiar determination that flashed through Declan's eyes sent a chill of warning down Archer's spine. He cursed as he heard the familiar sound of groaning metal behind him. He didn't need to turn around to know that Declan had focused his rage on the metal poles of the marquee. And he knew his brother well enough to know that once he'd tapped into his elemental power of fire, not much would stop him. Thanks to the hundreds of candles and fire torches that burned throughout the garden, Declan had all the ammunition he needed. The flames flared, burning brighter and stronger, extracting surprised reactions from the guests in the garden. One by one, the metal poles of the marquee weakened from the intense heat and gave way, creating a stir of panic and confusion amongst the unsuspecting guests. "Declan, stop it. You know the rules. There are people here."

"They shouldn't be here."

"You'll hurt someone."

Archer spun around as a series of frightened shrieks echoed across the lawn. The band had stopped playing, and there was a mad scramble of people as they frantically tried to escape the collapsing marquee. Surprised guests poured out from beneath the tent in a whirl of frightened screeches. Moments later, the roof caved in, swallowing everything beneath it.

"Declan!" Archer snapped, punching his brother's shoulder.

"Stop it."

"Back the hell off!" Declan growled, breaking focus. Using both arms, he shoved his brothers off him and took a steadying step backward.

In perfect unison, Ethan grabbed Declan from behind whilst Archer slammed a hand on each of Declan's shoulders.

"Get a grip, Declan," Archer said firmly, trying not to show how rattled he was from his brother's outburst. Sienna had been right. They'd all taken Sarah's death hard, but for Declan, it was different.

"Let me go, Archer."

"Hell no."

"He took her powers!"

Silence fell as all three brothers took the blow that came with those words.

"I know," Archer said with a brief nod. "I know, Declan. And he'll pay for what he did to Sarah. But it'll have to wait. There are too many witnesses here tonight, and too many people could get hurt in the process."

"She would've hated this, dammit."

"I know." Archer eased the pressure on Declan's shoulders and lowered his voice. "Trust me, brother. I get it. I want to rip his head off as much as you do – and we will. Just not here and not tonight." Sensing that his brother had regained some control, Archer gestured to Ethan with a brief nod. "The party's over. I've got this. Find Sienna and check that's she okay. Then find Rose."

Ethan hesitated, eyeing Declan. "If I let you go, you won't try anything stupid?"

"Screw you, Ethan. I'm not ten years old."

"Maybe not, but your silent temper tantrum just killed the party." He slapped Declan on the head. "You could've set something alight, you ass. Show some control."

"If I wanted to set something alight, I would have. I didn't.

That is control, brother."

Ethan came around Declan and settled his brother with a hard, unbending stare. "We're all pissed at Warrick, and we all want him to pay for what he did, but raging through his house wielding anger and a sword in front of his guests is not the way to avenge Sarah's death."

Declan inhaled sharply and nodded toward the house. "Just go find the women."

Ethan glanced at Archer and released Declan. "I'll meet you at the cars."

"And give Pam a call and tell her she needs to find a way into Warrick's study." Archer turned to Declan, keeping a firm grip on his brother's shirt. "Are you cool?"

"He's using Sarah's powers. The asshole has her ring."

"Which makes him stronger than we anticipated. And more dangerous. It also means that he's connected to Sienna through Sarah." The thought that Warrick had that access to Sienna, a very treasured, deep part of her, sent a bolt of fury through him. He quickly pushed the thought aside where it could be dealt with later. For now, he had his hands full with his brother's anger.

Declan turned his head and looked at Archer, a thunderous expression twisting his features. "Warrick threatened Sienna, threatened us."

"And we're not about to let that slip by. Sienna made it clear what she thought of his threats. Let's take a beat, and we'll find a way to deliver the same message. Only stronger."

Something sinister and quiet flashed in Declan's eyes as he processed Archer's words. "All Sienna's done is rile him up."

"And shown him that she's stronger and more in control of her powers. What Sienna did to him tonight would've yanked his chains, but I bet she purposely provoked him in an attempt to get him to reveal his powers. At least now we know what we're dealing with."

Archer felt the fight lessen, and Declan blew out air. "So when do we get to rip his spleen through his throat?"

Archer released him and stepped back. "It's late and we're all riled. Let's get Rose and Sienna home, sleep on it, and come up with our game plan in the morning."

****

Sienna glanced at Archer during the ride home and frowned. She'd expected all three brothers to come guns blazing and swords wielding. Instead, there'd been an eerie silence that had creeped her out.

Calm before the storm?

"Archer," she said softly, her voice slicing through the thick silence in the car. "We should talk about what happened tonight."

Archer didn't reply, kept his grip on the steering wheel and his eyes on the road. His frown became more pronounced, the only indication that he'd heard her.

"Are you mad at me?" she asked.

"I'm mad at myself."

That surprised her.

"Why?"

"Because Warrick's right."

"About what?"

"We're hard-wired to protect a Beckham witch, to protect you. It's as natural to us as breathing."

Sienna frowned, waiting for him to continue. When he didn't, she placed her hand on his arm. He surprised her by shifting his arm out of her reach. She swallowed, her eyes never leaving his face. "Archer, what's wrong?"

"It's not unnatural for a Keeper and his witch to develop a bond

256

after all the time they've spent together. But we're different. We've known each other forever and there's a lot of history between our families, our parents, and us. That changes everything."

An uneasy feeling prickled through her as she realized what he was getting at. "Archer, you're not my weakness."

Archer laughed, but the sound was empty and held no humour. "Oh, that's where you're wrong. Warrick was spot on when he said we're your weakness, Sienna. We're your biggest damn weakness. Despite our differences and our arguments, the relationship we share between the four of us is unique. We would die for each other, and Warrick knows that."

"We couldn't help but develop a solid relationship, Archer. I've known you all my entire life. You're my best friends, my Keepers, and I'd do anything for you."

"Even reverse a spell and break a curse?"

She sucked in air, staring straight ahead of her, and thought of several responses.

But she didn't offer any. Instead, she kept quiet, relieved when Archer turned the car into the driveway leading up to the house. His brothers weren't home yet, the house mostly in darkness. The garden was well illuminated with soft lighting that masked the mansion in a warm glow.

Archer parked the car beside Declan's motorcycle at the front door, not bothering with the garage, and killed the gentle hum of the engine. He shifted his weight so that he was facing her. "Because of the bond we all share, it's easy to forget that we fight for the greater good and that our aim is to maintain the balance between good and evil. That should be our first and utmost concern." His voice was steady, even, and succeeded in sending a slight shiver down her spine. "The problem is, Sienna, when it comes to choosing between the safety of one of your Keepers and choosing what's best for the greater good, you'd pick us. Every damn time."

Sienna didn't look at him. Couldn't look at him. He was right. Somehow, over the years, they'd become more important to her than her destiny, her promise, or her constant fight to maintain the balance of nature.

Not if it meant sacrificing one of her Keepers in order to do it.

"Warrick was right when he said we've become your greatest weakness. That's why he's threatened us. He knows that through us, he can get you to do whatever he wants, including breaking that damn curse."

"No."

He raised an eyebrow at her weak answer. "Even if it meant one of us dying?" When she didn't reply, he closed his eyes and sighed. "Precisely," he said and made to exit the car.

"Archer." She placed a hand on his arm, and he glanced back over his shoulder, brushing off her touch as though she'd scalded him.

"We better go in. It's late."

"Archer, don't do this to us."

"Sienna," he said, meeting her gaze, "there is no 'us.'"

CHAPTER TWENTY

Archer hated the way her eyes rounded and her lips parted, as though he'd sliced through several layers of her. He saw the confusion in her eyes and ached to rectify it.

No.

"I don't understand. You were the one who said you were willing to fight for us," she said.

"And you weren't. You shot me down."

"I changed my mind."

"And I've changed mine."

"Why? Because of Warrick?"

"Damn right, but more so because of everything that stands between us, between me as your Keeper and you as my witch. I was stupid to think we could be anything more than what we are now." A furrow appeared between her delicate, curved brows, and she lowered her long lashes. It took everything he had not to brush away the hurt he'd caused. "It's bad enough that our existing relationship has put you in danger with the likes of Warrick. I'm sure as hell not about to put you in danger with The Circle."

And everyone knew that nobody messed with The Circle. Only senior witches like Rose and Lora could contact The Circle but even so, they rarely did.

Determined to maintain the balance of nature, The Circle would stop at nothing to achieve their goal and see that order was upheld. Even if that meant trashing a relationship between a Keeper and his witch.

Thanks to some cranky dead witches, the woman in front of him was everything he wanted, yet everything he couldn't have.

Sienna looked away, staring out the window ahead of her. "Last night it was all rockets and fireworks, and now you won't even let me touch you."

"Last night was a mistake," he said, needing space between them. He pushed open the car door and slid out the car, not bothering to look back.

He couldn't bear to see the sadness reflected in her eyes, or the way her lips had thinned into a disapproving line.

Screw the damn Circle. Screw Warrick Brogan. And screw the fact that they were all right.

He went inside, tossed his keys onto the kitchen counter, and rolled his shoulders, inhaling slowly.

Sienna marched into the kitchen, green eyes blazing with something sharp and unrelenting. "No."

Archer raised a brow. She crossed the room and stopped a few feet away from him. He had no choice but to look at her.

"I'm not letting you back away from this now, Archer. Not after everything we've been through. I know you feel something for me, and I refuse to walk away from that because of some rule."

Archer stared at her lips, trying to resist the urge to lay claim to them. Everything he'd ever wanted was right here before him, and his gut twisted with the knowledge that he would never truly have her. He could never risk hurting her and the curse that threatened them was too real, too dangerous.

"We can't do this, Sienna," Archer murmured, his voice low and insistent. Through sheer force of will, he pulled back, needing the distance between them.

"Don't push me away, Archer. Please don't do this to us."

"There is no us, Sienna!"

"Only because you won't give us a chance." She reached for him, her eyes widening in surprise when he stepped out of her reach.

"This is for the best."

"For you maybe. What about what I want?"

"I'm doing this for you, dammit. It's because I care about you that I won't let this happen." The urge to leave her conflicted with the urge to hold her, and he dragged in a ragged breath.

"We'll find a way to beat Warrick and break The Circle's curse, Archer."

"We don't even know what that curse is, Sienna, or how to break it. The Circle hasn't exactly offered a guidebook to their crazy-assed rules."

"Rose said it would take a blood sacrifice and a counteracting spell."

"A spell we don't have and blood sacrifice we'd never offer." The tone in his voice cut like a knife, and his gut twisted even more when she flinched.

"Archer."

"Warrick. The Circle. I can't risk hurting you." Her look of anguish kept him transfixed, unable to look away. He flexed his fingers, reaching for control. Wrenching his gaze away from hers, he headed for the kitchen door.

A gust of wind whooshed past him with such force that it unsettled a vase on a nearby table. Simultaneously, the vase toppled over with a resounding crash as it hit the floor, and the door slammed shut before he reached it. Clearly, she wasn't going to let this go. Archer blew out a breath and closed his eyes, not daring to turn around. He didn't need another glance to know that her expression was twisted with pain and confusion, and he refused to lay claim to the reason of their existence.

"This is not just about you, Archer," she said softly, her voice shaking with emotion and fresh anger. "I know you care, and I know you feel what I feel. I'm here, and I'm willing to fight for us. If this is really over between us, it's because you walked away."

"Sienna."

"Archer, look at me." When he didn't move, she repeated the instruction and moved toward him, but he heard the slightest crack in her voice. "We'll find a way to deal with Warrick, and I'll do whatever it takes to find a way to break this crazy curse."

"Sienna, I can't."

"I can." She stopped in front of him, her eyes filled with an emotion that rocked him. Her hands came up around his neck, her fingers brushing the side of his jaw. "I'm not afraid, Archer," she whispered, pressing her lips to his. "I'm not afraid."

Her words stirred something untouched, sacred, inside and he felt the slightest chip in his resistance.

"Sienna."

She pulled away, the familiar steely look back in her eyes, and he knew he didn't stand a chance.

"I love you, Archer. I've always loved you."

Their gazes met and everything that mattered came into focus. Everything that didn't simply fell away.

Throwing caution to the wind, Archer captured her face in his hands, and kissed her.

The kiss held all the intensity of their emotions, their heated argument, and when he broke away, they were both breathless.

He pulled back, searching for signs of hesitation. There weren't any. "I would never forgive myself if –"

She silenced him with a finger to the lips. "Ssh. We'll figure this out." Leaning forward, she touched her lips to his. "You're stronger than Hercules, and I'm a Beckham witch. We'll figure something out.”

Archer stroked her face with his thumb. God, she was beautiful. Her hair hung in a mass of wavy curls around trembling shoulders, and although a flush had broken out on her cheeks, hope had fired in her eyes.

“Trust me,” she whispered against his lips.

“Dammit, Sienna –”

She silenced him with another kiss, and he felt the last of his resistance melt away. With a groan against her sweet lips, he shoved his hands in her hair and ravished her.

****

Everything inside Sienna tingled as though Archer had ignited hot little tendrils of electricity throughout her body.

His mouth plundered hers until she was breathless. His hands scoped across her body, his gentle, possessive touch making her shiver. He’d invaded every one of her senses, brushing away everything that didn’t matter.

It was only them, now, here.

His body stiffened and he tore his mouth away from hers, cocking his head in the direction of the door.

Sienna gasped. “No, don’t stop.”

“My brothers are back,” he grumbled and grabbed her hand.

A smile broke out on her face when he pulled her toward the kitchen door and headed for the stairs.

With a low growl that sounded like a caged animal, Archer tugged her into his bedroom, slammed the door shut behind them, and pushed her up against it.

“I have to have you,” he murmured before capturing her mouth with his again. He caught her wrists in his hands and held them above her head.

His taut body held hers in place against the door, pressing against her, unable to move, sending delighted quivers of desire straight between her thighs.

She gasped, rolling her head back as a shiver ran through her when his teeth nipped her earlobe. "For a second I thought you were going to stop."

Archer leaned back and gave her a predatory smile. "Hell no."

She smiled and inhaled sharply when he pressed his hips against hers, his erection hot and hard against her pelvis. He kissed her again, his tongue sweeping against hers in soft, teasing motions that had her groaning against him.

Without breaking their kiss, she tugged her hands free and pulled at his shirt. So far, he'd done all the touching and tasting and she wanted some of her own.

He stepped back, dark green eyes filled with desire and anticipation, searing into hers. The heated look he gave her was so intense, so raw, that her breath caught. Without looking away, he reached behind her and unzipped her gown, the material dropping to the floor in a soft whoosh of champagne flutters.

Sienna stepped out of the dress, and Archer tossed it aside with his foot. His jacket and shirt quickly followed, and she flashed him a predatory smile of her own when she saw the hard wall of sleek muscles that beckoned to her.

She brushed her fingers across his tattoo on his shoulder. His muscles bunched beneath her fingers, his satisfied growl making her grin. His hands came up to cup her face, and his mouth took possession of hers in a kiss so gentle, but so powerful, that she quickly grabbed onto his shoulders in order to ground herself.

"You're so beautiful," he whispered, trailing a hand across her smooth skin. She felt the gentle scrape of his ring across her skin, a fleeting reminder of everything he stood for. The thought thrilled her rather than frightened her. She trusted him with her life, and the notion sent a fresh wave of sexual determination though her.

When his hand reached her breasts, he pulled back to cast a leisurely gaze across her body. He teased her nipple beneath his fingers and drew in a sharp, appreciative breath. Moments later, his hands slid around her and his mouth took over.

Her thoughts shamelessly scattered, and she lost herself in the delicious onslaught of pleasure.

His mouth returned to hers and this time, his kisses were hotter and held a sense of urgency that thrilled her. Still holding her, still kissing her, he moved backward toward the large bed in the corner of the room, bringing her with him.

She followed, quickly working on his belt, his zipper, and pushed the material over his hips.

Completely naked and with growing excitement, he turned around and nudged her backward onto the bed, covering her body with his.

She trembled as he shifted between her legs, gasped when he kissed her, and sighed as the surging heat rumbled through her.

"Archer," she said, her voice raspy and thick with emotion and desire. "Now."

Her body burned for him, needing the release only he could give her. She touched a hand to his face, looking up at him, her other hand moving around his body and capturing the hard wall of muscle she found there.

He paused and met her gaze, his eyes searching, questioning. "Sienna?"

She knew what he was asking, and her hand curled around his neck. Drawing him closer, she kissed him softly on the lips. "I'm sure, Archer."

He nodded and in a fluid movement, he captured her mouth and her body with his.

They moved together, slowly at first, in perfect harmony. A

rolling rhythm, a moment in time when nothing else mattered, a connection like no other.

Fingers laced together, bodies entwined, tidal waves of pleasure.

And then suddenly, the tenderness gave way to an urgency that had them both gasping against each other, frantic with need. The heat intensified and he increased his pace, pumping into her, filling her.

She cried out as she came and wrapped her arms around his neck, needing to hold onto something while she soared. Her release brought on his and with a low groan, he buried his face in her neck and gave way to the incredible sensations that rolled through them.

An incredible feeling of lightness, of overwhelming joy, of absolute pleasure.

They fell silent, still, for a long while as their breathing levelled. Sienna held onto him, not wanting the moment to end, not wanting to give room to any of the doubts that threatened.

He shifted above her, leaving a trail of feather light kisses along her neck until his mouth was against her ear.

"I love you," he whispered.

And all her doubts vanished.

CHAPTER TWENTY-ONE

"Rise and shine, brother," Declan said, walking into Archer's room the following morning. "We have a busy day ahead of us."

"Declan!" Archer bellowed, bolting upright in bed. He turned, quickly tugging the sheet across Sienna's body.

Declan skidded to a stop and gaped at them.

Unknowingly, Ethan followed directly behind Declan, tugging a white t-shirt over his head. He smelt of the shower, a smell that quickly permeated the room, and although his hair was still wet, he'd already combed it into his usual spiky style. "And just for the record, brother, Declan's insisting on serving a dose of revenge and malice for breakfast." He sidestepped Declan to avoid colliding into him, quickly realizing the reason behind Declan's unhinged jaw – a rarity for his brother. Ethan's expression quickly resembled his brother's. "Sienna?"

Sienna closed her eyes, willing them to go away.

They didn't.

Damn.

At least she'd pulled on a tank top and her panties at some point in the night. She may be in Archer's bed, but at least she wasn't naked. Now.

"Go away," Sienna groaned, dragging the sheet over her head.

"Since when did you move into Archer's bed?" Declan asked her, his tone edged with surprise and a tinge of laughter.

"Declan, get out of here," Archer said, throwing a pillow at his brother.

Declan caught the pillow and tossed it aside. "No need for this to be awkward. We all knew it was coming." He smiled. "And since we're all here together, we can have a quick brainstorming session."

"Now?" Archer and Sienna said in unison.

"Word is that Pam is sniffing all over Warrick's ass and he's on the move because of it."

Archer frowned and cast a quick glance at Sienna before settling against the pillows with a sigh of resignation. "What do you mean? Where's he going?"

"See?" Declan said with a half smile. "It's about time you two untangled those sheets and got out of bed. Evil doesn't wait for sleepy heads."

"Declan."

Ethan laughed and shoved a hand against Declan's shoulder. "Let's get out of here, brother. We can discuss this later. Besides, you have a guest of your own waiting for you."

"She's asleep, and hell no. I've been up for two hours waiting for you lot to surface."

Sienna leaned up on her elbows and eyed Declan. His usually untidy hair had been finger combed into submission, and he wore dark jeans and a grey shirt that did very little to hide the bulging muscles across his chest and abdomen. Although his eyes were alive with amusement, his entire body bristled with energy. No wonder he wreaked havoc with the likes of Tara. "Seriously, Declan? Right now? Right here? I'm as eager as you are for a brainstorming session, but that's not going to happen for at least another hour. I need coffee."

Declan shrugged off her request and walked toward the window, the sound of his heavy boots clunking across the wooden floors as he moved. He whipped open the heavy curtains, blasting bright sunlight across the room, and ignored the protests coming from the bed. Turning, he folded his arms across his body in a guard-like stance. "We need to pay a visit to Mason."

"What?" three voices echoed through the room.

Declan nodded, glancing at Sienna. "Since you spelled the tomb shut, we know he's still in there. You can't break the spell on Mason without the stones, the Grimoire, and…you. But you can open the tomb without breaking the spell, can't you?"

"Yes. But why would we want to do that?"

"Warrick's hell-bent on breaking the spell to wake his brother so they can take over the world," Declan said, the last few words said in a mocking singsong voice. "He may be evil but he doesn't have half the balls his brother does. It's crucial that he never frees Mason and he can't do that if he doesn't know where his brother is."

Sienna sat upright, her jaw dropping. "You want to move Mason?"

Declan grinned.

"That's just creepy."

"Warrick's already surprised us once. Now it's our turn."

"Where the hell would you put a mummified dead body?"

"He's not dead," Ethan added, the brief notion of his head indicating his agreement with Declan. "If we move Mason, it'll make it harder for Warrick to break the spell. He'd have to find the stones, the Grimoire, get you to agree to unspell them, and find his brother."

"And hopefully, with his hands so full, he'll forget about wanting to turn your Keepers into road kill," Declan said with a fake smile.

Sienna sighed and glanced at each of her Keepers. So incredibly handsome, so powerful, and so utterly devoted to protecting her and avenging Sarah's death.

The thought sent a warm trickle through her as it so often did, and she leaned back against the pillows with a soft sigh.

Declan had a point.

But it was still creepy.

Archer glanced at her. "If you open the tomb, who would go in?"

"That's the tricky part," Declan said with a grimace.

Because an elemental witch had sealed the tomb with a spell, the seal prevented anyone with elemental powers from entering or exiting – even once she'd lifted the spell.

That eliminated everyone in the room.

Declan waved a casual hand of dismissal. "We'll figure that part out."

"Warrick's going to be furious when he discovers his brother's missing," Archer said.

A satisfied, evil look crossed Declan's expression. "He pressed a few of our buttons last night. It's sweet justice to push a few of his."

Archer looked at Ethan. "Have you been in touch with the Keepers assigned to the four witches harbouring the stones?"

Ethan nodded. "I spoke to three of the four. The fourth one isn't answering his phone and neither is the witch."

Sienna tilted her head, her eyes narrowing. "Who's the fourth witch?"

"Lexi."

She frowned at the mention of her friend's name. "Can you keep trying?"

"Of course."

Archer waved a hand at his brothers. "Get out of here. We'll meet you in the kitchen." He grinned at Ethan. "Are you making breakfast?"

Ethan shrugged and headed to the door. "Yeah, yeah." He pulled Declan toward the door. "Come, brother. You're on coffee duty."

Declan paused in the doorway and looked back over his

shoulder, his expression sobering. "You two ready for the crap you're going to get from The Circle?"

Neither Archer nor Sienna replied.

"Just asking," he said with a quick shrug of his shoulders and left.

Ethan merely cast them a lingering glance before closing the door.

Exhaling loudly, Sienna fell back against the pillows and covered her face with her hands.

Oh, brother.

****

Archer threw back the sheet and went to lock the door. The mess in the room had him raising an eyebrow. Clothes, bedding, and pillows littered the room. Furniture had been shifted, the bed a mess of tangled sheets, and they were both half-naked.

Wow. They'd been busy.

He was surprised his brothers hadn't had more to say about the state of his usually immaculate room.

His gaze settled on the woman in his bed. Images of their night together sprang to mind and he grinned.

"Stop looking at me like that," Sienna groaned, throwing back the sheet and marching to the bathroom.

"Like what?"

"Like you're about to devour me all over again," she replied over her shoulder.

He laughed. "Is that an invitation or an objection?"

"Neither."

The roar of the shower swept away his reply, but he followed her, pausing in the doorway to watch her strip and step under the water. A perfect vision of pale skin and wild red hair. Beautiful. He couldn't resist the grin, and suddenly had a new appreciation

271

for the double shower he'd had installed several years ago.

Without waiting for an invitation, he pushed off the long cotton pants he wore and slipped in behind her. He slid his arms around her waist, turned her around, and tangled his hands into her hair.

He saw the flash of unguarded hesitation, felt the slight withdrawal.

She was having doubts.

Dammit.

He tipped her chin upward. "Sienna, don't do that."

A small smile relaxed her features. "I'm fine."

"Then why the frown?"

"Reality, I guess." Sensing his question, she slid her hands up his arms. Her gaze lingered on his scarred arm before meeting his. "Last night was wonderful, Archer, and I don't regret it. At all."

"You sure?"

She leaned up and touched her lips to his in a kiss so tender, sealing her promise. "Absolutely."

"We have to contact The Circle."

"Yes, but for now we have bigger fish to fry. Warrick's not going to bide his time, and the only way we can beat him is to think faster and act before he does."

"Like moving his brother?"

"It will buy us more time to figure out what to do about Warrick."

"I say we fry his ass."

She smiled. "And I second that."

Archer kissed her forehead and reached for the shampoo beside her. Adding a generous dollop of soap into his palm, he began to wash her hair. An act so intimate, reserved for lovers. Lovers. He smiled, unable to shake off the euphoria summoned by that thought. Despite the challenges they faced because of it.

"It sucks that your brothers walked in on us," she said.

"Rather this morning than last night."

She laughed, the sound light and tinged with relief. Her expression cleared, and she looked up at him. "Isn't there a small part of you that has any doubts?"

Images of their night together resurfaced and Archer's body hardened in response, a reaction that immediately drew a grin from her as she peered down at him.

Her hand swept across his rippled abdomen, moving lower, until her fingers wrapped around his hard length. "Hm, I'm starting to think that perhaps using the word 'small' around you is way off-base."

"Oh, you're good for my ego." He laughed, slid his fingers into her hair, and pulled her back into the spray of water. Rinsed, he moved closer and kissed her.

"Really?" she asked. "Again?"

He didn't reply and rolled his hips against hers as his arms came up around her, drawing her in.

"Wow, Bennett," she said in a breathy sigh. "I'm not sure if I've had multiple orgasms or simply one long continuous one."

He threw his head back and laughed. "More like a handful and you're definitely good for my ego."

Archer's smile quickly disappeared when he pulled her in for another kiss, his tongue sweeping against hers in wave of flickering sensations that left them both gasping for air.

"Your brothers are waiting," she panted, putting a hand to his chest.

"A few more minutes won't kill."

"But they'll know what we're doing."

"Like I care."

CHAPTER TWENTY-TWO

When Sienna sauntered into the kitchen a while later to find the three brothers seated at the breakfast table, an array of food sprawled in front of them, she was relieved that no one brought up her newest residence in Archer's bed. She should've known they wouldn't say anything. Archer would've issued a firm warning to keep their mouths shut.

But it would probably still come up. Later. For now, she needed the kick that only caffeine could give her.

Tara's voice had Sienna glancing up from the coffee pot. "Tara," she said, trying to keep the wariness out of her tone. She hadn't heard their newest houseguest come in. Tara had changed out of the red cocktail dress from the night before and now wore a neat white work suit that added an angelic appeal to her. And yet, the look Tara had pinned on Sienna was anything but angelic. "I see you brought an overnight bag."

"A girl can never be too prepared."

Tara was sweet and friendly, with a bite, and somehow always managed to send Sienna's instincts flaring. Although Tara had always been friendly with all three brothers and tolerated Sienna simply because she had to, she'd always had her sights on Declan. The obsession was eerie, even though Sienna seldom brought it up. Declan seemed to have fun with her and Tara made him laugh, despite the bitchy comments that rolled off her tongue as though they came with honey.

"I see you're back in the Bennett mansion," Tara said evenly.

"I live here."

The simple statement brought a brief frown to Tara's perfectly made up eyebrows. "And why is that again?"

Sienna almost balked at the rehashing of the familiar dialogue. Apparently, Tara's fascination of Sienna's relationship with the Bennett brothers was an ongoing one. Pouring herself a coffee, she joined them at the table, dropped a kiss on Archer's lips, and sank into the vacant chair.

Tara's eyes narrowed as understanding dawned, and she shifted her gaze to Declan. "As I don't have the luxury of living off my family's fortune like some of us in this room, I have to get to work. At some point, I need to pin you three into a boardroom so we can finalize the details for the upcoming harvest."

"Later. You don't want breakfast?" Declan asked.

Tara shook her head. "I'll grab something at the office. I'll see you tonight?"

Declan didn't reply but stood to walk her out.

Once the kitchen door closed behind them, Ethan chuckled. "It's as if nothing's changed."

Sienna smiled, shaking her head. Despite the underlying competitiveness between them, mostly instigated from Tara, they'd still managed to form a basic level of friendship.

Even if that level was a very basic one.

Declan returned, minus Tara, carrying a rolled-up sheet of paper in his hand. He spread it across the kitchen counter in a quick movement, smoothing strong hands across the paper. The bulky ring he wore on his right hand caught the blaze of sunlight streaming through the window.

"Mixing business with pleasure again?" Sienna asked, grinning at Declan.

He shot her a fleeting glance, a cheeky smile breaking free. "Always."

Smiling, Archer handed Sienna an empty plate, kissed her head, and joined his brother. The affection felt strange, new, the openness of the action bringing an odd sensation that was hard to decipher.

"What are you reading?" she asked, helping herself to a slice of toast. She was ravenous. Go figure.

"The blueprints to the Bennett Estate." Archer jabbed a finger on the paper. "There it is."

"There what is?" Sienna asked.

"One of the old underground storage buildings in the forest on the estate. I knew it was here. I often heard Rose and Mother talking about it."

Sienna gaped at him. "You want to move Mason into our home?"

Archer glanced at her, a small smile hitching his lips. "He won't exactly have guest privileges, Sienna. And I'd hardly call an abandoned storage building in the forest home."

"But still, that's just creepy."

"He'll be underground, locked away, all lonely and desiccated."

"Not to mention spitting daggers at us." She shuddered. "That's one warlock I'd rather not have sleeping anywhere near me."

"Scared?" Declan asked, not bothering to hide his amusement.

"No, just wary. And although I was the one to desiccate and spell Mason, I still find him creepy. Ever seen what a desiccated man looks like? Ugh."

All three brothers laughed and turned back to the drawings.

"So why here?" Sienna asked.

"Because it's dark, underground, and hasn't been used in decades." Ethan traced a finger along the sketch, indicating the area of the underground rooms. "It consists of one room leading into a series of others but as they were never used when our family took over the estate, they became neglected and overgrown. The entrance was eventually destroyed years ago. Even if we knew where to find the entrance, it's probably impossible to penetrate."

"There's a tunnel leading to the room." Archer circled the buildings in a bright red pen and pointed to an underground tunnel. "We once stumbled upon it as kids but were forbidden to ever go inside. It leads from the old well at the river." Archer jabbed a finger to a spot on the opposite side of the river. "This is the abandoned church tomb in the forest where Mason is. There's a bit of distance between his current lodging and his new one, but once we figure out a way to access the tomb and haul Mason's dead-weight ass out of there, we can work our way through the forest along the river and into the tunnels."

Declan nodded in agreement. "No one but our family has access to the forest and the river anymore so moving Mason without being seen should be easy."

They'd put a stop to anyone entering their estate years ago. It had caused a few heated arguments, but the Bennett brothers had stood firm in their decision. After all, it was a decision made to protect their friends in town. With the supernatural elements that often lurked on the Bennett estate, they'd had no choice.

"Do either of you remember the tunnel's location?" Sienna asked as a wave of unease washed over her.

"My memory is sketchy, but the well marks the closest spot so we'll start from there. With any luck, the tunnel's still clear and the rooms are still habitable." Archer smiled at Sienna's grimace. "Don't worry, we'll be with you."

"Doesn't ease the creepiness of the whole idea," Sienna replied and bit into her toast. She flashed an appreciative smile at Ethan, the breakfast he'd made hitting the spot. "So now that we know where to put Mason, how are we going to get him out of the tomb?"

All three brothers turned to look at her, stooped for an answer.

Archer spoke first. "What do you need in order to break the seal on the tomb?"

"I'd need the Grimoire and the stones."

Declan hitched a brow. "And you're sure that breaking the seal on the tomb won't affect the curse on Mason?"

"No," Sienna replied, shaking her head. "We used a separate spell on Mason."

"Both spells you used on Mason that night were powerful ones, Sienna." Archer tossed the pen and straightened. His attempt to keep his expression even would have worked had it not been for the worry that lurked in his eyes. "Are you sure you're strong enough for a spell that powerful?"

Had he asked her that question a week ago, maybe not. But a lot had changed in a week. Warrick's sudden reappearance to Rapid Falls and the threat he stood for had sparked a renewed connection to the elements of nature and a determination to master her powers over them. She still had a lot to learn, but since her return to Rapid Falls, the intensity of her powers had lost the terrifying factor that had kept her from using them.

"I'll be fine, Archer. Rose will be there to help me." Sienna set her mug on the table and turned to face Archer. The mug rolled, unsteady, and toppled over. As it tipped off the table, Ethan was there in a flash that startled her, a hand in place to catch the mug before it shattered on the floor.

Sienna gave him an appreciative smile. In battle, their power of speed was a life-saving essential. In day-to-day life, when it came to simple things like saving a coffee mug, it was a luxury.

Ethan winked at her and handed her the empty mug. "You're sure we wouldn't be able to access the tomb once you and Rose break the seal on the door?"

"Not whilst Mason's still inside," Sienna replied. "It'll still be sealed to us because of our magical connection."

"So do your witchy crap and break the seal so that we can go in," Declan said.

"I can't, Declan. It was a difficult spell with a double seal designed so that it's impenetrable to anyone with magical elements."

Clearly unimpressed, Declan gave a brief shake of the head. "Witches. So fickle and full of nonsense."

"The only one here that's full of nonsense is you, brother," Archer said, smacking Declan on the back of the head. He turned to face Sienna. "So who would be able to enter the tomb?"

"We'd need someone that has no link to the elements of nature. That eliminates all of us."

"We can use Tara," Declan said without emotion.

Sienna tilted her head and looked at Declan, a small smile playing on her lips. "Yes, Declan, I'm sure your lover will happily oblige to entering a creepy tomb to remove an even creepier semi-dead guy from a cement slab."

"Tara's usually quite happy to oblige anything I ask of her."

"So I see by her quick return to your bed."

"Jealous that you're not the only one having fun?"

Sienna smiled. Fun seemed too simple a word to describe what she'd shared with Archer the night before, but she quickly dismissed the thought the moment she felt herself blush. "As fascinated Tara is with your manly charms, I still don't think she'll do this."

"Have you got any other suggestions, witchy?" Declan asked.

Standing, Sienna considered. "Having the Grimoire and the stones together with Mason and Warrick around is very risky." She headed to the coffee machine, her body bristling with a vengeful energy she hadn't felt in years. "If Warrick catches onto what we're up to he'll come at us with guns blazing."

"We'll have to take the necessary precautions to ensure that doesn't happen. Warrick will never suspect that we'd move his brother," Ethan said with a confidence Sienna didn't feel.

Having the Grimoire and the stones – and her – together made it so much easier for Warrick.

Declan slapped his hands together. "I can't wait to see his expression."

Sienna smiled. "Our plan has some flaws but we can make this work. Rose will need to summon the stones."

"And you'd need to bring the old Grimoire out of hiding."

Sienna's stomach twisted at the idea. The book was so treasured, and so valuable to an evil warlock like Warrick. But they'd protect the book at all costs. As they always had.

"I'll go talk to Rose this morning while you guys find out where Warrick's headed," she said, swiping a hand across her forehead. A sudden unease had swept over her, sending her instincts on high alert. Nerves? She reached for the coffee pot. "We need to be…" Sienna paused, swallowed, as heat seared through her body, starting from the centre and spreading its way out, threatening to suffocate her.

Archer rose. "Sienna?"

She shook her head. "We need to be sure that Warrick – oh!" she gasped, dropping the coffee pot. It shattered on the kitchen tiles, hot liquid splashing across the floors and up the cupboards.

All three brothers were beside her before she sank to the floor. Archer scooped her off her feet and away from the glass.

"What's wrong?" he asked, casting a quick glance across her writhing body.

While she gasped for air, she clutched her chest, blinking rapidly. "I can't breathe."

"Sienna!" he yelled, grabbing her chin and forcing her to focus on him. "What's happening?"

Sienna groaned as a powerful heat washed through her in

agonizing waves. She swatted him away, her breaths coming out in choppy gasps of air.

"Sienna!"

She drew in a ragged breath and looked up at the three brothers crowding around her. "It's Lexi," she gasped, fear joining the ranks of the heat already threatening to burn her. "She's channelling me. She's in trouble."

****

Archer pointed at Ethan. "Get them on the phone. It has to be Warrick."

Ethan was already dialling but was quick to curse. "The phone's dead." He dialled the number for Lexi's Keeper and shook his head.

"I can help her," Sienna said softly, drawing in several deep breaths. Her skin, clammy from the heat that still gripped her, was hot to touch.

Archer frowned and reached for the water Declan produced. "Here, drink this."

She did, almost finishing the bottle. Handing it back to him, she grimaced but looked at them. "I can help Lexi. Now that I know it's her, I can allow her to channel my energy. Our combined powers should help her."

"Do you know where she is?"

Sienna didn't answer. Instead, she'd already disappeared into a world created by a mystical magic that only she understood. She'd stopped writhing, although her body was still on fire. Droplets of sweat ran down the side of her face, and Archer grabbed a towel to swipe them away.

"Damn, she's burning up," he grumbled.

"She knows what she's doing."

Sienna closed her eyes, leaning back into the couch. For a brief moment, she relaxed, almost as though she was granting Lexi access, allowing the endangered witch entry into a very deep, very treasured part of her.

They felt the tension escalating, felt the connection. Sienna gripped the sides of the couch, her knuckles whitening with the unruly grip. Her body arched forward and she groaned, and everything inside Archer demanded that he put a stop to her personal torment.

He was all for helping those in need, but watching his woman in such pain was torturous.

"Archer, she's fine," Declan said softly, placing a hand on his brother's shoulder.

He nodded and drew in a choppy breath that came out in a huge sigh of relief when Sienna's eyes suddenly flew open.

"Sienna?"

She blinked rapidly, trying to clear the fog that lurked.

He helped her to sit up and handed her more water. "Are you okay?"

"It worked," Sienna said, her voice croaky and merely a murmur. "They've left but Lexi's in pain and she's alone."

Declan cursed, a clear indication of his hatred for any woman, especially a woman of their kind, to be hurt at the hands of Warrick. Another score to settle. "If she's alone it means they've killed her Keeper."

"If Warrick's killed her Keeper then he has added powers," Sienna warned.

Archer met the cold glare in his brother's eyes. "Go, I've got this."

Declan nodded. "You two iron out our plan to move Mason. Once that's done, we're thrashing out a new plan on how to deal with his delinquent brother. We'll be back as soon as we can."

"The stone," Sienna added. "Don't forget the stone."

"Chances are Warrick has it."

"I don't know. She would have used the stone to channel me. It means she might still have it." Sienna wiped the towel across her clammy forehead. "Please be careful. I don't sense her danger anymore but we have no idea what Warrick's up to."

Seeing her tight frown, the worry etched across her face, Declan stepped forward and pulled Sienna into his arms. "We'll be fine. You did great, Miss Witchy. You're making me think twice about messing with you."

Sienna smiled and watched them go.

"Are you okay?" Archer asked turning her toward him. He sensed the lessening of the tension, the lack of fight, the beginning of exhaustion. A given after a channelling session. Even for a powerful witch like Sienna.

"I'm fine. I need a shower. I'm drenched."

He drew her into his arms and held her. "Declan's right. You did great. You saved Lexi's life."

"But not her Keeper's."

"We don't know that for sure. My brothers will have answers for us soon."

She pulled away and headed for the door. "I'm going to shower and then we need to find Rose."

"While you shower, I'm going to make some calls to warn the other three Keepers and their witches. If Warrick's struck once, it's a given that he'll strike again."

CHAPTER TWENTY-THREE

Rose was ready and waiting for them when they arrived at her cottage. She stood outside, the image of a pentagram drawn in the sand around her. In one hand, she held a tattered book, yellow from age. Her other hand clasped four locks of hair in varying colours and length, hair belonging to the witches who harboured the four precious stones, no doubt. Although Rose appeared calm, worry lined her features.

"Rose?" Archer said softly, careful not to startle her. He'd had enough experience to know that startling a witch during a witchy moment was never a good idea.

"Gran, you've already cast the circle. Were you waiting for us?" Sienna asked, approaching her grandmother. She shouldn't be surprised. Rose had always had a keen sense for when one of their witches were in trouble.

Rose looked up, frowning. "I knew you'd come." Without offering more, she carefully placed the four locks of hair in the centre of the pentagram, handed Archer the book, and held out her hand for her granddaughter. "We need to protect the witches who harbour the stones."

"Lexi's already been attacked."

"I know. But they didn't get her stone."

Rose gestured to the pentagram etched in the sand. Placed strategically within the symbol were all four stones.

Sienna gasped. "You've already summoned the stones?"

Rose nodded. "They're in danger, and you'll need them to open the Grimoire."

How the older witch knew of their discussion over breakfast was anyone's guess.

"Warrick won't know that we have the stones, but he'll still go after the witches who harbour them. Come," Rose said to Sienna, "they're going to need all the help they can get."

"The other three witches are fine, Rose. I've just spoken with them," Archer said.

"Let's keep it that way," Rose said, reaching for Sienna's hands.

Silence fell and Archer stepped back to watch them, familiar with the scene. Together the two witches stood in the centre of the pentagram, holding each other's wrists above the four locks of hair.

For a long while, they stood in complete silence, eyes closed, breathing quietly as they made their connection.

They looked incredible together, a force to be reckoned with. So in control, so focused, so connected and the power that emanated from them was breathtaking.

Their sudden gentle chanting snapped the silence, bringing Archer's attention to the ceremony at hand. He hoped the protection spell worked. He hated the idea of anyone being hurt at the hands of Warrick Brogan, more so if they harboured the four stones that would unlock everything the warlock sought.

The air grew warmer and a gust of wind swept through the trees, whistling softly as it unsettled the peaceful forest.

Fire, Sienna's central power. Strong, if tapped into alone, but lethal if channelled with Rose.

He took a deep breath of dry air, almost coughing at the lack of moisture. Stifling, hot, arid. A contrast to the cool fall air they were used to. With the wind, came more heat, and he glanced at the two witches still quietly chanting over the pentagram.

A moment later, the locks of hair burst into flames on the floor, sizzled for a few seconds and died out, leaving behind the acrid smell of burnt hair.

The two women grew quiet and a moment later, two pairs of eyes flew open.

"It's done," Rose said, piercing Archer with a confident stare.

He nodded and went to them. "We've alerted their Keepers. That and the protection spell should keep them safe."

"Warrick's determined." Rose gathered the four stones and stepped out of the circle. She straightened her arm, and a moment later, the sand shifted, covering the remains of the pentagram.

Never one for leaving signs of witchcraft.

"Gran, come inside, I'll make you some tea," Sienna said, reaching for her grandmother's arm. They went inside together, and Sienna quickly assembled the tea.

The faint aroma of herbs wafted through the kitchen, piercing several memories Archer had of growing up in Rose's kitchen. Her brews and potions had always fascinated him, the power they wielded even more. Large windows overlooked their house in the distance, the massive spans of lawn and forest that separated them. He'd often invited Rose to stay in the house but she'd remained adamant the cottage was her home. He could see why. It was homey, warm, comforting, everything a grandmother's house should feel like.

The older woman looked tired, but less worried. "Lexi might walk without a Keeper."

Another death. Another Keeper. Another witch exposed.

A thought that tugged at all Archer's protective instincts. He nodded at Rose. "We don't know that yet, Rose. My brothers will call as soon as they get to Lexi."

Something shifted inside Archer, cold and determined. Warrick Brogan's days of funfairs and candyfloss were over. He'd been marked the moment he'd killed Sarah. Now Lexi and her Keeper.

They had a score to settle and settle it they would.

He just hoped like hell that he'd be able to protect Sienna in the process.

Archer glanced at Sienna as she poured tea for her grandmother and filled her in on the plan to move Mason. She wore her hair pulled back into a ponytail, a style that scraped years off her age and lessened the impact of her fiery red hair. She'd opted for skin-tight jeans, long black boots, and a suede black jacket pulled over an olive green t-shirt. She looked elegant and graceful as she slipped into the vacant seat beside Rose. It was hard to reconcile the tiny woman in front of him with the power he knew she was capable of.

"Lifting the seal on Mason's current tomb will take a lot of strength and power but together we could do it," Rose said.

"Are you sure you can both pull this off without either one being hurt in the process? It's a powerful spell." Archer felt the irritated glare shot his way but he ignored Sienna.

"We'll be fine, Archer," Rose said with a half smile. "We witches aren't as feeble as you think."

Archer had never considered either of the Beckham witches as feeble. No, that word was the complete opposite of what they stood for. "We still have to figure out how to get Mason out. Neither of us will be able to enter the tomb."

Sienna grimaced at the idea of moving a desiccated man, and Archer smiled. The final image of Mason had haunted her since the day they'd spelled him.

"What about Declan's suggestion about using Tara?"

"You shot Declan down with that idea," Archer said. "Why the change of heart?"

"Lack of options. She doesn't usually like to get involved with anything magical but she'd do it if Declan asked her to."

Rose fell quiet, mulling over her tea. A moment later, she looked up. "It's a full moon tomorrow. We can draw energy from the moon, which will help us lift the spell. Once the door's open, Tara can get in, get him out, and we can move him to his new lodgings." She smirked, holding up her teacup in mock salute. "It may not be the Ritz but it'll do."

****

Sienna flashed Archer a satisfied grin when the lock on the door to the tunnel burst open. If the map to the Bennett estate was accurate, the old storage rooms waited at the end of the gloomy tunnel. Standing back, she watched as Archer shoved the door open.

"All these years we've lived here, explored these forests as children, and only once stumbled upon the entrance to the tunnel," Sienna said.

"Our parents probably had something to do with that."

Finding the entrance to the tunnel had been a challenge, as it hadn't been used in years. Overgrown and hidden, perfect for their quest to keep Mason hidden during transit, but creepy nonetheless.

She winced at the dark, gloomy tunnel, and wrinkled her nose at the musty smell. It had been sealed for years, starved of air, and home to God knows which type of creatures.

Archer scanned her expression and smiled. "Frightened?"

Yes. "No. More like not in the mood to have an army of Incy Wincies crawling on me."

"You're happy to fight off warlocks and warriors yet you're afraid of a few spiders?"

"They might be hungry. Or hairy." She couldn't think which was worse. She shuddered, and Archer chuckled. "Don't laugh at me."

"You're such a girl."

"I am a girl. Now do your man thing and go check the tunnel."

"You're not coming with me?"

Sienna nibbled her bottom lip, eyeing the tunnel, the cobwebs, and the darkness that went on forever in the distance. "No. I'll wait out here."

Archer smiled, drawing her closer. "My fierce warrior witch is afraid of spiders."

"And dark, gloomy tunnels that haven't been used for decades. Besides, with your super speed power thingy, you can be in and out of the tunnel in a flash. I, on the other hand, move at the pace of a normal person."

"There's nothing normal about you, Sienna."

He tilted her chin, and she had no choice but to look at him. Despite the humour reflected in his eyes, he gave off a heated intensity that stirred an instant butterfly sensation in her stomach. The man practically gave off sparks. "You're beautiful – even when you're scared," Archer said, a sexy grin playing on his lips. His hands slid up her arms, into her neck, and dark green eyes shifted with amusement.

Sienna drew in a deep breath, all too aware of the inner tingly sensations that were far too distracting. How he managed to stir such a wicked, delicious awareness in her in the same conversation as spiders was anyone's guess.

"Yeah, yeah. Stop delaying the inevitable."

He kissed her softly, silencing her weak attempt to cover her fear, and Sienna sighed against his lips, savouring the sweet moment.

Pulling back, Sienna held out a hand toward the tunnel. A moment later, several lanterns that hung from rusty nails in the roof lit up in a steady stream of candlelight.

Archer shot her a smile that made her heart lurch. "Thanks,

witchy."

"I'll wait for you here."

"You'll be okay?"

"Just peachy."

"Call out if you need me."

With another quick kiss planted on unsuspecting lips, he flashed her another smile and entered the tunnel.

Sienna watched him retreat into the tunnel. All confidence and strength. He cocked his head in her direction, gave her a final wink, and vanished. Something stirred inside, and she smiled.

Her man. Her warrior.

As though to mock her back into reality, a small black spider came sailing down its web spun from the roof at the entrance to the tunnel. Sienna stepped back, unable to suppress the slight shudder. Ugh.

Turning around, Sienna crossed the dry scatterings of twigs and leaves, her feet crunching against the floor debris, and made her way to the edge of the river. Her gaze travelled along the gentle ripples of water that resembled a mirror reflecting a forest of trees in the distance. The silence comforted rather than unnerved her, and Sienna settled beside a cluster of rocks at the edge of the water, enjoying the tranquillity. It was hard to reconcile the peace she found here with the craziness her life had become in the last few days. When taking in the breathtaking beauty around her, it was impossible to believe that warlocks, warriors and other supernatural creatures lurked nearby, searching for every opportunity to wreak havoc. It was something that they constantly lived with. Their worries and battles were so different from the ordinary humans surrounding them and Sienna had often wondered what it would be like to be one of them.

To worry about simple, everyday things as opposed to fending off power-hungry, greedy warlocks and their warriors.

With a soft sigh, her head fell back against the rock and she closed her eyes, enjoying the sunlight on her face, the sound of the water gently lapping in the nearby distance, and the absolute stillness of nature. A rustle of leaves sent a ripple of warning through Sienna and she opened her eyes, unmoving. She listened, her senses in prime form.

More rustling, more movement, followed by the sickening realization that she wasn't alone. Archer? No one else knew they were here. Sienna slowly inched onto her feet, careful to remain hidden and silent. Peering around the rocks, she looked for signs of her visitor. When silence greeted her pounding heart, she blew out air. It must have been one of the many forest animals that called the forest home.

A soft, low growl above her had her freezing, the quiet sound sending a shiver of warning jolting down her spine. She drew in a level breath of air, needing a moment to settle the bolt of panic taking hold of her gut.

Slowly, not to alarm her visitor, Sienna looked up. Her breath caught as she saw the large wolf standing on the rock above her. Grey coat of fur, black eyes, and white canines flashed behind upturned lips. He growled again, perched, ready to pounce if she moved.

Oh, God.

Black eyes met green ones in a moment of unspoken challenge that had her heart rearing with warning. The eyes of a wolf that spelled everything evil.

Archer. Archer!

He'd sense her danger, be quick to get to her, but she knew that one pounce and the wolf would be on her.

A second growl behind her had Sienna reeling around. Horror struck another chord within her when she saw two more wolves circling her. Where'd they come from? She hadn't even heard their approach.

Knowing her fight would be a hopeless one, she drew on the energy brewing within, reaching for the only part of her she knew would keep her alive. Her powers.

A deep, scary emptiness greeted her and she drew in a deep breath as weakness washed over her. Panic rose, fought with her grasp on composure, and she glanced frantically at each wolf. And then the realization hit her. First a cold trickle of fear that quickly turned into raw horror as she saw the small brown bags neatly tied around each wolf's neck.

Ashwood.

A powerful herb that bound a witch's powers. Not often used or well-known, but clearly whoever had sent the wolves after her knew all about Ashwood and the effect it would have on a witch. They also knew that the only way to activate the debilitating actions of the dreadful herb was to place it in a triangular form around a witch.

A shape the wolves had mastered.

A perfect ambush.

CHAPTER TWENTY-FOUR

Everything inside Archer had him on full alert, his powers ripe, his senses sharp. And one look at Sienna, surrounded by three snarling wolves, only fuelled the strength that exuded from him.

It didn't take him long to figure out that the wolves weren't simply on a hunt for their next meal. The brown bags tied around their necks and the perfect triangle they formed around the witch sent everything reeling into place.

They'd been sent for her.

Powers depleted, Sienna dragged in air and almost choked when she sensed Archer's arrival. Wide eyes flashing with fear settled on his, and he could see by the quick rise and fall of her shoulders that she was terrified. He approached slowly; careful, wary. Not the sudden charge at full steam his protective instincts demanded. But he knew an ambush when he saw one, and he also knew better than to startle a pack of wolves in attack mode.

"Stay calm, Sienna," he murmured.

"They've bound my powers," she whispered, staring at the wolf closest to her.

The wolf reacted by snarling at her, a fierce sound that made Sienna flinch.

"It's okay. I'll get you out of this."

Almost as though they sensed they were about to be challenged, the wolves took a determined step closer, enclosing their prey. Their soft growls simultaneously turned into loud snarls, each one taking random turns to snap their warning at her.

"Sienna, don't move," Archer said softly, eyeing the wolves, his mind scrambling for a defence attack.

The sight of Sienna, surrounded by the animals, tore at him and he drew on his powers, needing the calm, the strength they would bring.

Knowing he had no choice, Archer charged.

In a flash of dust, vicious blood-curling growls, and a horrified scream from Sienna, Archer reached her, yanking her away from the fierce jaws that sought her out. With a speed that fuelled the excited wolves, he grabbed Sienna and bolted into the river.

The wolves snarled, set chase, the water slowing them down, but their attack mode had been triggered and everything about them spelled determination as they charged their prey.

Holding onto Sienna, he leapt out of the water and sped to a nearby rockery. A few more leaps put enough distance between them and Archer slowed down to check if Sienna was hurt.

They were both panting, drenched, adrenaline working every nerve they had. Archer quickly ran his hands across her face, her shoulders, checking for injuries.

"I'm fine," she gasped, peering over his shoulder. "I'm okay."

Her body shook and a fierce jolt of anger tore through Archer in response. They'd made a move on his witch. Again. With a damn pack of wolves!

Fire sparked inside, and Archer dragged her into his arms. "I'm sorry," he panted, kissing her head. "I'm so sorry."

"I'm okay."

Before he could respond, his head jerked up. In the distance, silent to Sienna, he heard the wolves' ragged breathing as they tracked their prey.

He grabbed Sienna's hand and started running, scanning their surroundings for a safe place for her. He eyed a huge rock formation that nudged the edge of the river and aimed for it, keeping a firm grasp on the frightened witch.

The wolves drew closer, their fierce snarls growing more excited as they sensed their prey nearby.

Archer saw the wolf leaping off a passing rock before it reached them and clutching Sienna, he tried to leap from its vicious grip.

The wolf connected with them, unbalancing them, and they all hurled to the ground in a tumble of screams, growls, and a rough curse.

Sensing the upper hand, all three wolves pounced.

****

Sienna scrambled away from the fight, gasping furiously for the air that evaded her. Her back hit a wall of rocks and she struggled to her feet, keeping her body against the protection of the rocks behind her.

Her entire body shook at the sight of Archer fighting off the wolves, snarling, snapping, biting, with all the strength he possessed.

A warrior in action, all his defensive impulses activated.

Dust rose up to surround them as fists and jaws fought a battle that left her breathless.

One of the wolves gave a piercing whine as Archer punched its jaw with enough force to send it reeling against a nearby tree. The other two wolves kept coming, determined to subdue him. Almost in sync, the remaining two wolves circled Archer once before charging him simultaneously.

But Archer was faster and grabbed each wolf by the back of

their heads, banging them together with such hatred and force that both wolves yelped in response. The brief moment of stunned silence gave Archer a chance to attack each wolf separately. In a flash, he pounced, snapping their necks as though they were poor unsuspecting bunnies.

With a warlike cry, Archer shoved their limp bodies off him and straightened.

Sienna watched as he stormed to the third wolf, still at the foot of the tree. He yanked off the bag of Ashwood and tossed it before shoving his hand against the wolf's throat. His eyes narrowed, and he cursed before snapping its neck in a swift movement that signalled the end of the attack.

A sob escaped Sienna before she could rein it in, and her hands flew to her mouth. She shook so violently, her legs unable to support her, and she slowly sank to the floor.

Archer was beside her before she hit the ground. "It's okay. It's over. They can't hurt you."

"Oh, my God," she choked, clinging to his torn shirt. Her fingers touched something cold and thick and she pulled back, wincing at the sticky blood she found. "You're bleeding."

"I'm fine." Strong hands encircled her face, and he quickly scanned her for injuries. "Are you okay?"

"Yes, but you're hurt, Archer."

"I'll be fine."

She pulled back, still trembling, and shifted the sleeve of his shirt aside. A deep, ugly slash on his arm oozed blood and her heart sank as she realized he'd been hurt protecting her. Again. "You've been bitten."

"I'm okay, Sienna. It'll heal soon enough." He glanced at the oozing gash, grimacing at the pain. "Sienna, Warrick sent them."

Her eyes rounded in disbelief. "Wolves? How?"

"I don't know. But I sensed his presence all over them when I touched them. The Ashwood, the ambush. All Warrick."

She sighed, closing her eyes. "He's stronger than we thought."

Archer rose, pulling her with him. "Let's get you home."

"Archer."

Her words had him pausing mid stride. Turning to face her, his dark hypnotic gaze took her in.

"Thank you," she whispered.

A small smile made his lips curl but quickly vanished as he pulled her into his arms, enveloping her in an embrace so tight, so fierce, that she could barely breathe.

A moment later, he drew back to peer into her eyes. "I will always protect you, Sienna."

She nodded, not trusting herself to speak, her throat constricted with a relief and emotion she couldn't express.

He kissed her forehead and took her hand, leading her home to the safety that awaited them.

CHAPTER TWENTY-FIVE

Archer pocketed his phone and glanced at his watch. It was late and his brothers were due back soon. Lexi and her Keeper were safe – injured, exhausted, but safe. Another witch and Keeper triumph. The thought brought a fierce bolt of pride to Archer, and a satisfied smile hitched the corners of his lips. His brothers' arrival would spark an entire series of conversations, and he was eager for their return, but for now, he needed Sienna. Grabbing the bottle of wine and two glasses on the kitchen counter, he went in search of her.

Dismissing the images of her surrounded by the vicious wolves was proving to be more difficult than he'd hoped, and every time he thought of the danger she'd been in, and how deliberate the attack had been, his gut clenched with renewed fury. He was itching for the return of his brothers so they could set the plan in motion for moving Mason and trapping Warrick.

The Brogan brothers had had their turn of evil and outright threats. Now it was time to return the favour.

Archer pushed open the bathroom door, blew out a deep breath to calm the anger that came with all thoughts of the warlocks, and settled his gaze on Sienna.

The lights were out, the room was illuminated with the comforting glow of candlelight. Sienna lay in the massive bath, her damp hair tied in a loose knot at the top of her head, her entire body immersed in the soapy water.

The image of her relaxed, safe, at peace, was such a raw conflict to the mental onslaught of the images of her attack.

Her eyes fluttered open, and she smiled when she saw him. "How's your arm?"

"Better." It had hurt like hell and taken longer than usual to heal, a thought that troubled him, but the wound had finally stopped bleeding. He'd cleaned it, covered it with a bandage, and hadn't given it much more thought until now.

"Have you spoken to your brothers?"

Archer nodded and went to her. Handing her the wine, he leaned over to kiss her lips. Curvy, soft, and full of promises of later. She took the wine and flashed him a breathtaking smile, a gesture that immediately relieved some of the tension that riddled him.

"How's Lexi?"

"They're both fine. Bruised, angry, but they're both safe." Archer sat on the edge of the bath and ran a finger along her jaw. "They targeted her Keeper, but he fought them off."

Damn right.

"We almost lost another Keeper, Archer. It's all my fault."

Although her voice was steady, it hinted at the sadness that lurked inside her, and his abdomen tightened in response. Archer set his glass on the basin and took her by the back of her neck, lowering his face so she could see how serious he was. "Sienna, none of this is anyone's fault. The only one responsible for all this violence is Warrick Brogan."

"Warrick warned me he'd go after the Keepers. I just never thought he'd dare."

"And we'll retaliate, avenge Sarah's death, and prevent him from hurting anyone else." Anger tinged his words, and he fought to regain an even tone. He stripped off his clothes, dropping the jeans and t-shirt in a pile on the floor, and slipped into the bath behind her. She shifted to make room for him and immediately leaned back against his chest, drawing his arms around her.

She sighed, a soft sound in the silence of the bathroom that drew at his gut. "No amount of vengeance will ever bring back our family. It will be a relief to witness Warrick's downfall, but it will only be a band-aid on the pain he's caused us."

"I know, but a wound with a band-aid is better than an open wound."

"I wonder if we'll ever know what really happened the night of the fire."

Archer frowned at the stark reminder of their parents, kissed her head, and tightened his grip around her. "I think if there were answers surrounding that night, we'd have found them by now."

"It's the anniversary of their deaths next week."

"I know."

"Does it ever get easier?"

"The longing?"

"Yes."

"Probably not, Sienna."

"I wonder if we'll ever be free of this."

"Free of what?"

Using both hands, she drew his scarred arm toward her and gently brushed her fingers along the disfigured skin. She laced her fingers with his, drawing his hand to her lips to kiss him softly. "Warrick," she said, lowering his arm. "Warrick and everything he stands for."

"We'll take down Warrick."

Words said with such conviction, and he almost shivered with the thought of it. He could hardly wait.

She reached for his other arm, touching the large white patch that covered the bite wound on his arm. "But what then? Will it truly be over, or will there be others like him? Is this the way we'll always live – constantly looking over our shoulders, afraid for ourselves, afraid for each other?"

It was a grim thought, one he'd often considered. "Our life is a risky one but this is who we are, Sienna, and I think the only way we can grasp any sort of a normal life is to snatch the moments where we can. Moments like this." Archer trailed a finger along the gentle curve of her hips. He tilted her head so he could kiss her. Their lingering kiss altered the course of their conversation, offering a respite from the gloom of their day.

"I think I need more of these moments," she sighed.

"I'm happy to oblige. No more talk of doom and gloom or anything Warrick," Archer said softly, his hands moving up her sleek curves to capture the perky, slippery breasts hidden beneath the bubbles. There'd been enough fear and fury for one night. For now, he needed this beautiful woman in a way that would chase away all thoughts of the war to come.

She closed her eyes, dropping her head back against his chest, and sighed. This time, the sound resembled more contentment than sadness.

He toyed with her nipples, nibbled her ear, and eventually captured her mouth with his in a gentle kiss that promised her more. She responded by shifting her body against him, tilting her head so that he could draw her in for a full kiss, hot, real, needy.

Fire sparked and she arched into him, needing more than he gave her. His hand left her breasts to continue the same onslaught of pleasure between her legs. Her thighs parted in the water, giving him all the access he needed.

Her body jolted in his arms when he touched the very core of her, and she cried out against his lips as he slipped a finger inside her.

"I can't get enough of you," he said, sweeping a tongue against hers. His voice was raspy, thick with desire, and his thoughts scattered as she quivered in his arms.

He shifted his hand, returning to the sensitive nub between her folds, drawing a soft sigh from the woman writhing in the water.

Her body tightened in anticipation of what was to come and trembled as he increased his pace. She threw her head back as she came, her body a rumble of jerky movements as she convulsed in his arms, crying out softly from the wave of pleasure.

He growled softly at her release, sounding like a caged animal, and quickly rose, drawing her with him.

"I need you," he whispered, flipping her around so that she faced the bathroom wall. He reached for both her hands, placing them against the wall, holding her there. His head dipped toward her, teeth nipped against the flesh he found there, and he rolled his hips against hers.

She gasped as he pushed inside her, cried out as he filled her body, her heart.

"You're mine," he told her, leaning over her, releasing her hands to take hold of her hips. He started his rhythmic pumping into her, slowly at first, but the urgency that rocked between them, her throaty cries, had him quickening his pace. Within moments, he was slamming into her, the slapping sound of their skin mingling with her soft moans. The erotic sound sent him soaring and his fingers gripped into her flesh, keeping her in place.

He felt her come again, her soft cry echoing through the steamy bathroom, and he quickly followed with his own release, groaning softly into her neck.

Moments later, breathing heavily, he withdrew, breaking their connection, and turned her to face him.

He wasn't done with her yet.

Covering her mouth with his, he kissed her.

When Sienna opened her eyes the following morning to find herself alone in Archer's huge bed, she wasn't surprised. Her warrior hadn't slept well, despite the eventful night they'd had. Although she'd eventually fallen asleep in the early hours of the morning, she'd sensed his restlessness, the worry that gnawed at him.

All thanks to Warrick.

Lifting herself onto her elbows, she winced as parts of her ached in places that hadn't ached in a very long time. Memories of another night spent in Archer's bed came to mind and she closed her eyes to ward off the explicit images. The things he'd done to her – and the way she'd reacted.

Wow.

And now reality loomed like a great big shark about to swallow her whole. Sienna threw back the white sheet, tangled to within an inch of its life. Not surprising considering the bedroom Olympics they'd shared during the night. The whole night. She felt the blush creep across her cheeks and groaned. She needed a shower, and not because she'd spent the night having hot, sweaty, toe-curling sex. No, she needed the comfort the water would offer.

She went into the bathroom and ran a hot shower, her mind spinning with their plan to move Mason today. A full moon meant it was ripe for all sorts of supernatural events and although the beauty of the moon always fascinated her, it brought its own eeriness.

She felt better once she'd showered, and she quickly dressed in jeans and a white shirt. She pulled a brush through her hair, leaving it loose around her shoulders, grabbed her jacket and scarf, and went in search of her Keepers.

She found them on the patio, mulling through their plans for the day over coffee and a heated conversation. They'd all showered, dressed, and wore fierce expressions that warned her they were brewing for a fight.

And about time too. If anything would bring some relief around Sarah's death, it would be avenging it and ending the life of the man who'd murdered her.

The day was clear and bright, a contrast to the gloom that surrounded them, and everything looked sharper. The sky was a clear aqua blue that matched the glistening pool at the foot of the stairs. Levi lay in the sun on the blanket of thick, lush green grass, looking lost in the huge spans of lawn. No doubt, she was far more relaxed than her owners were.

Archer saw Sienna first and stood. He went to her, reached for the scarf in her hands, and wrapped it around her neck before drawing her closer to kiss her. He smelt of soap and man, a scent that quickly stirred fresh memories of their night together. "Sleep well?" His green eyes remained serious, but a smile eased his expression.

"Better than you. So, have you three devised the plan to take over the world?"

"Just about. We could use some of your witchy expertise."

She nodded and joined the other two men at the table. Archer appeared beside her, a mug of fresh coffee in hand. As he handed her the mug, the sleeve of his shirt shifted, exposing the bandaged bite wound. She reached out, taking his arm in her hands. "You're still bandaged."

Archer quickly withdrew. "I'm fine."

Alarm prickled down her spine, and she shifted her gaze to his. "It hasn't healed yet? Why hasn't it healed yet?"

Declan's hand shot out, grabbing his brother's arm. He pulled back the sleeve to look at the white bandage. "You were bitten?"

Archer shrugged him off and pulled his sleeve over the wound. "It's healing. I'm fine."

"It should have healed by now, brother."

"It has."

"Archer!" Sienna said.

"I said I'm fine!"

Sienna sat back in her seat, watching him. The wound should have healed. Her stomach rolled at the idea that he was still hurting and she looked at him, wanting to say more but knowing from the steely look in his eyes and the tension in his shoulders that he'd already dismissed the topic. She sighed and looked at Declan. "Have you spoken to Lexi today?"

"They're both fine," Declan answered, keeping his gaze pinned on Archer. "The surprise of the attack has worn off and given way to anger. They're both spitting mad and ready for a fight should we need help."

The thought brought some comfort to Sienna. It was always nice to know they weren't alone in their quest to keep evil in check. Never underestimate the bonds of the witch world. Hurt one, hurt them all. Same with the Keepers.

"It was fortunate that Rose summoned the stone before Warrick got his hands on it," Ethan said. "According to Lexi, Warrick was in full swing yesterday with his newfound powers."

"Sarah's powers," Declan said through clenched teeth. The idea that the warlock was using Sarah's powers stung and Declan's eyes clouded with something sharp.

"It still doesn't explain how he managed to control the wolves yesterday."

Sienna released a breath of air at the curt reminder of the attack. "He knows about Ashwood."

Ethan cocked a brow. "Where did he even find Ashwood? I thought the stuff was impossible to find."

"Warrick seems to have too many resources for my liking. As I'm not about to be wolf food, I'd really appreciate it if you guys can kick his ass once and for all."

"We're moving Mason tonight," Archer said, his voice clipped with anger. "And once that's done, we're going after Warrick. He won't know that we've moved his brother so we have that advantage."

Sienna brightened. "Then we could lure him back to the empty tomb with a fake offer of peace and the return of his brother."

"Once he's inside the tomb, Sienna could perform the same spell on him that she did on Mason," Declan added.

Archer frowned. "He'd never fall for that."

"He's desperate to get his brother back. Maybe he will."

"He might be gullible enough to believe it if I approach him alone," Sienna said, preparing herself for the onslaught of objections. She wasn't wrong and she saw all three Keepers grow instantly restless with frustration. She held out a hand to silence them. "Hear me out before you all go King Kong on me. Warrick approached me wanting to make the deal that I free his brother, they both leave town, and no one gets hurt. I'll make him the offer to free his brother in return for exactly that."

"So the plan is to lure him to the tomb, thinking you're about to unspell his brother, but instead you spell him," Archer said, looking at Sienna.

"It's a simple plan but I think it'll work."

"Providing he falls for it. And what about his warriors?"

"I'll make the condition that we meet alone, no warriors."

"You're not meeting him alone, Sienna."

"Fine, then you three can lurk in the background where he can't see you. You'll know if I need you."

"You could get hurt. The attack on Lexi, the wolves, it just shows that Warrick's unstable and brewing with all sorts of evil antics of his own. I don't trust him."

"Of course not, but what other choice do we have? He's the one who made this offer in the first place. If I'd listened to him, neither Lexi nor her Keeper would have been hurt. The car accident, the wolves. It's only going to get worse from here."

"But Warrick has Sarah's elemental power," Declan said. "Won't that keep him from entering the tomb?"

Sienna shook her head. "The spell that keeps us out of the tomb only holds if Mason's still in the tomb. Once he's out of the tomb, the spell will be broken."

"We need to bring out the Grimoire," Ethan said, watching Levi as she sauntered up the stairs toward them. He held out a hand and stroked the dog, that promptly collapsed into a sighing heap on the floor beside his feet.

"Archer and I will fetch the book today," Sienna replied, immediately uneasy at the thought of uncovering her precious Grimoire.

"Sienna can make contact with Warrick as soon as we've moved Mason," Archer said with a grim expression.

Although not happy, there were nods of agreement all round.

Declan rose first and looked at Sienna. "Fine. Fetch your witchy book. Ethan and I will fetch Rose and her stones, and we'll all meet back here. Once it's dark, we'll go for Mason."

The air prickled with a sense of excited energy and revenge. Everything that had transpired since the night of Sarah's death, the hurt, the pain, the sadness, and everything that had happened since Sienna's return to Rapid Falls a few days ago, all culminated in one thing. Warrick.

And tonight, if everything went as planned, karma would whip around and bite Warrick in the ass.

Damn right.

CHAPTER TWENTY-SIX

Sienna hugged the Grimoire to her chest, a flash of pride mingling with the unease that came with having the book exposed. But it was inevitable if they were going to move Mason. The moment he was in his new lodgings, she'd have the book back in its hiding place.

She held the book to her nose and drew on the musty scent of years of knowledge, legends, spells, and potions. Every Beckham witch in her family had added to the book over the years, and the book was bursting at the seams within its leather binder. Running a finger along the pentagram symbol that bound the book closed, she smiled. Life as a Beckham witch may have its challenges, but she couldn't deny the fierce sense of honour that came with the title.

A Beckham witch. And according to Rose, she was *the* Beckham witch, whatever that meant. She still refused to explain her reasons for transferring all her powers onto Sienna – according to Rose, she would find out when the time was appropriate.

Sienna fingered the four stones in her pocket that were the key to opening the book and made her way to the kitchen, hoping to have a moment alone. As a child, the book had been one of her favourites and she'd often spent many hours paging through it with her mother. She hadn't touched it in two years and seeing it again now stirred up so many memories.

Her breath caught when she spotted her Keepers through the kitchen window. They were outside on the lawn, each of them standing in their own quiet stance around the pool. Knees apart and slightly bent, arms up, facing each other. They were all dressed in white cotton pants, all shirtless, rippled muscles glistening in the sunlight.

Wow.

She made her way onto the patio, pausing at the top of stairs to watch her Keepers. Without their shirts, their legacy and identity was clearly visible, the mark of a Keeper boldly sketched across their tanned flesh. Archer's tattoo had been crafted across his left shoulder, Declan had opted for the tattoo to be drawn on his back between his shoulder blades, and Ethan wore his tattoo on his right arm.

Their feet rooted to the ground, their arms and upper bodies followed a series of flowing movements, slow, controlled and in perfect harmony with each other. They looked so strong, so powerful, and she gaped at them in fascination.

Individually, they were striking. Together, they were breathtaking. A total force to be reckoned with.

The subtle brush of air across Sienna's skin hinted at a sudden change in weather. Sienna folded her arms to ward off the chill, and watched the three brothers in awe. Moments later, the bright sunshine disappeared as grey clouds began rolling across the sky with gloomy intentions, casting a dark shadow across the estate. The wind picked up momentum, and the weather turned dark and eerie. The low rumble of thunder echoed in the distance, rolling closer, and seconds later, a flash of lightning lit up the sky.

Ethan.

Sienna watched in fascination as Declan reared up, taking advantage of the flash of lightning to create a spark that he quickly assembled into a ball of fire by using a series of controlled hand movements. He sent the fireball soaring through the sky where it exploded into a flash of sparks, reminding Sienna of fireworks. Another ball of fire followed in quick succession and within seconds, there were sparks flying everywhere.

Fascinating, but a scary sight for someone not used to their powers.

Sienna smiled, in awe of the magic at work, but her smile quickly vanished when several bushes surrounding the pool area caught alight. Fuelled by the windstorm Ethan had created, the bushes went up in flames almost immediately.

"Archer!" Declan snapped, breaking his trance-like position and whirled to face his brother.

Sienna frowned, immediately zeroing in on Archer who seemed oblivious to the burning bushes. He still maintained his own position, arms outstretched, staring at the water in the pool. His eyebrows were drawn together in a deep, intense frown, his expression coloured with a darkness that had Sienna sucking in air.

The water in the pool bubbled, as though someone had flicked a Jacuzzi switch.

"Archer, put the damn fire out!" Ethan yelled, snapping out of his own trance and straightening. With the change of his movement, the wind lessened and the lightning stopped. The clouds began thinning, giving way to the sunlight.

Another bush caught alight and Sienna felt everything inside her clench. Nervous, uncertain, Sienna stepped forward, calling Archer's name.

But he remained focused on the water, muttering softly to himself.

Sienna placed the Grimoire on a nearby table and bolted down the stairs, a rumble of energy herself. She drew on her powers, focusing on the bubbling pool, the pull of the water stronger than ever. With several flowing arm movements, she sent three water lashes directly to the burning bushes, dousing the flames instantly.

The smell of smoke immediately permeated the air, along with the eerie realization that something was way off.

"What the hell, Archer?" Declan called from across the pool, staring at his brother as though he'd lost his mind.

Archer stepped back, breaking form, and cursed loudly before turning around and storming toward the house. A thunderous expression clouded his features and fury raged through dark green eyes.

"Archer, what happened?" she asked as he brushed past her and pounded up the stairs.

"Nothing," he snapped without looking back. "I lost focus, that's all."

****

Something was wrong.

Archer stormed into the bathroom, trying to shake off the worry that tore at him. He felt strange, different, and he shook his head, hoping to deny the truth that gnawed at his gut, mocking him, taunting him to face his worse nightmare.

He peeled back the sleeve of his shirt and unravelled the white bandage wrapped around the wound on his arm. A wound that hadn't yet healed.

What the hell?

Archer frowned, grimacing at the bite wound. He'd often been hurt, always felt the pain, but the war wounds had always healed quickly and without scars. A perk that came with his title, his destiny, of being a Keeper.

A perk that seemed to be fading.

Archer flexed his hand, refusing to admit the truth. His powers were all he had to protect Sienna. His witch. His woman. Without them, he was still strong and agile, but when facing anything Warrick and keeping Sienna safe, he needed all the advantage he had.

How could his powers be fading? He'd never heard of a Keeper losing his powers, not unless someone had bound him, stripped him. And with the battle looming ahead of them, he needed his strength and powers more than ever.

And the wound hurt like hell.

"Your expression resembles something out of a sinus headache commercial, brother."

Archer glanced in the mirror and scowled when he saw Declan standing in the doorway behind him. Damn, he hadn't even heard his brother's approach.

Declan's gaze shifted to Archer's exposed wound that drew an instant tightening of brows. "You're hurting?"

"No."

"Bullshit. Why hasn't it healed?"

Archer clenched his jaw, refusing to voice the truth. He looked away, not needing to see the worry reflected in his brother's eyes, and quickly shoved his sleeve back in place.

"Archer, what's wrong?"

Archer stepped back when Declan moved forward, yanking his arm out of reach. "Nothing. I'm fine."

"So you keep saying but we both know you have a wolf bite on your arm that's not healing." Declan reached for him again. "Don't be a jack-ass, Archer."

Archer shoved his brother away and stalked out the bathroom, Declan hot on his heels. He should've known his brother wouldn't let it go.

"I'm all for bravery and crap, Archer, but defeating Warrick and his men will take a lot more than Sienna's magic."

"Don't underestimate Sienna's magic, Declan. We saw the night

Sarah died how vicious she can be if crossed. She'll handle Warrick."

"True, but once Sienna has entombed Warrick, we're the ones left facing his army of unhappy warriors."

"Since when does combat of any sort scare you?"

"Since I'm not sure my brother's being entirely honest with me."

Their eyes met in a fierce stare, tension prickling between them as they both faced a truth that would unsettle everything they knew.

"I told you, I'm fine," Archer said, anger dripping from his words.

"Archer, if you're not at the top of your game, it would be nice to have a little heads up."

"You're being an ass, Declan."

"Am I Archer? I'm just forcing you to face the truth so man the fuck up and do that."

Archer spun around, colliding with Declan, and slammed a hand against his brother's chest. "Back off, brother."

Declan scowled, his eyes honing sharply on his brother. Without saying a word, his hand shot out to grab Archer's wrist. Unflinching and with steely determination to prove his point, Declan tightened his grip.

Archer tried to break free, usually an easy reflex, but he struggled to break his brother's hold. "Declan, cut it out."

He didn't. Instead, Declan stepped closer, his fingers digging into Archer's flesh.

"Come on, Archer, admit that something's wrong."

"Screw you, Declan!" Archer snapped, bringing up his free arm and taking a swing at his brother. His fist connected with a force that had Declan reeling back, breaking the firm hold.

Declan stumbled backward, steadied himself with a rapid speed, and stared at his brother. He stroked his jaw, his mouth opening and closing as he flexed the pummelled muscles. "You just hit me."

"I said back off."

Doing the exact opposite, Declan charged, grabbing Archer around the waist and pushing forward. Archer soared backward from the impact, crashing into the wall. With a grunt, Archer swung his fist, connecting with his brother's cheek. Declan returned the favour and in a flash of irate curses, swinging fists, and unresolved brotherly frustration, the two brothers communicated with an effectiveness that didn't involve words.

But the fight was uneven. A novelty for them and an eerie revelation at that.

Ethan arrived in a speedy blur and a string of curses. He wedged himself between the two brothers, quickly separating them into neutral corners. "What are you two fighting about?"

Both panting and cursing, Declan was the first to step back. He dragged a hand across his bleeding mouth and pinned Archer with a furious glare.

He pointed to Archer's arm. "Still want to spew me some crap-assed bullshit about that bite wound being nothing? Because that's what it is, Archer. Bullshit. Our wounds heal faster than Warrick can say the word 'warlock'. That wolf bit you last night and you're still hurting."

Ethan looked at Archer, his gaze flickering to the loose sleeve that covered the wound. "What's Declan talking about, Archer?"

"Tell him," Declan prompted. "Tell him that your powers have weakened since the bite."

Ethan raised an eyebrow. "He didn't look weak to me when he was pummelling your head in, Declan."

Archer levelled Declan with a hostile look, seething with a rage that threatened to consume him. The wolf bite and the weakening of his powers had nothing to do with Declan, but damn him for being right. He dragged in an aggravated breath and looked at Ethan. "The bite hasn't healed yet."

"And your strength? The rest of your abilities?"

"Still there but weakening." It slammed everything inside him to hear the words aloud, and he fought not to flinch at the reality of what he'd just said.

A heavy silence hung between them as they all absorbed the impact of his words.

"Don't say anything to Sienna," Archer murmured, dragging a hand across his face. He sighed, cursed, and turned to the window.

"Archer, it may be the bite from the wolf," Ethan said, "but taking your recent shift of gears in your relationship with Sienna into account, have you considered that this might also be a bad-assed punishment from The Circle?"

Ethan's words sent a bolt of hot fury through Archer, and he slowly turned to face his brothers. Of course. The Circle. But really? Would they really put one of their own in danger by stripping her protector, her Keeper, of powers needed to keep her safe? If that was the case then they were in a whole new realm of selfishness.

Declan marched into the bathroom and returned with a wet towel pressed to his bleeding lip. "So what does this mean?"

Scowling, Archer stormed toward the door. "I'm going to see Rose. We're still going through with our plans tonight and if either of you spill a word of this to Sienna, I'll have your ass in a sling before either of you can blink."

"Yes, brother," Declan replied with a fake smile. "May I remind you that you're the one with a glitch in his power supply?"

"You're an ass, Declan."

"I'm trying to help you!" Declan called after him, but Archer ignored the final comment and raced down the stairs.

If anyone had answers for him, it would be Rose.

And dammit, he needed answers.

CHAPTER TWENTY-SEVEN

It was finally over.

Or at least, the first part of their plan was. They'd broken the spell that kept the seal of the tomb in place.

Now came the creepy part.

Rose broke away, releasing Sienna's hands, and wiped her brow. The spell had been easier this time, surprising them both.

"Are you okay?" Archer asked, approaching the two witches.

They both nodded, their attention on Declan and Ethan who were in the process of moving the heavy stone door that sealed the tomb, that sealed Mason.

The four lanterns placed around the tiny room outside the tomb offered some relief from the darkness around them. The roof was low; the room made of sandy floors and stone walls, still blackened from the fire Sienna had created the night Sarah had died. The stuffiness and warmth of the room brought a light layer of perspiration to them all. The air was stifling, the acrid smell of burnt hair making it almost impossible to breath. In the centre of the room, a small fire had already started fizzling out. The Grimoire, surrounded by the four precious stones, lay on the ground beside Rose. The mood was sombre, tension dripping from the walls, and Sienna knew it would remain that way until they'd safely relocated Mason.

Their plan was a risky one, but essential to buy them time and leverage.

Archer joined his brothers and together, grunting, they slowly shifted the rock slab to one side until a huge black hole gaped back at them.

A shiver raced down Sienna's spine and she forced all thoughts of what they'd find in the tomb to the back of her mind. Mason's fate had been a cruel one, but he'd caused enough pain and death to so many innocent people that their decision to desiccate and entomb him had been an easy one.

It was still eerie, though.

Both Ethan and Declan turned to look at Archer, a moment of heavy silence passing between them.

Sienna frowned, her instincts flickering. "Archer?"

Without replying, Archer stepped toward the dark doorway, dragged in a quiet breath, and went inside.

"Archer!" Sienna gasped, rushing to the door.

Declan and Ethan drew her back in an instant. She tried to slap them away, but they kept a firm grip on her, her efforts useless against their strength.

"Sienna," Declan said, stepping around her so that he faced her.

"How did he do that? How could he go inside?" She tried to keep the panic out of her voice, but confusion shook her words. Only someone without any elemental powers could enter the tomb. Their hasty decision to leave Tara out of their plans for tonight suddenly made sense. They'd known all along that Archer would be the one to enter the tomb.

Worry escalated to anger, and she pinned Declan with a fierce glare. "What are you keeping from me? How the hell did Archer get into that damn tomb?"

"Sienna," Declan said softly, his tone sending a fresh shiver of panic through her. "Archer's been stripped of his powers."

She gasped. "What? All of them?"

"His Keeper powers are still there but slightly weaker. He's lost his connection to the water. That's why he couldn't douse the fire at the pool."

"His elemental power? How? What happened?" She spun around to face Ethan, Rose. "Did you know about this?"

The old woman didn't reply, didn't have to. Sienna saw the raw truth in her striking green eyes and the sadness etched on her face.

Sienna gaped at her. "You knew about this and didn't tell me? How could you keep this from me?"

"Archer didn't want you to know, Sienna," Ethan said, his expression matching his brother's.

"But how did this happen? And why now?" Her gaze flickered from those of her Keepers and settled on her grandmother's as understanding dawned. Her skin prickled with the realization, and her abdomen tightened as the air whooshed out of her lungs in a swift blow. "Oh, my God. It's The Circle, isn't it? They're responsible for this?"

Declan spoke first, reaching for her arm. "We're not sure."

"Sienna, you knew there'd be consequences," Rose said softly, stepping closer. She reached for Sienna's hand, enclosing it within her own. "I didn't realize that things had escalated so far. I always knew The Circle would object to your relationship with Archer. I just didn't realize how strong that objection would be. According to Lora, they're spitting mad."

"They're punishing us? Are they mad?" She tried to keep the hysteric hitch out of her voice, but failed. The idea that Archer had lost his elemental power because they'd fallen in love was absurd. "In weakening Archer, they've put us all at risk. They've weakened me!"

Before either of them could respond, Archer appeared in the

doorway, dragging a long wooden box that contained Mason's lifeless body. A thin layer of perspiration covered Archer's face and arms, and he breathed heavily from the heat of the room and the exertion that came with hefting Mason through the tunnel of the tomb. He didn't flinch when his brothers went to help him but was quick to shift the weight more evenly. Together, they replaced the heavy rock slab across the doorway and moved to the exit.

Sienna stared at Archer, her entire world shaking around her. She'd done this to him. This was all her fault. "Archer?"

Declan whipped her a warning glare that immediately silenced her. "Not now, Sienna. Not now."

Sienna opened her mouth to object but her three Keepers were already moving through the low door at the back of the room. She looked at Rose, wanting to cry, reaching for strength and any explanation.

And found none.

"Gran?"

Rose gathered the four stones and reached for Sienna's hand. "Come, child. Let's deal with Mason first and then we'll contact Lora. If anything, she'll know what to do."

Lora, the messenger of The Circle. Right now, Sienna wasn't sure if she wanted to listen to anything The Circle had to say to her, but she knew that if Archer was ever going to regain his elemental power, she'd have to suck it up and take their rulings.

But she knew what they'd want, and the thought tore through her like a wild wind on a stormy night. Her heart sank, and she shut her eyes in a feeble attempt to block out the truth.

Yes, she knew exactly what The Circle was after.

****

Sienna knew.

Archer punched a nearby tree, felt the pain that came with the blow, but ignored it.

She hadn't said anything since leaving the tomb and had remained focused on the spell that sealed the entrance of the old storage building, but Archer could see from the heaviness of her shoulders and the worry reflected in her eyes, that she knew.

Damn it.

He loathed the idea of admitting to her that he'd weakened, knew the conversation was imminent, but it would have to wait for later.

Hearing a soft rustle of leaves above him, Archer glanced up at the tall trees that loomed overhead. An owl hooted softly, the sound echoing in the quiet darkness of the night. He'd left the lanterns inside the storage rooms, needing the blackness to cloak his thoughts as he waited quietly outside for his brothers and the witches.

Their plan had gone smoothly and Mason now had a new home, sealed with a spell that would keep him locked inside. And the best part of it all was that Warrick Brogan had no idea where his brother was.

The thought brought a satisfied smirk to Archer's face that quickly disappeared when Sienna came out of the tunnel. The lantern she carried illuminated her features, masking her in a glow of warmth. She was sombre, quiet, and hot from the airless rooms. Her clothes were dirty, her hair pulled back into a thick ponytail, exhaustion splashed across her features.

She looked up at the moon as she exited the tunnel and took in a deep breath of fresh night air. A luxury after the staleness of the underground.

"Everything okay?" Archer asked quietly and she nodded. He went to her, pulling her into his arms. "You did great."

"Rose and your brothers are gathering the Grimoire and the

stones. They'll be out now."

"Everything went well. Better than planned."

Wide eyes swung back at him and her eyebrows drew together in a tight frown. "Why didn't you tell me, Archer?"

He sighed softly, stroking her chin with his thumb. "Not now, Sienna. We'll discuss this later."

"You should've told me."

"It's not an easy thing to say aloud and I haven't even processed the impact of what this means."

"It's all my fault."

Her words surprised him, and he scowled at her. "I wanted this as much as you, if not more. This is a choice we made together."

"But you're the one who's suffering because of it."

"You're the one needing protection."

"You'll always be my Keeper, Archer."

"That'll never change."

Her shoulders dropped and she looked at the ground between them. "If you're ever going to get your powers back, we can't be together anymore."

"Sienna."

"It's over between us, Archer. It has to be."

"I know," he whispered, closing his eyes. His insides twisted uncomfortably and he pulled her into his arms.

She fell silent, holding onto him with an urgency that left him raw. The peace he felt when he held her, knowing she was his, contradicted his fear of losing her. He closed his eyes to savour the moment as he always did when he held her. Their life was a risky one, filled with threats and worries unbeknown to normal people. Everything could change in an instant. They'd learned that many times over the years.

Archer kissed her head, taking a deep appreciative breath of the woman in his arms. Right now, she was here. Still his.

And the idea that she might not be because of the damn Circle made him want to punch something again.

The sound of footsteps at the entrance of the tunnel had them breaking apart.

Rose came out first, drawing in a deep gasp of fresh air that was quickly replicated by her two Keepers as they stepped outside directly behind her.

The underground rooms had been torture for them all.

Archer went to Rose, took her hand, and helped her down the steps. Her movements were slower, her eyes weary, and her lips drawn together in a thin line. All testament to the fatigue that had taken hold of her. A powerful witch, scary to most, but her ageing body felt the strain that came with the magic. "Everything okay, Rose?"

"Nothing a scotch won't fix."

Her words broke the tension that rippled between them, and they all smiled.

The route home along the river was an easy one, relief etching the tones of their quiet conversations. They'd moved Mason, concluding part one of their plan. The relief that came with that was huge, despite their mutual worry about Archer's loss of his elemental power.

It was only when Ethan, walking up ahead, stopped moving and cocked his head in the distance of the forest, that alarm prickled.

"Kill the torches," Ethan said through gritted teeth. A moment later, complete darkness surrounded them. The full moon offered some light but with the huge trees overhead, it was minimal.

"Ethan?" Archer said, joining his brother. Everything about the way Ethan stood, staring straight ahead with a harsh frown, spelled trouble. "What is it?"

Declan was beside them in an instant. "Levi's barking."

A sound Archer would normally have heard too. A string of curses went through his mind, but he bit down from spewing them.

Ethan shot them a worried glance. "They're here."

"Archer, what's wrong?" Sienna asked, coming up behind him.

Neither of them answered and they stared straight ahead, their ears pinned to the noises surrounding them, their bodies switching to defence mode.

To Archer, the forest appeared silent and at peace, but to his warrior brothers, the darkness of the night spelled an impending war. Frustration, anger, and adrenaline gripped him and Archer glanced back at the two women.

He may not have all his powers but he was still their Keeper, a warrior, and there was no way he'd let anyone hurt them.

Hell no.

"You think they've spotted us?" Archer asked.

Ethan nodded. "They're surrounding us."

"They've brought the wolves," Declan added, his voice a low grumble of anger in the silence of the night.

"We have to assume they've brought Ashwood so the witches won't be able to use their powers if they're caught in position." Archer looked at each of his brothers, a moment of intense understanding crossing between them. "We have to split the women."

The idea of separating was a thought that sent the tension soaring. But they had no choice. If the wolves, the Ashwood, surrounded either witch, the other witch would still have use of her magic and powers.

And knowing the evil and hatred that spurred on their attackers, they'd need all the help they could muster.

Ethan shifted, looking at Archer. "You and Declan take Sienna. I'll take Rose."

"Fine. But we can't take them home," Archer said. "They'll only follow."

"So what's your plan, brother?"

"They're moving into place to set up an ambush. We're going to return the favour. Only, we're going to be smarter."

CHAPTER TWENTY-EIGHT

Sienna was grateful for the darkness of the forest as it hid her fear and the trembling of her hands. Everything had gone so well and they'd pulled off their plan without any hitches. She should've known that in their world, there was no such thing as a flawless plan and that evil always lurked around them, nipping at their heels like an irate dog.

She worried about Rose, her insides twisting with anger at the thought of her ageing grandmother in the middle of the woods about to be wolf food.

Not that Ethan would let that happen. Her grandmother should be asleep in bed, having spent the night drinking her beloved scotch and watching old reruns of The Golden Girls, not traipsing through the woods with a pack of wolves and God knows what else hot on her tail.

Her Keepers' presence brought Sienna some comfort and she drew on that to settle her nerves. Tension and anger radiated off them in a power of its own, and she glanced at them with a mixture of pride and worry.

They'd fight to their deaths to protect their witches. A destiny they never resented, a duty they saw as an honour. And she loved them all so much. The thought of losing another Keeper ripped at a part of her she constantly fought to keep buried.

The initial peace of the forest had whipped around to blanket them in a fear and attack mode that had both her Keepers on the full alert. Although it was dark, she saw glimpses of their fierce expressions through the moonlight filtering through the rooftop of huge trees above them. Muscular. All man. All warrior. It was a scary sight, impressive, and it took her breath away.

An eerie silence enveloped them as they walked toward their attackers. The sound of their feet softly crunching on the blanket of forest debris on the ground echoed through the quiet that surrounded them, the sound ridiculously loud in the stillness of the forest.

A flutter of wings in a nearby tree had them all whirling around defensively. An owl set flight, aiming for the ground. With expert grace and ease, he snatched a running mouse and disappeared into the darkness. An unpleasant reminder of where they were and what they were about to do.

Hopefully their fate would fare better than the mouse's.

A shiver ran down Sienna's spine, and she shook her head to shake the gloom. Not that it was remotely possible considering they had wolves and warriors nearby.

Declan halted, his head cocked to one side. "They've found Ethan and Rose," he whispered, his words barely audible. "They're at the bridge."

"We should hurry," Archer said, taking Sienna's hand and moving forward.

The tension escalated the closer they got to Rose and Ethan, the sound of water gushing between mossy rocks becoming louder with their approach.

They reached the valley between the two forests, separated by the river below, and nestled down amongst a blanket of thick fern bushes. A perfect camouflage. Tall trees, stripped of their bark from years of age, lined the edge of the forest on either side of the rocky valley, hovering high above the water. An old wooden and metal bridge hung from one side of the valley to the other and Ethan and Rose stood in the middle of the bridge. Part of their plan, a risky one at that, but one that would hopefully work. Gathered in a huddle of hatred on the opposite side of the bridge stood Warrick and his warriors, carrying burning torches, two wolves behind them.

Fury reached a level Sienna had never felt before. Her powers churned inside her, mingling alongside the rage and threatening the shaky control she had begun to master over her magic. Never a good mix, but this was Rose and Ethan, and she didn't care about keeping her magic in check. Not tonight.

And no doubt, their attackers carried Ashwood. Clearly their new weapon of choice.

"Easy, Sienna," Archer said softly, reeling her in.

She ached to charge, to annihilate everyone in her way until she had her grandmother and Ethan out of harm's way. Judging by the way her Keepers bristled with restless energy beside her; she wasn't the only one with thoughts of revenge.

Rose stood behind Ethan, the wooden railing of the rickety bridge against her back. Despite her age and the Ashwood, there wasn't a hint of fear in her expression. Her grandmother had always known their Keepers would protect them. That, combined with the magic and the power they possessed, was currently brewing a dangerous concoction inside Sienna, ready to explode.

Sienna drew in a deep breath of air and control, paused to shift her focus where it mattered most, and slowly exhaled.

"Where's the rest of your merry little gang of powerhouses?" Warrick yelled out to Ethan, his tone laced with more mockery than amusement.

"They went home." Ethan replied. Even though his voice was calm, level, his body was rigid in preparation of the inevitable attack.

Warrick turned, scanning the area. "Leaving you two alone? Right."

Although they were hidden in the thick blanket of ferns that surrounded them, and basked in darkness, Sienna still had the urge to shrink back.

"Your warrior skills must be waning, Bennett," Warrick goaded. "I'd have thought you would have smelt us from a mile back."

"Although the stench of evil desperation should've hit me, sniffing has never been my forte, Warrick," Ethan retorted.

"Evil desperation? Is that what you call this?"

"Why else would you mess with the Beckham witches? You know the wrath they can dish out."

"You know I'd do anything to free my brother."

"And you know we'd do anything to stop you."

Warrick held out a hand, focused on a pile of rocks beside him. With a brief flick of the wrist, a few rocks went hurtling through the air toward Ethan.

Senses in top form, Ethan stepped in front of Rose, shielding her body with his, and flung out his arm. A gust of wind followed suit, connecting with the rocks and sending them off course. To show his disapproval, he sent another gust of wind toward Warrick and his warriors.

Several of their torches blew out from the wind, darkness enclosing them in one quick gulp. Without much light, there were several yells of confusion that sparked a series of loud snaps from the two wolves.

Ethan grabbed Rose and bolted to the opposite side of the bridge.

Sensing their escape, the warriors set chase, their heavy boots scraping against the wooden bridge. Several shouts filled the air, warrior calls that unsettled the peace of the forest.

Just as Ethan and Rose reached the end of the bridge, he took a large leap into the forest.

Declan rose up from the shelter of the ferns, staring at the bridge with an intensity that came whenever he channelled his powers.

The bridge began to shake, followed by panicked shouts as the warriors realized they'd run into a trap. There was a frantic collision of bodies as they all tried to get off the bridge before it collapsed.

Not waiting for that to happen, Declan stepped forward, channelling more power, more anger. The bridge groaned under the pressure of his powers and slowly began to crumble as the metal bolts and nuts gave way to the intense onslaught of heat. It was an eerie picture of destruction and desperation, the warriors shuffling with frantic speed to get to the edges where safety existed.

But Declan was too quick for them. The bridge folded, collapsing with a crunching of metal, sending a dozen of Warrick's warriors plunging into the water below. Their screams echoed through the darkness, muffled by the sound of the bridge crashing against the rocks.

Sienna heard the whiz of the retaliating arrow past her ears seconds before it slammed into Archer's chest. He stumbled to the ground with a soft groan. In quick succession, several arrows followed from all directions, shattering the darkness with panic.

In a swift movement, Declan flung himself toward her, shielding her body as they tumbled into the ferns. The air whooshed out of her lungs from the impact, and she gasped air.

"Declan!"

"Stay down. They know we're here."

"Where's Rose?"

Declan glanced over his shoulder, his heartbeat thumping a

frantic rhythm against her chest. "I can't see her but Ethan won't let anything happen to her." He swung around, crushing Sienna with his weight, and tracked Archer. "Archer! Are you hurt?"

"I'm fine," Archer replied, his voice low and tinged with a soft wheeze.

"Stay there, brother. I'll come for you."

"I'm fine, dammit. Stay with Sienna."

"I've got Sienna," Declan said, doing a quick scan of the area in an attempt to track their enemies.

But Warrick had doused the rest of their torches, using the darkness to his advantage. The blackness had swallowed their enemies, and they had no way of knowing which direction the attack was coming from. The eerie sound of the howling wolves tore through the sudden silence that had engulfed them.

"Declan, I can't breathe," Sienna said, slapping his chest. She gulped air, unable to breath from Declan's weight on top of her. He shifted his weight, looking back at her.

"We have to stop them," she said.

"Their arrows are lethal, Sienna, and we don't know where their archers are hiding."

"We can take them down. You know we can. We're more powerful than them."

"How the hell are we supposed to defeat them if we can't even see them?" Declan glanced around, spotted the several large rocks overgrown with bushes nearby. It was the perfect respite from the danger that lurked. "I'm going to help you get to those rocks. You stay hidden; stay safe until I come back for you." He shifted his weight, preparing to move. "We're going to run on the count of three."

A batch of arrows, this time alight with flames, came hurtling through the air, landing on the ground around them. A fern bush went up in flames beside Archer, and Sienna gasped at the sight of all the blood on him.

"Archer!" she screeched softly, panic taking a vicious grip.

"Sienna!" Declan snapped, tipping her chin back to his. "I can't help Archer until I have you out of the aim of the damn arrows. We don't know if Warrick has men on this side of the river too so we have to act fast."

She nodded, struggling to regain her composure. "On the count of three."

His nod of agreement was brief, and he quickly started counting.

On the count of three, in the quick pause between the next batch of arrows, Declan pulled her to her feet. Holding her, he raced for the rocks, moving so fast that Sienna's head rattled.

Their attackers set off another batch of burning arrows. Declan spun around, shielding Sienna's body with his own, and flung out an arm, diverting the flaming arrows with ease. He grabbed her hand and took the last few steps into the safety of the rocks.

"Are you okay?" he asked, quickly scanning her body for injuries.

"I'm fine. I can take care of myself. Go."

"They're not after us, Sienna. They're after you. Stay here until I come for you."

"I will. Go!"

Declan vanished as another batch of flaming arrows tore through the air. Keeping hidden, Sienna scanned the horizon, frowning when all she found was blackness.

A rustle in the bushes had her whirling around, relief flooding her as Ethan tumbled into the rocky shelter with Rose in his arms. They were both panting and Sienna raced to them, reaching for Rose.

"Gran, are you okay?"

"She's hurt," Ethan said breathlessly, lowering Rose to the ground.

Sienna sank to her knees beside her grandmother, a new realm of fear taking a firm hold of her. Rose appeared exhausted, bloody, and dirty, the night having taken a toll on her. "What happened?"

"She was struck by an arrow, but it's a shallow wound. She'll be fine." He swung around and headed for the forest. "See what you can do for Rose. I'm going for Archer."

Ethan disappeared and Sienna turned to her grandmother. She moved Rose's hand away to examine the wound, the smell of fresh blood making her stomach roll. If it weren't for the raw adrenaline that coursed through her, numbing her senses, she would've gagged. The lack of light prevented her from seeing much, but her fingers fumbled along the wound, stopping when they brushed against the remains of the arrow stuck in her shoulder.

"Ethan snapped off most of it. You have to pull out the rest," Rose grunted.

"Gran."

"Do it, Sienna."

She did, cringing at the sucking sound the wound made as she withdrew the arrow from Rose's flesh. She tossed the offensive weapon and quickly ripped a piece of material from the hem of Rose's skirt. Rose reached for the material and placed it against the bleeding wound with a grimace.

"I'm so sorry, Gran," Sienna said, covering Rose's hand with hers. "We'll get you home soon, I promise."

"I'm fine, Sienna. Really, it wasn't deep. Had Ethan not pushed me out of the way when he had, it would have been a different outcome. Some healing herbs and a wound dressing and I'll be fine."

"There's so much blood."

"Typical of a superficial wound. Where's Declan and Archer?"

Sienna's head shot up to peer at the opening of the rocks. The fire had taken hold of several plants and bushes, the burning blaze providing enough light for them to see. The crackling of forest debris hissed through the forest, adding a fresh bout of panic.

She heard Ethan shouting Archer's name and frowned when he returned. Alone.

"Where's Archer?" she asked, scanning the area behind Ethan.

"I can't find him." His words came out through gritted teeth.

"What do you mean? Where is he?"

"He must have gone for cover."

"He'd never leave me, Ethan. And he has an arrow in his chest. Where is he?"

"I don't know!" He knelt beside Rose. "You okay, Rose?"

"Yes. Sienna removed the last of the arrow."

Declan's arrival had Sienna and Ethan whirling around on high alert, defences primed. "It's okay," he said quickly, sensing the defensive attack. "It's me."

Sienna glanced behind him. The fires still burned but the onslaught of arrows had stopped and silence had rolled through the forest. "Are they –?"

"The archers are dead. Warrick and his warriors have gone. Where's Archer?" Declan asked, scanning the area around them. "He wasn't where I left him."

Ethan grunted, straightened. "Archer's gone, Declan. I went back for him but he wasn't there."

Declan spun around to face Ethan, his eyebrows drawing together in a tight frown as understanding dawned. "He would never leave. They must have taken him."

Ethan shoved himself forward. "We should be able to track them."

"Stay with the women," Declan said and disappeared in a flash. He did a quick sweep of the area and returned with a grim expression. "No sign of them. They probably used the river. Let's get Rose and Sienna home."

Sienna's chest tightened as though Declan had struck her. She flew toward him, gripping his arm. "You can't just leave Archer, Declan. We have to find him."

"Rose is hurt and we have no clue where Archer is, Sienna," Declan said.

"They have him. They'll hurt him."

"Archer can handle himself."

"They will hurt him!"

"They won't kill him, Sienna. The only reason they took him is to use him as a bargaining tool to make you more pliable."

"So we'll do it. We'll do whatever they want."

"No."

"Declan, he's your brother!" Sienna gasped, as his words sank in. "We have to find him."

"Don't you think I know that, Sienna?" he snapped, gripping her shoulders.

"He needs us. His powers have weakened. He's hurt."

"I know."

"You know what they will do to him. We have to get him out, Declan."

"I know, Sienna."

"Declan, Warrick will –"

"Sienna, I know!" he shouted, tightening his hold on her. She gasped at the force of his grip, a strength he seldom used on her. Declan was quick to reign in his temper, and his expression softened as his hands came up to cup her cheeks. "Sienna, I get it. He's my brother. Trust me when I say that everything inside of me wants to charge ahead and find him, but I don't know where to look for him. Rose is hurt and we're under attack. Our first priority is getting you and Rose to safety. We don't know how many warriors are still out there. We're no use to Archer if we're all dead. Safety first, then we'll look for Archer. We'll find him, I promise."

Sienna nodded, trying to get a grip on the panic that tore through her. Her insides twisted at the thought of Archer at Warrick's mercy, but Declan was right. They had no idea what other dangers lay in waiting for them.

Her gaze flickered to Rose who leaned against a rock for support, one hand clutching her injured shoulder. Through the soft glow of the dying flames behind her, Sienna could see the red blood that covered Rose's hand.

Anger soared, and she averted her gaze to Declan. "Warrick will be in contact, Declan. You know what he's going to ask me."

He gave her a brief nod. "No matter what he threatens, there's no way in hell you're going to release his brother, Sienna. We always knew that Warrick was the lesser evil of the two and if Mason's ever freed, he's going to be out for vengeance and won't give a rat's ass who gets hurt in the process."

"Sienna," Rose said, straightening. "Declan's right. Releasing Mason would mean unleashing an ocean of evil upon this town."

"And sacrificing Archer in order to keep Mason entombed is okay?" Sienna said through clenched teeth.

"No, but you're duty bound to maintain the balance of nature. Setting Mason free would unsettle that balance."

"Killing Archer would do the same."

"We'll find Archer another way – one that doesn't involve freeing Mason. Your involvement with Archer has dampened your senses, Sienna. Deep down, you know what the right thing to do is."

"I am not sacrificing Archer!" she snapped, hating the fact that they were all right. Nausea took over and she pushed Declan away, needing space from his intense gaze, and the heated rage that oozed from every pore. Drawing on anger to steady her composure, Sienna went to Rose and slipped an arm around her shoulders. "Let's get you home. We'll figure this out once we've stopped the bleeding."

Declan caught her free wrist, swinging her around to look at him. "Promise me you won't do anything stupid, Sienna."

"Hell no."

CHAPTER TWENTY-NINE

Sienna didn't look back as she closed the front door of the mansion. She turned off her phone and slipped it into her pocket. Ethan and Declan were with Rose, patching her wound. With some proper lighting and a gentle clean, the wound seemed less fierce. Her flesh was torn, and she'd swallowed a few painkillers for the pain, but Sienna figured that with Ethan's careful stitching, Rose's concoction of magical herbs, and some much needed sleep, Rose would be fine.

Without making a sound, Sienna pushed Declan's motorcycle to the end of the driveway, ignoring the surge of energy needed for the effort. Anger and worry fuelled her strength and pushing a heavy motorcycle down a long driveway so she wouldn't be heard when the engine started, was of little importance to her.

All that mattered now that Rose was safe and on the mend was that Archer came home.

The engine of the Harley Davidson roared to life and shoving on Declan's helmet, Sienna climbed onto the bike and took off with a vengeful fury churning inside.

Their parents and one of her Keepers were dead, the other injured, all of them tortured.

It had to stop.

And she was the one to do it. After all, everything Warrick was after ended with her.

She made the quick trip to Warrick's mansion with ease and parked the bike directly outside his front door. Her days of hiding and coming through back doors were over.

Storming up the steps, she stared at the warrior on duty who immediately stepped forward to stop her. Sienna cursed and swung out her hand, fingers spread, delivering a quick, debilitating mind blast to the man who threatened to sound the alarm of her arrival.

He dropped to his knees with a groan, and she went to stand in front of him. He slumped toward her and she stepped back, not bothering to check if he was still breathing.

Hell no. He supported Warrick, fed on Warrick's evil crap, and that was enough for her. Any man on Warrick's team was in the path of her wrath tonight.

They'd all crossed her and she was itching to dig into the powers she'd been keeping on a tight leash.

Until now.

The front doors burst open from the intensity of her determined, vicious glare, and she stormed into the foyer of the house. Sienna flicked a glance at the expensive marble tiles, extravagant chandelier, and the enormous staircase, the stench of money fuelling her anger.

Two more men came rushing to stop her, but another blast of mental energy sent them to their knees with a loud groan. The three men who followed were quick to hold back once they'd witnessed her ability.

"Where's Warrick?" she demanded, the tone in her voice sounding foreign to her own ears.

One of the men pointed toward the pool deck and Sienna followed suit, not waiting for an invitation.

Warrick stood on his immaculate patio beside a rectangular

pool, barefoot, dressed in jeans and a long sleeve shirt. He had a drink in his hand and an amused expression on his face, looking far too relaxed after the stunts he'd pulled tonight.

"Where the hell is Archer?" she demanded, walking right up to him and slapping the drink out of his hand. The glass shattered against the ground, his drink splattering across the paving.

He wasn't surprised to see her. No doubt, he'd been expecting her. "Easy, Sienna. You're in my territory now," Warrick warned, his tone edged with a defensive hitch.

"Considering how you've stomped all over my territory, you don't know the meaning of the word."

"Your sidekicks aren't too far behind you, I presume?"

"No. I came alone."

"Really?" He lifted an eyebrow, a brief smile making his lips twist. "That makes for a refreshing change. I'm not sure whether I admire your gutsiness or question your stupidity."

"You'd better be careful with name calling, Warrick. After all, I am a witch."

"Oh, I haven't forgotten. I'm simply curious as to why you think you can challenge me alone."

"Need I remind you what I'm capable of?"

"We both know your powers are sketchy, Sienna. And what's the use of a witch having such strong powers when she's too afraid to use them?"

"You killed Sarah, sent us spiralling into the river, went after the witch who harbours the Beckham stone, you've taken Archer, and you hurt Rose. My list of paybacks has grown to mammoth proportions so you might want to stop antagonizing me."

"Bad me," he said with a sarcastic drawl. "It appears I've been a busy boy."

"All you've done is rile me up, and trust me when I say that emotions fuel a witch's powers."

"I'm not scared of you, Sienna."

"Yes, we established that the night of your party." Images of the fear splashed across his face as she set fire to his study came to mind and she didn't bother hiding the smug grin. She turned off the fake smile instantly and narrowed her eyes. "Where is Archer?"

"He's…rather tied up at the moment."

Sienna stared at the warlock's face, as her energy began to rumble through her, violent and frantic as though it had no choice but to flow outwards. A rustling of nearby trees at the bottom of the well-lit garden hinted at her anger. A rush of air rippled through the trees as a gentle gust that quickly grew stronger, gathering into a small whirlwind.

"Where's Archer?" she repeated, keeping her gaze pinned to Warrick's face, her concentration on the whirlwind hovering at the edge of his garden.

"A slight weather hitch won't deter me, Sienna." Warrick glanced at the whirlwind and smiled. "In fact, I dare you to show me what you have. We both –"

The sudden onslaught of harsh wind swept away the last of his words and he blinked rapidly, a brief flash of surprise replacing his cocky smile.

The wind grew stronger, the whirlwind gathering speed across the lawn, increasing in its size and intensity so fast that it quickly formed a small, but powerful tornado.

Keeping them pinned in the centre of its wrath, the tornado wrapped around Warrick's house with such force that the wide-eyed warlock stepped back. Several of his warriors tried to rush to his assistance, but the wind prevented them from moving forward.

Sienna drew on more energy, more strength, empowered by revenge and hatred for the man in front of her who'd done every-thing in his power to destroy them. Fuelled by her rage, the tornado wrapped around the house faster and more powerfully, lifting everything in its wake. Garden furniture, pot plants, rocks, and bushes were pulled into the circle of madness around the house, gathering momentum with reckless speed.

Glass shattered, roof tiles were ripped away from the roof, and everything that could be lifted was thrown into the air.

"Sienna, stop it!" Warrick yelled, grabbing her shoulders.

"Where's Archer?" she shouted back, her voice barely audible above the noise of the wind. "You bring me Archer, and I'll stop."

"Fine."

"Now, Warrick."

"Then stop, dammit!"

Just like that, the wind stopped, and everything circling the house mid-air came crashing down around them. Warrick's garden, his house, was trashed.

Damn right.

"Bring me Archer," she said to the stunned men.

Warrick nodded at one of his warriors who went inside, returning a moment later with a small, flat screen. Warrick glanced at the image on the screen, grunted, and held it out to Sienna.

The image served as a powerful punch to her gut, and she fought for composure.

They had tied Archer with ropes around his wrist and he hung mid-air in a dark, gloomy room. Blood gushed from the arrow wound in his chest and several other injuries they'd given him.

"What the hell have you done to him?" Sienna threw the screen at Warrick and charged forward.

Warrick caught the screen with one hand and held up the other to fend her off. "Easy, Sienna. One word from me and they'll kill him."

"Killing him would start a war you would never want, Warrick."

"All I want is my brother."

"I can't do that. Your brother is more evil than all you warlocks added together. Setting him free would unleash an evil upon us that would hurt many innocent lives."

"My brother deserves to be free and I deserve to have the powers that were mine. You and your grandmother had no right to strip us of either."

Sienna stepped forward, jutting out her chin in quiet confidence. "We had every right, Warrick. We are Beckham witches, designed to keep everything pure and good about the world intact. You and your brother stand against everything we believe in. Had you used your powers for the greater good, we'd never have interfered!"

"This time, Sienna, you're the one who can huff and puff all you want, but we both know that you'd never sacrifice Archer's life to keep my brother entombed."

His words of truth whipped at her control but she kept her gaze on him, unflinching. Warrick showed her the screen again, the image of Archer striking her where he knew it would.

Hurt, injured, bleeding.

He nudged the screen at her. "Undo the spell, and I'll give you Archer."

"Give me Archer, and I'll undo the spell."

"Ah, so we're at a stalemate."

"I have no guarantee that you won't kill Archer once I've freed Mason."

"You have my word."

"Your word is as good as the word of a chipmunk, Warrick. You either bring Archer to me or you say good bye to any chance you have of seeing your brother again."

"Fine," Warrick snapped, tossing the screen to the man closest to him. "But Archer's not here."

"Then take me to him."

"Meet me at the tomb where my brother is, and I'll bring Archer."

Sienna nodded, although everything inside her rebelled at the idea. "And your warriors?"

"They go where I go."

"Hell no. If I'm going alone, so are you, Warrick." She gave him a final glare and pushed past him, knocking her shoulder against his. "I'll see you in an hour. Come alone, or I go home. And that includes your damn wolves."

He flashed her a wicked grin. "You've met my wolves?"

"They had your stench all over them."

"Nifty trick I picked up last year. Pity Archer had to kill three of them."

"A given considering they were after me."

"Ah, your White Knights are forever at your service."

"Of course. One hour, Warrick. No warriors, no wolves. And bring Archer." With a final glare, Sienna turned around and stormed out the door.

CHAPTER THIRTY

Sienna paused as she reached the clearing in the forest that housed the old church tomb. Old rocky steps led the way to a cement platform, once a popular place for rituals and ceremonies. Now it was abandoned and falling apart. Lining the back of the platform was a huge rock formation, overgrown with a thick creeper; the ancient church tomb buried within the thick stonewalls. A heavy wooden door marked the only entrance into the tunnel that led to the tomb, also overgrown and hidden with greenery.

The tomb held an ocean of memories, sadness, and regret.

Refusing to recall the tragic events of that night again, Sienna climbed the steps and shoved aside the green branches to reveal the door to the tunnel. She shoved her weight against the heavy wood, and pushed it open, the sound scraping across the sandy floor. Unable to suppress a shudder that had nothing to do with the crisp morning air, she stood back to stare at the blackness that beckoned throughout the tunnel.

Entering the tunnel with her three Keepers had somehow been much easier than going inside alone.

She glanced at the small opening, edged with old cobwebs, and looked down the long, low passage. The tunnel descended into the ground with several rocky steps marking the way. Ancient brown stones made up the side of the walls. At the end of the tunnel was the tomb that Warrick sought.

Sienna narrowed her eyes, staring beyond the darkness at a soft flicker of light at the end of the tunnel. A light? Had they left a lantern burning when they'd moved Mason?

She turned around, scanning the forest. A red glow had seeped through the tall trees, hinting at the sunrise beckoning over the hills. A pretty sight that brought her comfort in knowing that daylight was on its way. Traipsing through a dark forest alone was creepy, despite the powers she possessed.

In her case, knowing she was there to meet with a warlock had her on high alert. Her Keepers would be furious with her, but there was no way she could trade Archer's life for Mason's.

He was her best friend, her Keeper, and she loved him. Losing him would be like ripping out her soul.

She turned back to the tunnel and sent a trail of fire along the gloomy passage to light the lanterns hanging from the rock ceiling. Once lit, the gloom of the tunnel eased somewhat, but it was still eerie enough to rip another shudder through her. With a grimace, she pushed through the tunnel, thankful for the light from the fire lanterns hanging above her head.

As Sienna neared the opening outside the tomb, the faint smell of blood shook her senses. Her head shot up, her heart began pounding, the eeriness of the tunnel forgotten. She began walking faster, the smell of the blood growing stronger with every step, and everything inside her rebelled at the idea of what she would find.

Archer.

She broke through the tunnel with a gasp and stared in horror at her Keeper strung mid-air in the centre of the room like a damn sacrifice about to be offered. His eyes were closed, his head hung forward, and everything about the way he hung, unmoving, terrified her.

"Archer!" Sienna rushed to him, reaching up to him. They'd taken his shoes and shirt, bound him with rope and chains. He was sticky and wet, his jeans and naked chest covered in blood. The arrow was still in his chest, his flesh ripped in vicious slashes across his body. His hair was wet, his body covered in a thin layer of perspiration from the stuffy tomb, and his skin gleamed in the flickering torch light. "Oh, my God, Archer!"

His head lifted, his eyes opened. "Sienna? What the hell are you doing here?"

She heard the anger that edged his words and ignored them. Her hands fumbled along the chains, tugging on them.

"Over there." Archer nodded to the wall where the chains were fastened.

Sienna whirled around and glared at the lock that kept the chains in place. Her energy along with adrenaline, and it didn't take long for the lock to pop open under the intense onslaught of heat. Archer slumped forward and although she tried to catch him, they both tumbled to the ground.

Anger, worry, and hatred stirred inside and she bit back from the spew of emotions that threatened to explode from her.

"Archer, we need to get you out of here."

"The arrow," he grunted, sitting up and reaching for the wooden spike in his chest. With a coarse groan, clipped with an angry curse, he tugged the arrow from his chest. The chains rattled with the motion, and he quickly loosened them with a tug to each wrist.

Sienna produced two painkillers and a bottle of water from the small bag slung across her shoulder. "Here, take this. It'll help the pain."

"You came prepared. How did you know I'd be here?"

"I didn't, but I knew I'd find you."

He threw back the pills, chasing it with a large gulp of water while Sienna quickly shoved several wads of gauze against his wound. He pushed her away. "I'm fine, Sienna."

"You're not, Archer. But the meds will numb the pain and the treated gauze will stop the bleeding. The rest of your wounds can wait for later."

He struggled to his feet, cursing from the challenge. "We have to get you out of here. Where are my brothers?"

Sienna grabbed his hand and headed for the door, but he yanked her back toward him.

"Sienna, where are my brothers?"

Her stomach lurched at the icy notch to his tone. She lifted her gaze to his, not willing to give room to any doubts for her decision. She would have chosen Archer over Mason any day. The rest of the crap that came with freeing Mason she would have dealt with later.

"Where the hell is Declan and Ethan?"

"They're at home!" she blurted, irritated with the anger in his tone.

Archer's eyes rounded and he flinched. "They'd never leave you alone. Why…?" His jaw worked, and he tugged her toward him, taking her by the shoulders. "You ran without telling them, didn't you? They don't know you're here, do they?"

"I had to do this, Archer, and they would never let me come if they knew what I had planned."

"Damn right!" he roared. His eyes narrowed as understanding dawned. "Where is Warrick?"

Sienna stepped back, keeping her gaze level to his. She refused to back down, to trash her decision, but the fire that burned in his eyes revealed an anger she'd never seen before.

"You made a deal with Warrick to free Mason, didn't you?" he demanded.

"I had no choice."

"Really, Sienna? Free Mason?" His words came out in a low

growl, his expression twisted with disapproval. "That goes against everything we believe in."

"Archer, it's you."

"It's the balance of nature first, dammit!"

"No!" she shouted back at him, yanking free from his grip. "I will do everything to maintain the damn balance expected of me, and I'll suck up the crap that comes with the life bestowed upon me, but there's no way that I'm trading you for anything, Archer. Anything. Don't you get it? I can handle Mason if he's set free. I can handle both Brogan brothers. But I can't handle losing you!"

Her words whipped away his reply and he stared at her with a harsh frown. Slowly, he blew out air and stepped closer, his hands cupping her face.

"God, Sienna. Do you always have to succumb to the urge for these Kamikaze missions?"

"The only mission I'm on here is to free you, Archer."

"And Mason?"

"I'll deal with him later."

Archer kissed her head and pulled back. "Let's get out of here."

"Are you okay?"

"Yes. I may not have the powers I once had but I'm still your Keeper, and there's no way in hell that Warrick is going to hurt you."

Despite the tension between them, she smiled and followed him out through the tunnel.

"What was the deal with Warrick?" Archer asked.

"That we meet at the tomb alone and make the swap."

"You really think he'll come alone?"

"I did."

Archer tilted his head over his shoulders to flash her a final glance before pushing against the heavy door that sealed the tunnel. He held it open for her, helped her through the opening.

The blast of fresh air had them both drawing in deep breaths, the cool morning air a welcome change to the stifling tunnel. The forest was still dark but more sharp rays of sunlight infiltrated the umbrella of tall trees ahead.

And littering the ground around the tomb were hoards of fierce warriors that surrounded Warrick. He stood at the bottom of the stone steps, amongst his warriors, his expression relaxed. He was all confidence, and the sight made Sienna's gut twinge.

He was up to something. The warriors, the amusement she saw in his eyes, his level expression, all hinted at a hidden agenda.

Sienna stepped forward, settling a menacing gaze on the warlock. "What's with the minions?"

"I needed company."

"Too afraid to confront me alone?"

"You're not alone." Warrick's gaze fell to Archer, a small smile tugging free at the corner of his lips. "I see you found your prize."

"He's been hurt. Not part of our deal."

"He wouldn't co-operate so my men had to use a little force to subdue him."

His confidence unsettled her, and she quietly scanned the group of warriors. Although they appeared at ease, they had attack mode splashed across their fierce expressions and guard-like stances.

One word from their leader and they would attack.

"This wasn't part of our deal, Warrick. We agreed to come alone."

Warrick nodded to the trees beside her. "I'm not the only one that broke our deal, Sienna."

Sienna tilted her head slowly and gasped at the sight of Ethan and Declan standing at the far edge of the rocky platform. The relief that flooded her, despite her inner objection, quickly gave way to worry. They weren't bound, weren't harmed. They simply stood facing Warrick and his warriors, ready for a defensive attack if needed. Two men against an entire army, and yet they hadn't backed down or walked away.

A bolt of pride landed in her gut, and she shifted her gaze to meet Declan's.

She saw the flash of guarded anger in the depth of his clouded blue eyes. His lips were drawn together in a tight line of disapproval, his eyebrows narrowed in a harsh frown.

No doubt he was spitting mad, and would dish out a good ass whooping once they got home.

If they got home.

Sienna dragged in a deep breath of air, glanced at Ethan, and nodded. She turned back to Warrick and his army of warriors. Two forces on the opposite sides of nature, two enemy sides. No wonder the tension was so ripe.

"You hurt either of my Keepers and you'll never see Mason again, Warrick," she said.

"We had a deal, witchy. You've found Archer – alive, I might add – and now I want my brother." Warrick stepped forward, leaving his warriors behind. "Everyone stays here. We go inside alone. Once you've broken the spell, you're all free to go."

Sienna's eyes narrowed. It was all bullshit. The stench was all over him, but what choice did she have? She glanced at each of her three Keepers, her beautiful warriors. Despite the glaring looks they gave her, she nodded at Warrick. "Fine. We'll go inside alone. I'll undo the spell on Mason and then I'm leaving with my Keepers. Once Mason's free, you leave town, Warrick. You leave town and never, ever, come back to Rapid Falls. Ever."

"Agreed. You have my word."

She rolled her eyes. "Chipmunk, Warrick. Don't insult me."

"Show some respect, Sienna. After all, I'm the one getting what I want at the end of this little soap opera."

"Evil doesn't deserve respect. Now let's get this over with."

"My pleasure." Warrick didn't bother hiding his smile, and

glanced back at his head warrior. A look of understanding passed between them and with a final nod, Warrick climbed the rest of the stairs.

Sienna immediately recognized the warrior. Harper. The man from the park. His gaze met hers, his eyes shifting with undisguised amusement that gave her the urge to send him into the nearby river.

Archer stepped in front of Warrick, blocking the entrance to the tunnel. His green eyes had darkened, his expression fierce and mixed with fury and hatred. Despite his injuries, her Keeper looked menacing.

Sienna put a hand on Archer's arm, willing him to back down. For a long while, he simply glared at Warrick, and then finally, his gaze faltered to hers. Without words, an ocean of understanding and emotion crossed between them, and he nodded.

Adrenaline coursed through her body, thick and plentiful, making her heart pound and tuning her senses into overdrive. The tunnel was still creepy, the air just as stale, yet none of it worried her this time. All that lay heavy on her heart like a dead weight brick of concern, were the three Keepers at the mercy of Warrick's warriors outside.

Sure, they were more powerful than their enemies were, but they were outnumbered by the dozens. A fact that Warrick was counting on should a fight break out.

They pushed through the end of the tunnel and into the clearance of the stuffy room. Sienna eyed the chains where she'd found Archer and glared at Warrick.

"Easy, Sienna." Warrick had the grace to mask his grin. He came to stop in front of the tomb. "The last time we were in this room together it was under such different circumstances, don't you think?"

"The last time we were here, you killed my Keeper."

"And you bound my powers, imprisoned my brother, and set me alight. I'd say we're even."

Sienna scowled at him, trying to get a grip on the flash of anger that soared through her. "I set the room alight. Tough luck for you if you weren't smart enough to haul ass outside. And nothing I did to you that night excuses anything you've done since then."

"Ah, Sienna. We can dredge up the past all you like but it still won't change the outcome of tonight." He waved a hand at the entrance to the tomb. "My brother, if you don't mind."

"You need to move the rock covering the doorway."

Keeping her emotions contained and without a word, Sienna left him to it and cast a circle. She pulled her Grimoire out of her bag and placed it carefully on the floor in the centre of the circle. Next came the four stones that she placed strategically around the book.

"Ah, the famous Grimoire and the four stones that open it." Warrick smiled, his eyes alight with pleasure as he stared at the book.

Sienna glanced at Warrick, irritated at his triumphant expression. He was practically drooling.

She stood back, immediately starting a gentle chant in a language foreign to Warrick. He fell silent, giving her the space she needed to perform the ceremony. Her trance grew deeper, her concentration focused on the entrance to the tomb. The fire torches flickered illuminating the room in bright sparks. She began rocking, chanting louder and louder, whilst the flames burned brighter, feeding on her energy.

Fire. A power so familiar to her entire essence that the magic rolled off her with ease.

And then it was over.

She fell silent, dropped her hands beside her legs, and concentrated on regaining a steady breath. Her shoulders were heaving, her heart pounding, the adrenaline soaring.

"Is it done?" Warrick asked, his voice hitched with excitement. "Is the seal of the door broken?"

Sienna nodded.

Warrick took three heavy booted strides toward her and grabbed her arm. "You're coming with me."

She yanked her arm away. "No way, Warrick."

He'd already grabbed her arm again, his grip unrelenting this time, and began tugging her toward the opening.

"It won't work, Warrick!" she snapped, slapping at his hand. She shoved him away, and quickly took several steps away from him. "I'm the witch who sealed the room. If I enter the tomb, everything I've just done will come crumbling down, and we'll never get Mason out."

Suspicion flickered through his eyes, but like a hungry dog ripe for his prize, Warrick shook it off. "So now what?"

"I'll wait here. Bring Mason to me, and I'll break the spell that binds him."

Warrick's eyes narrowed, and he slowly turned to look at her. A moment later, he marched toward her, grabbed her tiny wrist in his large calloused hand, and slammed it against the rock behind her. She didn't flinch when he reached for the shackles, unperturbed by the chain he quickly slapped around her wrist.

Locks were of no deterrence to her. Clearly, the warlock's senses were overshadowed by his desire to see his brother freed.

Warrick tightened the shackle on her wrist and stepped back to admire his handiwork. "My insurance policy."

Right.

"I'm not going anywhere," she said, trying not to sound too sweet. She simply needed the warlock to get into the damn tomb.

He didn't reply, turned around, and disappeared into the tomb.

Sienna closed her eyes and breathed a sigh of relief.

Everything they'd fought for culminated into this one moment for Warrick. Freeing his brother and regaining his own powers. Like hell.

CHAPTER THIRTY-ONE

Sienna had barely freed herself from the bloody shackle that bound her right wrist when Warrick came hurtling toward the entrance of the tomb.

"Where's Mason?" he shouted. He tried walking through the doorway but an invisible obstacle kept him from leaving. Roaring with fury, he slammed both hands against the sides of the rocky doorway. "You crazy bitch! What have you done?"

Sienna tossed the shackles, and wiped her hands on her jeans, the sticky blood adding another notch to her anger. Archer's blood.

Unable to suppress the satisfied smirk, Sienna turned to face the warlock. He kept trying to walk through the door but the spell she'd cast on him remained firm, the barrier locking him inside the tomb. His face was red from rage, his eyes rounded in disbelief, his nostrils flaring.

"Where is my brother?" he roared, slamming a hand against the wall.

"Relocated, Warrick. We moved him." She was pleased with the even tone in her voice, revelling in the triumph that he'd walked into her trap so easily.

Warrick's warriors were still outside, but they'd handle them. With luck, they might flee once they learnt the fate of their leader.

A leader now incarcerated in a gloomy, rocky tomb, about to live out the same fate as his older brother.

Sienna thought of the mysterious faces strewn across the floor in his study. A torturous end for a man, but a fit punishment for evil.

She walked toward the doorway of the tomb, ducking her head to avoid colliding with the roof lantern. She stopped in front of Warrick, a fierce jolt of triumphant pride settling inside. Aside from what he'd done to her Keepers, he was also responsible for so much pain and misery to so many innocent people. Leading up to the night they'd bound the Brogan brothers, Mason had been the more evil leader of the two and Warrick had stood by while many lives were wrecked in their quest for power and control. At some point, he'd decided to take a stand and he'd become just as evil as his brother.

But no more.

"We had a deal, Sienna!" he shouted. "Where the hell is Mason?"

"In similar lodgings to this, Warrick."

"We had a deal!"

"I told you before; I don't make deals with the devil."

"You bitch!" he snapped, spittle flying out of the corner of his mouth. Fury raged in cold black eyes, his face scrunched in hatred and fear. "I'm going to kill you, Sienna. You and your pathetic Keepers!"

"Go ahead, Warrick. You'll have all the time in the world to plot your revenge against my Keepers and me." She gave him a wicked smile. "Pity you can't get out."

"You've messed with the wrong person, Sienna. Mark my words. You will all die. DIE!" he spat with such hatred that she stepped away. "And when I'm done with you lot, I'm going after every witch and Keeper I can find!"

"Knock yourself out, Warrick." She headed for the door, needing to get away from him, needing her Keepers.

"Sienna!"

Ignoring him, Sienna stopped in the doorway of the tunnel and glanced back. With a quick swoop of the arm across the room, the fire lanterns blew out, plunging the small room into blackness. Not wanting to stay in the eerie room any longer, Sienna turned toward the tunnel and hastily made her way to the end.

Warrick's vicious shouts could be heard all the way down the tunnel, and she ran the rest of the way.

God, the tomb was torture.

Hands shaking, she swiped at her brow. With a giant gasp of air, she broke through the doorway and froze, gaping at the chaos that reigned throughout the forest.

"Oh, no." Her mouth dropped, her eyes widened, and everything inside her clenched in revulsion.

Whilst she'd been in the tomb with Warrick, a full-blown war had broken out between his warriors and her Keepers.

They'd destroyed the forest, trampled bushes and flowers, uprooted trees. Various weapons lay scattered across the ground, whilst other weapons were clutched in the hands of the warriors that surrounded her Keepers. Fire surged through the trees, the ground splattered with burning embers. The smell of smoke, mingled with raw fear and fresh blood, filled the air with sickening reality. Warlike cries echoed through the forest, followed with screams and shouts that made her blood curl.

There was so much destruction, so much blood.

An arrow surged past her with a hissing noise, and Sienna quickly rolled to the ground. Jumping to her feet, she crouched low, staring at the bloody mess around her.

She spotted Archer first, in true hand-to-hand combat, with three of the warriors. With a loud roar, he plunged a fist into a warrior's jaw, knocking him out, and swung around to fend off the second warrior. More punches and kicks were thrown with a violence she seldom saw from him. Blood gushed from his enemy as Archer broke his nose with a swift punch to the face. Archer whirled around, aiming a lethal kick at the third warrior's chest that sent him hurtling backward into a nearby tree. The warrior crashed against the ground, dazed and confused, but struggled to his feet.

A bolt of fire surged past Sienna, annihilating a warrior headed her way. The man tumbled backward down the stairs in a pile of flames and horrified screams. Sienna spun around, scanning the war for signs of Declan.

Surrounded by fire, his weapon of choice, Declan fought the onslaught of violent warriors. Fireballs hurled through the air, along with several lashes of red heat that resulted in painful screams from the men at the tail end of his wrath.

Two men charged Declan from behind, hoping to neutralize his brutal powers by overpowering him, but a sharp gust of wind hit them moments before they reached their target. As though they were weightless, the blast of vicious wind sent them soaring through the air and crashing against the hard ground.

Ethan charged toward Declan, swinging around so that their backs were against each other. Fighting their way through the army of warriors, they reached Archer who had begun to take strain from his injuries. Together, her Keepers formed a circle, back to back, and faced the continuous onslaught of men together.

They were as bloody as their attackers, worn, weary, and exhausted.

But they fought on.

With piercing war cries, several of the warriors charged the trio of powerful men. Declan reacted with several defensive fire bolts that plunged the approaching men to the ground in a burning inferno. The fire quickly fizzled out, and the warriors struggled to their feet.

Sienna gaped at them in horror. They were black from the burns, their skins a mangled mess of burnt flesh from the intense heat of the fire, yet they were still fighting. She scanned the forest, realizing they had all risen.

What the hell?

Sienna's gaze zeroed in on the warrior closest to her, scanning his body, and she cursed when she spotted the chunky round pendant slung around his neck.

A protection spell.

Damn. Warrick had linked them all with a protection spell, the spelled pendant they all wore protecting his warriors from harm. And no doubt, Warrick had linked the spell to himself.

An icy hand crept across Sienna's heart, and she drew in a sharp breath of air as realization hit her. She spun around, glaring at the entrance to the tunnel, horror washing over her.

The door to the tunnel scraped open to reveal the warlock she had just entombed with a spell of her own – a spell that wouldn't work if he too wore the protection pendant.

Without checking, Sienna knew that he did. He'd been a step ahead of her the entire time and had faked a perfect reaction to her entrapment spell. No, no, no!

Warrick pushed through the heavy door, sweaty, angry, and flushed. A wicked grin crossed his face as black eyes found Sienna. "I had you fooled, didn't I? I deserve top points for that performance, don't you think?" He laughed, the sound tinged with a triumphant evil that made her skin crawl.

"Warrick." His name came out on a whoosh of air, her heart thudding a frantic rhythm as her brain quickly rerouted a plan.

Warrick charged toward her, his smile vanishing. He lunged for her, but she quickly sidestepped him. "You bitch! You would have left me there to rot like you did with my brother."

His warrior, Harper, stormed to the bottom of the stairs, and let out a loud, eerie warlike cry that had all the other warriors stand down.

Silence fell across the forest, the crackling of the blazing trees and groans of pain from the injured men the only sounds that echoed through the tension.

Warrick walked to the edge of the rocky platform and scanned his army of followers scattered throughout the forest. They were dirty, bloody, injured, and charged with adrenaline, but they waited for further instruction from their leader.

Her Keepers maintained their position, exhausted from the fight, but not backing down. They kept their backs to each other, each brother offering protection to the other, their gazes pinned on the warriors around them.

Warrick's expression brightened when he saw them and he flashed an evil smile at Sienna. "Your Keepers look a little worse for wear."

"They are three men against an army of yours." Sienna was unable to keep the hatred out of her voice and gave him a hard, unblinking stare. "Considering your men are covered with a protection spell, I'd say my Keepers aren't fairing too badly."

"Ah, the protection spell. A helpful spell I picked up from one of the witches I killed."

"Release my Keepers, Warrick. This is between you and me."

Her words sent a flash of fury across his face, and his eyes clouded with darkness. "You broke our deal, Sienna. If it wasn't for the protection spell I cast upon myself, I'd be rotting in a tomb like my brother."

She heard the bitterness and resentment laced within his words, but refused to flinch. Her plan had backfired, but her mind scrambled for another one. And all the while, her entire body ached with the truth that this was one fight that her and her Keepers might not win.

She met Warrick's angry gaze. "You deserve the same fate as Mason."

"And you've just signed the death warrant for everyone you've ever loved." Warrick nodded to Harper who quickly disappeared behind the rocks. When he returned, he had a woman slung over his shoulder. With a satisfied laugh, he dumped the woman on the platform beside Warrick. She fell to the ground with a thud, groaning softly before opening her eyes.

"Gran!" An icy chill of horror chased through Sienna, and she rushed to her grandmother's side, breathing a sigh of relief when Rose blinked. She looked so pale, her clothes were dusty, her hair matted with a smear of blood. Sienna frantically wiped it away, her heart pounding with anger. "What happened? What did they give you?" Sienna whirled on Warrick, blind with rage. "What have you given her?"

"A dose of revenge."

"Rose Thorn?"

"Maybe."

She hated the way he said it, as though he'd simply given her grandmother an apple pie on a merry occasion. But this wasn't apple pie and there was nothing merry about the moment. She glanced at her grandmother, weakened from the dreadful herb.

"Take her inside the tomb," Warrick ordered Harper with a curt nod. "And kill her if I don't come back."

Sienna stepped in front of her grandmother, everything inside her aching for the older woman. She didn't have to look around her to know the dangers that surrounded them. Even though it killed her to have her grandmother inside the tomb, she knew it was the safest place for her amidst the fight that brewed.

"I'll come for you, Gran," Sienna said, putting her arms around Rose. "I'll fix this, I promise."

Weak and weary, Rose held her tightly, placing her lips to

Sienna's ear. "You can do this, Sienna," she whispered. "You are the chosen one. The Pure."

Sienna nodded, not understanding her grandmother's ramblings, but quickly brushed it aside as Harper stomped toward them. "I love you."

"Remember Sarah," her grandmother whispered as Harper hoisted the older woman to her feet.

Sienna's heart shattered as she watched her grandmother disappear into the tunnel. She raised blazing eyes, full of hatred, toward Warrick. "If you hurt her, Warrick, I will spend the rest of my life making yours a misery."

"Oh, you've already achieved a great deal of that, my love," he said with a fake smile. His expression cleared, and his jaw flexed. "I'd instructed my men to harm your Keepers but keep them alive. My patience is running out and I'm about one breath away from ordering their deaths. Tell me where Mason is."

Sienna looked at her Keepers, torn between the men she loved most and the destiny she lived for.

"Sienna, no!" Archer shouted, his voice gruff, tortured.

"Tell me, Sienna, or I will set my men on your beloved Keepers," Warrick warned.

"Sienna!"

Deciding he'd had enough, Warrick glanced over his shoulder toward his warriors. "Kill them!" he roared, his thick rumble of words shattering the silence. "Kill them all!"

"No!" Sienna screamed, rushing forward, but a string of leafy ropes slid across her path and grasped her ankles with such speed that she gaped in surprise. A quick glance at Warrick told her what she already knew. Sarah's powers, now his powers. A master of the earth element, meant for protecting the good. And Warrick had perfected the use of Sarah's powers with ease. More leafy vines raced toward Sienna, crowding the others, sliding around her body in a tight grip that had her gasping. Trying to tug free from the tight vines that bound her, she sought out her Keepers. "NO!"

They'd already sprung into action, fighting for their lives against the men instructed to kill them. And this time, the fight was worse.

Vicious, brutal, an end goal of death in sight.

Warrick laughed, the sound loud and tinged with madness. He came to her, a syringe in his hands, and a triumphant spring in his step.

Rose Thorn.

So that had been his plan all along. He'd weakened Rose, her Keepers, and now her.

She stared at the liquid in his hand with such intensity and hatred, not even blinking when the syringe exploded.

"I have plenty more where that came from, Sienna." Warrick said, discarding what remained of the syringe. He lunged for her, grabbed her from behind, and wrapped an arm around her neck in a death grip. He turned her so that she could face the destruction of her beloved Keepers, an image he knew would devastate her.

"Look at them," he breathed against her ear, his voice dripping with sick satisfaction. "Look while we slaughter them."

"Warrick, this is between you and me!"

"But hurting them will destroy you. Just like the death of Sarah and your parents. After tonight, you will have no one, Sienna. No one."

"And neither will you!" she cried, her voice cracking from the sting of his words.

"True, so while we're on the subject of crippling truths, there's something else you should know." He tightened his grip on her, tugged her closer against him, and pressed his lips against her ear. "I killed your parents. My parents set it up, but when they lost the nerve and left, I was the one who lit the match."

She gasped, but before she could reply, he threw her to the

ground where she landed in a tumble of leafy vines and anguished cries. As she got to her knees, Declan's fierce roar had her head jerking back in their direction just in time to see the warriors closing in on them.

Sienna closed her eyes in disbelief, unable to bare witness to the destruction of her Keepers. She'd already lost so many people and losing her Keepers or her grandmother would be unbearable. They were all she had left in the world to call hers.

Sienna reached inside, searching for the one thing she knew would alter their fate.

And then everything changed. Suddenly, despite the chaos around her, everything became still. Everything slowed down, became quieter, calmer, more controlled.

The will to survive and her fierce determination to protect her loved ones took over, and a slow movement of energy shifted through Sienna, sending her to a place she'd kept guarded for two years.

Rose's elemental powers. Now her powers. All of them.

The surge of energy that came with the acceptance of her destiny was exhilarating, and she drew on it in a way she'd never done before.

Despite the resistance, the leafy ropes holding Sienna captive broke free, scattered to the ground, and withered away. She stepped forward, scanning the bloody battle as everything fell into place.

With several calm movements, she focused on her Keepers and everything evil surrounding them. Drawing her energy from the fire element, she sent bolts of fire across the warriors. Shouts mingled with the smell of burning flesh, and everyone scattered for cover. Several warriors charged toward her, and she sent several lashes of fire their way. The blaze engulfed them in a foul swoop of terror, and they tumbled back down the stairs, howling in pain.

Keeping the fire element flowing, Sienna drew on her second

element. Water.

The nearby river provided plenty of ammunition, and she used it in a way she'd only ever seen Archer do. Torrents of water whipped across the warriors, plunging them to the ground. With quick precision, Sienna sent a second set of lashes across the frightened warriors. She raised her left arm, gathered several water balls that went hurtling through the air like bombs, the destruction just as deadly. Water exploded across the warriors with a force that sent them reeling.

Wind came next – cruel whirlwinds that tore apart the gathering of men, scattering bodies along its unrelenting path. Slashes of wind whipped across the frightened men, adding to the confusion and terror. Several of the men started running, despite their protection pendants, and Sienna set chase with blasts of fresh mini tornados.

Maintaining the chaos brought about by the elements of fire, water, and wind that crashed their brutal ambush, Sienna turned her attention on Warrick.

Hatred dripped from his expression, and sensing a challenge, he charged her again. In his right hand was another vile of Rose Thorn.

Sienna glared at him with all the strength she could muster and sent a thick ball of fire his way. Warrick dodged, rolled to the floor, the vile shattering within his palm. He retaliated in quick succession by sending a shower of lethal rocks her way, but with a quick swipe of the arm, Sienna diverted them. Using them as ammunition against Warrick's own warriors, Sienna hurled them toward the warriors with such force that they dropped to the ground on impact.

"You can't win, Sienna!" Warrick shouted at her, his voice barely audible above the noise around them. "No matter what you do to us, we'll keep coming back. And I won't rest until I've killed every witch and Keeper there is."

It all came down to the protection spell, a niggling warning amidst the fury that had been unleashed in Sienna.

Warrick was right. Despite the pain and power she unleashed upon their attackers, the protection spell would keep them safe. As long as Warrick was alive, the spell would hold. Their injuries would be brief and short-lived, as the protection spell would bring a zap of energy, along with renewed determination to fight.

With a gut wrenching roar, Warrick faced her Keepers, focusing his full energy on the three weakening men. Several large rocks rose up from the ground and hurtled toward them.

"Ethan!" Sienna screamed, the high-pitched screech of warning immediately drawing his attention from the battle.

He whipped out a warning to his brothers and held up a hand to divert the shower of dangerous rocks.

Unrelenting, Warrick sent several fresh rock showers their way, distracting them from the ground warriors that rushed toward them.

A warrior rushed up behind Ethan, shoving a sharp knife deep into his back. Ethan yelled, his eyes rounded in disbelief, and he dropped to his knees with a loud growl. Ethan's shield against the rock missiles momentarily disabled, the onslaught of rocks and stones rained down upon them.

Arms up to shield themselves, her Keepers scrambled together, their worry heightened as they realized that Ethan was badly injured. More rocks followed, delivering a brutal blow to Declan.

Sensing their weakness, more warriors charged, engulfing her Keepers.

"NO!" Sienna screamed, as everything began to fall apart. She felt the weakening of her powers, a brief hitch in her energy source as horror came crashing down around her.

She screamed their names, her fear etched in the snapped words.

She flung around to face Warrick, turning her entire focus on the warlock, on everything that he was, everything he stood for.

All this madness came down to him.

Remember Sarah.

Sienna gasped as the meaning behind her grandmother's words washed over her, triggering a wave of renewed hope. Remember Sarah.

Everything became clear, vanquishing the rollercoaster of fear and emotions. With fresh determination, Sienna turned toward the battle on the ground below her.

Drawing her energy from the earth, a power she hadn't yet used because of the tortured memories that came with it, Sienna sent out a batch of her own leafy ropes slithering along the ground. They worked their way around several pairs of ankles, pulling tightly, and hoisting the unsuspecting victims into the air. Suspended mid-air, their shouts fell on deaf ears.

Her other elemental powers subsided, and she focused on the one elemental power that would set them free.

Earth.

The ground shook as several creepers, trees and plants roared to life around Warrick and his men, slithering along the ground with frightening speed, and attacking with brutal force. A soft rumble of earth had them all staring in horror as the ground shifted and broke apart to reveal a gaping hole in the middle of the war that immediately sucked in a handful of men.

A sand storm rose up, engulfing them in a thick spray of dust that muffled their vision and clouded them in confusion.

Stone, rock, sand, plants, trees, shrubs – all earth elements that Sienna drew on with such fierce determination that she began to tremble.

A shower of stones came next, targeting the warriors with brutal impact.

The sky grew murkier, the air thick with the sandy storm she'd created, and just as she thought everything would explode around her, she felt the hitch of energy inside her.

Knowing she'd reached her limit didn't deter her. Instead, she lashed out more power, drawing more energy from the earth, driving it home with a force that had everyone around her diving for cover.

Through the cloudy madness, Archer struggled toward her. "Sienna, stop!" he yelled, holding an arm across his face to shield himself from the ruthless sand storm and the shower of stones. "Sienna!"

She ignored him, kept her focus on Warrick who had started to weaken. Wind whipped across her face, the sand stinging her skin. Warning bells flared within her, blood poured from her nose, and everything inside her rumbled in pain. Instead of backing down, Sienna glared at Warrick, digging deeper, reaching further than she'd ever reached.

It was the only way to destroy him.

"Sienna, you're going to kill yourself!" Archer shouted, trying to reach her through the treacherous sand storm. "Sienna!"

Warrick stumbled, swayed, and coughed. Gasping for air, he clutched his chest, and whirled toward Sienna as horror set home.

She'd tapped into his energy source, threatening to drain the very essence out of him. He'd killed Sarah and used her powers for his evil means, but with the transfer of powers, came the same connection to Sienna as her other Keepers. A connection that Sienna could use to destroy him.

"Sienna!" Warrick bellowed, staggering toward her. Weak and exhausted, he collapsed at her feet with a twisted gasp of sandy air. "Stop. You're going to kill me."

Sienna closed her eyes, her body saturated. Everything inside her demanded she stop, but she couldn't. He'd hurt them all, hurt others, destroyed lives. He'd ripped away her beautiful, kind, and loving parents in one flick of a match. Beautiful Sarah, gone in a flash of his hatred. He was a threat to everything they believed in, the man who threatened to unsettle the balance of nature they fought so hard to maintain.

"Sienna, stop!" Warrick begged, softer this time. He reached for her, drained. "Harper will kill Rose if I don't return."

Sienna's head snapped back as a sharp pain tore through her. She cried out, breaking the connection she had to the earth.

Everything collapsed around them, became still, quiet, a complete contrast to the craziness she'd bestowed upon them.

Sensing her weakness, Warrick hurled toward her as she opened her eyes, a dagger clasped in his right hand.

A brief flash of recognition collided with the brutal memory of the day he'd stabbed Sarah. Sienna screamed at the sight of the dagger charging toward her, her body too weak to move out of its way.

Archer charged, throwing himself against Warrick. The two men tumbled to the ground in a pile of fists, warlike growls, and ruthless punching. The dagger scattered to the ground, slid across the rocky floor, and crashed against the door of the tunnel.

Declan was there in a flash and without hesitation, he swiped the blade off the ground and tossed it to Archer. "Archer, the dagger!"

Archer's head snapped up as he flung out an arm, his fingers snatching the dagger midair. With a thunderous roar, Archer twisted his body and plunged the dagger into Warrick's heart.

Warrick's jaw dropped, his eyes widened, and he slumped to the ground in shocked silence.

Everything became a blur for Sienna as her legs gave way beneath her. She heard the shouts of the warriors in the distance as they scattered, heard her Keepers yelling her name.

As she slipped into the blackness that beckoned, there was only one thought that tumbled through her mind.

It was finally over.

CHAPTER THIRTY-TWO

Archer shoved Warrick's limp body off him and scrambled toward Sienna. "Sienna!" He cradled her head, checking for a pulse, and gulped air when he found one. "Sienna, open your damn eyes!"

Her head rolled back, and she murmured softly, but her eyes remained closed. Her red hair and pale face was streaked with blood from her violent nosebleed, her body saturated with perspiration. And she was so cold.

Declan appeared on the stone steps, helping Ethan to rest beside Sienna. They were panting, bloody, and battered. "How is she?"

"She's weak. Dammit, she refused to stop. She knew that weakening Warrick would weaken her."

"It shouldn't kill her, Archer. She's too strong for that." Declan dropped beside them, quickly scanning Sienna for any injuries. "She's weak, but she should be okay."

Archer nodded, knowing his brother was right, but the sight of his woman in such a weakened state tore at him. He flicked a glance at Ethan. "You okay, brother?"

"I'm fine. Declan removed the knife." Ethan moved toward them, a mass of ripped and bloody flesh, and grimaced. "This has got to go down as the worst damn day in the history of my life as a Keeper."

"You and me both, brother." Archer put two fingers to Sienna's pulse again. His stomach lurched, and he hoisted himself to his feet. "Her pulse has weakened. Help me, Declan."

Declan swiped Sienna into his arms, hers falling open as though she were a limp rag doll. Declan cradled her, and headed toward the entrance of the tunnel. "Let's get her into the tomb. Rose can help."

"Harper —"

"Hauled ass the moment Warrick went down. And by the terrified look on his face, Rose had started spewing some sort of witchy crap on him."

"Rose." Archer pushed open the heavy stone door, not waiting for an answer. Although he was hurt and exhausted, the bleeding to his arrow wound had stopped. The painkillers Sienna had given him and the surge of adrenaline had long destroyed any signs of pain. Spurred on by anger and worry, he led the way through the tunnel toward the small clearing outside the tomb.

The tunnel was dark but he trudged on, unperturbed. His senses were on high alert, driving him ahead like a silent captain. A soft glow of light at the end of the tunnel marked the place of the tomb, and he headed toward it, ready for what he might find.

Rose sat against the stone wall on the far side of the room, weak but awake. Her head snapped up the moment they entered the small, stuffy room outside the tomb.

"Is it over?" she asked, her voice hoarse and etched with worry. "Did she weaken Warrick?"

"Yes," Archer replied, going to her. "He's dead."

"Dead?"

"He attacked her." Archer left it at that and helped the older woman to her feet. She was pale, her breathing shallow, and her damp hair clung to the sides of her face from the heat of the tomb. "Sienna's weak, Rose. She needs your help."

Declan arrived, carrying Sienna, and placed her unconscious

body on the sandy ground. They towered around her in mutual tension, panic, and worry.

They all loved her, were all bound to her, and seeing her like this ripped them apart.

Rose dragged in air and slowly leaned over her granddaughter. "What happened? She's completely drained, depleted."

Archer quickly filled her in, hating the way Rose's worry intensified with each passing moment. The witch was supposed to fix this, to help Sienna, but the look on Rose's face wasn't hopeful. "She'll be okay, won't she?"

Rose didn't reply as she placed a finger against Sienna's pulse. She leaned over Sienna, a sob escaping her.

"Rose, what's wrong?" Archer asked, unable to keep the panic out of his tone. "What the hell's wrong with her?"

She lifted a tearful gaze to meet his and slowly shook her head. "She's too weak, Archer. Tapping into all the elements at once and then pushing herself to weaken Warrick has drained her."

"But she's strong, she's powerful. She should be able to handle this."

Rose shook her head again, tears pouring down her cheeks. "When the transfer of powers took place, Sienna's essence became linked to her powers. Four elemental powers of nature. She also became linked to each of you. With each broken link, she grows weak. Under normal circumstances, she should be fine, but she hasn't yet learnt her limits and has pushed herself too far."

Archer stroked Sienna's hair, willing her to wake up. "Warrick was connected to her because of Sarah's powers. Now he's dead —"

"She no longer has the access to that element of nature. It's weakened her. As have you."

Archer's head whipped up to look at Rose. "Me?" Before Rose could explain, her meaning struck him with a vicious blow to the gut. "The Circle's curse. My elemental power."

"Stripping you of your elemental power had little effect on Sienna when tapping into the water element because you're still alive. But her essence is still tied to the four elements. With your powers bound, she'd still be able to access the water element but there'd still be a weak link. The kind of magic and power you saw tonight would take a toll on the strongest witch, Archer. Added to that, are Warrick's death and the binding of your powers. It's simply too much for her. In this state, she can handle the loss of one elemental power, but two…"

"What are you saying, Rose?" Declan asked, his voice unlevel and shaky.

"She's too weak. She might not find her way back to us."

"NO!" Archer yelled, his voice thundering across the stone room. He held Sienna's face in his hands, everything inside him rebelling at the idea of losing this beautiful woman. "There's no way in hell! We have to do something." He whirled toward Rose. "Do something, dammit!"

"There's only one thing I can try."

"Will it work?"

"It's risky."

"For Sienna?"

"No."

"Rose…"

"You have to trust me." Rose lifted her gaze to meet Archer's. "This shouldn't be happening, Archer. She has a greater purpose and we need her alive. The world needs her alive. Archer, listen to me. We don't have much time." Rose struggled to her feet, holding out a shaky hand for Declan to help her. "Sienna was carrying her Grimoire and the stones in her bag. Bring them to me."

"You can help her?" Declan asked.

"If we hurry."

Declan took Rose by her shoulders, scanning her face. "Rose.

You're not strong enough for this."

Scowling, she swatted him away. "I can do this. I have to do this."

"But the —"

"Declan, we have no choice!" she snapped, pushing against his chest.

Declan hesitated, but then nodded and disappeared in a flash to locate the abandoned bag.

"What are you doing, Rose?' Archer asked, watching as the old witch quickly cast a circle in the centre of the room. She reached for one of the lanterns, used the flame of the burning candle to start a small fire in the middle of the circle. When Declan appeared with the bag, she placed the stones around the circle and opened the Grimoire.

"She's going to hate me for this." Rose reached down, lifted a rusty nail from the ground, and straightened. She looked ill, withered, and had aged ten years since the day before. "Neither of you will understand what I'm about to do, but you all have to trust me."

Declan stepped forward. "Rose, what the hell's happening?"

Rose placed the Grimoire on the ground beside her, opened on a spell that made no sense to them, and turned to face them. "I have loved you three like you were my own. Thank you for protecting my family the way that you have."

"What is this, Rose?" Archer asked, her words striking a fresh round of unease within him.

"I'm going to help Sienna."

"How?"

"By breaking the spell that binds the curse on you and Sienna. If I can break it, it should automatically destroy the bind on your powers."

"You can do that?"

"Yes. She'd still be without the earth element, but without the bind on your powers her essence would stand a better chance of survival."

Archer nodded, pulling Sienna in his arms so that her head rested on his lap. He stroked her hair, holding onto everything that mattered to him. "What do we need to do?"

"Don't interrupt me. If she wakes up, don't let her come to me. No matter what happens, you let me finish."

The three brothers nodded, watching as Rose took the nail and slashed the palm of her hand.

"Rose!" Ethan snapped, stepping forward, but Rose held out a hand to stop him.

"I have to do this, Ethan. She's meant for great things and we need her. You have to trust me." Without waiting for a reply, Rose stepped into the circle she'd cast and closed her eyes.

A gentle whispered chant filled the silence of the room, growing louder and louder as she gathered more energy. Fuelled by the renewed energy, the flames burning in the several lanterns in the room exploded into more light, burning brighter and stronger.

The sound of the blaze mingled along with Rose's chants, and the three brothers looked on in awe.

Her chanting became more powerful, with added determination. Rose held out her bleeding hand above the fire, her blood dripping into the glowing flames. They flickered, splattered, sizzled. They burned brighter, hissing as it consumed her blood. Her words whipped through the room, resonating against the stonewalls, filling the tiny space with a power so strong that the Keepers were unable to move.

Sienna moved in Archer's arms, groaning softly. Her eyes fluttered opened, and she blinked several times to clear her murky head. "Archer?"

"I'm here," he grunted, his words sounding more like a growl of relief at the renewed strength he sensed in her. Whatever Rose was doing seemed to be helping. "You're okay, Sienna."

Her head turned and she looked at Rose in the centre of the room. "What is she doing?"

"Ssh, she's fine. She's doing what she needs to do."

Sienna listened, connecting to the magic that filled the room. Her eyes widened, and she struggled from Archer's grip. "No."

Archer kept his arms around her, her shoulders against his chest. He felt her resistance, the urge to rush to Rose and put a stop to whatever she was doing. Although Rose's ceremony seemed to bring more life into Sienna, his uneasiness intensified.

"Gran!" Sienna called, trying to sit up again.

Rose didn't answer, didn't even register that she'd heard her granddaughter. She continued with her chanting, louder and with added vigour. Her clear voice echoed across the walls, her chants and her blood fuelling the burning flames that hissed loudly like a snake zeroing in on its prey.

"Stop her, Archer!" Sienna shouted. "She can't do this."

"Sienna, she's performing a spell to break the curse on us. Without it, you'll die. She knows what she's doing." The urge to stop Rose grew stronger, but he knew the witch had an insight into their world that they didn't. She knew what needed to happen, and he had to trust her.

"It's not a spell, Archer, it's a sacrifice!" Sienna yelled, breaking away. She tried to rush to Rose, but Archer held her back, her words washing over him with a bite of reality.

A sacrifice?

Archer's gaze zeroed in on Rose, took in the blood pouring from her nose, a sign that their witch was weakening, the powers and magic having drained the very essence of her. The reality of what Rose was doing kicked in, triggering his age-old protective instincts, and he quickly slid out from beneath Sienna. He raced across the room, growling loudly when he hit the invisible barrier around the circle. "Rose! Rose, STOP!"

"Stop her, Archer!" Sienna screamed.

"I can't get to her. She's spelled the circle shut. Rose!"

"No! Gran, no!" Sienna started wailing, hysteria taking a firm grip when Rose collapsed to the ground.

The intensity of the flames lessened, signalling the end to the ritual.

Archer charged, dropping to his knees beside Rose. He quickly felt for a pulse, struck by devastation when there was none. "Rose!" he growled fiercely, shaking the older witch in his arms. "Don't you dare do this, Rose. Rose!"

"Gran!" Sienna screamed and scrambled across the sandy ground until she reached her grandmother. Sienna grabbed the lifeless woman. "Oh, my God. Archer! Archer, she's not breathing!"

Ethan and Declan sank to their knees beside them, struck by the tragedy, the reality, of what had just happened.

"NO!" Archer yelled and leaned forward, placing his hands across Rose's chest. He covered her mouth with his and breathed air into her lungs whilst his hands pumped rapid compressions against her heart.

It was only when Declan grabbed him by the shoulders a while later, snapping his name, that Archer stopped.

It was over.

"I'm so sorry, Rose," he ground out, stroking the older woman's face. "I'm so damn sorry."

"She was poisoned," Declan said, kneeling beside them. His words grabbed their attention and they both turned to look at him. "The arrow that wounded Rose last night was poisoned."

"Are you sure?" Sienna asked in a strangled voice. "When I left her, she seemed fine."

"She would have died anyway, Sienna. The symptoms started shortly after we got home last night and she knew immediately."

"Rose was dying?"

Declan nodded. "She knew which poison they'd used and she knew there was no hope. Ethan went to look for you but you were gone."

Sienna started crying, her shoulders racked with quiet sobs as she reached for Rose's hand. "I'm so sorry, Gran. I should never have left you."

"Sienna, in the end, it was your magic, your strength, and your powers that saved us."

"But I couldn't save her," Sienna wailed softly as the sobs came.

"No," Declan said, shaking his head. "And she knew there was no saving her, which is why she sacrificed herself to save you."

Still holding Rose in one arm, Archer reached for Sienna as she sobbed uncontrollably over her grandmother's body. He shifted his gaze to Rose, the woman who'd spent her life protecting the good, protecting them. A woman who'd sacrificed her own life in order to save her granddaughter's. She was like a grandmother to them all, and they loved her dearly.

Closing his eyes to ward off the image of the lifeless woman in front of him, he held Sienna while she sobbed.

CHAPTER THIRTY-THREE

Three months later

Sienna replaced the book of potions on the bookshelf in Rose's living room and looked around. It was exactly as Rose had left it, a room decorated in white couches and curtains, splashed with Rose's favourite colours – pink and red. Tasteful, neat, and comforting.

She'd searched Rose's cottage, studied every page of the Beckham Grimoire, recalled dozens of past conversations with her grandmother and she was further away from an explanation than she'd ever been.

The transfer of powers, the secrecy, and the details surrounding Rose's final, fatal sacrifice was still a mystery.

Archer appeared in the doorway, his strong and quiet presence snapping her attention away from her broody thoughts. He wore jeans and a white shirt underneath a black suede jacket. He leaned against the doorframe, his muscular arms folded across his chest. "Are you done? It's getting dark."

Sienna nodded, turning off the lamp beside her.

"Are you okay?" he asked.

"It's hard coming here. I can't believe that it's been three months already."

He scanned the books scattered across the coffee table. "Any answers yet?"

"No. Nothing."

"Maybe we should stop searching. Maybe we should simply trust her."

"No," she said, shaking her head. "I need to know why she chose to die in order to break the spell on us. I know she loved us and I get the whole binding of your powers and the fact that I needed them restored in order to regain my strength. But she sacrificed herself, Archer. For us."

Archer's frown became more pronounced. "Rose knew she was going to die anyway, Sienna. She chose to have her death mean something. She loved you and believed you're meant for greater things. You dying in a tomb was not part of her master plan."

"I wish I understood her plan. So far, all I have are a dozen questions and no answers."

He went to her, pulling her into his arms, his manly scent and the feel of his arms around her bringing her the comfort she'd grown so accustomed to. "Rose wanted you to have her powers, and although she wasn't willing to disclose why, she always said you were meant to have them. She believed that, Sienna, and you have to believe that too. She was so determined to protect you, protect your powers, that she was willing to sacrifice herself in order to accomplish that."

It was hard to explain the guilt that racked her, but Archer understood. He carried his own guilt over Rose's death, and he was processing it in his own way. With the curse against them destroyed, his powers were at full throttle.

Archer pulled back, catching her chin between his fingers. "Poisoned or not, Rose died to save us. She gave me back my powers and she gave you back your life. Her death means something,

Sienna. We'll always have a lifetime of guilt and gratitude toward Rose, but we have to trust her. She knows more about this world than we'll ever know and she had her reasons for doing what she did."

Sienna nodded, captivated by his words and the intensity of his gaze. When she looked at him all she saw was love and a sincerity that had her rooted to the spot. "Rose gave me you," she whispered.

Archer closed his eyes, absorbing her words. When he opened them, his eyes were clouded with a sadness she'd often seen since Rose's death. With a soft exhale, Archer pulled her into his arms again, kissing her head. "She didn't die for nothing, Sienna. You're here because of Rose. We're here because of Rose. Her death matters."

Sienna's eyes filled with tears and she pulled back to wipe them away. "I miss her."

"Me too. She'll always be watching over us."

"Hopefully drinking her scotch and tending the rose bushes."

Archer smiled, reaching into his pocket. "I have something for you."

Sienna glanced down, her breath catching when she saw the necklace in his hands. Her necklace. The one she'd spelled years ago to keep him from finding her. Despite that, he'd still found her. Fell in love with her. Fought for her. Almost died for her. And after all that, he was willing to return the necklace to her.

Archer reached for her hand, placing the pentagram within her palm. "I said you could have your necklace back when this was all over."

"I also said that once this was all over, I'd be leaving."

Archer raised a brow, but didn't say anything. Sienna's gaze flickered from his face to the necklace in her hands. The pentagram stood for everything they were – their connection, their destiny, their bond, and their love for each other.

With a small smile, Sienna handed the necklace back to him, closing his fingers around it. "I don't need it anymore, Archer."

His expression darkened with an emotion she seldom saw, and he stared at her for a long while before finally breaking away to look at the pendant in his hand. "Are you sure?"

"There's nowhere else I'd rather be than here, with you. With your brothers. You're my Keepers, my life, my only family. This is my home, and I was stupid to run all those years ago. There may be others like Warrick and we might always be in battle against men like him, but if that's the case, then there's nowhere else I'd rather be that fighting them by your side."

Archer exhaled quietly and closed his eyes, seemingly reaching to maintain a sense of calm that had been rattled at the warlock's name. Warrick's admission that he'd started the fire that killed their parents had been tough for them to process. They'd all reacted differently, the main emotion being absolute fury for the one man that had seemed hell bent on destroying their family.

Sienna cupped his cheeks in her hands. "He can't hurt us anymore, Archer. You killed him and avenged the deaths of our parents and Sarah. It's over."

Archer's eyes glassed over and he pulled back. Pocketing the necklace, he slid an arm around her shoulders. "Come. No more talk of Warrick. We have something for you."

They walked outside onto the front porch, now in darkness, and Sienna froze at the top of the stairs, gaping at their surprise.

Ethan and Declan stood in Rose's garden, surrounded by dozens of glowing paper lanterns. They both wore jeans, thin jackets, and similar sombre expressions. Their eyes held the weight of the grief they all shared, but the quiet strength and power that emanated off them was breathtaking.

They were her warriors. Her Keepers.

Declan stepped forward, lighting the last lantern, and handed it to her.

Sienna walked down the stairs, glancing at each of her Keepers, and drew in a deep, calming breath. Her emotions were so raw, so real, so overwhelming, and the fact that they'd done this for her brought a fresh bout of tears. Not trusting herself to speak, she took the lantern with a small nod.

Archer moved behind her, slipped his arms around her waist, and rested his chin on her shoulder.

No one said anything, they didn't have to. Their emotions matched hers, their grief just as great, and the moment just as powerful.

They all missed their parents, Rose, and Sarah, but in truth, their cherished loved ones were finally free.

One by one, they released the lanterns and watched the gentle glow of light peacefully float away into the darkness. It was liberating, and touched a part of Sienna that had been numb for so long.

She rested her head against Archer's, felt his gentle breathing beside her cheek, and closed her eyes. There were still so many questions, so much sadness and a lifetime of guilt, but the only thing she was sure of at that particular moment was that she'd lost, she'd come home, and her life was filled with a love that most people only ever dreamed of

Rose's death mattered.

****

By the time they broke out of the forest and crossed the lawn toward the patio, it was late and the house was in darkness, an indication that Declan had gone out instead of returning home as he'd said. Declan had never been one for emotions so the memorial service they'd shared for their family had been a quick one for him and he'd quietly returned home ahead of them.

Archer eyed Sienna as she walked up the stairs and sank into the corner couch. She was exhausted, quiet, weary, but peaceful. It might be short lived and he doubted she'd give up her quest for answers, but for now, she looked more relaxed than she had in months.

Ethan swiped the bottle of whiskey on the coffee table and sank into the couch opposite her. He grinned at Sienna and shook the bottle. "Want some? It's a perfect numbing agent."

Sienna smiled. "Although I'm all for the numbing part, I think I'd prefer a glass of wine."

"I miss Rose. At least she shared my taste in alcohol," he grumbled and poured himself a shot of whiskey.

Archer reached for the soft blanket neatly folded across the couch and draped it across Sienna's shoulders. "I'll be right back," he said, dropping a kiss on her head and went inside to fetch the wine.

As he headed to the small cellar beside the kitchen, a soft thud in the living room next door had his head rearing up.

"Declan?"

The sound of glass breaking had Archer bolting into the living room. He skidded to a stop in the doorway just as a black-clad intruder aimed a lethal kick at Declan that sent him crashing into the window behind him. Wood splintered, glass shattered, the noise a striking intrusion to their newfound peace.

Declan sprang to his feet and charged his assailant, who swiftly sidestepped him, swiped a vase off a nearby table and crashed it across his head. Declan cursed as glass rained down on him and he charged forward. This time, he was faster, and he sent his attacker to the ground.

Rolling on the floor in a struggle of fists and grunts, they fought each other with similar strength, but Declan was still stronger and faster and quickly got the upper hand by launching his full body weight against the black cloaked figure. Trapped beneath Declan, the stranger hit back until Declan grabbed the flailing arms and pinned them to the ground.

"Who are you and what the hell do you want?" Declan demanded breathlessly.

"Get off me!"

Declan and Archer gaped at the feminine voice beneath the hoodie. Declan released her arm and shoved back the hood of her coat. "You're a woman?"

Using their brief moment of surprise, the woman broke free and shoved Declan with such strength that he flew backward across the ground, crashing into the coffee table. She sprang to her feet, swung around, and launched herself across the room toward the three daggers against the wall above the fireplace.

Archer was there as she reached them. As he lunged for her, she whirled around, stabbing one of the daggers into his shoulder. He gaped at her, the small woman with big dark eyes and long black hair. He groaned, releasing her, and wrapped his fingers around the handle of the dagger. She gasped, staring at his shoulder. Wide eyes swung back to meet his, and for a brief moment, Archer was caught off guard by the flash of shock that splashed across her expression.

Declan charged her, grabbing her by the neck in a death like grip. She screeched, the sound shattering the quiet undertones of their scuffle, and reared backward in an attempt to dislodge him. Declan's grip never faltered and together they struggled around the room, tripping over the coffee table in a crash of curses and grunts.

"What the hell's going on here?" Ethan demanded as he and Sienna rushed into the room. They paused in the doorway, gaping at the intruder caught in Declan's grip.

Before either of them could react, the room started trembling. Everything rattled, shook, shivered, the noise screeching through the room in an eerie realization that their intruder was not a normal burglar. Cupboard doors burst open, glass shattered, books flew across the room, and the light bulbs exploded.

Taking advantage of their brief moment of surprise as they stared at the chaos she'd created, the woman grabbed the two remaining daggers off the wall, not risking the third dagger still shoved in Archer's shoulder, and bolted through the nearest broken window. As everything came to an abrupt stop inside the living room, she landed on the grass outside with a gentle thud.

The three brothers raced to the window but she was already across the lawn, headed toward the forest.

"What the hell?" Declan said breathlessly as she vanished into the darkness with a speed they easily recognized. "She's a bloody Keeper."

The three brothers stared out of the window in stunned silence.

"What just happened?" Sienna asked, gawking at the mess in the room.

Simultaneously, they all turned to look at her, their shoulders heaving from the unleashed adrenaline that came with the struggle. They scanned the room, the explosion of destruction, trying to piece together exactly that.

"Archer, you're hurt!" Sienna exclaimed, rushing toward him.

With a grimace, Archer tugged at the dagger in his shoulder and tossed the weapon onto the floor. Sienna disappeared into the kitchen, quickly returning with fresh towels that she shoved against the bleeding wound.

"She stabbed you?" she asked, checking the wound. "With your own dagger? How did you let that happen?'

"She surprised me," he replied with a grunt.

Sienna turned to look at Declan. "You're also bleeding," she said, nodding to his face where a streak of blood gushed from a slice to the forehead.

Declan swiped at his head, glaring at the blood on his hand. "That bitch!"

"Why was she here?" Ethan asked, reaching for a towel beside Sienna and tossing it to his brother. "What was she after?"

"She was after the daggers," Declan said, anger lining his words. He walked to the fireplace, pointing to the spot where the three daggers had hung. "I was sipping a whiskey on the couch when she simply walked into the living room and helped herself to the daggers."

"She walked in?"

"I didn't bother with the lights and by her calm demeanour it appeared she thought we were out. I tried to stop her but she turned into a crazy woman."

"A hitch in your manly powers, Declan?" Sienna goaded. "How could you let a woman trash the living room and steal your daggers?" Sienna held up the remaining dagger, bloody and sticky from Archer's blood. "Well, she made off with two of the three daggers."

Declan tossed the bloody towel and scowled at her. "She surprised me, witchy."

"Why would she want the daggers?" Archer asked, his breathing more level. "They've been in our family for generations. How does she even know about them?"

"Who is she?" Sienna asked.

Declan flexed his jaw, dark blue eyes still smouldering with rage. "She's a Keeper."

"No way, Declan." Sienna shook her head. "She's a witch. I know a witch when I see one."

"And I know a Keeper when I see one. That woman had the abilities and strength that resembled ours, Sienna. She's definitely a Keeper."

"Well, she's definitely a witch too. She trashed this room with a power that resembled mine. A keeper doesn't have that ability."

Silence fell as they absorbed the meaning of her words.

Archer's hand fell away from his wounded shoulder and he tilted his head toward the broken window. "A witch and a Keeper? That's absurd."

"Maybe not." Declan reached for the bloody dagger and wiped away the blood. "Maybe she is. She had the ability and power of both."

"A hybrid?" Archer asked, turning back to them. "Is that even possible?"

"In a world of warlocks, witches, and Keepers?" Declan said, reaching for a piece of rolled up paper beside the couch. "Anything's possible."

"If she's one of us then why was she fighting us? We don't normally fight against our own kind." Sienna nodded to the paper in Declan's hand. "What's that?"

"She dropped it. She had it in her hand when I tackled her."

"You tackled her?"

"She attacked me."

"You're mad at her because she outsmarted you."

"She surprised me. It's not every day a woman comes busting in here looking for our daggers, dammit," Declan countered, clearly agitated that Sienna was right. "And besides, she caught me off guard with her Hulk-like tendencies."

"Still doesn't change the fact that a woman just kicked your ass," Sienna said with a smile.

Archer peered over Declan's shoulder, looking at the scroll. It was worn from years of use, yellow with age, and made from thick paper they hadn't seen before. There was a small triangle set within a larger one and each point of each triangle held a symbol. Inside the smaller triangle was a blackness that overshadowed the inner triangle.

"Oh, my God," Sienna said softly, reaching for the scroll. "It's the legend. The legend of the blackness."

Declan rolled his eyes. "That's a bedtime story."

"Declan, we have a scroll that resembles everything in that legend. If it's true, a blackness will be unleashed upon earth." Sienna pointed to the shadow inside the smaller triangle. "This is that blackness."

"Then what are the other symbols?"

She pointed to the three matching symbols at each point of the larger triangle. "Those mean protection." Her finger trailed along the scroll to the top symbol on the point of the smaller triangle. "This is fire. And this here," she said pointing to the bottom symbol on the left, "is the symbol for a Keeper. The last one on the right represents three swords."

"Or daggers," Archer added, reaching for the dagger from Declan. He turned it over in his hand before lifting his head. "Maybe they're not swords." He held up the dagger. "Maybe they are three daggers, like the ones that were on our wall."

Sienna's eyes widened. "The daggers are linked to the legend?"

"The legend is a myth," Declan said.

"We've been told since we were kids that there was an evil coming."

"Those were stories told by our parents to keep us in bed at night. They're not true."

"Then explain this," Sienna said, shaking the scroll at him. She pointed to the dagger in Archer's hand. "And explain that. Those daggers were hanging on our wall for decades and suddenly, tonight a woman holding this scroll comes busting in here wanting to steal them? These daggers must be part of the legend. Our ancestors knew about the legend. We know about the legend even though the details are a little sketchy."

"A little? All we have is a bunch of symbols surrounding a

black shadow."

"The blackness represents evil and the symbols are the key to destroying that evil."

"We don't even know what that evil is or how the symbols fit together," Declan argued.

Archer stroked his chin as he studied the scroll. "The symbols seem to indicate that a Keeper using fire and three swords, or daggers, are the key to destroying the evil."

"Our lovely intruder?" Ethan asked.

Sienna shook her head, trailing a finger across the symbol on the scroll that resembled a Keeper. "It can't be her. The symbol doesn't fit. Not if she's a hybrid."

"We don't even know if there is such a thing," Declan said.

Sienna rolled up the scroll and glanced at her Keepers. "Well whatever it is, she ran off with two of the daggers. Think she'll be back?"

With a thunderous expression, Declan headed for the window.

"Where are you going?" Archer asked, instinctively knowing that his brother was stewing for some answers, along with vengeance.

"I'm not sitting around here waiting for her to come busting in again. I'm going to go find her."

"You don't even know where to look."

"She may be fast, but I'm faster. And she must have left a trail." Declan stood on the large wooden window frame and glanced back at them. "Find out more about the scroll. I'll call you when I find her."

"Declan!" Sienna called, but her Keeper had already disappeared into the night. She shifted her gaze to Archer's. "What just happened?"

He glanced at the dagger and the scroll, and gave a brief shrug of the shoulders. "I wish I knew."

"This isn't over, is it?"

"Not by a long shot." He handed Ethan the dagger and the scroll and went to her. He slid an arm around her shoulders, drawing her close, and kissed her forehead. "We're a witch and a Keeper, Sienna. This is our life. We knew it would never be over."

She sighed, her long, lowered lashes hinting at a kind of surrender. "It was good while it lasted."

"It always is, my love."